More Than Love You

MORE THAN LOVE YOU

MORE THAN WORDS SERIES BY

SHAYLA BLACK

MORE THAN LOVE YOU
More Than Words, Book 3
Written by Shayla Black

This book is an original publication by Shayla Black.

Copyright 2018 Shelley Bradley LLC
Print Edition

Cover Design by: Rachel Connolly
Photographer: Sara Eirew Photographer
Edited by: Amy Knupp of Blue Otter

Excerpt from *More Than Want You* © 2017 by Shelley Bradley LLC
Excerpt from *More Than Need You* © 2017 by Shelley Bradley LLC

ISBN: 978-1-936596-47-8

PRAISE FOR *MORE THAN WANT YOU*

"Highly recommend! Shayla Black delivers once again with this passionate and sexy novel… A beautiful love story with a twist that you'll never see coming!"

—Meredith Wild, #1 New York Times Bestselling Author

"Amazing! Everything I didn't even know I needed or wanted in a romance novel. Hot. Spicy. Addicting."

—Rachel Van Dyken, #1 New York Times Bestselling Author

"Sexy, passionate and oh-so-clever! An intriguing love story!"

—Lauren Blakely, #1 New York Times Bestselling Author

"You'll hate him and then you'll love him! A sexy read with a surprising twist."

—Carly Phillips, New York Times Bestselling Author

"I'll play house with the hot real estate mogul Maxon Reed any time! Shayla Black's fans are gonna love this new series!"

—Lorelei James, New York Times Bestselling author of the Need You series

PRAISE FOR *MORE THAN NEED YOU*

5 Stars! "I adore Shayla Black! She masterfully delivers story after story full of passion, love, heartbreak, and redemption."

—Chasing Away Reality

5 Stars! "I love this book!!! It has all the elements that takes you on an emotional rollercoaster."

—Romance Between The Sheets

A True Gem! "More Than Need You took me on an extremely emotional, realistic, passionate journey towards an HEA for two people, who each went through emotionally scaring events yet finally were able to come together in a beautiful HEA, one that will remain one of my all-time favorites!"

—Guilty Pleasures Book Reviews

"So real and so raw! Be prepared to fall in love, have your heart broken, and then carefully mended back together by a master."

—Shayna Renee's Spicy Reads

5 Stars! "Ms. Shayla Black has once again reached inside my chest and shaken my heart with this emotional story…"

—Amuse Me Books

ABOUT *MORE THAN LOVE YOU*

I'm Noah Weston. For a decade, I've quarterbacked America's most iconic football team and plowed my way through women. Now I'm transitioning from star player to retired jock—with a cloud of allegation hanging over my head. So I'm escaping to the private ocean-front paradise I bought for peace and quiet. What I get instead is stubborn, snarky, wild, lights-my-blood-on-fire Harlow Reed. Since she just left a relationship in a hugely viral way, she should be the last woman I'm seen with.

On second thought, we can help each other...

I need a steady, supportive "girlfriend" for the court of public opinion, not entanglements. Harlow is merely looking for nonstop sweaty sex and screaming orgasms that wring pleasure from her oh-so-luscious body. Three months—that's how long it should take for us both to scratch this itch and leave our respective scandals behind. But the more I know this woman, the less I can picture my life without her. And when I'm forced to choose, I'll realize I don't merely want her in my bed or need her for a ruse. I more than love her enough to do whatever it takes to make her mine for good.

There are infinite ways to tell someone you love them. Some of the most powerful don't require words at all. This was the truth rolling through my head when I first conceived of this series, writing about a love so complete that mere letters strung together to make sentences weren't an adequate communicator of those feelings. For this series, music was my go-to choice.

I *love* music. I'm always immersed in it and spend hours a day with my ear buds plugged in. I write to music. I think to music. I even sleep to music. I was thrilled to incorporate songs into the story I felt were meaningful to the journey. I think of it this way: a movie has a sound-track. Why shouldn't a book?

So I created one.

Some of the songs I've selected will be familiar. Some are old. Some are newer. Some popular. Some obscure. They all just fit (in my opinion) and came straight from the heart. I listened to many of these songs as I wrote the book.

For maximum understanding (and feels), I seriously recommend becoming familiar with these songs and either playing them or rolling them around in your head as you read. Due to copyright laws, I can't use exact lyrics, but I tried to give you the gist of those most meaningful to Harlow and Noah's story. So I've made it simple for you to give them a listen by creating a Spotify playlist.

Hugs and happy reading!

I WILL REMEMBER YOU – Sarah McLachlan
GOODBYE TO YOU – Scandal (with Patty Smythe)
HAVEN'T MET YOU YET – Michael Bublé
I WANT TO KNOW WHAT LOVE IS – Foreigner
(YOU'RE) HAVING MY BABY – Paul Anka feat. Odia Coates
I CHOOSE YOU – Sara Bareilles
I WILL FOLLOW YOU INTO THE DARK – Daniela Andrade
THE LONG AND WINDING ROAD – The Beatles
UNBREAKABLE – Fireflight
CAN'T HELP FALLING IN LOVE – Elvis Presley
ALL OF ME – John Legend
UNCONDITIONALLY – Katy Perry
HERE COMES THE SUN – The Beatles

CHAPTER ONE

Noah

I HAD NO idea when I purchased my dream home that it would come with the woman straight out of my fantasies.

As I stare down at the brunette reclined on a chaise by my pool, a smile spreads across my face. I have no idea who she is, but I stare. And I stare some more. I can't stop. In fact, I can barely keep my tongue in my mouth. *Holy shit.*

A floppy hat covers the top half of her face. A fat paperback lies by her side. I'm guessing she fell asleep in the sun, but that only gives me an opportunity to appreciate the hell out of her uninterrupted.

Inky hair flows down her shoulders to a truly spectacular pair of breasts and banging curves. Even her navel is somehow sexy. I'm sure I've seen her tiny screaming-red bikini in a dirty dream or two. Would she notice if I ran my tongue up her fair, now slightly pink skin? Yeah, I've always had a thing for that. My mom's family is from Hawaii with ancestors from Samoa. And there's nothing I love more than seeing my darker hand glide across the silk of a pale woman's skin. I can't see this stranger's eyes, but her lips... Rosy. Bee-stung. Wide. They would look great wrapped around my cock.

Now I just have to figure out who she is and why she's squatting at the very private estate I recently bought. In fact, this is the first time I'm seeing it in person. It's everything I wanted. My rep, Lian, was spot on. Sick views of the Pacific. Beach, swaying palms, infinity edge pool that goes on forever, all on incredibly secluded grounds. It's perfect.

But all I want right now is to stare at my unexpected guest.

"Are you just going to stand there and block my sun or will you explain why the hell you're trespassing on private property?" She lifts the brim of her hat to peer up at me, her expression somewhere between curious and annoyed.

Her green eyes nearly knock me over.

I want to fuck her. With the kind of urgency I haven't felt since I was twenty-two, new to the NFL, and discovered a sea of pussy eager to get down and dirty with a newly minted pro athlete.

"Funny, I was going to ask you the same question. I'm here because I own this place as of yesterday. But I have no idea who you are or why you're on my property."

That made her sit up. "Shit. You're the buyer? Noah…" She snaps her fingers like she can't remember my name. "Noah…"

After being the star quarterback of one of the NFL's highest-profile teams for the last twelve years, having someone not recognize me is a fairly novel experience. And a little humbling. I almost laugh. "Weston."

"Noah Weston. That's it." She plops her book on the small table beside her lounger and stands, sticking out her hand.

She's tiny. The top of her head barely reaches the middle of my chest. Another turn-on for me.

I put my hand in hers to shake it. The cursory touch feels anything but casual. My blood scalds, turning to lava in my veins, which rushes, hot and thick, to my cock. If my T-shirt wasn't so long and loose, she would know exactly what I'm thinking.

"And you are…?"

"Sorry. Harlow, your house sitter. No one expected you for another few days."

I give my Realtors props. They have damn fine taste in house sitters—and women. Have they set her up at my place and used it as a temporary love shack? Gotta say, I wouldn't blame them. She's raging hot.

I've only ever spoken to Maxon and Griffin Reed over the phone, when we finalized the sale of this twenty-five-million-dollar pad. The price is steep, I know. But I wanted the privacy. And the islands aren't cheap. Hey, it's paradise. More importantly, it's home. My roots. It feels so damn good to be back in Hawaii while I figure out what comes next in life.

"I decided to come early, Harlow the house sitter. Nice to meet you."

"You, too. I'll...um, gather my things. I've been here for nearly a month, so I've made myself at home. It will just take me a couple of hours to get out of your hair."

"No rush," I assure. "I thought I'd grab a little pool time myself. If you're not in a hurry, I wouldn't mind the company."

Actually, when I walked in the door ten minutes ago to set down my luggage, I was thinking more like nap and solitude after my long flight from Dallas. Now I'm wide awake and attuned to this woman. Maybe some flirtation in the water will convince her to get horizontal with me. The view of the crystal ocean and tropical scenery is pretty damn romantic, after all.

"Really? You don't mind?" At my nod, she breathes a sigh of relief. "Thanks. It will take me a while to arrange a ride. I don't have a car on the island since I'm just visiting."

So if I want to tap that, I'll have to work quick. "Where's home?"

"San Diego."

I nod. "What's waiting back there? Job? Boyfriend?"

She wrinkles her nose. "No boyfriend. I finished my master's program earlier this year. I have a job offer close to my apartment. I'm taking some time off to ponder if that's what I really want. You're...um, a football player, right?"

"Just retired." I peer at her. I'd suspect her non-response to my name and occupation was disingenuous if I wasn't already convinced she's for real. "Not into sports, huh?"

"I grew up with brothers. When I was little I tried to keep up. Then I got older and discovered shoes were more fun."

I laugh. In her defense, I'll bet she looks good in sexy, strappy platforms. Hell, she probably looks good in dollar-store flip-flops…or nothing at all. How on earth does she not have a boyfriend? Too busy with school to bother? That's the only explanation that makes sense, because there's no way men haven't noticed her.

"I have a sister who feels the same way about anything requiring a ball," I explain. "At least I have my brother, Trace, to talk pigskin with."

"Lucky you. I'm the only girl, so I'm outnumbered. My brothers won't debate with me whether Choo or Louboutin makes a better shoe. I don't understand why." With a facetious sigh, she sits again, then sprawls her shapely legs out on the lounger, ankles crossed.

I smile and look for something to keep the conversation rolling. She's more interesting than the usual jock groupie I meet. I kind of want to know this woman. Of course I want to get her bikini off. But laying the verbal groundwork for that is a little tougher than I expected. I can't remember the last time I had to do more to attract a woman's attention than walk into a room and crook my finger.

"How long will you be staying in Maui?" I ask.

"I haven't decided."

Harlow doesn't say more, but her reticence suggests there's more going on than simple school fatigue or job avoidance. If she's got a master's degree, she's a smart, probably ambitious girl. She didn't accomplish that by being lazy. I wonder what's up.

"Want to talk about it?" I offer. "An impartial ear is sometimes best, and I've got nothing but time for a few months."

"Thanks but…" She shakes her head. "No."

That's all she says. No niceties. No explanations. No apologies.

She's hard to read. I'm surprised by how much that intrigues me.

Harlow cocks her head at me. "So what are you going to do with the rest of your life since you're obviously way too young to sit in your front-porch rocker and watch the grass grow?"

Isn't that a great question? "Like you, I'm pondering my options."

It's another reason I'm hanging out in Maui now. I left the NFL after my last injury. As I played my final game, I knew I would never suit up on a Sunday again. Everything I'd devoted my life to since age six…suddenly gone. To take the field any more would risk my long-term quality of life. Already I have side effects—but I don't talk about that. The team's doctors refused to clear me to play next season. My agent absolutely threw a shit fit when I even suggested rehabbing to get back in the game. Truth is, no franchise will gamble the huge salary I command under their cap since they seem to think I have one foot out the door and the other in the old folks' home. I always promised myself I'd go out on top, so I did— with a really tough press conference and a slammin' after party.

But now, I have no idea what to do. At thirty-four, I'm old by pro football standards. Endorsement deals are lucrative but not a career. I'm a man used to doing, not sitting back and counting my money. That's never been why I worked my ass off. I need purpose.

That only makes the offer recently extended my way so hard to re- sist…but impossible to accept. Still, I can't bring myself to turn it down.

"You know, I'll just go." She gathers her book and makes to stand. "It sounds like you've got heavy stuff on your mind and you bought this place for privacy, so I should let you have it."

"Stay." I look her way, hold her gaze. "It's been a long-ass flight, and I'd rather not be alone. You're…interesting. I wouldn't mind getting to know you better."

She hesitates, and I see her weighing her options. Something that looks like regret crosses her face, and I know I have to act fast. My name doesn't entice her. I get the sense money doesn't, either. I have to try something else. I don't know if my conversation is sparkling, but I know damn well how much time I spend pumping iron. I've been snapped a few times for both bodybuilding mags and *GQ*.

I whip off my shirt. And I see her eyes go wide. *Bingo.*

Finally, I've impressed her.

With her eyes glued to my pecs, she nods. "I-I guess I could do that."

The smile that curls up my lips feels slow and wide and so, so satis- fied. "Good. We got any food and booze in this place?"

"If we didn't, I wouldn't be here," she vows with attitude. "I've been slow-cooking a side of cow all day. I'm a red-meat girl. But I'm also not uncivilized. I've got a nice selection of wines to serve with that slab of meat. I'll even give you a fork and a glass."

"Cow sounds awesome, but I'll pass on the vino. Got anything stronger?"

She raises a brow at me. "I'm breathing, aren't I? Booze is essential. But I'm warning you, I can drink most men under the table."

"Not me," I promise her. "I will crush you."

Harlow scoffs. "You wish. Ever had a liver transplant?"

"The operation?"

"The drink." She laughs at me. "There's a reason it's called that. If you're not careful, I'll get you plowed."

I'd rather be the one doing the plowing, but I digress… "You're on. What's in this drink?"

"Rum, vodka, four flavors of liqueur, a few fruit juices, along with some sweet-and-sour mix. It goes down smooth like a punch because it's loaded with sugar, but it packs a hell of a wallop. It will sneak up and set you on your ass."

After the last few months of malaise, an evening with strong booze and an even stronger woman sounds fantastic.

"I don't know… Is that some fruity girls' drink?" I can't resist teasing her.

"They all say that—at first. Come with me."

She heads to the kitchen, which I hadn't even been able to find on my first pass through the enormous house. I didn't realize how big over eight thousand square feet really was until I roamed the joint. Trace will come visit me now and then. But otherwise, what am I alone going to do with this much house?

Another problem for another day.

Right now, I far prefer to focus on Harlow's fine ass, swaying gently from side to side as she leads the way toward the heavenly scent of slow-roasting meat and potatoes.

"That smells so good. And you eat that?" I nod at the Crock-Pot once we reach the kitchen.

"You don't?"

"I love it." And it isn't as if I have to maintain the strict chicken-and-rice diet I did during my pro quarterbacking days. I can splurge every so often now. "Most women I know are too busy watching their figures."

She snorted. "I may be carrying a few extra pounds but if I have to choose between being a bag of bones and eating hearty, I'm totally picking food. Separate me from cupcakes, and we'll have a real problem."

I laugh. Nothing about this woman is artificial. Not her hair, her nails, her breasts, or even her glow. Certainly not her personality.

I can't remember finding my last five girlfriends put together half this amusing.

"Wouldn't dream of it. Mix me a drink, woman. Some booze and beef is just what I need."

Harlow has an easy way in the kitchen. It's not organized or neat, but somehow she makes a few homemade biscuits, which are ready at the same time the roast and veggies come out—all while mixing the drinks. We talk. And we laugh. My own mother hasn't directed me to set the table since I was maybe twelve, but Harlow does it with a snap of her fingers and without missing a beat.

I'm still smiling as I sit to eat. She presses a few buttons on her phone and some old-school Nirvana roars through built-in speakers. It's like she's speaking my language.

Then I take my first bite of the roast and moan.

"Good?"

"Amazing." I sip the drink. Like she warned, it's sweet but not syrupy or cavity-inducing. I gulp down half of it in a few long swallows. "So is the booze. You're gorgeous and have good taste in music. You know, I think we should get married."

Harlow laughs me off. "Oh, god. None of that for me. I'm happy with just sex."

I can barely swallow the bite of roast I just shoveled in my mouth. Now there's a subject I can warm to.

Bracing an elbow on the table, I set my fork down and level a smoldering stare her way. "I can make that happen."

A little smile dances across her face. "I'll bet you can." Her gaze slides over my shoulders and chest, and I swear she's so potent it almost feels as if she's touched me with her hands. "You look more than capable to me."

I see interest and speculation on her face. She's wondering what I'd be like in bed.

"I'll give you whatever you want, Harlow. However you want it. As long as you want it. As hard as you want it. All you have to do is say the word."

She doesn't speak for a long moment, merely sips her liver transplant from a red Solo cup and stares at me over the rim. "How do I know you're not an ax murderer?"

She's teasing. I think. "You weren't worried about that when I approached you all laid out by the pool."

"Yeah, but I was watching you. The only harm you were causing me then was blocking my rays. I figured that if you had murder on your mind, you would have done far more than stand there gawking at me."

"I wasn't gawking."

"You totally were. I know I surprised you by being here, but once you got over that you checked me out. You going to deny it?"

"No, I am not. That is one banging bikini you're wearing. You look damn fine in it."

"Thank you. My brothers hated it and suggested something with a skirt down to my knees."

"They're your brothers. When my little sister got married last year, I winced every time someone talked about what they'd be doing on their honeymoon. I just...can't think about that."

Her smile turned into a sparkling laugh. "I hear you. My brothers are newlyweds. It's one reason I've stayed here. Their wives are sweet as pie, but if I bunked with them until I head back to San Diego... Let's just say I don't want to hear my sisters-in-law crying out in passion or whatever." She winces. "Just no."

I laugh. "How do you know there'd be screaming?"

"Please. My brothers are macho enough that they'd insist on that whole conquering, chest-beating thing. I also suspect they're trying to get their wives pregnant, and I'd rather not be under the same roof for that momentous occasion."

I pause and consider. There's no way I'd want to hear Samaria conceiving. "I see your point. Yet another reason for you to stay the night."

Harlow leans back in her seat and sips her drink. "Back to the sex thing, huh?"

"You brought it up," I remind her.

"So I did." She shrugs, and I get the feeling she's used to saying whatever's on her mind. "Did I surprise you?"

"A little bit. But in a good way."

"Aren't you pro athletes used to women throwing themselves at you?"

"It happens." A lot. And I've grown more discerning over the years. But I still haven't run across one like Harlow in the last dozen years. Maybe ever. Most of the women looking to collect a "trophy" by sleeping with a celebrity sports figure lure the guy with her body, not her personality. Harlow seems to have tons of both. "I don't often say yes these days."

She raises a dark brow at me as she lifts a forkful of meat. "But you once did?"

I think about dodging, but she's pretty straightforward. This likely won't be a long-term relationship, so there's no reason for jealousy or accusations. "I admit that I was once twenty-two and stupid."

"We all were." She rolls her eyes, seemingly poking fun at herself, too. "I did a lot of ridiculous things as an undergrad. Thankfully, I outgrew it. I'm guessing you did, too."

"I like to think so." Though when it comes to Harlow, I suspect some parts of me are smarter than others. My brain is trying to keep up...but most of the blood in my body is flooding to my cock. The two heads don't always work simultaneously, and right now I'm having trouble keeping up with the conversation. First, Harlow has boobs. Great boobs.

And I'm just a man with an oral fixation. Second, the time difference is catching up with me. It may only be seven p.m. in Hawaii, but my body is still on Dallas time, where it's midnight. I don't want to think about why being tired distresses me so much.

And right on cue, my head up north starts a dull throb. After all, why should the one down south be miserable all alone?

"If you're all enlightened and mature now, why didn't you ever tie the knot?"

It's a question I've asked myself more than once. A lot of my teammates started out wild and have since settled down. "Maybe I never met the right person. You?"

She hesitates. "I thought I might get hitched once but it didn't work out and splitting up was for the best. I'm not really cut out for attachments and commitments."

I frown. "Maybe you just haven't met the right person, either."

Harlow looks as if she might argue, then she wipes the expression from her face and gives me an easy-breezy shrug I don't believe for a minute. "Maybe so. Seconds?"

I don't argue. What's the point?

When I glance at my plate, I'm surprised to see it empty. Ditto for my bright plastic cup. "I think I'm good for now."

She stands and heads to the kitchen counter she's turned into a make-shift bar, then proceeds to pour herself another drink. "Sure thing, lightweight."

At her teasing, I lounge back in my chair, arm slung over the back, and watch her. "When I haven't spent all day traveling and I'm not feeling like I'm in the wrong time zone, I'll prove you wrong."

"You're on. I'll cut you a little slack tonight since you've been on a plane." She stirs her drink, then sits back in her chair. When she lifts her lashes and pins me with a flirty gaze, I know I'm in trouble. "Does that mean you're too tired for sex?"

"I don't think I've ever been too tired for that." I refrain from mentioning the marathon with the blonde bombshell after my last Super Bowl win. All I needed after one of the hardest games of my career was a shower. Then I was good to go. Don't see why tonight will be any different…

As long as we don't have to talk.

She sends me a sultry glance. "Good to hear."

"You're serious." About the sex. About us having it. I don't ask her because it's not a question.

She lifts a shoulder in an offhanded shrug. "I'm single. You're single. We have this damn nice place to ourselves. I'm attracted, I admit. I think you'd only block my sun to gawk at me if you liked what you saw. So why not?"

Honestly, she isn't using rationale I haven't used myself. It seems logical. Obvious, even. But something about the way she's coolly propositioning me gives me pause. I want to get to know her more. Spend time with her. I'm not sure why, exactly. Maybe because she's not my same old-same old. But I have a nagging suspicion that if I take her upstairs and give her a very personal tour of my master suite, she might well be gone by morning.

Normally, that would seem like a great outcome. So why am I not down with her vacating the house I bought for my private retreat? No idea, but there it is. I'm rolling with it.

"Why don't we swim first? I never got to test the pool before you fed me this amazing meal."

"Sure." She stands as if she doesn't have a care in the world, but suddenly she won't look at me as she lifts our plates to clear them from the table.

As Harlow bustles to the sink, I follow her, wrapping my fingers around her arm. "Hey."

Somehow, she manages to ease out of my grip yet still set the plates in the sink. "If you're not interested, it's no big deal. I've heard no before."

From a blind man? "Baby, I'm not saying no. I'm just saying that I'd rather not rush this. We have all night."

Some of the ice melts from her chilly posture. "All right."

"And not to sound like a fainting Victorian belle or anything, but I have a bitch of a headache."

Concern creases her face. "Do you want something for that?"

I wish a good, old-fashioned orgasm would cure it...but probably not. "Ibuprofen and a cup of strong coffee?"

"Sure. I'll start the pot. Tablets are in the pantry over there." She points me in the right direction.

"Thanks," I call over my shoulder as I walk into the enormous closet off the kitchen that Harlow has stocked with a few spices and canned goods. I shake out withdraw a couple of pills before putting the bottle back on the shelf.

When I emerge from the pantry, Harlow is staring at the coffee brewer, watching it drip. "How do you like it?"

Then it happens, just like before. One minute I'm in the moment. The next...nothing. And I know what's coming. I start to sweat. Still, I try to open my mouth and form words.

I know if I push the sounds through, nothing coherent will come out. I'll blurt some sound that can't even pass as a "huh?" or "what?" I close my eyes, grit my teeth, and try again to remember the conversation. What did she ask me?

"You okay?"

Since there's nothing wrong with my motor skills, I merely nod.

"Want your coffee black? Or do you just want to call it a night?"

I still can't find my words, but at least I know she was asking me about coffee before I spaced out. Fuck. Why is this still happening to me?

I shake my head and try to snag the cup from the brewer. If I whip it up to my lips, maybe she won't notice the silence. Black coffee is my preference. Why can't I say that right now? I know the words. They're in my head. I just can't seem to get them to my mouth.

"Sit down." She smooths out a frown. "I'll wash the dishes and clean the kitchen."

I'm afraid to look at Harlow again. Confusion on her face would be bad, pity way worse. I grip my mug and stare down into the dark brew, wondering how long the episode will last this time. I know sleep will help, but damn it, I don't want to give up tonight with this woman. I'm not sure the chance will ever come again. Until this shit, I didn't have much in the scintillating conversation department anyway, but to have zero? How can I get naked with her if I can't even talk to her, ask her what pleases her?

Stubbornly, I shake my head.

She frowns. "Really. I've got this. Why don't you hang on the sofa and I'll join you when I'm done. It will only take ten minutes."

I want to argue, but without words, how? Then Harlow makes everything easier when she leads me to the living room and fluffs a cushion on the island-casual couch, then gives me a saucy wink. "When I'm done, if you still want to have your wicked way with me, I'm totally game."

Finally, I look her way. Really look. I don't see pity. I see concern. Weirdly, that turns me on.

Unfortunately, I can't seem to summon the verbal skills to thank her. I promise myself I'll show her my appreciation in bed later.

When I hear water running in the kitchen sink behind me and the pop of the dishwasher opening, I close my eyes. Maybe a ten-minute power nap will resurrect my verbal agility. If not, I'll simply have to show her that I'm really good with my tongue.

CHAPTER TWO

I JOLT AWAKE. The kitchen is dark, as is the living room. I look around
and find the place empty.

"Harlow?"

Thank fuck my ability to speak is back. The sleep must have restored
me. It usually does.

I pull my phone from my pocket and glance at the time. My eyes
nearly pop from my head. I conked out for three hours?

What. The. Fuck?

Worse, she didn't answer. Did she decide I'm a deadbeat who can't
put out and catch a ride to one of her brothers' pads? Or worse, decide she
was better off finding someone else more capable of scratching whatever
itch she has? Normally, if a hookup was too horny to wait and didn't care
who she dropped her panties for, then she would be more than welcome
to find some douchebag to cozy up to for the night.

Thinking that Harlow might be on the prowl both angers me and fills
me with a dread that makes zero sense.

Seriously, what is wrong with me tonight?

Stomping up the stairs, I call her name again. No answer.

Quickly, I figure out which bedroom she occupies. It's the one that
smells like her, island vanilla and gardenia. It's the one with lacy panties
folded on the dresser next to a strappy bra. A pair of red wedges are strewn
around the room as if she kicked them off the second she walked in. Her
suitcase peeks out from a luggage rack in the closet, visible through the

cracked door.

At least if she left, she hasn't left for good.

On her nightstand, I see her tablet, a thick biography about Elizabeth Blackwell. I have no idea who that was or what she accomplished. But after I find Harlow, I'll Google it and figure out what fascinates the woman who's beginning to fascinate me.

Right now, I just want to know where the hell Harlow has gone.

A check of the other seven bedrooms in this place, including mine, proves pointless. I stomp back downstairs and look from room to room—office, formal living, formal dining, exercise room—empty. I rake a hand through my hair. Where has she gone?

Then I hear splashing outside, along with the distinct sounds of Evanescence.

Darting for the pool, I see Harlow's little red bikini lying on a lounger. She's skinny-dipping? I glance around for confirmation and find the woman herself clutching a pool noodle with one hand and a glass of wine with the other.

"Hi, Sleeping Beauty." She grins my way.

"Sorry about that. I can't remember the last time I just fell off."

"You obviously needed it. Feel better?"

"Tons. Thanks. How about you?"

"Great. I love drinking alone." Her smirk says she's poking harmlessly at me again. "But you gave me time to finish the dishes, do some laundry, read *War and Peace*..."

"Stop," I groan. "Three hours is a long nap. I admit it. You going to ease up now?"

"When teasing you is so fun?" She raises a brow. "What do you think are the odds?"

Shitty. "How can I make it up to you? If you want to hop out of the pool and come to my bedroom, I'll do my best to put a big smile on your face."

"I'm intrigued," she admits. "But in between chapters of the sad Russian saga, I Googled you. You're, um...a big deal."

I feel heat rush to my face. I'm used to people talking about me, but I've never been completely comfortable with it. "I'm told I was. But like I said, I'm retired now."

"Hall of Famer, for sure."

"So my agent assures me." I shrug. "I'm trying not to linger in the past. I still have a lot of life to live."

She splashes around a little more. "I don't know. You're practically ancient compared to me."

Is this woman going to rib me about everything? Probably. And I still think it's oddly adorable. It's way more entertaining than the bowing, scraping, and yes-sirring I've been hearing for years. "How much older?"

"Almost nine years. When you were graduating from high school, I was starting junior high. These days, do you need vitamins before sex or a little blue pill?"

Now she's laughing, and I find myself smiling in return. "Fuck you."

"That *is* the idea…"

"Come here, baby."

Her eyes sparkle under the moonlight, and it's all I can do not to jump in after her, clothes and all. I want my hands on her now.

"Why don't you drop trou and come in after me?"

"You're all wet."

She purses her lips together, and I know she'll make one hell of a sexy bad girl. "Don't you want me that way?"

The way I feel now? Every day, all day. "Just your pussy. That should be juicy and swollen and ready for my cock. The rest of you shouldn't be wet unless I'm making you sweat in pleasure."

"You sweet talker, you…"

I'm wondering if I'm really going to have to take my shorts off and jump in after her when she finally kicks her way to the steps of the pool and shoves the noodle toward the deep end. I wish the moonlight were a little brighter or that the surrounding deck had better garden lighting. Yeah, I can see her vague shape under the shallow water, which looks damn fine. But it's all shadows and dusky grays in the dark. I want some damn LEDs out here so I can really see her.

I put that on my mental list of home renovations.

"If it gets you out of the pool and into my arms, I'll keep talking."

Harlow smiles. "It just might. But in all seriousness, I have a question."

"Shoot."

I haven't seen this woman be serious yet, so I'm expecting her to ask about my condom size or lasting power. That's not at all what I get.

"How many concussions have you had over the course of your career?"

I rub at the back of my neck. It's a sore subject since it's the reason I was forced to retire. "Five officially. But a couple more in practices, peewee, and high school leagues. I'm better now."

Well, getting there. But some days I struggle more than others...like today.

"And your last one was in January? During the NFC championship game two weeks before the Super Bowl?"

"Yeah. Why the interest in my medical history? You want my blood tests, too? Find out if I'm sexually-transmitted-disease free?"

"Are you?" she asks as if her question is a passing curiosity. I'm not sure if she actually wants to know or is downplaying her nosiness.

"Of course. I've always been careful." Meticulous, actually. I met a lot of women in the NFL...many of whom had made the rounds. I wasn't keen on my bare junk rubbing against some chick who'd been banging my teammate the week before. "You?"

"Practically a monk. I haven't had sex in at least six months. But that's not where I was going with this. Your concussions... You often have those verbal fogs? Lose track of the conversation? Find yourself tongue-tied?"

Her words feel like a bullet, fast and unavoidable, nailing me right between the eyes. I try not to stagger back at the impact. But she definitely scored a direct hit, and I'm trying to figure out how to answer her without sounding defective.

"I was just tired," I hedge.

She purses her lips at me. I don't know this woman well, and nothing else on her face changes…but I see she's not pleased. "Does it happen more often when you're tired?"

"What are you getting at? I was beat and I didn't feel like talking." I hear myself getting defensive and I realize I'm being an ass. But I don't want this woman seeing my vulnerabilities. Hell, I don't want anyone seeing them.

"Look, my master's degree is in speech pathology. What you're experiencing following repeated trauma to the brain is not uncommon. Have you ever heard of Chronic Traumatic Encephalopathy?"

I put my fists on my hips and resist the urge to back away. "Of course. I played for the league for a dozen seasons. I know what the players who came before me say they've endured after repeated hits to the head. But I'm not depressed, impulsive, moody, or aggressive. I don't lose my memories." Just blip out in conversations once in a while. "I'm not emotionally unstable. And don't have tremors. I don't have trouble seeing or smelling or walking or talking."

"But you are experiencing intermittent problems with your speech. Have you had a brain scan?"

She sees right through my denials. I let out a breath and look away with a shake of my head. "What do you want?"

"I'm sorry if I'm upsetting you. I just want to help. It sounds as if you're experiencing some apraxia of speech. It's a motor speech disorder where the messages from the brain to the mouth are disrupted. Do you feel as if you can't move your lips or tongue the way you need to form words sometimes?"

"I don't want to talk about it." I can't afford to. Okay, so it's partially a macho thing. I hate the idea of looking weak in her eyes. But it's also my second career on the line. I can kiss my chance of being a football commentator good-bye if word gets out that, at random times, I can't speak a word.

"I know it's frustrating."

"You don't know anything."

"I've never had the condition personally. You're right," she goes on as if I didn't just refute her. I can't miss the empathy in her voice…but it still rubs me wrong. "I've heard you speak, so I know the muscles you need to move your mouth aren't weak. So you seem to have some aphasia, which is a speech disorder as a result of neurological damage. How often does it happen?"

I press my lips together. "I'm done talking. Do you want to fuck or not?" Now that she knows I'm broken? I scoff. "Of course you don't. I'm going to bed."

Before this conversation goes further south, I turn away and head for the house. I suspect I'll be spending the night with my cock in my hand, thinking about Harlow. My head was already banking on the fact that I'd be getting horizontal with her and my dick certainly didn't need convincing that sex between us would be spectacular. Now I'll have to resign myself to pointless jacking off. Goddamn it.

"Noah?"

At the sounds of splashing, I turn to find Harlow emerging from the pool, walking up one step at a time, dripping, swaying with every step, and completely blowing my mind. Her long hair clings to her pretty breasts, flirting with her plump nipples. Her waist dips in, then flares out to a pair of hips I want my hands on. She's sleek and sexy and stunning.

I can't find words for an entirely different reason than before. She leaves me speechless.

"Can you hand me a towel from over there?" She points to the patio table.

On autopilot, I back toward the surface, never taking my eyes off her. When I bump into the glass, I grope behind me until terry cloth fills my hand. Then I race toward Harlow. "Need anything else?"

She takes the towel from me, and we're standing so close I can smell her scent mixed with a tinge of chlorine. "A shower. Then an orgasm or two, preferably that you give me."

Did I hear her right? "You sure?"

Harlow nods, her gaze tangling with mine. "I want to fuck."

It takes a split second for her declaration to sink in. I was convinced she wouldn't want me after she figured out I'm just a man with flaws. Then again, she was never looking to get laid from someone ESPN hailed as a football god. She just wants pleasure.

The way she holds my gaze singes me with heat. It sizzles across my skin, burning the flesh under my surface. I can't quite breathe.

I have a feeling she's going to be trouble—and I don't care.

"Let's do it." Taking the towel from her grip, I jerk it until it unfolds, then wrap it around her back, covering the dripping ends of her hair. Then I tug her against me. Her skin feels cool pressed to my overheated chest. I don't dare kiss her now. The way I want her, I'll lay her out on the first available surface, and I'd rather save my knees the agony of looking for the leverage to fuck her properly on a chaise lounge.

Digging for restraint, I drag in a rough breath. If I'm already having trouble resisting her, how bad will the craving be once I've had a taste?

I shove the thought aside. "I won't go easy on you."

"I never thought you would."

"I won't be gentle."

"Good. I may be small, but I'm not fragile."

"I won't be quick. Expect me to be at you all night."

A sly smile curls up the sides of her lips that turns me on even more. "I'll hold you to that."

I run out of ways to warn her that I intend to turn her inside out and wring her dry before I let her leave my bed. But fuck it, I'll let my body do the talking.

Bending, I lift her to my chest. She's a tiny thing. Given her boobs and hips, I thought she would be heavier to carry, but I've curled barbells that weigh more. "Then let's go."

Her smile becomes a grin as she wraps her arms around my neck. "Consider me happily along for the ride."

We head inside the house, and I'm glad as hell for the accordion glass doors along the back. Nothing to open or close, just open air, the Hawaiian breeze, and a hot woman.

Inside, I take the stairs two at a time. I'm impatient; I admit it. I can't wait to lay her across my bed, turn on every light in the room so I can have a good look at her, then watch her face as I sink inside and see the sensations overwhelm her. I can do that to her. I was damn good on the field, but I've also been told I'm a legend in the bedroom. Lots of practice through stupid years of partying. I might be a little rusty now. I haven't trusted myself around a woman not to have a lapse in speech at the most inopportune moment in months. But riding a woman is like riding a bicycle, right?

When we reach the master suite, I kick the door open and make for the bed. Before I can set her down, she wiggles out of my arms and heads for the door.

I frown as she leaves. "Where are you going?"

"Um, I'll just be a minute. I need a shower."

Why the hell would she think that's necessary now? "You don't."

"Ten minutes. I promise."

She darts away before I can stop her, and I'm left scratching my head. This woman gives off more mixed signals than a malfunctioning traffic light.

Since I'm not standing here with my dick in my hand while she rinses off, I open the first of my two giant suitcases. Moving from the mainland was an undertaking and the rest of my things should arrive in a few weeks. For now, I pluck out some toiletries and rinse off in my own shower. I should march down the hall and hop into Harlow's with her. If we're going to have sex, why not get naked together now?

But I give her privacy. The downside is, I shower in less than five minutes and emerge from the bathroom, towel wrapped around my waist. The overhead spray revived me a bit and cleared my head, sure. But now I'm alone and waiting impatiently.

I turn down the bed, put a few things in my suitcase away, and open the balcony doors to the full-frontal ocean breeze. Still no Harlow. I haven't stared at my empty doorway much longer than ten minutes, but as far as my cock is concerned, that's nine and a half minutes too long. She doesn't need to groom for me. She just needs to be naked and willing and in my bed.

Scowling, I prowl down the hall and across the open loft space that separates the master wing from the rest of the upstairs bedrooms. The first thing that assaults me is the whirring sound of her hair dryer. The door to her bedroom is cracked, and I can see straight through to her attached bath.

The sight of her bent over, dark hair dangling as she wields the handheld device, her gorgeous ass waiting for my hands, nearly stops my heart. God, her derrière is pale and pert and round. I want to run my lips across those globes, sink my teeth into them.

My stirring cock stands up straight, ready to perform—or beg. Whatever gets her attention.

On silent footfalls, I sneak up behind her and grip her hips, fitting that pretty ass against my raging erection with a groan.

Harlow shuts the hairdryer off and tosses it on the counter, standing upright with a flip of her head. A rush of breath slips from her lips. "Noah…"

"I couldn't wait anymore for you, baby." That's doubly true now that I can see every one of Harlow's valleys and curves under the bright bathroom lights.

Mercy… The woman is a work of art, full of symmetrical dips and swells. Slender shoulders, round breasts, a tapered waist, and a smooth, bare pad between her legs.

Our eyes meet in the mirror. Hers are a moss green, verdant and bright. As I raise one hand to her breast and cradle it in my hand, I exhale roughly. In response, her pupils enlarge. Her nipples tighten. Her cheeks flush. And her body melts against mine.

"Your touch feels good."

A woman who communicates. I like it. "I can make you feel so much better. Come to bed with me, baby."

"That's my plan." As I pinch the taut tip of her breast between my thumb and finger, her eyes slide shut. "My hair is almost dry."

I skim my other palm up her waist, over her ribs, then plunge my fingers into the thick, silky mass. It's barely damp. "Close enough."

"I'm trying not to leave wet spots on your sheets."

No way I can resist a sly grin. "Oh, I'm hoping you do. C'mon, Harlow. I need to be inside you."

I met this woman a few hours ago and slept through most of them. I haven't even kissed her yet. But I already feel as if I've waited far too long for her. It's insane. And I don't give a shit. Something about her just feels right at the moment.

Harlow reaches behind her head to grip the back of my neck at the same time she sways her hips, grinding against my cock. Only a towel separates us. It would be easy to set her on the bathroom basin, spread her legs, lose the terry cloth, and thrust inside her. But it would be too quick, like skipping over a scrumptious feast and eating only a bite of dessert. Nothing wrong with it when that's all you want. But I'm hungry for more. I want this woman under me, where I can take her in every way I'm craving.

For now, I let my lips skate a path from her shoulder to her neck. Even fresh from the shower, I inhale a teasing whiff of her vanilla gardenia scent that revs me up. Then I give a gentle tug to her scalp until she cedes more of her velvety skin to me. A little gasp slips from her lips before she tilts her head so I can explore her throat at will. I feel as if I've won an important skirmish. She's stopped stalling and started surrendering, and nothing could be more arousing.

"Noah…"

"I'm here. Tell me what you like."

"Exactly what you're doing," she breathes.

"Tell me what you want."

"I wouldn't complain if you kissed other parts of my body."

I grin. "Oh, I plan on that. Let's go back to my room."

Her lashes flutter. Her eyes open. She looks at me, then glances at the bed behind us reflected in the mirror. I see the moment she dismisses whatever crossed her mind. "Lead the way."

"I'm not letting you put any space between us tonight." Before she can say a word, I turn her to face me and haul her body to mine, grabbing her ass in my hands and hoisting her body up. "Wrap your legs around me."

Harlow does as commanded, folding her arms behind my neck, too. Our gazes meet. I feel the impact of her stare down to my cock. Even without a speck of makeup, she's one of the most hypnotic women I've ever seen. I may have glimpsed—even dated—females more beautiful. But none who flip my switch quite the way this one seems to.

Is that because my dry spell has been way longer than usual? Or because there's something special about Harlow?

"You going to kiss me yet?" she asks.

"Once I get you in my bed, sure."

"Why not now? Am I supposed to just stare at you as you walk down the hall carrying me?"

"Yep. Anyone ever tell you that you ask a lot of questions?"

A little smile curls up the corners of her lips. "All the time."

And she's not going to change her behavior a bit. I don't know Harlow well, but I suspect that she'll always march to her own drum and anyone who doesn't like it can fuck off.

I can't help but grin back at her as I head for the master suite. "You'll thank me later for not kissing you now. I doubt you'll miss the rug burn on your back. My knees already appreciate my restraint."

She bites her lip and sends me an amused glance. "Impatient, are you?"

Why lie? "Like I might come out of my skin in the next three minutes if I don't get my hands and my mouth on you."

I reach the threshold of the master suite and save her from a reply. It's not her conversation I want right now anyway.

Arms wrapped around her, I plant one knee on the bed and let her fall to the mattress. Before she's even settled, I follow her down and tumble on top of her, pinning her with my legs. I anchor my elbows on either side of her head and grab her hair so she can't look away.

Her breathy little gasp turns me on even more.

"Now I'll kiss you, and when you come up for air a few orgasms later, I swear you'll be completely satisfied."

"Those are big promises," she taunts.

"I'll deliver."

Something about her strips my usual cool reserve. I can normally hold back, maintain casual distance. Nothing about her or this moment feels casual at all. I don't understand it. I only know that my whole body is tightening, my heart thudding, as I snare her gaze and lower my head.

Harlow meets my kiss halfway. She might have teased me earlier, but there's nothing coy about her response now. Her fingers grip my neck and press me closer in silent demand, even as she parts her lips and her thighs, allowing me between both. Sexual heat smolders down my spine. As soft as her lips feel, it's her flavor that shocks my system with a fresh jolt of desire. I taste wine on her tongue. But under that, I also taste her strength, her sensuality, her need.

Grabbing more of her hair in my fist, I settle my hips between her legs and give my towel an impatient tug. It's damp and it won't budge, damn it. With a pissed-off snarl, I rise up to my knees and whip it free, tossing it who knows where. It's out of my fucking way and nothing else matters but pressing my skin to Harlow's again and getting inside her.

When I focus on her again, her lips are slightly swollen. Her pupils have dilated even more. And she's looking straight at my cock.

"Problem?"

Her gaze never wavering, she shakes her head. "I'm looking forward to getting every inch of you in my mouth."

Oh, fuck. She couldn't have said many other things that would have thrilled the hell out of me even half so much. "Baby, I'm dying for that moment, too. But first things first… I promised you orgasms."

She lifts her gaze to my face with a grin. "So you did. Do your worst, jock."

The snappy comeback on the tip of my tongue dissolves as she arches her back and spreads her legs wider. I wish like hell I'd turned on more lights in the room, and I vow I'll fuck her tomorrow too, when sunlight floods this suite and I can see every inch of her ivory perfection.

"I plan on being your best fuck ever." I mean that sincerely as I lower my body over hers again, pressing skin to skin, fitting my cock against the soft pad of her bare pussy.

Before she can come back at me with a saucy reply, I seize her mouth again, take her lips, delve deep. When she hits my senses, the impact makes me groan. She melts on my tongue. She's sweet and tart and addictive. I'm going to have to have more of her, I can already tell. A night may not be enough. But this works in my favor. She needs a place to stay until she returns to San Diego, one where she won't have to hear her brothers procreate. I can give her that. She can stay in my house, in my bed, where I'll be able to sink into her any time I want, day or night, until I sate this raging need clawing at my self-control.

Beneath me, all her sass and teasing turns to eager compliance. She's in the moment with me in every way, her hands busy mapping my back, her lips clinging to mine, her legs folding around my hips.

How easy it would be to notch down her body enough to slide inside her, feel her without any barrier between us, and take her the way I've never taken any woman. The urge is there. I don't even understand why I want her bareback so bad. But that's a decision we have to make together.

"Are you on the pill?"

"Yeah," she pants into my face.

I know another teammate who fell into this trap, believing his one-night stand was on the pill when it was a total lie. She's wrung a fortune from him and made him jump through ridiculous hoops just to see his son ever since. But Harlow isn't the sort of girl looking to get pregnant for a payday. I'd bet my life on that.

"I'm clean, I swear," I tell her.

"I am, too," she promises, trailing kisses up the column of my neck and nipping her way toward my lips.

It's really hard to think when she does that…

"Can I have you bare? I might sound crazy, but I want to feel all of you. I don't want latex—or anything—between us."

Harlow breaks away and blinks. "I-I... I'm not sure that's a good idea. I went off the pill for a bit and I haven't been back on it that long. I might still be able to get pregnant."

On the one hand, I'm disappointed that I can't just tunnel inside her and enjoy her without a barrier separating us. On the other hand, I'm grateful for her honesty. For a moment, I wonder why she just started the pill recently when she said she hadn't had sex for months. Female issues? I don't know and it doesn't matter. What does is that I've got all night with her and I intend to make the most of it.

"Totally understand. I've got condoms."

She gives me a halting smile. "I'm glad one of us is a good Boy Scout."

"I'm not quite that good, but I always try to be prepared."

"There you go. So, about those orgasms... What did you have in mind?"

"I could tell you, but I think it will be far more fun to show you."

Because I can't help myself, I dip my head for another sweet taste of her mouth. It's like crack. I can't make myself back away. I can't stop tasting her over and over, feeling her grasp me, melt into me, beg me for more with her urgent fingers digging into my skin. *Yeah...*

But I can't kiss her to climax, so I start making my way down her luscious body with a sweep of my lips across her jaw, a nip at her neck, a tongue tracing her collarbones. Right away, I remember the other reason I love fair-skinned girls. Not only do I get a perverse satisfaction of seeing her pale flesh under my bronzed hands, I see the flush of her arousal right away. With every touch and whisper, her response is obvious. The rosy stain blooms in her cheeks and works its way down her body as I do. It follows me wherever I plant my mouth, wherever I glide my palm across her flesh.

When I hover over her nipples, they not only blush but tighten even more, especially when I swipe gentle thumbs across the tips.

Her fingers curl around the back of my head in demand. "Suck them."

"Is that a please?" I can't resist teasing her.

Harlow's lashes flutter open, and I'm stunned by the aroused green of her eyes. I'm trying my best to rob her of breath, but everything about this woman is stealing mine, too.

"It's a request. I'm telling you what I want. You're not one of those who demands manners in bed, are you? Please, Sir and thank you, Sir and all that?"

I never have been before. I've always preferred equal partners. But the thought of bending Harlow to my will with the pleasure I give her trips my trigger more than I would have thought. "What if I am?"

Something passes across her face, so quickly I can't tell what she's thinking. But I get the impression she actually doesn't hate the idea.

"Well, that's not my thing."

Now I know she's lying—whether that's to me or herself, I'm not sure. I can't even put my finger on the reason I'm convinced she absolutely wants a man to command her in bed. Maybe the breathless way she denies it? I tuck the knowledge into the back of my head for now and shrug. "Whatever you say, baby. I won't make you beg."

At least not at the moment.

Harlow bristles. "I don't do that."

I think I can make her—and I will…when the time is right. I'll ease her in, let her get comfortable, until she thinks she knows exactly what sort of commodity I am between the sheets. In the meantime, I'll learn her body, read her cues, see how she responds. I'll pounce once she's ripe and she least expects it.

"No sweat. I assume you have no issues with me putting my mouth on your clit and sucking until you scream your throat raw?"

She inhales a sharp breath and struggles to find her voice. "None at all."

"Excellent. You told me to do my worst, so…"

I let the insinuation dangle. She can interpret that however she wants. I intend to get busy.

Out of the corner of my eye, I catch Harlow's shaky nod. But I'm already fixated on her nipples—and the rest of her body I haven't had the opportunity to explore yet.

Cradling one breast in my hand, I dip my head and lave the distended tip. The bead is hard against my tongue. I drag it in and nearly moan at how plump it feels as I suck it deep. I've always been oral during sex. I enjoy getting my mouth on a woman and watching her squirm and pant as she races to climax. Already, I suspect Harlow will be different. She won't lie back passively and let me go down on her. She'll want to put in her two cents so she has some semblance of control.

That's not happening.

She threads her fingers through my hair. There's not much to grip, but she manages to dig the tips into my scalp enough to send a tingle racing through my entire body. I shudder as I shift to the other breast and wrap my lips around the taut bud.

"Harder," she demands.

"How hard?" I admit I have a caveman streak. I love being rough with a woman's nipples. I love to squeeze, bite, torment, and suck them until they're red and throbbing and sore. "I can make them ache, baby."

"Can you make me feel it tomorrow? So that every time they rub against my bikini top I'll bite my lip and remember?"

Besides food and music, this is another place where we're absolutely in sync. "That's like asking if I know how to breathe. It comes natural. If that's what you want, I'll be more than happy to give it to you."

Her breath sounds choppy as she nods. "Do it."

I give her a lazy smile. She has no idea what she's inviting…

When I bend my head and lick one hard tip again while pinching the other, she gasps. I don't even let her recover before I hoover her into my mouth, add a bite of teeth, then soothe it with my tongue again. As I switch to the other nipple, her hips move restlessly. She gives a not-so-subtle tug of my hair. The arch of her back, lifting her breasts closer to my mouth, tells me she's loving this.

That makes two of us.

I keep at her, and the sounds of her whimpers grow louder, closer together. She wraps her legs around me and digs her nails into my scalp with every drag and draw on her nipples. They're swelling in my mouth, and I swear the flavor of her on my tongue is only getting sweeter. I can fucking smell her arousal in the air between us, and it's all I can do not to grab the nearest condom and start plowing her until she screams. But I have to make this so good for her that she'll never forget. I need her to be as desperate to have me inside her as I am to get there.

I've always been competitive. Succeeding has been bred and hammered into me since my first peewee football coach, my dad, insisted that I should never try less than my best and that dreams unfulfilled are merely aptitude wasted. No way am I not succeeding at arousing Harlow—what's her last name?—out of her head with desire.

"Holy hell…" she pants out. "That's so good."

"Your nipples sore yet, baby?"

She nods almost unconsciously. I wonder how much control she has over her brain with all the desire coursing through her blood. Her hugely dilated pupils say it's not much. "Yeah."

"You like it." I don't ask; I know.

"Love it." She cradles her own breasts and gives the nipples a tweak, tossing back her head and digging her heels into the mattress.

Have I ever been with a woman who arouses me this much? If I have, she's gone from my memory bank now, replaced solely by this one.

"I feel everything now. Every lick, every pull, every nip. My nipples and my clit seem connected, and every drag on one"—she pinches the hard tips again and groans—"pulls between my legs."

As it should be. "How you going to hold up when I get my mouth down there, baby?"

Her lashes flutter. Her lips part. I'm enjoying the hell out of undoing strong-willed Harlow. "I'll come hard."

"That's exactly what I want to hear," I murmur as I take over pinching her taut beads.

Her nipples are probably reaching max stimulation, but I can't quite let up. I toy and tease, just one more slow, soft pass of my tongue or a tiny brush of my knuckles over the tips. She shudders, writhing under me. She doesn't need much stimulation now to feel my every caress, and watching the unvarnished reactions pass over her face is like magic. For sure she'll be tender after her orgasm—and probably for the next few days. But I don't want these sensitive buds so worked over that I can't indulge in this oral treat again tomorrow.

Still, I'm reluctant to let up. The gentlest lick against them has her tensing and struggling to breathe. I exhale on them, kiss all around them, skim the barest touch over them. She closes her eyes, whimpers, and melts into the mattress.

This girl is so fucking responsive. She makes me feel less like a guy who knows his way around a bedroom and more like a man commanding his woman's body. A few hours ago I would have resisted that idea. First, I've known how the female form works since Leilani Iosua during my tenth-grade season. I can get women off. But Harlow is different. This is so heady. And that's scary. My whole attitude and approach to her feel oddly possessive. I'm not in the market for attachments. My life is too up in the air.

But everything about this woman sizzles me and fries my brain.

"Noah, show me how hard you can make me come," Harlow says, her voice not quite even.

It's not a demand…but it's more than a request. I'm happy to oblige. "I've been looking forward to this." I slide down her body, kissing my way across her tummy, then down again to that bare, puffy triangle of flesh, so wet now I can already see how slick and welcoming she's going to be. "Spread your legs wider for me."

When she does, my jaw nearly drops. She's all pale and pink and perfect. If a pussy can be pretty, hers definitely is. Between the swollen lips, I see a hint of rosy folds and the tiny opening I'm desperate to fill with my cock.

I spread her open with my thumbs as I settle my shoulders between her thighs. I'm getting comfortable down here because I intend to stay until she cries for mercy. Maybe longer.

Under my hands, she's turned still, anticipation freezing everything except the air shuttling in and out of her lungs. Those are working overtime as she stares my way. Yeah, she wants it. I can't wait to blow her mind.

"I hope you're a screamer," I growl because I'm too aroused to find my normal tone of voice.

"Not usually."

With a sly glance up her body, I zero in on her watchful gaze. "Let's see if we can change that."

Then words are no longer necessary, and I turn my attention to the pouting flesh inches from my lips. I'm practically salivating. She's so ripe and juicy, and my oral addiction needs another fix, especially when I see how red and engorged her clit is before I've even touched it.

This is going to be so easy…and so satisfying.

I stroke my tongue through the furrow between her folds, ending at the apex. I lave the knot of nerves in a slow swipe that has her gasping and fisting the sheets. She grinds her ass into the mattress, then lifts up to my mouth, restless and eager.

"Oh, Noah…"

"You like that?" I know the answer but I want to hear her admit it. I have a feeling that, usually, she's a tough nut to crack.

"Yes," she says on an outrush of breath.

"You want more?"

"Yes."

Say please. The demand is on the tip of my tongue. I'm not normally that sort of guy, but with Harlow the urge is almost compulsive. I'm not even sure if that's because I merely want to bend her or totally own her in this moment. But I stifle the urge to push her now. If tonight is all we have, I don't want to spend it fighting a battle of wills. If I can hook her now, the power struggle that may come later will be much easier to win. And victory will be so sweet.

Until then, I stiffen my tongue and flick her hard pearl. As I do, I fit a pair of fingers inside her. The sweltering heat of her nearly burns me.

Jesus, she's snug. And as I take her clit between my lips and suck in gentle pulls, I feel the corresponding clamp of her vaginal muscles on my fingers.

She's going to be so tight to fuck. That will be a thrill all by itself. But I love the idea of turning this woman inside out and wringing every ounce of pleasure out of her I possibly can. I want to addict her. I haven't even fucked her yet, and already I fear she'll be like heroin. The pull to her will be strong, the craving too hard to resist. Hours after one fix, I'll need another…and another…and another.

Or maybe it's just been so long since I've had sex and I'm so horny that everything about Harlow feels new and different and amazing. Yeah, I'll go with that.

My internal BS meter is pealing in alarm. But I'm ignoring that for now.

Instead, I dive into Harlow headfirst, opening my mouth on her pussy as if I can kiss every part of it at once. Her tangy-sweet cream is abundant and addictive. Holy shit, I've always loved pussy, but this woman… I moan and grip her thighs. If she'll stay beyond tonight, I'm going to make her my breakfast. I'll need snacks during the day, too. I wonder how she'll react if I suggest she take to wearing skirts and ditching her panties. I want twenty-four-seven access. I want this cunt—and this woman—to myself.

Harlow's breathing edges up a notch. Every exhalation sounds shakier and noisier. I flick her clit with my tongue again, finding the very tip and working it with the flat, absorbing everything about her into my taste buds. In response, she whimpers and plants her feet on the bed, lifting her hips to my mouth.

I open wider, take her flesh in deeper, at the same time I turn my wrist and flick my fingers against her most sensitive spot. It's not hard to find. It's the one that feels smooth and flat and makes her cry out and bow her back when I rub it.

"God, you taste good," I tell her as I wrap my free hand around her shin and shove the leg up to her hips. "Grab your knees and hold yourself open for me. I want to taste every part of you."

She hesitates, watching me lick her essence from my lips, then dip my tongue through her folds again. Then she shudders, struggles through another breath, and complies.

Good girl.

I duck my head and focus all my attention on her wet, swelling flesh once more. If anything, she turned sweeter, headier. I stroke her from her soft opening all the way to her knotted clit in one long swipe before I circle around the distended pearl again and again.

"Noah! I'm going to…" Her breath catches before she can finish. "It's big. I don't know if I can hold out."

"Then don't. Believe me, I'll be doing this again."

I already have plans. I think I'll lay her across the dining room table and make a brunch out of her come Sunday. No, that's too many days away. Besides, I can have brunch any damn day I want. The idea of pouring champagne over her and licking it from all the intriguing dips and valleys of her body, watching the bubbly trickle to her pussy and tonguing it from her, is enough to jack up my desire even more.

She fists the sheets even tighter. "Suck my clit in your mouth and rub that spot again."

I will…in time. "You're awfully demanding."

"Because you're driving me out of my mind. Oh, my god…" She bucks and tosses her hips up, trying to force me to put more pressure where she needs it.

Perversely, I ease back. "You like this?"

"I've never been much of a fan of receiving oral before but…wow."

That's pretty forthcoming for Harlow, and I realize I must be getting to her if she blurted that. Vaguely, I wonder who are the inept assholes capable of botching oral pleasure. Whatever. They don't matter now. I'll show her what it should be and have a shit ton of fun doing it, too. I love being this close, this intimate, able to sense every rise in her pleasure way before she's willing to admit it. Guys who don't get the beauty of that are fucking losers.

I give her a lingering look. "I've always been an enthusiastic giver, but you're a special treat. I'm going to insist on more of this."

She doesn't answer, just wriggles with the next drag of my tongue over her sensitive flesh. And the one following. She's definitely close—right on the edge. This is the perfect time to press my position.

"You're going to give me more, right?"

"What?" Her breathless question tells me she can barely follow the conversation, and I smile. Almost there…

"You'll spread your legs and let me put my mouth on your sweet pussy whenever I want, won't you?"

"Tonight? Yes. Hell yes."

"Tomorrow, too." I caress her sensitive inner thighs with a drag of my thumbs up, then back down…just shy of her steely red clit. "I want tomorrow."

I don't mention that will probably extend to the day after, too. Hell, probably the next week. Why not give myself plenty of time to really work this beauty out of my system?

Providing such a thing is even possible. Maybe she's simply my sexual Kryptonite, and I'll always be willing to gnaw my way off my leash to have her. It's a crazy thought, but if that ends up being true… Well, I'm willing to live with it if I can have her.

Harlow doesn't answer right away, so I stop everything. I let up stimulating all the nerve endings I've been skimming and strumming with my tongue. A split second later, she bolts up enough to grab my head in her hand and urge my mouth closer.

I back away. "Promise me tomorrow, Harlow. Promise me a day with your legs spread and my feast waiting."

"Yes. Tomorrow. Whenever you want," she concedes.

I don't think she knows just how serious I am…but she will. "And wherever I want."

I'm thinking hard about that long dining room table downstairs, about sitting at the head of it and pulling her right up to my chair so I can enjoy her like a meal. The more I visualize it, the more I want that.

I've never in my life failed to pursue what I want until I get it. Harlow won't be different.

"If there's privacy, yes."

I can appreciate that caveat. The last thing I need now is any sort of scandal threatening my future. I have to be squeaky clean to keep my endorsement deals, and especially if I'm even going to entertain the notion of accepting this broadcasting offer. I would never want to embarrass or jeopardize Harlow in public, either. But in private, I want to be dirty as hell with her.

"Done," I promise. "And I'll hold you to it."

"Fine," she pants. "Just make me come. Please…"

Ah, those are the sweetest words. One little breathy plea, and my cock feels as if it's ready to burst. I'm going to enjoy wringing even more begging out of her soon.

"My pleasure, baby," I assure her as I focus my undivided attention on her pussy again, lapping and licking, stroking, flicking, and nipping.

Within seconds, she's heaving air in and out of her lungs, every inhalation a bit louder as she keens her way up and up. Finally, her body freezes, her bliss breaks, and her voice splits into a wail that bounces off the walls, peals around the room, and fills my ears with the sweet sounds of her ecstasy.

Nice to know she's a screamer, after all.

Her orgasm seems to go on forever, and her body bucks and shudders. I grip her hips, hold her down, and keep at her until I wring every last bit of shivering pleasure from her body. Until she falls limp against the mattress with an exhausted sigh.

I can't remember the last time satisfaction was so sweet—and I haven't even found my own climax yet.

"What did you do to me? My legs are Jell-O," she murmurs.

"How about the rest of you?" I ease away long enough to reach for a condom.

A little smile spreads across her rosy lips. "I'm floating. But who knew I could see black spots and stars during climax?" She opens one eye to look at me. "I admit I was skeptical when the clothes started coming off, but you were amazing. Is that oral technique something they teach you in training camp? Maybe you learned how to lob the ball up one day and go down on a woman like a god the next?"

I laugh. "I'm afraid training camp was never that entertaining. I might have liked it a whole lot better. But instead, I was trapped for weeks with sweaty dudes in hot climates, wishing like hell fall would hurry up."

"So you're just naturally orally gifted, then?" She sighs and goes on as if she doesn't expect me to reply. "I feel like a lucky girl."

"Good. Then you won't regret agreeing to let me eat my fill of you tomorrow." I give her a wide grin.

Harlow struggles up onto her elbows. "You were serious?"

"Why would you think I wasn't?"

"I just assumed it was...you know, sexy talk."

"Nope. I expect to have my mouth on you tomorrow whenever and wherever I want. You agreed."

She nods slowly, some of the flush receding from her cheeks and chest. "I did. You can go down on me, but since you haven't had your orgasm yet, I think it's the perfect time to make a bargain of my own. I'll throw in sex now and whenever you want tomorrow—if you agree to let me help you with your post-concussive speech issues. If not, well... I got mine. I feel damn good. I could roll over and sleep like a baby all night now. How about you?"

CHAPTER THREE

I SIT BACK on my heels, staring at Harlow. Smart, sly woman. I did not see her turning the tables on me...and I should have. She seems like the sort of woman who gives as good as she gets—plus a bit more to let people know she means business.

"I don't have speech issues." The words come out more clipped than I mean them to.

"So you don't have more difficulty speaking when you're tired or nervous or in stressful situations? So it hasn't been holding you back from conversations, social situations, or maybe even future career plans? I saw a rumor on the Internet that several networks are looking to bring you on to their broadcasting team and that you haven't indicated your interest one way or the other. Most people suspect it's a ploy to wheedle more money out of them, but I think you're worried about being able to actually do the job. You don't want your legacy to be the once-in-a-lifetime quarterback who sucked in the broadcasting booth, do you?"

I drop the condom. "I'm not talking about this now. I've got a hard-on from hell, and I thought we were having sex. Did you change your mind?"

"No. I really, really want you inside me." Her face softens. "But I want to help you, too. And I can."

"Why do you give a shit?"

"Well, I wouldn't have earned a master's degree in speech pathology if I didn't have a passion for the subject and didn't want to help people improve all the verbal, listening, and processing aspects of their lives. You have a great voice. You clearly know the game. All your fans think you'd be amazing as a commentator. I also think you're too young to retire and live for decades off your glory days."

"I have the money."

"Clearly, or you couldn't have afforded this house. That's not what I'm saying. I just can't picture you sitting idly until you're too old to care what people think. That doesn't seem like you. If it was, you would never have reached the pinnacle of professional sports and led your team to multiple Super Bowl victories. And your Wikipedia bio says you've been playing your whole life. So I ask myself, if a man like this can't play anymore, how could he lend his expertise and be an ambassador for his sport? And what would hold him back from saying an obvious yes?"

Goddamn it, she's seen right through me. I feel way more exposed in the wake of her little speech than I do sitting in front of her stark naked. "Harlow…"

"Let me try. That's all I'm asking. It's a win-win for both of us. If I help you past your current challenges, then you have a great second career. If I don't, at least you won't be wondering what if. You'll know because you'll have tried. And if I succeed in helping you, then I get a step up professionally. Speech following traumatic brain injury is sort of my thing. I was looking to help children, but this would look great on my resumé. I don't see the downside here."

Other than my utter humiliation at being broken? She's right.

"And the truth is," she goes on, "I don't think I'm ready to go back to San Diego. There's a lot going on back home. Drama I just don't need. But I'm not one to sit idle, either. I've done it for a month now and I'm bored silly. Working with you would keep us both occupied and making progress toward a better future."

"What about sex?"

She gives me a big grin. "It could be a great side benefit."

I'm considering her words really hard. Harlow would have made a hell of a litigator because she knows exactly when and how to press her point to maximum advantage. "Let's say I'm thinking about this."

The satisfied rise of her brows tells me she thinks she's won. Hell, she probably has. But...I'd have to confront the problems I've been avoiding for months. Which is probably smarter than burying my head in the sand. Even so, I'm not so sure I want every jock junkie and *Sports Illustrated* reader knowing about my deficiency.

On the other hand, what if some of my peers or teammates have been suffering in silence, too? What if I make enough progress to take this job and can use my mic and the network's platform to give other players, past and present, hope?

Plus I'll get to fuck Harlow now. And later, too. Like she said, win-win.

I sigh and hope I'm making the right decision—or rather that the right head is making it. "All right."

A big smile perks up her face before something more cautious takes over. "It's not an overnight process, though. I can't wave my magic wand or anything."

"How long?"

She shrugs. "Hard to say. I need to have some idea how much you're impaired and what your triggers are. Obviously, when you're tired."

"Especially then."

"And if you're going to be jetting across time zones to cover games, that's likely to be a lot. Does it happen when you're nervous, too? I was guessing but..."

I shrug. "I haven't tested that."

I haven't been willing to, but if being a little rattled affects my ability to find words, I won't be terribly surprised.

"I'll need to do a few assessments on you to be sure exactly what I'm dealing with but I have a decent idea. How long before you have to know whether you want to take this kind of job?"

"About a month. Maybe six weeks if I push it."

She nods. "We'll have to work fast—and diligently. I think it's important we replicate situations that may challenge you and work on your speech then."

"You mean therapy when I'm tired or nervous?"

"Exactly. So maybe late at night or really early in the morning, in stressful situations. That kind of thing. It will require some planning but it will ultimately be worth it, I think. It will definitely be the best way to help you progress and see where you might need a little more focus."

A stroke of genius streaks through my brain.

"You should stay here while we work. I have plenty of room, and neither of us will have to be driving to the other in the middle of the night." When she looks uncertain, I press my advantage. "I need a therapist and you need place to stay where you're not hearing your brothers making babies. Win-win," I toss her words back at her.

"You're serious?"

"Totally."

She shifts and stretches. "Let's do it."

The conversation is over. And with that visual of her dark hair spreading over my white sheets, I lose my patience with talk.

"I'll call my attorney and have a contract drawn up," I murmur as I prowl my way up her body, spreading her legs with my knees and making some mental notes about clauses to insert to make the most of having Harlow close. "How about we get back to the situation at"—I pause when she wraps her fingers around my stiff, aching cock—"ah…hand."

Everything this woman does to me feels new and mind-blowing—like an experience I'm going to want to repeat.

Harlow grins as she teases me with tormentingly slow strokes. "You mean sex?"

"Yeah," I choke out, fisting the condom wrapper so hard the corner of the foil packet jabs my palm. "I need to be inside you."

"But I want to explore you and—"

"Later," I bark as I loom above her and rip the square open with my teeth. "Let me fuck you, then you can do whatever you want to me."

The laugh that slips past her lips is light and infectious, but I can't share in the jolly while she's jacking up my need with that molasses stroke.

Instead, I'm single-minded as I get the condom open and roll it down my length. Then—finally—I press my naked body on hers and turn my entire focus her way. My hot stare drills down into her eyes as I settle my full weight between her legs.

As I glide my cock against her slick sex, her laughter dies. "Noah?"

The tremble in her voice both worries and thrills me. But her expression doesn't convey fear at all, just pure sexual desire.

"What, baby?"

"Hurry."

So despite that massive orgasm I gave her five minutes ago, she's already restless and achy again? Excellent.

I clench my fingers in her hair. "Absolutely."

When I dip my head to capture her lips, I root around to align my cock with her soft opening. As if she were a magnet for my iron-hard dick, I find the right spot almost immediately and begin to sink the head inside. I test my welcome—an inch in, an inch out. Repeat the process. She's like warmed silk gripping me, and when she rolls her hips and digs her nails into my back in silent demand for more, I can't stop the groan that tears from my chest.

I also can't stop myself from plunging completely into her with one harsh, teeth-baring stroke. But once I'm in? *Oh, god...* Have I ever felt anything half as euphoric as being inside Harlow? I'm thinking she must feel the same since she gives me a long moan and tosses her head back. Her lips part. Her nails pierce my skin. Her legs wrap around me tight. Her pussy envelops me like a wet dream.

I want to do her slow and do her right, hold out until she comes a couple of times, chanting my name in dazed satisfaction. The minute I feel her all around me, I know that's not going to happen.

"I won't hold back."

"Thank god," she breathes.

"Grab on tight."

She grips my shoulders with even more insistent fingers as I drag my palms down her body to lift her hips into my waiting hands. I watch her face. Harlow meets my stare. Her eyes are a dark, hypnotic green, and I'm ensnared. I'm ensorcelled.

I'm screwed.

That's my last thought before I crash into her, full force, one unrelenting stroke after another—until the bed rattles, until she begins to flush rosy once more, until she makes the sexiest little whimpers at the back of her throat. Until she tightens on me like she's close to climax.

Pleasure isn't even the right word to describe the sensations coursing through my body and screaming down my spine. It's more than bliss, more than ecstasy. It's not like anything I've ever felt. I'm dizzy. I'm breathless. Every inch of my skin feels seared with fiery tingles. But it's worse because I swear I feel her inside me, too. Like she's squeezing my thudding heart. Like she's cutting a deep valley through my soul.

What the hell is going on?

I don't know but I can't stop. I'm compelled to thrust deeper, harder, build the need higher. And as if some force bigger than both of us is coercing her, too, she nips at my shoulder, kisses my neck, skimming her lips over my jaw, all but trying to inhale me.

It's the single most erotic experience of my life.

Unfortunately, it can't last. I'm burning too hot, too bright. Too close to the edge.

"Harlow?" I growl out the question between a hard thrust and the next, which is even rougher. I can't stop drilling into her. It's as if some primal part of me is convinced I can somehow leave my stamp of ownership on her and make her mine.

"Now," she keens out. "Please. Oh…yes!"

Suddenly, she convulses around me, and I'm a split second behind her, lava charging through my veins and jetting from my cock.

I'm dying, and it's the best feeling I've ever experienced. My vision closes in on only Harlow. My breath bellows. My body pumps of its own volition—whatever it takes to get closer to this woman. The sensations are like a brick wall slamming me at a hundred miles an hour and flattening me, but it's not pain I feel. No, she leaves me with the most amazing high.

I want to feel it again right now.

Hi, my name is Noah Weston and I'm an addict. Harlow is my drug of choice.

Admitting the problem might be the first step, but I don't want to recover. In fact, I don't want to change a thing—except to get more of her. Instantly, I start planning to get as much of this woman as I possibly can.

THE FOLLOWING MORNING, I sit up abruptly. A glance around tells me I'm alone. The bathroom door is open. There's no one in the adjacent walk-in closet or on the balcony overlooking the majestic Pacific.

"Harlow?" I call her name in low, experimental tones.

No reply. But I see a gray SUV in the driveway on the side of the house. Did she decide to leave after last night and find a ride off the estate after all?

Damn it.

We had a deal. Why would she suddenly change her mind?

Tossing the sheet back, I grope around for shorts and snag my toothbrush off the bathroom counter, squeezing a dollop of paste from the tube and brushing my teeth as I jog down the stairs. I've got to stop her. First, last night we had the best sex I've ever had and I'm nowhere near done with that woman. Second, the more I think about her proposition, the more I suspect she's right. Speech therapy could not only help me, but her—and all the other guys in the league who may be too hesitant to come forward and admit that concussions have screwed with their mental faculties. Maybe I can do more good with my position than win a trophy and a few rings.

At the bottom of the stairs, I spot the powder bath. I also hear the mumble of a distinctly male voice.

Shit. Who is this interloper and what is he doing in my house?

Totally disregarding the fact that I haven't scrubbed my pearly whites for two minutes, I duck into that guest bathroom, do a quick spit and rinse, then haul ass toward the kitchen.

"I'm fine," I hear Harlow say to her mystery guest I can't see around the corner.

She sounds defensive. If I were whoever she's talking to now, I wouldn't believe her. Besides, anytime a woman says she's "fine," she's definitely not.

"What does that mean?" he demands.

"It means that nothing is wrong and that I'm perfectly capable of making my own decisions."

"Five days ago, you were—"

"I know what happened. I don't need the reminder." Now Harlow sounds thoroughly annoyed. "I wasn't all in your business when—"

"My life was falling apart? Yeah, you were." He snorts. "So I'm not stepping out of yours."

What is this guy talking about? I have no idea, but I intend to find out.

"Don't do this," she implores.

"Do what? Care? You mean the world to me, and I refuse to leave you now."

My insides seize up. So here's another guy with a thing for Harlow. I shouldn't be furious. I shouldn't even be surprised. If I was one of her exes, I'd be fighting for her, too. I get where he's coming from. No idea why Harlow let him into my house, but I'll be damned if he's staying—or taking her with him. She's here, and unless she tells me she's completely in love with him, she's mine. At least for now. He can go fuck himself.

I storm into the kitchen. Harlow barely has time to turn to me with a gasp before I give my competition a steely glare and wrap my arm around her waist. Yes, I'm marking my territory. I feel possessive. Hey, at least I didn't lift my hind leg.

Harlow tries to shimmy and slink away. I hold firm.

"Problem?" I growl because I don't like the way he's talking to her, as if he has a right to meddle in her life. Hell, I don't like him talking to her at all.

Harlow glances between me and the competition, who's got dark hair and a very serious expression. He looks younger than me and he's definitely dressed smarter. I also notice he's wearing a wedding band. *Fuck*. Does that mean Harlow is his mistress…or his wife?

I expect the guy to growl at me, tell me to get my goddamn hands off his woman—something appropriately cavemanish. Instead, he stands and thrusts out his hand. "Mr. Weston, it's an honor to meet you."

I hesitate, then realize he's sly after all. I have to let go of Harlow in order to shake his hand. I don't do it happily.

"Thank you. Who are you and why are you here harassing my girl?"

"This is so awkward," Harlow sighs as she shakes her head. Then she holds up her hands to ward the other guy off. "Before you freak out, Griff, just listen…"

Scowling, Griff takes in my shirtless form and then the slinky robe Harlow has wrapped around her body. Her well-worked nipples poke through the silk of her garment and tell me that she's not wearing a stitch underneath. Unless he's blind, I'll bet the other guy noticed, too.

Maybe that's not a bad thing. At least now he knows that if he wants Harlow back, he's going to have a fight.

"His girl? You fucking slept with him?" Griff explodes. "Do you have any idea how many notches are on his bedpost?"

I glare at Griff. So much for being honored to meet me.

"It's none of your business," she insists. "Like I said, I've got my life handled without your interference."

"I was willing to accept that when I thought that meant you'd re-solved to put the past behind you and had found another job on the island so you didn't have to head back to San Diego. I didn't think that meant you'd found someone to shack up with."

"Hey," I challenge him with a scowl. "What she and I do is none of your business, asshole. So stop whining, accept that she's moved on from you, and dust off your man card. While you're at it, get the hell out of my house."

I expect a lot of reactions, but again, this guy surprises me when he plants himself on my barstool again and bursts out laughing. "She will *never* move on from me. Ever. I will be in her life for the rest of her days, whether either of us wants that or not."

I frown. Do they have a child together? Harlow doesn't look as if she's ever given birth but I know women who are in great shape following pregnancy. It's possible. But Harlow baps him on the shoulder none too gently with an annoyed tsk, which doesn't seem at all like something ex-lovers do when they're having a disagreement.

What's going on here?

"Stop being a douche, Griff. Don't yank his chain." She turns to me. "You don't have to play possessive or whatever this act is. Griff isn't my boyfriend. He's my brother."

It only takes a second for her words to sink in. Once they do, I feel like a fucking idiot. She told me she had brothers living on the island. I just never put two and two together. And now I see the resemblance. They both have the same striking green eyes.

"I'm also one of your Realtors." He raises a brow at me. "Griffin Reed."

I remember that name. And I feel like an even bigger ass.

We have this uncomfortable stare-down thing, and I'm trying not to look guilty until another voice interrupts our pregnant silence.

"What is taking so damn long? If Weston is here, Harlow should be ready to go." Another well-dressed suit strides in. He's got impeccable golden hair and shiny shoes. I'm betting this is her other Realtor brother. He and Griff both look like a proverbial million dollars—which I paid them in commission to buy this house. "So let's pack up her shit and—" When the guy notices me, he freezes. "Mr. Weston."

Harlow intercedes. "Noah, this is my older brother, Maxon."

He gives her barely dressed form a once-over. I doubt he fails to catalog her mussed sex hair and the faint hint of whisker burn on her cheeks. It's a small blessing that the Reed brothers can't see her inner thighs right now.

I search for a greeting or some light chitchat that will break the tension in the room. I come up blank. Not only don't I have a topic in mind but my tongue feels glued to the roof of my mouth. I take deep breaths. I sweat. I try to push through. I need whatever verbal skills I have now. No, the guys in suits might not beat me up for getting horizontal with their sister, but I have no trouble believing they're clever enough to plot some insidious revenge when I least expect it. Besides, they're Harlow's family. I don't want to make waves for her.

Thankfully, she saves me from the awkward silence. "As you can see, I'm fine, which is what I've been explaining to Griff. I appreciate that you heard Noah had arrived on the island early and decided to come 'rescue' me, but it's not necessary. I'll be staying here for a while."

Maxon scowls at her. "You did a great job house-sitting, but I doubt he needs your services anymore. I don't want to know anything about the welcome you gave him last night, but now it's time for you to vacate and let him have the privacy he paid for."

I want to jump in and tell them both that I've hired their sister to help me secure a broadcasting gig. But they don't have any idea I've had intermittent problems with my speech, so who knows if they'll even believe me. And I certainly don't want them telling the world. Besides, I can't even speak at the moment.

Well, shit. I guess I *do* have trouble getting my words out when I'm rattled. What a great time to find out...

"Actually, he does still need my services, so I'm staying for a while. You and Keeley have your hands full now that the bed-and-breakfast is open. Didn't you just host those bigwig honeymooners from D.C. for a couple of weeks? I know you've got other bookings coming up." Then she turns to Griff. "You and Britta are moving into a new house and you're both eager to conceive a new brother or sister for Jamie, so I'll only be in the way. I swear, I'm fine here."

Maxon looks unmoved as he turns to me. "You want her staying?"

I can't find words, but I'm glad as hell he's asked me a yes-or-no question. I give him a firm nod. End of discussion.

He looks as if he's biting back a curse. Griff's mien looks equally reluctant. I want to tell them I'll make Harlow deliriously happy. But they're men, so they'll interpret my meaning as I intend to keep their sister happy in bed…which is true. Maybe it's a good thing that I can't talk just now.

"There you go." Harlow gestures to me and catches my stare. When a little frown appears between her brows, I know she understands what's up with me.

In truth, having this unpredictable disability is both frustrating and humiliating. I've never been incapable of anything in my life, except maybe ballet. Yes, my college coach made us try it a few times for balance training. Or that's what he claimed. I still think he meant it as punishment. Either way, I'm not used to feeling helpless. And right now is the worst. Harlow could use the backup against her protective brothers, and I'm out of commission.

Finally, Griff sighs and rises from his seat. "All right. If you change your mind, my door is open. I teased you about possibly crashing my newlywed, baby-conceiving bliss, but I wasn't serious. You're always welcome. Britta would say the same, and you know Jamie loves his Auntie Harlow."

She nods, looking both relieved and grateful. "Thanks. You good now, big brother?"

Maxon glances my way, gritting his teeth. "I don't like it because I know your reputation, Weston. If you hurt my sister—"

"Stop!" Harlow looks horrified.

I want to jump into the conversation and defend myself. I'm not an asshole. And I'm not led around by my dick. Well, I'm not when Harlow isn't around. I'd at least like to assure them I'm not going to hurt her.

But I can't say a fucking word.

"What?" Maxon tosses his hands in the air. "I'm just saying—"

"Don't," Harlow cuts in. "There are eight bedrooms here, as you know. I can choose any of them I want and I'll be fine." When Maxon still looks unconvinced, she glowers at him. "Noah hired me to do a job, so I'm going to do it. I'll be helping him, and he's helping me by letting me stay for a bit."

"What kind of job? Will you be taking care of more than his house?"

"It's the kind of job we'll do with our clothes on, so butt out, big brother. Seriously. He's a decent guy."

"With a sexual track record so long it's more like a marathon."

If Maxon wasn't taking shots at me, I might laugh at his turn of phrase. Instead, I shake my head. I've had my share of women, sure. I won't lie about that. But I'm not a man whore.

"I don't care," Harlow argues. "We're *working* together, and you're embarrassing me. Once the job is over, I'll let him have the place to himself and go on with my life. I'm not looking for romance, so you don't have to worry about whatever delicate heart you think I have. Just...go. I've got this."

Maxon grits his teeth. "Why are you the most stubbornly independent female I know?"

"You mean other than your wife?"

"I'm starting to think you even have her beat, and that's saying a lot."

"Oh, I'm so going to tell Keeley you said that."

He snorts. "Threats won't work. Promise you'll call if you need us. We're worried. Five days ago—"

"Is not something I'm discussing. Pick up and move out, guys. Aren't you going to be late for work?"

Griff glances at his phone with a grimace. Maxon whips his arm up to stare at the vintage-looking Cartier on his wrist, then swears.

"Fine. We're going." Griff crosses his arms over his chest. "Call us if you need *anything*."

"I will," she assures softly. "Um, are Mom and Dad still on the island?"

"Unfortunately, yes. Mom isn't shy about showing off how happy she and Marco are right now. Dad's feeling like he needs to keep up."

Maxon nods. "It's a shit show. And they both want to talk to you."

Harlow looks disturbed by that. "Oh, please tell them you have no idea where to find me."

"Only if you two promise to have dinner with us in the next few days."

They want to check up on their sister, watch us interact together. I'm annoyed but I don't blame them. Well, not entirely. I just hope I can form goddamn words by then.

"Fine. Just keep them off my back."

"Let me clarify: a nice sit-down dinner. With Keeley and Britta." The oldest brother's expression softens. "They're worried about you, too."

Regret passes over Harlow's face, and I wonder what the hell has been going on in her life. "I didn't even consider that. I'm sorry. Tell them both I'll call soon. Maybe we'll do lunch one day this week if they're free."

"Thanks." Griff leans in to kiss his sister's cheek. "It would mean a lot to Britta."

Maxon follows suit. "Same with Keeley. Her mom and Phil went back to Phoenix. She's been a little weepy since. Oh, and I'm supposed to give you this." He reaches into his suit pocket and pulls out a CD. "My wife says this is a warm-up. She'll have more for you soon."

Harlow glances at the disc, then gives Maxon a rueful smile. "You've got a keeper. Thanks. Give both girls my love. And ruffle Jamie's hair for me."

"Will do."

She glances at me before turning back to her brothers. "Did…anyone else leave the island?"

Their grim faces say they understand her question. I'm totally lost.

"About an hour after you took off," Griff assures.

That makes her sigh with relief. Clearly, she wants to avoid someone. I wonder who that might be and what's going on. I want to ask but I'm pretty sure my words would come out like gibberish.

I curse a blue streak in my head, then realize the brothers are focused on me. We don't say a word, but there's a whole lot of Alpha male testosterone floating through the air. They want me to know they both think the job I've supposedly hired Harlow to do is bullshit and they don't appreciate me banging their sister. I want them to know that I'll treat her well as long as we're together, but otherwise, they can butt out.

After our silent conversation, they give me curt nods, then head out the front door.

As soon as it snicks shut, Harlow turns to me, hands on my shoulders. "Breathe. Everything is fine. Thanks for not losing your cool with my brothers. They mean well. And believe it or not, that actually went smoothly. They usually hate any guy I see."

I press my lips together, swallow, then drag in a deep breath. My nerves evaporate. And suddenly, the words between my brain and my lips begin to flow. "That was good?"

My enunciation isn't perfect, but I get the point across.

"Totally. Don't worry about them. Coffee?"

"I'll make it. What happened five days ago?"

Harlow doesn't meet my gaze. "Stupid family drama. I walked away from it. Everyone is worried about me because I might have lost my shit before I hustled out more abruptly than I should have. A lot of it has to do with my parents. They're separated and it's ugly and…" She grimaces as if the conversation is painful. "Can we talk about something else?"

She's dodging me, and I don't love it. But I understand. We've known each other fifteen hours. It feels longer, or like I know her way more than I actually do. Or maybe I'm simply more invested than I should be. Either way, she's put up a verbal KEEP OUT sign, and I have to respect that I have no place in her family issues. She's helping me with my speech, and I'm giving her a place to stay. We're going to share orgasms. That should be it. But there's no reason we can't be friends, too, right? Her brothers' behavior gave me the impression that whatever is going on with her is a big fucking deal. Like any friend, I want to be here for her if she needs help.

"Sorry to hear that. We can talk about whatever you want, but I'm willing to listen if you need to get something off your mind."

"Oh, god. The last thing I want to do is talk. I'm going to grab a shower and do some research on how best to tackle your challenges so we can get started." Then she gives me a second, lingering glance. "But you look mighty fine without a shirt. I'm tempted to chuck responsibility for a few hours and go back to bed. What do you say?"

I love Harlow's suggestion, but I don't like feeling as if she brushed me off. Still, I can't force her to confide in me. "Why don't you grab that shower while I make some coffee and call my attorney. I want to get your contract set up today so you can sign it. Then…we'll see."

"Sure thing, hunk. I'm excited. This is going to beat the hell out of a traditional eight-to-five job. And if last night is any indication, the sex will be an awesome perk." She winks at me, then swishes toward the stairs.

I watch her, both aroused and vaguely irked that she seems to like our sexual chemistry—and my penis—more than she actually likes me.

With a frown, I watch Harlow walk away, her sway happy-go-lucky. Her brothers' visit suggests she should be anything but. Seemingly, she's using sex to avoid personal interaction and wants orgasms more than the guy giving them to her. Since she's not a man-trophy collector, it's unexpected. The woman is a mystery. She's intriguing. I'm usually a brute-force kind of guy…but I already know that solving her is going to take finesse. But something is making her tick, and I want to know what.

CHAPTER FOUR

TWO CAN PLAY games, and I didn't survive league and team politics by not being aware of the people around me. Across the table at the seaside steakhouse, Harlow sparkles as she smiles like she doesn't have a care in the world. She flirts like a pro as the wind ruffles the loose tendrils of her dark hair around her face. She's stuffed the rest in an artfully mussed bun and tossed on a maxi dress and sandals, yet somehow manages to look both casual and put together.

"So there we are, ten sorority girls and a dead hamster named T-Rex, who had lived a grand life. We're giving him one hell of a Viking-style funeral on a raft in the pool at, like, two in the morning. We saluted him. One of my sorority sister's boyfriends had been a priest for Halloween, so he came over all dressed up to preside over T-Rex's funeral. I delivered a eulogy we all tossed together on a napkin at the last minute. I held the little speech in one hand and a bottle of Wild Turkey in the other. We literally couldn't stop laughing the whole time because it was so absurd. And we all needed the break from studying for finals." She sips her wine. "So while the raft is on fire and we're singing Sarah MacLachlan's 'I Will Remember You' at the top of our lungs, the raft that was supposed to send this hamster to Valhalla turns into a floating bonfire. Actual heat flared off the sucker. The smell of melting plastic was awful. Yes, we were young and stupid. But the elderly woman who lived in the house behind us woke up and called the fire department. I kid you not, they rolled two trucks with ladders, thinking they had a serious blaze on their hands. When they arrived, they scolded us for being careless—which we totally were. But a few of them stayed behind to hang, and one of them asked out my roommate. They're married now. I was one of her bridesmaids, as was Masey, the friend whose pet crossed the rainbow bridge that fateful night. The bride was originally from Texas, where they do a groom's cake for the reception, so theirs was in the shape of a hamster. Hardly anyone got the inside joke, but it was hard to keep a straight face through some of the pictures."

I laugh because I can imagine how ridiculous the fiery hamster funeral probably was. Of course, my frat brothers and I did stuff way worse than that. We were a bunch of jocks with something dangerously close to carte blanche from the university's dean and board of directors, as long as we won games and kept the alumni money flowing. But this swapping of tales isn't a competition. I'm not about comparing pasts, either. I just want to keep Harlow talking so I can learn more. I especially want to know what's up with her.

"You're lucky no one got arrested," I point out.

"I know! And poor Masey really was broken up about losing T-Rex. So we got her plowed and rigged up the funeral to give her closure. She aced her finals after that. And her boyfriend said she started putting out again. So the girls and I considered it something close to a public service." She winks. "Probably not as crazy as things you've done. Aren't you professional athletes all ridiculous party animals? Booze and drugs and girls everywhere?"

I shrug. "There was a time. I was no saint in college. I went from being the hero of my high school football team to the starting quarterback of my college team. So yeah, we partied hard. But we were a team in the middle of rebuilding. In four years, we managed to turn the program around and ended our senior season ranked number four in the nation. If we'd had a defense, we might have won it all. But sports were easy then. The NFL was much harder. Everyone was bigger and faster and smarter. Football went from being the sport guys played because it got them a free ride through college and got them laid to being the career they took very seriously. I almost wiped out my rookie season because I didn't get that. But after having my ass sacked over and over that year, I starting hitting the gym, working on drills, and paying attention to film a lot more. I devoted more effort to practices and mental preparation out of self-preservation and it paid off."

That rookie season also saw two of my concussions, one of them the most serious. I was unconscious for nearly twenty minutes. One moment I had a Detroit defensive back in my face, plowing me to the turf. The next I woke up in one of the Motor City's ERs with a member of the team's medical staff trying to calm my mother over the phone. In the last few months I've wondered if I had started taking my job and my health seriously a few months sooner, would I have saved myself that concussion and some of the crap I'm going through now?

Harlow props her chin on her palm and stares at me across the table. "That's amazing. I can't imagine my job being that physical. The craziest thing I do now is crouch down to find the right toy or exercise to help speech-impaired kids learn whatever I'm trying to teach them. It has to be daunting to be on the field with a bunch of well-trained maniacs bent on your destruction."

"When you put it like that, what was I thinking?" I laugh. "Actually, I'm grateful to football. It kept me out of trouble as a kid and gave me a future I never imagined growing up in Honolulu's poor neighborhoods. You wouldn't get it, being one of those rich kids."

She tsks at me. "Why would you think I grew up wealthy?"

I snort. "Are you kidding? Privilege drips off you. You have this easy air of assurance about the world, like you've never wondered where your next meal would come from, like you could take or leave money. But I'll bet you've never been without it. You're accustomed to nice houses and fancy cars. Not in the 'I could get used to this' sort of way, but as if having them is completely normal in your world."

"How could you possibly know that?"

"It's not a bad thing," I assure her. "But I know because I was a kid who didn't have air conditioning until I went off to college. We had one old TV. I didn't even have a cell phone until after I signed my first pro contract. When I bought my first house in Dallas with my signing bonus, I kept walking in and staring in awe because I couldn't believe I had a place with marble floors and didn't have squawking chickens in the backyard I was waiting to get fat enough to eat. The way you look at the world is different. I want to hear more about your past."

That's what started this discussion. So far, Harlow has regaled me with tales about her sorority sisters and the hamster funeral, along with a couple of stories about her brothers' childhood antics. Nothing about her parents, her childhood, or her romantic history. She's only sharing the pleasant parts of her life. Because she's giving me only the easy-breezy bits she wants to think about?

She cocks her head as she swishes the wine. "Not much to tell that you don't know. My dad is a workaholic, and he was always good at making money. My mom pushed me into group activities the other kids did, forever sucking me into this dance studio or signing me up for that beauty pageant. I think she lived vicariously through me sometimes and never wanted to hear that I wasn't interested in cheerleading or modeling or whatever she thought I should be for appearance's sake."

"She must be proud of you now. A master's in a degree that can really help people, and especially if you're focusing on children who really need you…"

Her smile turns stilted. "I think she would rather me make something of those acting classes she dragged me to. Or at least marry well. Since I'm disinclined to do either, I'm pretty sure she's disappointed. What about you? Your parents must be extremely proud of all you've accomplished. And your siblings. What do they say at family gatherings?"

"They treat me like they always did. Trace tries to be bigger and badder, so he gets into these mock wrestling matches with me. Samaria still rolls her eyes at me and tells me to make myself useful. When we had Christmas dinner at her house last year, that meant doing a mountain of dishes. Mom clucks around me, like always. Still protective, as if I'm nine, not thirty-four. Dad passed away a couple years back. He always struggled with asthma. He had an attack when no one was home and he couldn't get to a phone."

Compassion softens her face. "I'm sorry. That must have been heart-breaking for you and your family."

Harlow means that genuinely. And I realize that's the dichotomy about her I don't understand. She can be so warm and genuine and easy to be with. But when I ask her about herself, she dodges and deflects. If I get too direct, she shuts down. She's not cold…but she's also not forthcoming.

Suddenly, I'm actually looking forward to having dinner with Maxon and Griff and their brides. Maybe I'll get some answers. Because as much as Harlow and I have sex—and we had a whole afternoon of it today—she's let me have full access to her body, no problem. But I don't feel as if she's let me any closer to the woman beneath all that gorgeous glowing skin.

It's bugging the hell out of me. Normally, I'd be high-fiving all the awesome, no-strings nookie. Not now. Not with Harlow.

I'm not even sure why. Maybe I'm bored and I have time on my hands?

"Thanks. Holidays are hard, for sure. I regret that none of us gave him the grandchildren he really wanted before he died, but I was too busy playing football to get domestic. Trace was too immature. Samaria was just finishing college. But now that my sister is married, I'm sure she'll make up for her deadbeat older brothers. That will make Mom happy, and I'm sure Dad will be smiling down on her, too."

"Don't you want kids someday?"

I haven't actually given it much thought. "I suppose." But the tone of her question makes me pause. "I take it you do?"

"Yeah. I've wanted them forever. A bunch of my girlfriends are al-ready married and have babies. They all say motherhood is the purest, most enduring form of love."

If a picture is worth a thousand words, I wish I had a camera so I could snap her face right now and capture that look of longing. I don't know if she's interested in romance or marriage or she simply wants a baby. But clearly standoffish Harlow craves love.

I never would have guessed.

I'm still turning the startling realization over when the waiter comes by to inquire about dessert. I pass. So does Harlow. Within two minutes, I've paid the check and we're heading out the front of the restaurant to wait for the valet.

As the trade winds blow gently and the sun takes a graceful bow over the horizon before disappearing, I take her hand in mine, liking how good it feels to just have this simple connection with her. Nothing about her tells me she's disappointed or lonely, but I sense she's troubled.

"You'll make a great mom someday," I tell her.

I think of her filling out and rounding with our child. My desire for Harlow, which is always hot, blazes to something shocking and scalding and insistent. I actually…like the idea of her being pregnant? Whoa, that's totally a new development for me.

"Thanks. I'd hoped to be one sooner rather than later. But…" She shrugs. "That's life, right? Unpredictable."

"Yes, it is. Just like meeting you." I lean in to kiss her. "But I'm glad I did."

I can't stop myself. Usually I'm not one for PDA because the press can take my first conversation with a woman and make it into the most dramatic breakup argument ever, but I don't know how to not touch Harlow. I'm still embarrassingly revved up from thinking about her pregnant. But an air of sadness lingers around her. I can't ignore it. I realize that's what's been snagging my attention over and over. She says things that are funny and light. Since we met, she's been the life of my party. Definitely the lay of the century. But it all feels like I'm barely scratching her surface. What pain is she covering up?

I palm the back of her neck and bend to kiss her. It's gentle and reassuring. Consoling. I don't think I've ever kissed a lover this way. I know that if I try to dig deeper into whatever she's hiding now, she'll just retreat behind her walls, but it's harder for her to evade me when our lips are pressed together.

Harlow clings sweetly, not rejecting my kiss or the comfort I give her. Moments later, she melts into me with a soft moan. I bring her closer.

Then several bright flashes of lights around us kill the moment. A small crowd of reporters and gawkers have gathered around us, some frantically texting pictures they've just taken of Harlow and me.

"Mr. Weston, how's retirement?" some random dude shouts nearby as I tuck her behind me.

"Are the rumors about you starting a second career in the broadcasting booth true?" asks a forty-something woman who looks like a shark seeking a scoop.

"How do you feel about being hailed as a hometown hero made good?" queries a seasoned sports reporter from the *Honolulu Star-Advertiser* whose name has escaped me.

"I gave statements to the press when I retired, folks. I'm just enjoying an evening out now that I'm back in Hawaii and I'd appreciate some privacy."

"Who's your date?" the woman demands to know as if I didn't just ask politely for them to shut the hell up. "Is it serious? Will the hearts of female Noah Weston fans be broken by an engagement announcement soon?"

I grit my teeth and smile, but when they start trying to snap pictures of Harlow, I'm genuinely annoyed. I turn to ask if she's all right and realize that, unlike most of my dates over the last twelve years, she's not seeking camera time. No, she's hiding her head and desperately trying to avoid it.

I search around the parking lot for any sign of the valet, but I see nothing except the starry Hawaiian evening and these shitheads ruining it. I wrap my arm around Harlow protectively. I'm sure the press will make all kinds of assumptions about that, but whatever. Right now, distress pours off Harlow as she buries her head in my arm.

"What's your name, miss?" asks the sports reporter. "How long have you been dating? Are you the reason Weston retired?"

"No comment." Her mutter is muffled by my sleeve and her refusal to show her face.

"You heard the lady. She has nothing to say. Neither do I. Have a good evening."

Finally, I see the lights of my rental approach. I'm looking forward to having my own car shipped over, but that will take a few weeks. This SUV will do until then, and I hustle halfway across the lot to meet it, Harlow in tow. Finally, the valet catches on to our dilemma and stops as we approach in the middle of the lot. He hops out and dashes around the car to open the door for her, but I've already beaten him to the punch. As soon as Harlow is settled inside, I shove a bill in his hand, then burn rubber out of the lot, leaving the small gaggle of gawkers behind us.

"You okay?" I cup her knee and will her to look over at me.

Instead, she nods, head bowed. "Fine. Can you just get me home?"

I notice that she considers my place her home. I'm not bothered. "On our way."

"Thanks." She looks up and sees we've left the restaurant behind, then exhales in relief. "How do you put up with that?"

"Reporters and nosy people?" I shrug and turn left. "Comes with the territory. In truth, I'm a little surprised to find them here. I'll bet someone in the restaurant tipped them off. Sorry if it upset you. I didn't expect this crap to last into retirement, especially after I moved closer to my old stomping ground. After all, I won't be dazzling fans anymore by breaking new touchdown or passing-yards records. Now I'm just a regular guy."

She scoffs. "I don't know that you'll ever be just a regular guy. I get that you want to move on with your life. I don't know if they ever will. Blood-sucking assholes."

I study her a bit closer as I stop at a red light. "You seemed kind of freaked by their intrusion. Have you had trouble with people barging into your personal life or something?"

Right on cue, here comes her plastic smile. "I'm not as important as you, fancy pants. Sure, I like attention as much as the next girl, but not when a bunch of vultures are trying to give it to me. Do you think they're so fascinated by everyone else's exploits because they've done nothing noteworthy in their own lives? What drives sad little people to care more about someone else's achievements than their own?"

That was a skillful deflection, and if I wasn't already on to Harlow, I probably would have fallen for that juicy question. "I don't know and I don't care. I'd rather know why they upset you."

She blinks at me as if I'm crazy. "Me? If I'm upset, it's for you. They totally disregarded your privacy."

"It's what reporters do." I grimace. "Are you sure you're not upset? Because once they started asking you questions, you turned an interesting shade of pale and stuck your nose in my armpit as if you wanted to know whether my deodorant was still working."

Since direct questioning and concern haven't yet worked, I'm trying sarcasm. She seems to speak that language. My question makes her smile.

"Is it?" She wags her brows. "Maybe you should drop your shirt now and let me get up close and personal with you. You know, as a public service. In case we run into anyone else. You don't want to reek."

"If you start something in this car, woman, we may be finishing it here, too. And I'm too damn tall and big for backseat action."

"I'm nimble," she offers. "I could easily reach across the console and unzip your pants. Do you think my head will fit between the steering wheel and your lap? I do."

My libido wants to find out. "I bet it will. But if you try, we may not make it home in one piece. I don't think it's smart to test my ability to drive safely with your mouth wrapped around my cock."

"But—"

"If we get into an accident, imagine how those headlines would read."

She grimaces, then sighs. "Who knew there are downsides to banging a famous guy? I thought it would be all laughs, glamour, and orgasms." She tsks. "You're such a disappointment."

I take her teasing in stride. "How about if I make it up to you when we get home?"

"Oh?" Harlow raises a brow. "You might be able to suck up to me for my forgiveness. What do you have in mind?"

My tongue takes a leisurely glide over my lips as I reach over to drag my fingertips up her thigh. "Dessert."

"Yes, please." She gives me an eager smile.

Now that she's seemingly happy again, I look for a backdoor angle to ask my question again that won't raise her defenses. "I'm used to reporters and the ridiculous things they say. I hope it didn't upset you too much."

"Do they usually go after your dates?"

"They dig enough to find out who she is. Then they try to invent some drama-laden relationship we've never had by telling their readers that an 'anonymous source' knows all the details. They're leeches." I don't mention that they sometimes dish my date's dirt, too. Harlow is already on edge. I just want to find out what's wrong without adding to the problem.

She gapes at me, then sits back against her seat, arms crossed. "I shouldn't be surprised. I just... I'm looking for peace right now, and getting press will only stir up the drama I've been dealing with."

"You mean your parents' divorce?" Not sure why she thinks anyone will care about that. I doubt they will, but clearly she doesn't want to deal with the situation at all.

"Yeah. And some other minor shit. How do you put up with having your life scrutinized?"

I suspect the "other minor shit" is anything but. There's a wealth of information in what she's not saying. "Well, when your final deal in the NFL makes you north of a hundred million dollars, you expect followers and idiots."

Her eyes widen. "Yeah, I can believe that."

"I don't pay those people any attention. You shouldn't, either. Whatever the press says about you will be hot news for less than fifteen minutes. Then some Kardashian will probably do something ridiculous, and they'll move on. Don't worry."

"I hope you're right." But she sounds concerned.

Everything about the conversation reinforces that she either has something that she doesn't want to talk about, something to hide—or both.

The rest of the ride home is silent while I contemplate. I already made the mistake once of assuming her brother was some stalker ex. I need to keep my assumptions in check and stick to facts.

When we pull behind the electronic gate protecting the estate, I make a mental note to have my rep, Lian, look into hiring a rotation of guards to keep press and nosy people out. But it's not as important as helping Harlow from the car and chipping away at her facade a bit more until I learn what has crawled under her skin.

We've barely cleared the garage and made it into the shadowy hallway just inside the house when Harlow sidetracks me by turning, dropping to her knees, and attacking my fly.

I grab her wrists. "Baby?"

She looks up at me, her eyes bright and desperate in the dark. "You promised me dessert."

"No. I planned to make dessert of you."

Her breath catches. "After I have mine." She grabs my hips and drags her lips up the front of my khakis, right over my rigid cock. "I'm hungry now."

At the thought of having her lips wrapped around me and sucking deep, I stagger back against the door. "Fuck."

"I want to," she says breathlessly. "So bad."

Then she rips into my zipper and shoves my boxers down to my thighs. As my cock springs free, she takes it in her hands. I can't stop the groan that slips past my lips as she strokes me with slow insistence. Then the tip of her tongue lashes the head. Sizzle zips down my spine. *Holy shit.*

With a long groan, my head falls back against the door. I'm a goner and I might as well accept that now. I spent the first half of dinner thinking that I'd rather be doing Harlow than dinner out and I've had an erection since. I'm not going to fight the sharp claws of arousal clawing my flesh far under the skin.

The thought barely clears my head when I feel the hot velvet of her mouth envelop my length. She cups my balls with one hand and wraps the other around my thigh, dragging me closer, taking me deeper.

If the speech pathologist thing doesn't work out for her, she could make a ton of cash giving blow jobs. I've had hummers from some really practiced mouths, but this? *Yeah…* On second thought, she can teach other women how to do this to their man. No one with a Y chromosome is getting near her staggeringly hot mouth. The thought of any other guy feeling this bliss from her has me gripping the strands of her long, inky waves in my fist and settling deeper in the back of her throat.

Mine.

It's ridiculous and over the top and I don't fucking care. It's how I feel right now. Every time I talk to Harlow our connection is so good that I think we could be really good friends. Then she does something to remind me that we have amazing, blinding, fucking hot sex. Who am I kidding? Everything she does reminds me that she's mind-blowing in bed. And in the shower. And on the balcony overlooking the ocean. I would know.

But this… I'm not sure I'll survive.

When she hums softly, I grip her harder. "Fuck, baby. You're undoing me."

She doesn't answer, but I feel her lips curl up. I groan as she sucks harder, her head moving rhythmically up and down my aching dick. Tingles begin brewing. I can't breathe. I gave up on coherent thought about something other than Harlow two seconds after she put her mouth on me and I don't regret it one bit.

The gentle glide of her teeth over the sensitive head makes me shudder. Climax is approaching. I'm racing to get there, groaning with each breath. I swear I can feel every layer of my skin slickening with sweat and every curve of her lips shuttling up and down my cock.

"If you don't want me to unload in your mouth, now is the time to stop." I'm amazed I get the words out and they're coherent. Everything else is a scramble in my brain.

Harlow answers by digging her nails into my thighs and sucking me even harder, tongue swirling around my length, teeth skimming up every sensitive inch. The suction is killing me. I'm shuddering as I'm pushing my way along her tongue, against her throat, as if I will the pleasure to overtake me now even while I wish it would go on forever.

If giving blow jobs were an Olympic sport, she would be a fucking gold medalist.

Oh, god. I'm not going to last.

"Harlow..."

Everything she's doing is turning me both on and inside out. I know the inevitable end is near. When my blood is churning and racing straight for my cock and I feel the growl of ecstasy screaming straight to the head, I'm seconds away from climax. But she sends me there even sooner when she brushes kisses over my thigh, not like she merely wants me. But like this somehow matters to her.

Yep, I'm a goner.

The second she fastens her mouth around me again and lifts her long lashes to stare up at me, I feel my knees buckle and the world implode. A groan tears from my chest as everything dissolves around me until I'm drowning in the kind of satisfaction I swear will leave blisters on my soul.

I'll forever measure my life by specific milestones: losing my virginity to a cheerleader two years older than me on a school bus home from the end of a great season, our team winning the state championship my senior year of high school, my first kegger, my first Super Bowl win, my father's death...and now the moment I'm realizing I might not be able to live without Harlow satisfying my every sexual need. It sounds crazy; I've known her twenty-four hours. But there's something about this woman that gets to me.

At my feet, she licks her lips, then softly laps at my erection before easing up my length and releasing me into her waiting hand. She presses a lingering kiss to my abs, then lays her cheek against me with a sigh, eyes closed in seeming contentment.

I could more than get used to this. Hell, I could more than get addicted to this. I could need this more than I know how to handle.

"Hmm. I knew you'd taste good," she murmurs.

I stroke her hair, soaking in her femininity and softness. "Once my knees start working again, I'll definitely return the favor and then some."

"No rush. I've been grinning big since last night."

Extending a hand to her, I help Harlow to her feet and wrap my arms around her, still wall-hugging the door for support. "If you're with me and you're not smiling, I've done something wrong."

She laughs. "I'll let you know when I'm in danger of frowning."

"So what did you do for fun around here before I arrived, besides lay out by the pool in barely legal bikinis?"

Her grin turns rueful. "Actually, I discovered that the previous owner left behind a gaming console, so I've been testing out a few of the games. I had no idea I could be such a badass, especially with conjuration and destruction spells in Tamriel."

I raise a brow at her. "I have no idea what you said. Did you just speak geek to me?"

"I totally did. Impressed?"

"Yes, and weirdly turned on. You'll have to show me what the hell you're talking about. I've got to keep up, you know."

"Why don't I pour a bottle of wine and I'll introduce you to my kick-ass Nord woman in gilded armor? She's hot."

"Let's do it." I like the playful side of Harlow, so I know I'm in for an interesting night.

Then once she's comfortable, has forgotten all about our run-in with the press, and I've had enough time to recuperate my mojo, I'll have dessert of my own—and find out what she's trying so hard to hide.

CHAPTER FIVE

A T NEARLY TWO in the morning, I set down the game controller with a groan. "I give up. You can't kill a giant."

"You can, but you need more stealth and better weapons. And way better armor. You kind of sucked at vampires, too. Get it?" She elbows me. "Suck?"

I roll my eyes. "I need a garlic necklace to ward off jokes like that."

"Ha ha."

The truth is I like Harlow's unexpectedly goofy sense of humor and the admittedly geek side of her I've seen tonight. In her defense, Elder Scrolls is a *huge* game, and I feel as if I've barely seen a quarter of the map. With a story centered around a civil war and an ancient legend coming true, I get why she's been drawn in.

But now I've got something else on my mind.

I wrap my arm around Harlow and help her to her feet, then I scoop her up against my chest.

She squeals. "What are you doing?"

"I never did have my dessert, and I've suddenly got a sweet tooth…"

Even in the room's low lighting, I see her flush. "I take it you don't mean a pie I might bake in the oven."

"Nope. You know I love to eat your pussy, baby. Let's grab a few things along the way to make this even sweeter." I cart her past a stack of towels folded on a table for pool and beach use, then double back to the kitchen. "Open the fridge and grab that champagne. Oh, and that bottle of chocolate sauce."

She takes the items cautiously. "What are you going to do?"

"Feast." I give her an unrepentant grin as I reach the pantry and search for what I want. "Pick up that jar of maraschino cherries, too."

Harlow wraps her hand around it with a halting touch. "This sounds messy."

"Yep, not to mention prolonged, sweaty, and dirty as hell."

When she's got everything in her grip, I haul her to the dining room, strip off her shirt and bra, then lay her across the table. She hisses and arches when the cool wood hits her back. I sit at the head, position the foodstuffs nearby, then grab her hips and pull her luscious ass to the edge.

I lift her skirt. "Panties?" I heave a long-suffering sigh. "I should forbid these."

"You can't do that. My panties are none of your business. What makes you think I'd even listen to you?"

"Don't you want to make me happy so I can make you even happier?" I send her a sly grin as I slide the little scrap down her legs and to the floor.

"Well, when you put it like that…"

"Glad you see things my way. Now spread your legs, brace your feet on the edge of the table, and lift your hips." I take hold of the towel.

"You're bossy tonight."

Despite her complaint, she does it.

I smile as I slide the towel under her ass. "Occupational hazard. I was the offensive leader of my team, you know. I'm used to taking charge." I wink her way. "And I know how to score."

"Talk about bad jokes…" She gives me a sour expression, but I see her smile peeking through.

"Yeah, but that's not why you like me." I skim my fingertips down the inside of her leg, satisfied when she shudders and her breath skips. I caress her thigh as my gaze latches on to her pussy. My mouth waters. I won't be able to keep my tongue off of her for long. "What comes next is."

With practiced moves, I pop the champagne open and set the cork aside. The bottle fizzles over and splashes bubbly over the rim, down my fingers, then onto her sex. She gasps at the cold. I heat her up by raking my tongue between her lips and into her folds, groaning when her flavor mixes with the sweet effervescence of the champagne. But I stop short of her clit.

Harlow wriggles. "You were almost to the best spot. Why stop now?"

"I intend to savor my dessert. Be a good girl, lie back, and let me."

Capitulating isn't her style, and I sense she's gearing up to mount an argument for argument's sake. I stop her by latching my mouth on her pussy again, opening as wide as I can to drink her all in at once. Her toes curl. Harlow grips the edge of the table and holds her breath. Her protest becomes a needy whimper.

God, I love giving her pleasure and having power over her body.

With a long lick, I ease back and grope for the champagne again and stand, leaning over her to pour a trickle of the chilled liquid into her navel.

Her stomach contracts and clenches. Her eyes slide shut with a sigh of pleasure. Her beaded nipples and rosy cheeks tell me how aroused she is.

And I've barely started.

I drink from her skin, relishing the way she writhes under me. Her responses are everything I've always wanted and like nothing I've experienced. When her fingertips curl around my shoulders, I can actually *feel* how much she wants this, wants me.

Swept up in my need, I can't resist dribbling some bubbly between her breasts and licking the fruity liquid away. I take a swig from the bottle and hold the sparkling wine in my mouth as I capture her nipple against my tongue. When the cold champagne meets her heated flesh, her back twists. Her head thrashes.

I swallow and repeat the process with the other breast, sucking and tormenting to my heart's content.

"Noah…"

I don't answer, just curl my tongue around her distended bud and suck deep. It's swollen from last night. Knowing she's still sensitive enough to shiver at every lick and nip on her breast turns me on even more.

Her hips start gyrating against my abdomen, as if her pussy is desperate for stimulation. For climax.

I wonder if she's figured out yet that it's going to be a long time coming…but sooner than I want if I can't get myself under control. The blow job she gave me a few hours past might as well have been a few decades ago. And her womanly scent is driving my primal urge to get in, sink deep, and fuck hard.

Easing back, I reach for the bottle of chocolate syrup, give it a shake, and send her a devious smile.

"You're not going to drizzle that on my pussy and eat it." She says the words in warning.

"Yeah, I am. You're going to be my perfect sundae. Sweet cream…" I swipe my fingertips through her drenched folds with one hand and open the spout on the plastic bottle with the other. "Chocolate…" I tip the bottle upside down and coat her pretty pink flesh with the liquid cocoa. As she gasps, the rich scents combine and waft to my nose. I set the bottle aside and reach for the jar at her hip, popping the lid open. "And cherries."

"Noah…" She writhes and tosses her head back, throat arching.

"What, baby?" I fish out one of the candied fruits and let it drip over the jar.

"Didn't your mama ever tell you it isn't polite to keep a girl waiting?"

I laugh. She's always got a comeback, and it's one thing I adore about her.

"Sure she did. But she meant for a date. We didn't exactly cover oral sex etiquette. Now lie still and let me enjoy." I set the jar of cherries on the other side of her thigh, still within reach.

"But you're going to torment me."

"I am." And I plan to enjoy every moment…even if I'll be tormenting myself, as well. Because, no lie, I'd love to strip off my pants and seat myself inside her in the next ten seconds, let my eyes roll back in my head as I lose my sanity to what I already know will be earth-shaking sex. Instead, I hold off. Wait. I want to make this so good for her. Mostly because I want her to want to stay around longer, even if it's just for the sex.

If I can make her like me, even better.

Watching chocolate drip down the pouty flesh of her bare pussy could easily become my new pastime. She's swollen here, too. Puffy. Perfect. Would she object if I took a picture and hung it on my wall?

I drag the cherry up the lips of her engorged sex, swiping it through the chocolate and her essence, then settle it between, trailing it up her distended clit. She gasps at the touch, body thrashing. I do it again, slow down the drag, swirl it around the hard, rosy bud. As soon as I lift the candied fruit from her, I follow up with a silken glide of my finger. She bites her lip and wraps her fingers around her breasts, squeezing as if she's desperate for more.

I revel in every moment of her sexual agony.

Using a slow hand, I watch her fall apart by degrees. It's a lovely sight, and she's a sensual thing twisting under my touch. I've always loved women—the sight, the feel, the softness of them. But Harlow Reed is in a class by herself. I'm captivated by even the littlest things she does, by the way her dark hair gleams on my elegant table, by the way she pants when I touch her, by the way her entire body flushes as she approaches climax.

But she isn't ready to surrender just yet.

Suddenly, her fingers glide down to the slick flesh between her legs, mixing her cream with the chocolate. She dips in, swirls around. Then she props herself up on one elbow and holds her digits out to me, letting the potent scents mingle just under my nose. "Noah… Take a taste. Just one. The rest will be waiting for you. Open your mouth. What can it hurt?"

I shouldn't. It's a distinct possibility I'll lose my shit once I get her flavor on my tongue. But that doesn't stop me from leaning closer. She paints my bottom lip, tempting me. Taunting me. Damn if I don't crave her.

I slide my tongue over my lip, then move on to her fingers. *Heaven. Paradise. Utopia.*

One taste is my undoing.

I suck her fingers into my mouth as I rise from my seat and push her digits against my tongue, moaning as I melt.

Harlow pulls her arm back, leading me closer to the source of her honey. With the other hand, she opens her sex, revealing her reddening clit pulling away from its hood. "It's not my fingers you want."

She's right. Vaguely, I'm annoyed at myself for letting her derail me, but not enough to refuse her.

I let go, take another swallow of the champagne from the bottle, then pour more over her puffy pink sex. When she whimpers, I set it down. To my surprise, she sits up enough to take a few long swigs. I stare.

"What's it going to be?" she challenges. "Champagne kisses or choco-late-covered pussy?"

They both sound fantastic, but…it's no contest.

Planting my palm between her breasts, I push her flat against the table, then grab her hips in my hands. As I sit once more, I drag my dessert up to my lips and dive in.

Her flavor hits me, grips me, sends me into a frenzy. I edge closer, take her hands and use them to hold her captive. There isn't so much as a breath between her sweetness and my mouth. I settle in, go deeper, drown in everything that's Harlow. Sure, I taste chocolate and champagne. Even her clit has a little candied-cherry flavor my tongue is enjoying. But it's really her I want. I burn for.

I open wider, lap her from bottom to top, then savor her sweetness as I suck the fruit juice clean from her flesh greedily until I can taste nothing but her pure, clean essence.

Her moans bounce off the walls. Her thighs tense, and she's holding her breath. Yes, her orgasm is coming. Her body tells me. Her scent thickens. Her taste deepens. I have no idea how she got sweeter, but I'm loving every moment she's on my tongue.

Suddenly, she's rising and bucking and growling out a throaty cry of completion that scalds my veins and makes my cock harder than it's ever been. I dip my tongue inside her center and feel her hard pulses as she bows like she has no control over her body or the ecstasy wracking her.

Moments later, she melts limply onto the table with a heavy sigh, panting hard. "Oh… Noah."

I lick and kiss her flesh gently, reluctantly easing back and weaning myself away from her—for now. "Do you feel good?"

"Yeah. I'll be even better if you fuck me."

While I want that—bad—I don't have a damn condom in my pocket. I used the last one before dinner. "You got it. Let me run to the bedroom and—"

"Now," she insists, shaking her head.

"I don't have a way to protect you."

Harlow frowns. I see her wheels turning. "My period ended six days ago. I'm not that far into my cycle and I've probably been taking the pill long enough now. It should be fine."

"You're sure?" I don't want to argue because I'd love to have Harlow with nothing between us…and because the thought of her pregnant still sets off my libido again like a fireworks spectacular. But as pushy as I can be with pleasure, I'd never coerce her into taking me bareback. "I can run upstairs and be back in less than two minutes."

"Two minutes will feel like a lifetime," she wails, hips lifting as she shifts restlessly.

I can't disagree with her.

"Baby…" I swallow hard at the thought of actually feeling her against me, bare all the way around me. "I want you so damn bad. I won't last long."

She smiles like she knows she's won. "There's always later. Let's get to enjoying now."

With a groan, I take my cock in hand and guide it to her splayed sex. Stickiness from the chocolate and champagne remains on her pussy. This is going to be messy. And I'll love every second of it.

Grabbing her hips, I push inside her slowly. The electric sensation of her naked flesh gripping me sends an immediate shudder down my spine. She's so tight, and without the latex, an inferno of ecstasy scorches my senses. Need steamrolls me. As I submerge all the way to the hilt, I grip her harder and toss my head back with a chest-deep groan.

Harlow is ruining me. Worse, I can't give a fuck about anything except fucking her.

"Noah!" Her entire body moves under me, shoulders pressed to the table, hips lifting in my grip.

The cry of her voice flips a switch in me. I have to go deeper, harder, wilder. I have to leave my stamp on her.

I need to make her forget about any man who came before me.

I don't know why and I don't question the urge. Time for that later. I devote my entire being to merging with Harlow, withdrawing as quickly as possible, then shuttling in again with all my breath and might. The rhythm takes hold of my body. The table starts to shake with every plunge deep. Everything inside me is attuned to her—to the flush rising across her skin, to the light sheen of perspiration now covering her torso, to the twist of her full lips as the pleasure breaks her down.

Watching her is stunning. Impactful. But I need her closer. I need our mouths colliding as our bodies do. I need to invade her in every way at once that I can.

I'm trying to get enough of her. I'm beginning to think that's not possible.

Still, I'm compelled to try, so I scoop her up, ignoring her startled yelp. Before she's even finished the sound, I've taken the few steps across the room to back her against the wall and press myself into her. I slant my mouth over hers, lifting her up my aching cock. Then I let gravity work in my favor. She takes me even farther inside her, and I'm happily going where I suspect no man has ever gone before. Because this penetration is unlike anything I've ever felt—or even imagined in my wildest fantasies. I'm probing her depths and hitting a spot that has her tensing and clawing and panting into me. Her fingernails dig into my skin, leaving a trail of fire. Her lips part wide with euphoric bliss that transforms her face.

God, she's beautifully sexy. All woman.

Mine. I feel that possessive impulse again.

I cover her mouth once more, pushing my tongue inside even as I shove my cock deep, using my whole body to push her against the wall so I can gain leverage, immobilize her, have her body entirely at my disposal.

"Pinch your nipples," I demand between kisses.

Harlow reaches one hand between us to roll and tug on a hard bead, even as she uses the other to anchor herself around my neck and ride me like a surfer on towering waves roaring up to the coastline. She puts her whole body into our pleasure, gripping me with her thighs, gyrating her hips, eating her way up my neck and back to my mouth.

Shit, she's doing way more to me than merely rocking my world.

As the pinnacle of my pleasure crests and I swallow the frantic wail of her shattering climax, I feel her pulse around me like a vise. My body short-circuits. I lose the ability to focus on anything except Harlow and emptying myself inside her—body, soul, and something else that's totally new. Something that feels dangerous.

But I'm too far gone to care. The only thing that matters is spilling inside her and hoping that she'll beg me to do it again.

As our movements slow and our breathing begins to even out, she blinks and focuses on me. "Oh, my god. What was that?"

"The most amazing thing I've ever felt," I admit.

"You're not kidding. Sex has *never* been like this for me."

Part of me loves the ego trip. Another part is rejoicing at being her best. But there's a sliver that can't stand the thought of her remembering sex with any other guy. "Ditto, baby. You're amazing."

She gives me a tired smile. "We're amazing together. Sex has been dull the last couple of years, so this is perfect."

I want to know why...and yet I don't. But curiosity wins out as I disentangle our bodies and set her on her feet. "Why the last couple of years in particular?"

Harlow shrugs and looks like she's choosing her words. She seems suspiciously focused on my Adam's apple—or anything that keeps her from meeting my stare. "You know… School stress, chaotic college life, immature idiots. I just never felt like myself with anyone before. Thanks."

I'm getting to her. It's a relief to know I'm not the only one feeling something besides arousal and tingling genitals. Yes, we're talking about sex, but the soft surprise in her expression tells me she's stunned by our connection. Like I am.

Where is it going?

I don't know. And I don't have to right now. But I need time with her. I need to spend my mornings, noons, and nights with this woman until I figure out what's going on between us. I can only keep her here with the promise of employment and good sex for so long. No, she hasn't made any noise about leaving, but I want to lock her down so that packing her bags and heading out before I'm ready to let her go is impossible.

"Shit!" Suddenly, she hobbles off, holding her inner thigh.

I follow with a frown. "Harlow?"

"I'm dripping…you. I'm so used to a condom."

Me, too. But I'm kind of smiling as she dips into the powder bath and slams the door.

Feeling like a supreme sex god, I exhale with satisfaction and make my way to the home office. My lawyer is in New York. It's well into morning for him. Maybe he's already had a chance to put together the paperwork I asked him for yesterday. Sure enough, there's a small stack of pages on my printer/fax. Greedily, I grab the pages up and scan.

With every word, my grin widens. This is exactly what I wanted.

I hear the toilet flush, the water run, then the door opens a few moments later. The light flips off. "Noah?"

"In here. I've got something for you."

"If it's another erection, it's going to have to wait. Every part of me feels wrung out and I need sleep. Don't even think about waking me up for hanky-panky tonight."

I can't promise her I won't.

"No erection." Yet. "Just the contract and nondisclosure agreement from my attorney."

"That was fast."

I pay him to be. "It's great, right? We can get started as soon as you sign."

When Harlow holds out her hand, I slide the pages and a pen into her grip. It's late, and I'm hoping she doesn't tell me that she'll read it in the morning. I will sleep so much better tonight knowing that she's signed, sealed, delivered—and all mine for the summer.

Pushing a mass of dark hair away from her face and over one shoulder, she cocks her head and scans the document. I can't think of a single woman who would stand there stark naked under the harsh LED lights of my office and focus her brain on business. Many wouldn't have the confidence to make themselves so bare in front of a lover unless they shimmied or crooked a finger to entice him or just got dressed altogether. Harlow merely seems to accept her nudity as yet another state of being that's neither good nor bad. It just is.

She flips the page over and reads the rest, then scans the accompanying NDA. "This is generous pay."

Sex is one thing, but business is another. I switch gears...but I can only do it by focusing on her face. If I look at her tits, I'll be a goner. "I doubt unraveling my speech problems will be easy. Late nights, odd hours, and dealing with me when I'm grouchy won't be a breeze. But my second career worth millions is on the line. Being a successful broadcaster will continue to feed my endorsement deals, too. I think it's fair to compensate you appropriately."

"The term of the agreement is through Labor Day?"

I nod. "That gets me through the end of preseason, more or less. If we need to extend, we'll renegotiate. But I plan to work hard so that I'm broadcast ready by then."

Harlow nods in acknowledgement. "I have no problem not talking about our professional interaction without your consent. I wouldn't, anyway. Practitioner-patient confidentiality is paramount to me."

"Later, if we're successful, you can tell everyone. I will be. I've been thinking about other guys in the league who may be affected and not speaking out. Someone's got to break the silence." I shrug. "Why not me? Maybe others will come forward and get help if they feel like there's hope."

She smiles. "That's noble. A lot of jocks wouldn't want anyone to ever know. They don't want to admit they're less than perfect."

"If disregarding my ego can help some of the others find their voice, it's a small price. And it's not always that players don't speak out. Some are just drowned out. By the teams and their owners. And by the league itself, which has been slow to admit the connection between repeated hits to the head and long-term impact on players' faculties. If I open the door for a discussion so some of these other guys can be heard and get help, then it's a bonus."

Without hesitating, she signs the forms, then sets the pen down and saunters in my direction, wrapping her arms around my neck. "Done. You know, you're so good in bed that it's not fair to actually make me like you, too."

"It's not a bad thing. I mean, I like you. And I like spending time with you. I'm glad we'll be spending more together. And maybe...we'll figure out there's more going on here than a fling."

For a moment, she freezes. Then she tsks at me and gives me a flirty shake of her head. "And ruin this great sexfest we have going? Why would we do that?"

As she walks away, her laugh seems almost nervous.

It's hard not to notice that every time I bring up romance or relationship, she damn near runs in the opposite direction. But she wants children, and I don't see her impersonally going to a sperm bank to conceive. Even more, I don't think she would have let me take her without protection if she didn't feel *something* for me. Or is she simply trying to get pregnant, even unconsciously? Doubtful, but I think what's between us is way bigger than she's ready to admit.

Sometimes Harlow is a walking dichotomy. And maybe the way to her heart is simply through her pussy. I don't know yet, but I'm going to figure her out.

MY PHONE RINGING three hours later startles me from a deep sleep. I sit straight up in bed and grab the damn thing. Harlow was resting fitfully after I rolled over and turned out the lights. I don't want to wake her now.

As I hit the button to answer the call, I look over to see if she's still asleep.

The woman is gone. The sheets on her side of the bed are cold.

What the fuck?

Shoving the covers aside and climbing to my feet, I glance at the display on my phone. It's my agent in New York. I growl as I press the phone to my ear. "Cliff, do you know what fucking time it is in Hawaii?"

"Ungodly early, I know. But the network is up my ass. They want to know if you're stalling about giving them an answer about the job because of the runaway bride."

The *what*? How do I answer when I don't understand the question? "I'm considering all my options. You know that. They know that."

"And they weren't antsy about waiting until you were snapped looking cozy with a woman who ran out on her groom less than a week ago. The fact you two are dating now—and so publicly—is sending up a red flag for them."

The words do a drive-by in my brain but I don't comprehend them. "What?"

"We can all understand why she would leave a boring businessman for you, but Noah… Why would you give up the opportunity to take a prime spot in the coveted A Team for the network to—"

"She ran out on some guy less than a week ago?" I hate to sound as stupid as I feel for not Googling Harlow sooner, but I don't have my computer handy and I need to understand right now.

Where the hell is she? After the reporters splashed her image across the tabloids, did she decide to leave?

I march out of my bedroom and go in search of Harlow. As I head down the stairs, I don't see any lights on. I'm more confused than ever.

"You didn't know that?" Cliff asks.

"She failed to mention it." And given her behavior, I know it was on purpose.

"How could you *not* know? If she left this schmuck for you—"

"She didn't. I only met her two days ago."

"So it's not serious, right?"

I hesitate. I'm not sure how to answer that but I've always been straight up with Cliff—speech problems aside. "I think it could be. Or I did until you called. You're saying she broke up with her fiancé last weekend?"

"Um…yeah, buddy. In a big way."

"What do you mean? How did you find out about this?"

"I'm going to text you a link. I hope you're sitting down. We'll talk again after you've had time to digest."

Once Cliff hangs up, I'm torn between staring at the phone while waiting for his promised link to arrive and finding wherever the hell Harlow has gone so I can ask her a billion questions.

She was engaged less than a week ago?

Who was this guy? Why did she break it off? Suddenly, I'm less surprised that she seems allergic to relationships. What I don't understand is why she hasn't so much as whispered a word about this to me.

The phone buzzes in my hand, telling me I've got a text. But I'm still intent on finding Harlow.

Stomping my way back up the stairs, I fling open the door to the room she'd previously used as her bedroom and find her tucked under the blankets fast asleep. It's dark. A fan circulates, keeping the room cool. She doesn't stir at all when I walk in.

Why is she sleeping here, instead of beside me? Why did she lie down with me only to leave?

I stop and stare. I can't look away as I wonder how and why this woman is turning my life upside down. I shouldn't care. But I do. I shouldn't even want to listen to her explanation. But I'm dying to hear it. I need to know if anything that's passed between us means more to her than an orgasm. If she's even in a place to care about me half as much as she does the sex.

My thoughts tell me more than I'd like about how invested I am in her. After a mere two days, it should be easy to write her off and walk away. But even when my head is telling me that would be smart, I won't. She's got a story. I've been wondering what's up with her—and I'm finally finding out.

"Noah?" A familiar voice resounds from downstairs, startling me. "You up?"

I dash out of Harlow's room and creep halfway to the first floor, peeking into the shadowy entryway. "Trace?"

"Yeah. I promised you a six a.m. workout on Saturday. Here I am."

Shit. It's so early, and I totally forgot. "Yeah. Give me five. I just woke up."

"Sure. When you get downstairs, you can tell me why you're banging a girl who ran out on her fiancé a week ago."

Harlow's dirty laundry must be all over the media if Trace knows it, too. *Oh, fuck.* She will not be pleased. I feel more than a little responsible.

"Be right back."

After a quick swish with my toothbrush, I toss on some gym clothes and haul ass downstairs, my phone and the link I haven't opened yet nearly burning a hole in my hand. Once I reach the kitchen, I see my brother nursing a cup of coffee and staring at me like I've lost my damn mind.

"Don't get me wrong," he starts in. "She's a gorgeous girl but—"

"I literally found out five minutes ago about her ex-fiancé when Cliff called."

"Oh, shit."

"Let me catch up to you." I bring up the messages on my phone and find the link waiting for me. I have a terrible feeling it's going to change a lot between Harlow and me. But maybe it will at least help me make sense of her behavior.

I press the link and wait. YouTube pops up. The subject of the video says BRIDE RUNS OUT ON FIANCÉ IN EPIC STYLE. It's currently trending and has over three million views. My gut clenches as the footage starts to roll.

Harlow stands at the back of the aisle with an older man I can only assume is her father. They exchange words that don't look happy or comforting before she anchors her hand on his arm with a scowl. I frown as she walks up the aisle. Clearly, she's pissed at her father, and I wonder if it has anything to do with the pending divorce from her mother. And why that would make her abruptly leave the man she'd once agreed to pledge her life to.

After Harlow and her father pass the camera, the angle of the shot changes. The video shows her from the back, her upswept hair revealing a mostly backless dress and a long veil that lends a luminous look to her silky skin. Her train dusts the ground behind her as she nears the altar. The camera sweeps up to show a shot of the unlucky groom. He's average height—which is still far taller than Harlow. He's got a typical stockbroker's haircut, a face I swear I've seen a hundred times in football stadiums all over America, with only a cleft chin to differentiate him. He clasps his hands in front of himself, seemingly not nervous at all, merely smug. But I get why the smarmy bastard would be. He's thinks he's marrying a beautiful woman from a wealthy family in a lavish ceremony. I recognize the ballroom at the Ritz Carlton here on Maui.

As she approaches him, the music changes, and giant screens at the front of the room show snapshots of the two of them together, mostly staged poses from a single shoot—her wearing her engagement rock, him looking somewhere between self-satisfied and bored.

I've never met the guy. I don't even know his name. And I already want to punch him.

Suddenly, the rotating images of the happy couple projected on the screens on either side of the makeshift altar disappear as the sound of a needle being dragged across a vinyl record echoes. Beside Harlow, the groom frowns in confusion as a different video flickers and starts to roll.

This one shows the groom with his pants around his ankles, bending a blonde over a linoleum countertop, a pot of coffee to their right, as he plows into her, racing to orgasm in a full-out sprint. She's wearing four-inch stilettos and has her pencil skirt hiked up to her waist, showing off a hell of a tramp stamp that's wide and flanked by inked filigree. The script writing flows and sways, spelling out one word: WHORE.

The wedding guests gasp, jaws dropping. The groom starts losing his mind, demanding someone kill the feed. No one does. They just stare.

As the footage continues, he huffs and bucks on film, his white ass clenching on every down stroke. "Fuck, Mandy. You're such a whore, just like your tattoo says, aren't you?"

"Yes," she pants. "Yes. Your whore."

"My pregnant whore. Do you think I knocked you up in this room?"

"Or on your desk. There's something about getting pregnant by your boss in the office that seems even dirtier. Do you think your girlfriend suspects?"

"She's oblivious," he assures as he plunges into his assistant again. "I'll make sure she stays that way."

The drag of the needle across an old LP sounds again, then Harlow's face appears on both screens at the front of the room, her smile acid. "Hi, Simon. Or should I say stupid fucker? I'm not oblivious. And I'm not marrying you. Instead of being a no-show at the altar and leaving you to awkwardly explain to our family and guests why I'd run out on such an awesome guy at the last minute, I thought I'd just show them. I hope you and Mandy get everything you deserve in life. Oh, and I think you'll find that Mercedes you just bought for our island vacations might not look quite so pristine."

On the screen, a pale gray European sedan appears. The words JUST MARRIED written in temporary ink across the back window have been crossed out with black spray paint. The words LYING SLIME have been painted across the trunk in big, bold letters instead.

When Simon barrels down on Harlow, motions angry and jerky, she tosses her bouquet in his face, flips him her middle finger, then marches down the aisle, glaring again at her father. Then the video ends.

I'm blinking and stunned. A million thoughts charge through my head, none I can voice past my shock.

"Holy shit." Trace looks almost as bowled over as I feel.

"That happened less than a week ago?" I breathe as pieces of Harlow's puzzle start to fall into place.

No wonder she's not eager to talk relationship. It's a gross understatement to say that her last one ended badly. I understand now why her brothers are worried about her.

"Holy shit," my brother repeats.

I don't blame him for being so shocked his vocabulary has been reduced to two words. If I wasn't so focused on what to say to Harlow—how to deal with her—I'd probably be repeating Trace's catch phrase, too.

Still, I can't help but wonder...why didn't she tell me that she'd just broken an engagement? Give me a hint? Even mentioned that she'd ever been engaged at all?

I head for the stairs. "I need to talk to Harlow."

"She's here?" My brother seems taken aback by that.

"Yeah. She lives here, has for a while. Long story. I'll explain later. I need a rain check on the workout. I'll call you when I can."

Now Trace hesitates. "Maybe you should just walk away, bro. She sounds like she's been through a lot. And you don't need drama now."

"No one ever does. But I think Harlow needs someone to..." What? Soothe her, reassure her, hold her? "At the very least, she needs someone to listen."

"That someone doesn't have to be you. She has family or girlfriends, right? Or there's plenty of other fish in her sea, bro."

He's not wrong, but I can't leave her. "I've got this. Seriously, I'll call you once I've talked to her."

Trace shrugs. He doesn't like it, but he's backing off. "Sure. I'll scram and grab some coffee at that great little diner. Um, can I borrow a ball cap? I lost mine and was followed by two reporters who thought I was you yesterday while I ran errands."

It happens. We both look so much like our dad. When I glance in the mirror now, I swear I'm looking at a darker-skinned version of the man from my baby photos.

"Sure." I bound up the stairs to find one. The sooner I get rid of Trace, the sooner I can confront Harlow. Once I pluck one from my suitcase, I toss it his way over the railing. "That work?"

He settles the new cap I picked up at the airport on his head, tags and all. It simply reads HAWAII. "Perfect. Thanks. Catch you later."

"Take it easy, man."

With a nod, my brother is gone. I turn around and head back up the stairs, directly to Harlow's door, trying to get my questions—and my shit—under control. It's not working. I know this conversation will probably be long and ugly. But I push my way into her bedroom, refusing to put it off for another moment.

CHAPTER SIX

A S THE DOOR squeaks open, I step into shadow. Sunlight is beginning to seep under the blinds in the room, enough to see Harlow splayed on her back across her bed, one hand over her chest, one dainty foot peeking out from the covers. She's wearing a simple cotton nightgown in a maroon color that reads I'M NOT ALWAYS SARCASTIC. SOMETIMES I'M ASLEEP.

Even when she's at her most vulnerable, Harlow still has her defenses up.

I hate to wake her. I don't know what to say, if I even have the right to demand answers. After thirty-six hours in the sack, I'm not entitled to much, but I think she deserves to know that her name is all over the press and the video of her wedding has gone viral.

Sitting on the edge of the bed next to her, I have to resist the urge to touch her—cup her soft cheek, cradle the intriguing curve of her hip—something. But I don't. I have to wonder if the fact she's sleeping alone is supposed to tell me that she only wants to be touched when there's sex involved. Of course I'll challenge that later. But now I just want answers.

"Harlow?"

She groans and blinks, pushing thick curls off her shoulder as she slowly sits up with a frown. "Noah? What time is it? What's going on?"

"The press ran with those pictures they snapped of us last night. I started getting phone calls a half hour ago." I pause, try to decide how best to get answers without becoming the enemy. "They figured out who you are and—"

"They're talking about what happened last weekend, aren't they?" She shakes her head with a bitter smile, looking wide awake. "So of course you know, too."

"Yeah."

She crosses her arms over her chest protectively. "I had my reasons for breaking things off with him."

"Absolutely. Any particular reason you didn't mention Simon to me at all?"

"He's a dick, and the whole wedding was a fiasco. I don't want to talk about him. Besides, you have problems of your own. I didn't see why you'd care."

Of course she didn't. But I do care…though I doubt she'd believe me. "He is a dick, and I do have my own problems but not so many that I can't give you an ear or a shoulder or a hand to hold if you want it."

Her face relaxes a fraction. "You're not going to call me a heinous bitch?"

"Your ex is the one who fucked around on you, and he deserved everything you dished out and more."

"Not everyone thinks so. When I announced to friends and acquaintances on social media that I hadn't gone through with the marriage, some were both creative and vicious in finding new ways to tell me I'm self-centered and immature."

"Social media gives a voice to that small but vocal minority of mean people who have nothing better to do than assert their unsolicited opinions. I'm sure the people who truly know you are behind you."

"Not really. Most everyone who attended the wedding thought I should have told Simon to fuck off in private and spared him the terrible embarrassment and possible professional fallout."

"Why should you spare that dirtbag anything? He doesn't deserve any consideration from you."

Harlow shrugs. "That's what I thought, but my dad told me to take off my rose-colored glasses and realize that men have 'needs' that no one woman can possibly satisfy. My mom backed him up and told me that if I wanted to continue to live in beautiful houses and drive sleek new cars, I wasn't going to earn enough money on my salary, so I'd better marry well and learn to put up with some of the less pleasant aspects of marriage."

Her parents sound fucking warped. "Do either of them understand what marriage is supposed to be?"

"If they did, would they be getting divorced?" she asks cynically. "The only people on my side through all of this have been my brothers and their wives. Most everyone else is telling me to grow up, get over myself, and grovel to Simon until he takes me back."

"Then everyone else is fucked up. That asshole should be thinking about the child he's got coming with his assistant and leave you in peace. After the way he hurt you, that's the least he can do. You loved him and—"

"I didn't." The words are a soft denial. "The truth is, I never did."

If she'd shouted her feelings, I wouldn't have believed her. But her expression is so resigned I know she's being honest.

"Even though you were engaged to him?" I ask in surprise. Sure, I've seen gold diggers work a teammate over until he's eager to walk down the aisle. I know those marriages will only last as long as the money flows. But Harlow doesn't strike me as that kind of woman.

I've never been tempted to get married before because I want what my parents had. Sometimes they didn't have two nickels to rub together, but they had love. They knew what it took to make marriage work in good times and bad, for richer or poorer, in sickness and in health. They stuck it out until the day my dad died. But if he'd done to my mom what Simon had done to Harlow, she would have kicked his ass and walked out, too.

"I know what you must be thinking. In retrospect, I *was* a moron. My dad introduced us. Simon does business in sectors my dad would like to break into, while Simon needs the contacts my dad has in the U.S. They began forming some partnership, but my dad didn't want Simon to have any opportunity to slip through his fingers, so he cooked up this notion that the two of us should get married. I was reluctant at first, but Simon and I dated for a while. He was busy…but so was I. That was fine. He seemed all right. Finally, we got around to talking about marriage. He didn't have annoying habits. He was polite. He gave me plenty of space. I liked him better than at least half the guys I'd dated, so I figured…why not."

"Baby, you're supposed to love the person you marry madly and completely."

She gives me an uncomfortable shrug. "I've never loved anyone like that. I figured friendship and companionship would make the whole thing workable, give us a decent environment to raise children. That's what I was looking forward to, holding my baby and being able to love him or her with my whole heart."

Because she clearly hadn't done that with her fiancé. But that begs the question, why hasn't she ever loved anyone madly and completely?

"So when you found out he was having a baby with his assistant, you showed him the door."

"It wasn't even that simple. I might have let it slide. Really. Simon wasn't in love with me, either. If he'd been mad about her, I would have let him go and wished them well. The thing I couldn't forgive was that he told me he wasn't ready for children. I'd gone off the pill about three months before the wedding, hoping I'd get pregnant on my honeymoon. Two days before the wedding, I told Simon and he blew a gasket, said we should make those decisions together. When he put it that way, I couldn't disagree, especially after he claimed he wanted to be more established in his career before he could devote the sort of time he thought children deserved. I was bummed but also glad that he intended to take fatherhood seriously. Since I'm young, I decided I could be patient for a year or two. So I made arrangements to go back on the pill at the beginning of my next cycle. The next morning, the video of Simon fucking Mandy and talking about their baby was sitting in my inbox. I don't know who sent it, and it really doesn't matter. The fact that he had no problem knocking her up, then giving me excuses that didn't apply to his mistress is what pissed me off."

MORE THAN LOVE YOU

"Simon is a massive bleeding hemorrhoid who deserves to have his balls whittled from his body with a paring knife."

"Probably, but he's not worth my effort."

She's right.

"Come here, baby." I reach for her, cup her shoulders, and try to pull her into my arms.

Harlow jerks back. "I don't need comforting. Thanks, but I'm not heartbroken. Other than being embarrassed, I'm fine."

I don't think she is but insisting otherwise will only raise her hackles. "Were you the one who uploaded the video to YouTube?"

Alarm skitters across her face. "Someone put that online? Oh, god."

"As of fifteen minutes ago, it's had roughly three million views."

She sits staring and gaping at me, not moving, not breathing. Then suddenly she dashes for the attached bathroom and tries to slam the door between us. She doesn't put enough arm into closing a door that heavy, and it drifts open again.

I hear her retching seconds later.

I stand in indecision for a moment before I go to her. She's already suffered alone. Yeah, she's probably isolated herself intentionally. She'd even say she prefers it this way. But under that tough-girl exterior is a woman who's bruised and angry and deserves more. And now that I know the truth, I feel even more compelled to be close to her, help her.

In the dark bathroom, she's on her knees in front of the toilet, gripping the side with one hand and holding her hair back with the other. There's nothing in her stomach to vomit, so she heaves and gasps. Then I hear a sob that tears at my chest.

I can't not go to her.

"Hey, it's all right. I'm here." Taking hold of her hair at her nape, I rub her back with a soothing palm.

She jumps like a startled cat. "Go!"

I try not to take her rejection personally. I suspect she's rejecting men and emotions in general, rather than me specifically. "I won't leave you when you're upset. Your situation is way more public because of me.

Because I was careless enough to kiss you in public last night, naively thinking that since I'm retired no one would care about my love life."

Harlow doesn't answer, just continues to pant and shake over the toilet. I notice that she'd rather hold on to it than to me.

"I'm sorry, baby. Let's talk."

She shakes her head, then manages to get to her feet. "There's nothing to say. It's done. Let's look forward and not back. You've got a job to prepare for and you're paying me well to help you. You don't have time for me to lick my wounds. How many hours of sleep did you have last night?"

"About three, but it can wait. You need—"

"I need to move on. Since you should be nice and exhausted today, let's get started, hopefully make progress with the evaluations." She washes her hands, then reaches for her toothbrush. "If you haven't had coffee, don't. Let me throw myself together and we'll dig in. Meet me in your office in ten."

Like nothing ever happened. Like her life didn't fall apart less than a week ago and she hasn't been trying to pick up the pieces by herself since. If she's not ready to talk, badgering her won't help. I don't like it, but there's not much I can do now.

More and more, I find myself wanting to talk to Maxon and Griff. They're on her side. They understand their sister. They might be able to help me know what to do next and why she's seemingly broken. Why she wants a baby so desperately. And why, if her ex didn't shatter her emotionally, is she rebuffing someone who wants to make her happy?

"All right, but we're going to talk about you, too."

"That's not going to help your situation."

"Paragraph three, clause B says that we'll take breaks at your discretion but I can insist we continue with therapy or engage in non-therapeutic conversation as a low-key way to continue my verbal progress. So when I need to rest, you can talk."

"You want to grill me."

"I just want to know you better, Harlow. I'm not the enemy."

She stares at me, arms crossed. "Everyone is, Weston. Despite your celebrity, you're no different. You hired me to help you with your speech issues. If you still want to fuck, I'm down with that. But I don't need you to be my hero and I'm not looking for some grand romance. Now get out of my personal space."

Harlow shoves me out and slams the door, but not before I see tears falling down her cheeks.

I STARE AT the bathroom door she slammed in my face for a long second.

That woman is *not* fine. Does anyone else know that?

Shaking my head, I back away. I have maybe five minutes before Harlow gets herself together and comes downstairs in some thought-robbing outfit, gumption firmly strapped in place, demanding that we get to work. I should be using this time to do more than splash water on my face and find my wits, but as I do, realizations pelt me left and right. She's been using sex as a newfound expression of her freedom from the ex-dipshit. She's also wielding it expertly to avoid actual intimacy. It's easy to fuck, so I understand why she's acted as if we're friends with benefits. I imagine it's much more difficult to open your heart and make love. I've never actually done that, I admit. But Harlow needs to.

The question is, if I tried with her—if I could make love to her—how would she respond?

Yes, a woman who wants a baby because she craves love should want devotion from others in her life. But trust is a thin commodity with her, and she can feel secure that a baby will never hurt or deceive her. Harlow acts as if she's otherwise avoidant of attachment. I've never been a huge fan myself, but I like this woman. *Really* like her. I want to be something more to her than the rebound stud.

I'm also second-guessing whether I should get that deep with Harlow. The guy who finally convinces her to open up and trust should be prepared to be a staple in her life for a long while. Our relationship already has an expiration date, per our contract. Is it possible we'll still feel as hot for each other by the end of the summer as we do right now?

I don't know. But I also know I can't do nothing while she's hurting.

After some grooming, I pick up my phone and scroll through my emails. I remember seeing phone numbers in messages about my house closing. It takes me a minute, but I finally locate a missive from Griff.

"I'm ready," Harlow calls from the top of the stairs. "I'm setting up in your office. Come down and let's get this shit started. You've got a second career to nail."

With a grimace, I duck into the bathroom. "Be out in a minute."

If I'm going to start understanding Harlow, I need reinforcements. Reaching her will be hard enough. Doing it in a couple of months sounds ridiculous. I'd leave it alone if I thought someone else could manage it...and if I didn't have some inexplicable urge to be the man to break through her walls.

Taking a deep breath, I dial the number in the email. Despite the fact that it's barely seven a.m., he answers on the second ring. "Griffin Reed speaking."

"It's Noah Weston."

A long silence tells me he's not thrilled. "What do you want? Unless it's to buy another house from me, I've got nothing to say."

The chill in his voice is unmistakable, but I push on. "I'm calling about your sister."

"What do you want? You better not be looking for permission to shine a neon light on her broken engagement and humiliate her even more in the tabloid press. Because if you are, you've come to the wrong place. If you mess with her again, I will cut you. And Maxon will help me dig the hole and bury your body."

Nerves tighten my stomach. I blow out a breath. Is it hot in here or just me? I've got to focus. If her family is already against me, how the hell can I enlist their aid?

"That was a mistake. I'm sorry. I just want to help her. I didn't know

94

about her ex until less than an hour ago."

"She didn't tell you?" His grunt sounds frustrated. "I shouldn't be surprised. That's how Harlow rolls. But not knowing doesn't excuse the fact that you made her private life public. She doesn't need that shit, asshole."

"You're right." I rush to get the words out because I feel my nerves seizing my guts. Sweat beads on my forehead. My words freeze. "Why?"

I can't finish the rest of my question, and the final word doesn't even sound one hundred percent right to my ears. But it's all I can manage. I'm tired and I'm anxious. Those are both triggers for me. But goddamn it, I need to get out of my own way and help Harlow.

"Why doesn't it surprise me that my sister didn't tell you? Because she's great at helping everyone else with their problems and completely ignoring her own. When she first came to Hawaii, she dove in the heap of shit I found myself in with my wife. Long story, but she kicked me in the ass when I needed it. After that, she had her own wedding to focus on. Maxon and I kept asking her if she was sure she wanted to marry this guy. She would laugh us off or change the subject or..."

Find one of the other hundred ways she knew so well to deflect the issue. "Hmm..."

It's not much of a response, but it's the best I can do. My brain is screaming at me, but my mouth just won't cooperate. I drag air in, let it out, try to find calm. It's not helping. My head is whirling like someone punched me stupid.

"Getting familiar with that tactic already? Took me a while to figure it out, to be honest. But she's a master at the bait and switch. My brother and I hadn't met Simon until he showed up a couple of days before the wedding. I knew immediately he wasn't in love with her. And he was chummy with my dad, which wasn't a good sign. Neither Maxon nor I could persuade Harlow to talk. Our wives both tried, too. My Britta was more successful, but she still only managed to get Harlow to admit that she's not into romance. That's it. I don't suppose she's told you anything else?"

"Hun-huh." I put a negative tone to my voice and hope he under-stands. Griff putting his pissed off aside to talk to me at all is a blessing, and I'm so fucking frustrated that I can't form the words to have a coherent conversation.

"Figures. As siblings, we're pretty tight. But neither of us had any idea what Harlow had up her sleeve for her wedding day. Apparently she didn't tell her bridesmaids that she had revenge, not eternal devotion, on her mind, either. Nor did she breathe a word of it to our parents, not that they would have been able to spare the mental energy to care."

Because their own divorce is so consuming? I have no idea and I fuck-ing can't seem to ask. I grit my teeth and focus hard on making the sounds in my head. I manage to growl out a "wow" that almost sounds intelligible.

Griff pauses, and I can almost feel his scowl over the phone. "Yeah. So if you're just going to keep taking advantage of a woman who's already in emotional distress and sling her name through the mud as your latest conquest, I wish you'd fuck off and stay out of her life."

"Nah." I try for a no, but don't quite get one. I'm hopeful that dis-torted sound makes enough sense for me to get my point across.

"No, you won't take advantage of her or no, you won't fuck off?"

A question that I can't answer with a yes or no. I'm screwed. I suck in harsh air and try to muster my verbal abilities but after an awkward silence, I realize there's no hope. With an angry grunt, I hang up on him, then instantly tap out a text.

Sorry we got cut off. The answer to your question is neither. I simply want to help Harlow, so I called you for answers. I'm trying to understand her. Talk later?

It takes a moment, but the three little dots tell me that he's replying.

"Are you coming sometime this century?" Harlow hollers up the stairs. "If you're still grooming, didn't any woman ever tell you that she can't deal with a dude who's prettier than she is?"

As I pocket the phone, I swallow a few times. The dizzy, overwhelmed feeling begins to subside. I stop sweating as I head out of the bedroom and down to the office. The selective loss of verbal ability is frustrating as hell. Why does this keep happening? Being tired never used to affect me half so much. I can't remember a time before this year when I was ever anxious, much less worrying constantly that a situation will spiral out of control and I'll lose my ability to talk it through. I want to hit a wall or growl out my anger. But Harlow can't fix me if I lose my shit. And I'm useless to her if I do.

Halfway down the stairs, my phone buzzes again. I pull it from my pocket and scan Griff's reply.

You're damn right we will. This conversation isn't over.

It sucks that he sees me as the enemy, but I don't blame him. I'm annoyed that I can't do anything about it now.

I canter down to the home office. When I arrive, Harlow has a pamphlet in front of her, two open books, a pencil tucked behind her ear, and a steaming cup of coffee in her hand.

"Finally, Mr. Ready-for-your-close-up arrives. Have a seat." She gestures to a chair opposite her. "I got you a bottle of water and one of those protein bars you like." When I eye her coffee, she hugs it protectively to her chest. "Don't get any ideas about this java. After we're done, you can have a whole pot. But for now I need your raw responses. And before you get any ideas, you can't seduce me into easing up on the caffeine ban, so save yourself the effort and embarrassment. This cup is mine."

I narrow my eyes at her and open my mouth. "Mean."

Relieved that the constriction on my words seems to be easing up, I watch as she laughs. "Yeah, I'm a regular bitch. Just ask half my Facebook friends. But name-calling won't stop me from getting the best assessment possible. It's critical that I know exactly what's happening with you. Our time is short and this won't be an easy problem to tackle. I want to see you succeed. I want to help you, so let's do this."

Suddenly, she's positive and upbeat, supportive and sweet. Like she didn't just slam the bathroom door in my face and shove me out of her private pain fifteen minutes ago.

"Sure." I take a drink of water and gnaw into the protein bar, hoping that, even if I can't have coffee, the hydration and calories will help me focus. "What's first?"

"I have to ask you a few questions for background. We'll discuss some of your medical stuff, too. Then we'll hop into the assessment. It's a few hours long."

It sounds like torture, especially when she sips coffee, flips through notes, and looks too damn beautiful doing it. "Sure."

I grit my teeth and grip the table so I don't jump on her—or her cup.

"Have you ever had a problem speaking before these episodes began?"

"Never."

She jots notes on the assessment. "Have you had a hearing exam in the last twelve months?"

"Yeah, the neurologist insisted we check everything from top to bottom after the concussion in the NFC Championship Game but before the Super Bowl. That came out clear."

"Brain scan? I know they aren't completely indicative of issues, but did your neurologist find anything? I know CTE can't be diagnosed without an autopsy, so he wouldn't have laid that label on you. Let's not resort to that to get a diagnosis, okay?"

She's teasing me. Leave it to Harlow to joke through a serious subject. I think she handles everything rough with humor or deflection, maybe a touch of sarcasm, too. "Let's not. The scan I had back around the first of February looked good but…"

"These things develop over years and decades, yeah. Tell me when you first noticed your difficulty with speech."

"I couldn't speak for a few hours after my last concussion. I could think, but that's the first time I became aware of the disconnect between my brain and my mouth." I don't admit how much that worried me. But I sweated until my words returned. "Then again after the Super Bowl, I was supposed to go straight from the field to the shower, then to a press conference. I got through most of my canned statement all right, but when the reporters broke in and started pelting me with questions about my future in football and what I intended to do if I wasn't extended another contract, I remember feeling my words freeze up."

That's when panic really set in.

"The idea of never playing again made you anxious, I take it?"

"I already knew I was done. For my health, I had to be. Admitting it felt impossible. I intended to announce my retirement that night, but I couldn't—literally. I cut the press conference short by stomping out. The press painted me as pissy about the question, but I was frustrated about being unable to make my announcement after a reporter handed me the perfect segue. Later, my coach covered for me, telling everyone that I'd been dizzy and severely dehydrated."

"I remember seeing a clip of you on the news. The press made a big deal about your curt responses and abrupt end. So that was the first time you'd been unable to speak in public? It caught you off guard?"

"Yeah. I was stunned that I suddenly couldn't talk. I was especially baffled since I hadn't suffered another concussion that day." I still have no idea why it happens selectively. I mean, I've pinned it down to being tired or anxious. The combination together is almost a guarantee that I'll fuck up.

"What did you tell your coach?"

"About that night? Nothing. I said I didn't feel good. He made up the rest of the cover story. I went to a team party that night that lasted into the wee hours before I had to be up for more interviews the next morning. I was fine. We did Disney World and the White House. No problems. So I thought I was all right, that the whole incident had been a blip. Then it happened again when I realized I couldn't avoid announcing my retirement. Then again when my sister got married. I couldn't finish the toast I had planned." I'd had to plead a migraine to everyone, lie that I couldn't read the words swimming in front of my eyes.

"It's happened twice in the past couple of days."

Three times if I'm being picky. But she doesn't need to know about my conversation with Griff just now. So I simply nod.

"Does anyone in your family have this same issue? Or ever had trouble in the past?"

I shake my head. "They all seem normal. No one has ever expressed any problem. Samaria is actually really good off the cuff. She's in sales."

Harlow taps the pencil's eraser against her temple and stares at the paper in her hand. "Any new medications in the last six months? Something that may have altered your brain chemistry?"

"No."

"Did you tell your neurologist about your problem?"

"I haven't seen him since February."

She gives me a long-suffering sigh. "You could have called him when the problem persisted."

"And admit I had a problem at all?" I send her a quelling stare in jest…mostly.

"Oh, I get it. You he-man, so you're macho enough to self-diagnose and self-treat." Harlow rolls her eyes.

"No. I'm manly enough that I don't have problems I can't overcome on my own."

"Ever think about changing your name to Conan LoneWolf?" she pokes. "A little suggestion: next time you have an unexplained phenomenon with your brain, maybe you should, you know, call a doctor. Get an expert medical opinion."

She's right, but I can't help teasing her back.

"Why would I do that when I can find a hot woman to help me instead?"

"Well, I hope I can help you. On that note, let's start with this assessment. It covers general speech and language. It's a functional communication profile and will help me figure out where to start. If I can isolate the problem, I'll be more effective in teaching you ways to cope with or overcome your issues. I reserve the right to make you call the neurologist and admit to him that, despite being the manliest man ever, you need help."

"Ugh, you're torturing me, woman."

"I suggest you get used to it." She gives me an acidic smile. "You signed up for a summer full of it."

"Maybe I should have my head examined after all."

"Glad you're admitting I was right. But it's too late now. You're mine, and I'm going to need you to concentrate. So that phone of yours that keeps buzzing has to shut up until this assessment is over."

The damn thing is blowing up more with every passing moment, as if the rest of the world seemingly insists I comment on my relationship with the runaway bride. Her cell should be blowing up, too. "Why can't I hear your phone?"

She shrugs. "I left it upstairs on the charger. I've already talked to Maxon's wife, Keeley, this morning. She'll talk to Britta. I'll deal with my brothers later. Anyone else who wants to talk to me will only get a 'no comment' and I don't have the time or energy to say that a thousand times over the next few days. They can all go to voice mail and kiss my ass."

That's such a Harlow response. The woman is an island. A beautiful one, of course. But she definitely isn't into answering to anyone for anything. "I can't argue with that. They're relentless. I've had to change my number multiple times. It's a hell of a nuisance."

"But it comes with the territory?" When I nod, she sighs. "Fine. I'll change mine tomorrow. And bonus, Simon won't be able to call me again."

"Is that son of a bitch harassing you?"

"Calm down. He hasn't tried to ring me since the wedding. His family has, but I can handle them. I'm just saying it would be nice to cut them all off so I don't have to deal with them again. I should actually thank my ex and his wandering sperm. Simon's mother would have been one hell of a meddling mother-in-law."

I can't help but laugh. I don't see strong-willed Harlow bending to any woman's will simply to keep family harmony. Compromising, sure. But she will stand her ground and fight for what she believes in, even if she has to go to the mat hard. I admire that about her. She'll never let anyone walk over her without her consent.

"You're welcome. I'll help you get everything changed tomorrow if you'd like."

"Thanks." She nods gratefully, then holds out her hand for my phone. As soon as I set it in her outstretched palm, she powers it down and sets it aside. "Let's ignore the people itching to talk to you and get going. The sooner we finish, the sooner you get coffee."

For the next two hours, we focus on just about everything communication. Auditory and visual cues, motor skills, attention span, silent gestures, and of course a whole host of expressive and receptive language. Subject changes, intonations, listening, syntax, rate of speech. She even checks my ability to swallow and asks to examine my tongue.

"Baby, you know my tongue works just fine." In fact, I'm hungry. Yes, for breakfast. But for Harlow, too. It seems way too long since I had my lips on hers, my mouth on her pussy. I'm definitely feeling deprived. "But if you can't remember, I'll be happy to remind you."

"Later, Casanova. We're almost done, but you have to behave for a few minutes more."

After we wrap up, she releases me to find some caffeinated nirvana in a pot while she closes herself in the office to assess my situation. I snatch my phone back and power it up as I wait for the hot java to brew. I scan my messages, looking down the list. Sports reporter, gossip columnist, Internet tabloid journalist, former teammate who likes to run his mouth, then a whole host of bottom-feeders who intend to drag me through the mud. I ignore them all. A message from Maxon jumps out.

What the fuck is going on? I know you talked to Griff, but Harlow is not in a good place for your limelight. Back off. Hire someone else for whatever "work" you've got.

I'm going to have to convince them—somehow—that the last thing I want to do is upset or hurt Harlow. It sure would help if I could fucking speak to them, but the last couple of times I tried... *Nada*. Why do her brothers make me so nervous?

"Any conclusions yet?" I ask while the coffee finishes. She emerges from my office as I finally pour myself a cup.

"No." The soft sounds of footsteps precede her arrival in the kitchen.

She's now sporting a messy ponytail she hadn't had a few minutes ago and a confused scowl. "Everything on this assessment shows you being somewhere between average and above average."

"That's good, right?"

"It gives us a baseline to work with, which is helpful. But this assessment isn't one I can give again anytime soon. Or administer very effectively if we wait for a time when you're having difficulty speaking. I was hoping your daily speech would have some hallmarks I hadn't yet noticed but could work on. Nothing, so I'll have to fabricate a situation that incites a verbal dry spell and find another assessment that may help me whittle down the exact problem." She sighs. "I'll be honest. Since I studied mostly developmentally delayed children, I'm not sure where to go next. I observed other clinicians with adult patients, but none of them had your specific issue. I'll keep researching and have some ideas to talk to you about tonight, okay?"

"Sure." I shrug. "All kidding aside, once this annoying shit slapped me in the head a few times with the fact that I can't predict it and it's not going away, I didn't think solving the problem would be simple. If I did, I wouldn't have hired you."

"You did that just to keep sleeping with me."

"I might have agreed to your proposition for that reason, but I agreed to get started because I finally admitted that I need help."

Her face softens. "You do. I want to help you in every way possible to lead a full, normal life. Besides, I enjoy a good challenge. But I also think you love football too much to leave it entirely. Broadcasting seems like a perfect next step for you, and I'm determined to see you succeed."

I'm struck again by how complicated this woman is. She wants to cast a bright ray in my life but would rather sit alone in the dark with her own woes. She's doing her best to help me, so I'm going to jump in and help her, too. Maybe by summer's end we'll both be ready to move on and tackle a brighter future. What more could I ask for?

CHAPTER SEVEN

T WO DAYS LATER, Harlow wakes me at the crack of dawn and tells me to dress in comfortable clothes while she makes us a lunch. Two things don't escape my notice: First, she didn't sleep in my bed again last night. She stays long enough for the amazing, explosive sex and waits until I fall asleep. Then I can only assume she slips out because I always wake up alone. Second, she hasn't said a word about where we're going or what we're doing today.

"What's going on?" I ask.

"I have a new assessment I'd like to try. I spoke with my master professor yesterday, and she gave me some great suggestions about where to go with your case next. I didn't use any names, of course."

I nod, acknowledging her discretion. Not that the world isn't still buzzing about that kiss captured on camera and whether I'm the reason Harlow ran out on her cheating ex. As promised, I helped her change her number. She also disabled all social media profiles except LinkedIn, which she kept for professional purposes. I also haven't seen her return a single one of those stacked-up voice mails except to her brothers or their brides.

"But in order to give this assessment properly, I have to change the test conditions. We already tried getting a read on you when you were tired and you performed better than expected. Since anxiety seems to be another trigger, we'll try this in a stressful situation."

I'm pulling on a T-shirt to go with my khaki shorts and hiking boots when her words stop me. "What do you mean?"

"Nothing public," she assures me. "Believe me, the last thing I want is a spectacle. I don't need more attention, either."

True. No one seeks less attention from the press than Harlow.

"Thanks for the reassurance, but can you be more specific?"

"No." And she looks cheerful about having the upper hand as she hands me a cup of coffee. "If I tell you, then you can mentally prepare for the situation. I need you to be off guard for this to work properly."

"That sounds ominous."

Her smile turns flirty. "Am I scaring you, big guy?"

"A little bit. You're small but mighty. And you can be fearsome when pissed off."

"Don't you forget it." She winks and lifts a picnic basket. "Ready when you are."

With a little more trepidation than I let on, I get behind the wheel and we head out of the estate. I'm semi-prepared when we open the gate to find a small cluster of reporters waiting for a photo op or a scoop. The second we emerge from behind the sweeping palm fronds, the snaps start. I can hear the speculation now. No one has seen us come or go for days, so they know damn well Harlow has been in my house. They'll likely guess she's been in my bed. Not as much as I'd like, but I'll fix that soon.

Harlow keeps her head down as we pass slowly because they aren't in a hurry to get off the damn road.

"Is your relationship with Ms. Reed serious or are you her rebound romance?" shouts one reporter.

I'm not going roll down my window to justify that stupid question with an answer.

"What do you have to say about the speculation that you're in talks to provide color commentary for NFL games this fall?"

Nothing. If they want to speculate, I can't stop them. But I'm certainly not adding fuel to their fire.

"Simon Butler says Ms. Reed's public display at their aborted wedding was a stunt to whip up public sympathy when, in fact, she's a... What did he call her?" He flips through his little notepad. "Yeah, a fame-seeking whore. Butler claims she cheated on him with you. What's your comment?"

By silent but mutual consent, we've ignored most everything on our phones and turned off the world. It's easy to do when you have no neighbors, your own beach, and utter privacy. For the past couple of days, I've done nothing but enjoy my moments with Harlow. We've gone skinny-dipping and built a sand castle on the beach. We've watched movies and cooked together. And we've had sex. Steamy quickies, followed by hours-long bouts of slow, heavy pleasure. We've christened the living room sofa, the kitchen counters, even the lounger on which I first spotted her. I don't know what it is about Harlow, but every time I'm sure I've fucked her so much I shouldn't want her again, I want her more.

"Was she seeing you while still engaged to her fiancé, Weston?" the reporter demands. "Is she the fame-seeking whore Butler claims?"

That's it. I stop the SUV and put it in park.

"What are you doing?" Harlow gapes at me like she knows exactly what I intend and is horrified by the prospect.

"Putting a stop to this bullshit."

She grabs my arm. "You can't beat a reporter up. He's only saying that shit to get a rise out of you, and I've heard worse. I'll be fine."

"You shouldn't have to put up with that. It's fucking wrong, Harlow. Butler screwed you over, and I'm going to set the record straight."

"You'll just fan the flames."

"Your ex shouldn't be the only one who says his piece, especially when it's all lies. I've been silent because I don't care what they write about me. They've been doing it for years. But you got dragged into this tabloid shit because I wasn't thinking. It's my fault, so I'm going to stop it."

"Please let it go." She bites her lip. "For me."

When she asks like that, I can't be the asshole who makes a stink, even if it's for the good cause of defending her.

"Why?"

"They're not worth it, and I can fight my own battles. I want to look forward, not back. Arguing with them just mires us in the past and drags us down."

I grip the wheel until my knuckles are white. "I don't like this for you. You're not fame-seeking and you're not a whore. Goddamn it."

Her fingers on me gentle. "And I'm touched that you want to defend me. But they're like a schoolyard bully, right? If we ignore them, they eventually go away. The minute we give them something to talk about, they sink their teeth in. Really. Just leave it. Besides, Simon is looking to save face, so he's putting the blame for his shit on me. I'm sure he hopes that will protect his precious reputation. Honestly, if that's all it takes so he never darkens my door again, I can live with whatever these guys write about me."

Letting out a frustrated breath, I stare her way. Harlow is right, but I don't like it. I want to beat the shit out of anyone who maligns her. But my impulse to defend her really only gives her situation more heat and Butler's claim more credibility.

I put the SUV in drive and crack the window. "No comment."

As I raise the glass on their shouting, I rev the car. The idiots lingering in the road are finally smart enough to jump out of the way. And as soon as we're clear, I step on the gas and we lurch forward.

"Thank you," she says softly, trailing her palm down my arm to hold my hand. "You did good."

I squeeze her fingers. "I don't want to upset you, baby. I just—"

"I know. And it's very chivalrous. But we have more important things to do. And far more fun."

Since she doesn't give me much choice, I let the drama go. "You going to tell me what we're doing now?"

"Nope. But I'll tell you where to go. Head toward Haleakala. Once we're in the vicinity, I'll give you more specific directions."

"You really are enjoying the upper hand," I accuse.

"Totally."

Her smile sparkles and for the moment before I merge into traffic, I simply stare. She's wearing only sunscreen and lip gloss. There's nothing remotely sexy about her athleisure outfit and sturdy sneakers. Yet I'm thinking she's one of the most gorgeous women I've ever met. It's not her physical beauty, per se. I've dated actresses and models galore in the past. Country and pop singers. Even a porn star. They were pretty and all that. But Harlow is lovely from the inside out. There's a vitality about her that's bright and glowing and irresistible.

I'm sounding sappy and I need to stop.

After she rattles off a series of directions, I find myself at the top of a tall crater. The landscape here is more desert-like than tropical. There's a guy waiting for us next to a tall pole with cables and harnesses attached.

My gut tightens. "We're zip-lining?"

"We are."

"How are you going to assess me while we're doing this?"

"We're doing it in tandem. More than a few times. Are you afraid of heights?"

"They aren't my favorite thing," I hedge. Actually, I'm somewhat terrified.

"Good. Hopefully this will be effective."

I don't really want to know how much this is going to cost me, both in money and guts. But none of that matters, I suppose, if Harlow is able to isolate my issue and help me. "All right. Let's do this thing."

And get it over with.

She gives me a little clap and a quick peck. I'd rather linger and go in for seconds, but she's already approaching the guy wearing the polo shirt with the adventure company's logo. "Hi, we're your ten a.m. appointment."

"Harlow?" he asks, checking his clipboard. Then he glances my way and does a double take. "Mr. Weston. Wow. Hi. I'm such a fan."

Pasting on a smile, I hold out my hand and make small talk. Out of the corner of my eye I see Harlow gathering supplies from her backpack.

Finally, our guide, Matt, straps us in hip to hip, facing each other. Harlow taps her thumbs over her phone like a maniac. "I'm just going to record your responses and I'll calculate the results later. Nervous?"

"A little." Okay, way more than that. I'm starting to sweat. I'm definitely having second thoughts. I wish like hell this was over with and I wasn't having visions of snapping cables as we fall to our deaths. But I've never been a coward and I won't start now. "Have you done this before?"

"Yeah. A couple of times. It's a lot of fun."

Dangling from a wire hundreds of feet from solid ground while whizzing toward another post I can see myself face-planting into? "Yeah, a blast."

Chuckling, she secures her phone to an armband built to hold the device, then withdraws a booklet she'd rolled up and curled inside her bra. When she flips to the first page, I gape at her. "This is a real assessment, not just you trying to take a swag at my situation while we fly down the mountain?"

"Of course." Harlow looks baffled. "Why would I waste your time?"

Matt approaches, checks a few harnesses and leads, then asks us how we're feeling.

"Great!" She sounds downright chipper.

I, on the other hand, wonder if I can keep myself from vomiting. "Do I have to answer that?"

They both laugh.

"You'll do great," the guide vows.

I'm less convinced but short of chickening out and ruining whatever Harlow has planned, there's not much I can do. "Thanks."

Matt steps back. "Give me a thumbs-up when you're ready, then I'll release you."

Daredevil Harlow sticks her thumb out immediately. No hesitation, just a confident enthusiasm I envy. Then they both turn to look at me. My heart is drumming. I'm definitely feeling overheated again. A touch dizzy, too.

Still, the sooner we start, the sooner we finish. So I manage to clench my fist and raise my thumb. With a wild shout, the guide lets go of the rope he's been holding. We start to roll down the cable, and I grab on to the handle above me—as if that will do any damn good if the support above our heads snaps.

A split second later, Harlow begins asking me questions similar to those from the first assessment and gauging my replies. I'm supposed to listen and reply and keep my thoughts screwed on straight while I'm racing down the side of a massive crater, leaves whipping past my face, my stomach knotting? Right... I'll attempt to keep my head screwed on straight, but it's hard when breathing isn't coming easy, my heartbeat is frantic, and my brain seems focused on fear.

"Noah?" she prompts.

I manage to answer, but as my anxiety flares, my brain slows on all functions that aren't related to curbing my freak out.

"Look at me." She hooks her leg around mine and gives me a reassuring smile. "These guys are top rated. The worst that can happen is that you're too anxious of heights to finish the assessment successfully, then we'll have to come back and try again."

That sounds terrible. "Keep going."

It takes us about six trips down the mountain and a whole lot of will to keep myself together before we finish. My ability to speak didn't seize up entirely but it felt close at times. Only her voice, her encouragement to keep breathing and her focusing me on the moment helped me to stay on top of the worry. If not for her, I'm almost sure I would have seized up.

As we unpack ourselves from the harness for the last time, I grab her and hold her like a lifeline, burying my head in her neck. Instantly, she wraps her arms around me and I feel comforted. Soothed.

She kisses my temple. "You okay, big guy?"

I nod. "I'll make it. I think."

"Good to hear. You take care of Matt, and I'll get our gear together and loaded in the car. We can find a nice picnic spot and eat."

Reluctantly, I let her go and I toss her the keys. Harlow catches them with one hand and starts shoving water bottles and her test booklets into her backpack. She's not doing anything particularly interesting, but I can't take my eyes off of her.

"Did you enjoy yourself even a little?" the guide asks.

"Sure."

He laughs. "You're not a very good liar, sir."

"Noah." I correct him with a shrug. "How about this, then? Once we got going, it wasn't as bad as I thought."

"Fair enough. I didn't realize you were afraid of heights." He sounds surprised, like he's just realized I'm human.

"A little," I admit.

"Well, you did great." He slants a glance toward Harlow. "She seemed to have a good time. You were a nice guy to do this for her."

I don't tell him that she really did it for me because that would raise too many questions. It's on the tip of my tongue to say that I'd do anything to make her smile. That sounds like a good-guy thing to say, sure. But it's surprisingly true.

I think I need to introduce her to Trace, get his feedback. He knows me probably better than anyone else. More and more, I suspect she's not just a summer fling. After the hell she's been through recently, though, I wonder if she's ready to feel more for me.

"She's an amazing person," I say with all honesty.

"She looked as if she was there for you during every moment of your ride." His boyish grin morphs into an apologetic grimace. "It's none of my business and I don't listen to gossip much, but she doesn't strike me as the sort of woman the press has painted her to be. What her ex did to her seemed really skeezy."

"Thanks." I could say a lot more, but it's always a good policy to neither confirm nor deny. Instead, I voice the minimum to let him know that I appreciate his kindness but don't give him enough to prolong the situation or feed to the press. And of course, I tip him well. "And now we're going to eat lunch and I'll hope that putting something in my stomach will settle me."

Matt laughs. "Good luck. It was an honor. And for the record, I'd probably go out of my way to watch more football games if you were providing the color."

"I'll take that under advisement." I give him a little two-fingered salute, then join Harlow at the SUV.

"Make a new friend?" she asks, one bud in her ear as she records responses from our session onto the paper in her lap.

"He seems like a decent guy." I jerk my head toward the test booklet. "Come to any conclusions yet?"

"Nothing firm. I have some thoughts but I need to do some additional research, have a few more conversations, maybe try another assessment or two. I'll let you know."

She knows way more about this subject than I do, so I shelve my disappointment that we can't just jump into the therapy part of this. "So what should we do, then? How about lunch somewhere?"

"Know a good picnic place?"

"No."

"Then let's find one."

Under better circumstances, I'd rather take her out and show her off, but that's not smart now. "Sounds like a plan."

As we head down the bumpy road toward the highway, Harlow glances at her phone, then curses. "Well, our peace and quiet has run out. Unless one of us wants to claim that we've contracted prolonged explosive diarrhea, my brothers are insisting that we get together for dinner."

That's good news...and bad news. I need some answers, but every fricking time I've talked to them, I've been unable to finish the conversation. How the hell am I supposed to sit across from the pair of them while they glare at me as if they know all the dirty things I do to their sister and still be able to carry on the conversation?

"When?"

"Tomorrow night."

"Do I have a choice?"

"Not really. I might be able to sidestep them for a while, but I'm pretty sure their wives are insisting, too. So I'm afraid there's no getting out of it if I want to keep any family peace."

I sigh. "Where?"

"Maxon and Keeley's place. They recently opened the Sunshine Coast Bed and Breakfast. It's a really relaxing place. Full of Keeley's kitschy charm. Britta's mom moved to Maui from Chicago to work for them, and let me tell you that woman can cook. It will be private and relaxed."

With her brothers staring and judging? Sounds like a blast. Still, this will keep harmony in Harlow's life and it's important to her, so I can't say no.

I sigh. "Tell them we'll be there."

AFTER A LOW-KEY afternoon at home, Harlow on the phone for most of it with professors and colleagues, I spend time watching other color commentators, past and present, to get a feel for what works and what doesn't. If I can pull this off, I'll have to develop my own style. If I can overcome my issues, I'll look forward to the challenge.

As the sun begins to set, I'm still watching clips on my iPad when Harlow shuffles onto the patio. I glance up to say something—then I realize she's completely naked.

I can't speak, not because my ability seizes up but because she's stolen my breath.

"Hey." She gives me a flirty smile.

Harlow is in the mood. I'm praising a higher power and singing hallelujahs on the inside because after one glance at her I am, too.

"Hey." I set the iPad aside and pull off my shirt.

That gets her attention, and her double take makes me smile. Her staring never gets old, either.

Her gaze dips down toward my fly. "What's...up?"

"My cock, and you know it."

She grins. "I love having a man I can count on."

I scoff. "Unlike earlier. I wanted to wimp out on the zip-lining. Not very manly of me."

"You were totally masculine about your abject terror. You only squealed and trembled for the first few rides," she teases.

"Come here, woman." I stand and saunter closer, reaching for my zipper. "I'll give you manly."

"I thought you'd never ask…" Harlow sidles closer, hips swaying.

I lose the rest of my clothes and join her naked in the dusk. She wraps her arms around my neck and smiles up at me. Her eyes sparkle with mischief, happiness, and invitation. I don't think before I speak next.

"Are you ready for me to more than like you, Harlow? To want more than just sex with you?"

I'm heading in that direction, and I'd rather not put my heart on the line if she's simply going to reject any relationship beyond hooking up.

She stiffens but doesn't pull away. "I don't know. I like you. I have fun with you. I want to help you. But those are easy to both feel and admit. I won't deny there's something between us. But I'm not familiar with the 'more' part. I've never really done the whole romance thing."

"Never?"

Easing out of my grasp, Harlow shakes her head. "We moved from San Diego to Hawaii when I was eight. You know Maui can be like a small town, and we weren't from here. Sure, we lived here, but we weren't locals."

It's true. People here are close-knit but they can be standoffish to outsiders and newcomers. "I understand."

"Besides, any guy who liked me, either my brothers would warn him away or I'd figure out he was a teenage hormonal prick and lose interest. If I was ever tempted to dip my toe in the relationship pool, I just had to get an eyeful of my parents' version of undying devotion. After that, I figured I was better off without."

"Did they fight a lot?"

"Not overtly. They both operate more underhandedly. With them, it's always passive-aggressive shit like my mom 'accidentally' spilling nail polish on Dad's favorite dress shirt or him 'forgetting' their anniversary and planning an overnight business trip instead. Their relationship was cool and contentious under the falsely polite surface. Love never seemed to make either of them happy, so I figured…why bother?"

Wow. And her fiancé only reinforced all her worst fears about marriage. No wonder she's gun-shy. "It's not supposed to be that way."

"That's what Hollywood tells us," she says tartly with a shrug. "But who knows? Can we just take whatever this is between us one day at a time?"

"Yeah. I like that idea. You need to know me and I need to know you. I just wanted to find out if we had any chance… You've been through a lot lately, and I could understand if Butler put you off relationships for a long while."

"I'm not giving the asshole that kind of power over me. But I honestly didn't expect to find anyone I liked well enough to spend more than a night or two with. So you've surprised me."

"You surprised me, too. I thought I'd be alone while I figured my life out. But this is way better. You're fun and smart. And a little mysterious."

Her light laughter is like a melody in my head. "What you're saying is that you'd be bored without someone crazy to shake up your post-retirement ho-hums."

"Something like that. But I'm happy you're here."

I'd like to get more personal but she's tensing up, like I'm creeping toward the boundaries of her comfort zone. The last thing I want to do is rattle her too much so she decides that she can't deal.

"I'm…um, happy, too." She sends me the mischievous grin I'm coming to know well. She's moving back into safer territory. "So how about some raunchy sex in the pool?"

Harlow buries emotional intimacy with either humor or sex—or both. I need to put a subtle stop to that if I want her to give me a chance to be in her life as something more than a hookup or summer fuck.

"How about you come here?" I open my arms.

She pads into them warily. "What is it?"

"I just want to hold you for a minute."

"Are you sure?" She rocks against me, rubbing herself against my hard dick. The woman really doesn't play fair. "We could be having more fun…"

I clamp one hand around her hips to hold her still. If I let her drive me to crazed sexual hunger—a distinct possibility—I'll never learn what we could have if only we stopped screwing long enough to figure it out. "In a minute. Humor a guy, huh?"

With a sigh, she finally settles into my arms softly. She's small. Warmth shimmers off her body. I can feel how nervous this makes her, but she's trusting me in the moment. She's not running away. I'm calling it a victory.

It would be even sweeter if we kept our sex about the connection of more than our genitals.

Dropping a trio of kisses on her shoulder, I lift my face into her neck, lips against her ear. "You're beautiful, Harlow. I love being with you. I love to make you feel better than any man ever has."

Her shoulders tense and she leans back enough to meet my gaze in the halo of the patio light. She's searching my eyes as if she's trying to understand me. For her, I'm approaching dangerous ground.

"What do you want, Weston? Really?"

She doesn't mean in the next few minutes when we have sex. She doesn't mean over the next days and weeks while we work on my speech issues together. She's grasped that I'm truly wondering if this might be a longer-term thing.

"I don't know, baby. Like we've said, one day at a time."

Her brows furrow and a little line appears between them. "Yeah. Fair warning: I don't think I'm built for any kind of happily ever after. Simon understood the rules. He wasn't looking for romance, either. But it sounds as if you are. That's not me."

I shrug. "It's never been me, either. I'm just feeling us out. No harm in that, right? Maybe this goes nowhere. Aren't you a little bit curious?"

Harlow weighs my words. "I might be. More than I want to be."

Her breathless acknowledgement is honest. She thinks she's not into romance, but I'm calling bullshit. I'd bet twenty bucks she doesn't sleep with anyone just because they're hot. She'll actually want to like or respect the guy she's burning up the sheets with.

"All I'm saying is, let's figure this out. Oh, and I don't think I can wait to get in the pool to be inside you."

"Good. I don't want to wait, either."

I lift her against me and set her ass on the patio table and slowly spread her knees apart. She's watching me, and I love feeling her stare all over my body. Being with her sends a shiver down my spine and spikes my blood with a thrill. But now it's making things in my chest suspiciously soft, too.

"Hey, anyone here?" I hear a familiar voice call from inside the house.

Harlow leaps off the table with a gasp. "Who is that?"

I hastily grab my shorts and zip them. "My brother, who I will soon kill for dropping in uninvited."

Sure, I wanted his feedback about Harlow, but not when she was stark naked and looking sexy as hell.

"Shit," she hisses. "I don't have a towel or a stitch of clothing out here."

I glance around the patio and I see nothing except my T-shirt. I toss it her way, and she pulls it on over her head. I want to groan. If anything, she looks sexier. Her nipples poke the meshy blue fabric. The hem flirts with her thighs. Seeing her in my shirt and having that stamp of ownership on her is definitely doing something to me. And it's really not good that I have no way to cover my obvious erection.

"Noah?"

I stop cold at that voice. It's definitely *not* Trace's.

Fuck me.

"He brought a woman with him?"

I sigh. "He brought my mother."

Harlow's jaw drops. Her eyes flare wide. "Are you kidding me? Is there a hole in the yard I can hide in?"

"Nope." I take her hand. "We've going to have to brazen it out, baby."

"If they've been reading the tabloids at all, they know we've spent the last few days together."

"Exactly." And because no one in my family thinks I'm a saint, they know I've been sleeping with Harlow.

Maybe this is a blessing in disguise. They'll get to meet this woman who's wrapping herself around me while she's not at her best. Maybe they'll see the real her. Hell, maybe I will. Maybe they'll be able to find faults that I can't...or they'll figure out she's every bit as amazing as I suspect.

I tug on her hand and head for the open accordion door. "Out here, *Makuahine*."

"What does that mean?" Harlow whispers.

"It's Hawaiian for mom or mother."

"Gotcha. Thanks."

"You're welcome, *ku'uipo*."

Before she can ask me what that word means, my mother and my brother both appear on the other side of the wide, retracted door that leads to the patio. Trace grins. My mother stops short and takes in our lack of clothing and clasped hands in a glance.

"Hi," I say into the awkward silence.

Trace breaks the ice with a laugh. "We should have called first."

I nod. "It might have been nice. This is Harlow, bro. Makuahine, say hello."

My brother dutifully extends his hand, pretending that Harlow isn't half-naked. "It's nice to meet you."

"You, too." Her smile is strained, but she's managing the situation with grace.

My mother looks her up and down before a little smile dances at the corner of her lips and takes her hand. "Hello, Harlow." Then she turns to me. "Is she your *nalohia*?"

My girlfriend. I don't know if Harlow would object to that term, but it will make my mother feel a lot better. "Yeah."

Harlow looks a little confused, but I give her an encouraging smile when my mom turns back to her and squeezes her hand. "From what I understand, you've been through a lot recently. I hope my son is making you happy. And that you make him happy, as well."

Harlow relaxes, and her smile looks genuine. "He's great at putting a smile on my face."

As soon as the words leave her mouth, she realizes how suggestive her reply sounds and closes her eyes, face flushing. Trace laughs. I do my best not to smile. Even my mom looks amused.

"That came out wrong. I meant he's easy to be with and he's a good listener. On that note, I'm just going to go upstairs and…" She shakes her head as if thinking twice about mentioning that she'll put on some clothes. "I'll be back."

"Looking forward to it," Trace calls after her.

I put a hand at the small of her back and kiss her temple as she hustles to the stairs. "We'll be here."

As soon as she disappears to the upper level, doing her best to inconspicuously tug my shirt down over her bare ass, Trace erupts in silent laughter. "She turned a hundred shades of red. I'm sorry, but it's funny."

I shrug. My hard-on will wait. I haven't seen my mother in a few days, and even if their visit is ill-timed, I'm happy they're here. "We can swim later. Come in. Have a seat." I gesture to the sofa on the other side of the room. "Something to drink?"

"Coffee," my mom requests.

"Got a bottle of water?" Trace asks.

I get them both the beverage of their choice, then rush back to the family room. Harlow will be down soon, and I want to get a few minutes alone with my family.

Once they're sipping happily, I sit in the chair beside my brother's. "Harlow is from California. She's just earned her master's in speech pathology and wants to work with developmentally delayed kids. She's…different."

"From anyone you've dated?" Makuahine stirs her coffee contentedly. "It sounds as if she is your equal."

I snap my head in her direction. "Yeah. But she's complicated."

"You need a challenge. When I've seen you with women in the past, you looked as if you could take or leave them. This one…perhaps not."

It feels that way. "After what her ex put her through, I have to take things slow with her."

"Of course." My mother gives me a smile like she knows something I don't.

Trace butts into my bewilderment. "I'm looking forward to talking to Harlow. Anything else we should know?"

"She doesn't want to talk about her ex or the wedding. She's close to her brothers and their wives, who live on the island. In fact, her brothers sold me this house. We met because she was house-sitting."

My brother and I exchange a glance, and I know what he's thinking. *Why isn't she leaving?* I haven't told them about my speech problems. I don't want to worry my mother, and as much as I love my brother…he's got a big mouth.

"So you two just hit it off?"

"Something like that. This is a big place, and she didn't really have anywhere else to go that wasn't with her brothers, both of whom recently got married and are trying to start their families, so she's staying for a while. She gets me out of my shell. In fact, we went zip-lining earlier today."

"You?" Trace looks stunned.

"I know. She sweet-talked me into it. I think tomorrow I'll teach her to surf. That will keep her occupied for a while."

"She cooks?" my mother asks.

"Yeah. That's the other reason I was happy to have Harlow stay. She makes a mean pork roast."

Trace adjusts in his seat and murmurs for my ears only. "I know that's not the only reason you want her around."

I smile blandly as my mother pretends she didn't hear a word. "She makes you smile?"

"Yeah." Sometimes she infuriates me too, but if I didn't care, she'd never be able to get a rise out of me at all.

"Excellent. And she gives you pleasure?"

Trace almost spits out his water. "Makuahine, what a question to ask."

"What? It's important. They must have more than a meeting of minds."

I feel myself turning slightly red. "Yes, she does. Can we drop it?"

Harlow sprints down the stairs in a pair of flowing pants and a shimmering black tank. It's somehow casual and elegant, especially with her smile firmly in place. "Sorry about that. Let's try this again. I'm Harlow. It's nice to meet you, Trace. You and your brother look a lot alike."

Trace shakes her hand, eyeing her with a grin. "We get that a lot. Great meeting you. And I swear, if Noah will keep his promise to call in the future, I won't drop in unannounced."

"Mrs. Weston, hello. It's lovely to meet you. Can I get you a drink?"

My mother looks her over with an approving little nod. "I'm Malya."

"I got them something. Sit and join us."

She does, and for the next two hours we chat about everything— places we love visiting on the island, the fact that everyone except Makuahine hates poi, what it's like to grow up here versus moving to Hawaii from the mainland. We talk some about my career, Harlow's plans to pursue speech pathology, and Trace's on-again-off-again interest in leaving his current job to pursue something that makes more money.

The easy conversation buoys me. It's as if Harlow fits right into my family. She and my mother bond over their mutual passion for home decorating shows and The Rock. My brother and I both shake our heads.

When Makuahine sets her coffee aside and stands, she takes Harlow's hand. "It was lovely to talk to you, but it's nearly ten o'clock—way past this old woman's bedtime. I hope we meet again." She turns to me. "Walk me out, *keikikane*?"

"Son," I interpret for Harlow. "I'll be right back."

"Nice to meet both of you," Harlow says to my family as she takes the dirty cups and empty bottles to the kitchen. "'Night."

I follow my brother out as he helps our mother navigate the path to the car.

"She's awesome," Trace says. "You seem really...complete when you're with her. Don't let her get away."

Complete describes how I feel with Harlow. His observations validate my feelings. "Thanks, bro. I'm going to try like hell."

"She likes you but she's reserved." My mother shakes her head. "Afraid."

"Yeah." But I've got to keep trying.

"I think she could make you very happy, *keikikane*. But you'll have to reach her heart and make her feel secure first."

So everything I've suspected and believed about Harlow is spot on. Now that people more objective about our relationship have confirmed that, I'm feeling way better about where I'm at with her. "That's what I plan to do."

No matter what it takes.

CHAPTER EIGHT

O NCE MY FAMILY leaves, I return with my gaze locked on Harlow. Regret is all over her face. "I'm sorry. I never thought trying to seduce you on your patio would embarrass you in front of your family."

"You didn't, baby. It's fine. They like you."

She relaxes a bit. "I liked them, too. Your mom really loves you. She's so proud."

Something about the envy in her tone gives me pause. I don't assume again that her mom is proud of her, not after she corrected me once. "Have you talked to your mother since last weekend? I know she wanted you to marry well and now you haven't."

Harlow shrugs as if it doesn't matter, but I think, deep down, it does. "Running out on the wedding is just the latest in a long line of disappointments I've dealt her. I didn't want to be the star of Ms. Hattfield's Dance Academy when I was six. I didn't want to be a child model when one of my dad's Hollywood clients mentioned that he could get me work. I didn't become Miss San Diego County when I was eighteen because I couldn't stand the artificial bitchery of a contestant who was sleeping with two of the judges to ensure her win, so I rubbed icy hot in her bikini bottoms. In general, I didn't add any razzle-dazzle to Mom's name so the rest of her country club friends could ooh and aah when she walked in the room. I've learned to live with the fact that she's always going to think that I've failed to live up to my full potential."

Harlow gave me more information than I expected. Generally, that's a good sign, even though her mother sounds totally bent. "Those were her dreams. You were right to pursue your own."

"Yeah, but she's forever telling me I'm too strong-willed. She tried to call me for days after I ran out on Simon. I haven't answered. I don't have anything to say that's going to make her feel better."

So they're not close, and I'm sad for her. If I'd suffered such a public breakup, I know I could count on my makuahine's comfort and words of wisdom. Harlow would never want to lean on her brothers when they're just getting started in their own happily ever afters. She must feel completely alone.

Well, she was. Now, she's got me.

"Anything you have to say, you can always tell me," I promise her.

"Thanks." But she doesn't divulge deeper feelings or let me in on her innermost thoughts. "Now that your family is gone, can we pick up where we left off before we had unexpected company?"

"I'd like that." And if I get to touch her when she's feeling a little more vulnerable, I might be able to open her up more. Every little bit helps.

We both know what we want and no words are necessary. I take her hand. She curls her fingers around mine and lets me lead her upstairs.

Inside my suite, I seduce her slowly, punctuating every move with a brush of my lips across hers, a nip at her neck, a whisper in her ear. Under my touch, her breath turns shallow. She shivers. The pulse at her neck picks up speed.

"Noah..."

"What's wrong, baby?" I thumb off the strap of her tank top and press my lips to the newly exposed skin.

"Hurry." She tries to force the issue by reaching for the hem to whip the top over her head.

I take hold of her wrists and stop her. "We have all night."

When she looks as if she wants to argue, I lay my mouth over hers and swallow her objection. After a little gasp, she slowly loses her will to resist. Her hands soften and wrap around my shoulders. Then her kiss deepens.

Her body melts against mine. Her sigh tells me she's surrendered.

Finally, she trusts me enough to give me control over something. Even if it's only sex and even if it's only temporary, it's a first step.

I'm slow to remove her clothes. I'm even slower to kiss my way down her body. I take my time inhaling her scent and telling her that I can't wait to be inside her. I linger over her skin, bathe her breasts with my tongue, then work down her body until I have my head between her thighs.

Gasping, she plunges her fingers into my hair and invites me in—deeper, longer, sweeter. She's ambrosia on my tongue, and I know her particular flavor is something I'll never get enough of.

After giving her a pair of gasping, throaty orgasms, I slide my way back up her body and inside her—tongue and cock filling her at once. I take her, wrap myself around her. As if by some mutual, unspoken agreement, we haven't used a condom since the first time we agreed we'd be safe without them. When I feel her enclose me in stunning satin heat, I groan long and loud.

Beneath me, Harlow bucks and circles her hips, urging me on.

I grab her hips and hold her beneath me. "Don't. Let me love you slowly."

She protests with impatient sighs of need. I'd think she was cute if her body and her furtive movements weren't driving me out of my fucking mind. I want to take my time and make this last, wring every ounce of pleasure from her body I can, but I can't stop myself from wrapping one fist in her hair and tilting her gaze directly to mine. I stare into her eyes as I plunge into her, drinking in her whimper.

I love Harlow on top of me, riding me. I crave another chance to take her from behind while she's on all fours and I'm gripping her hips until my fingers leave faint marks. But more than anything, I absolutely love being on top of her, mastering her body, having her totally in my control. I'm sure that says something about me, but I don't care. And I'm pressing myself into her body, just like I'm hoping I'm pressing myself into her soul.

With a groan, I start to ride her. She responds, flattening her feet on the bed, hugging me with her thighs, lifting her hips up to meet my every stroke. I never take my gaze from hers.

"Tell me you want me inside you," I growl.

"I-I want you inside me."

Her frantic whisper lights me on fire.

"Tell me you want me deeper."

"Yes..." she pants. "I want you so deep."

"Tell me you're mine."

Harlow hesitates. "Noah... Don't play games."

"Why do you think this is a game?" I'm fucking serious.

I keep up the slow, steady strokes, trying not to give in to her incendiary touch and burn alive. This is important. *She's* important. If I want more than sex from her, I'm going to have to be both coaxing and assertive.

"I don't want to talk now."

"You just want to fuck. Guess what, baby? I'm the one on top, calling the shots. And I want more. I want to get up in your head. I want to know what you're thinking. I want to know if you're ready to admit that you're mine."

"For now, yes. Faster..." she croons.

I slow my pace. "I'm not rushing to orgasm. In fact, I can slow this down even more until you talk to me." I do, easing inside her with a molasses thrust. "I've got all night."

"No!" She sinks her nails into my shoulders and tosses her head back.

"Then look at me," I demand. "Are you mine?"

It takes her a moment, but she untwists her spine and focuses on me again. As our stares connect, a zing zips down my spine. She feels it, too. I can tell. I hear her sharp little intake of breath and see the goose bumps flare across her skin.

"Say it. Tell me you're mine."

"Don't do this," she cries as I slide inside her. Her body bucks up. She loses her breath. Her eyes slide shut again.

I take hold of her chin and force her stare back. "At least for the summer, Harlow. Give me that much."

"You said we'd take it one day at a time," she pushes back breathlessly.

"And we will. But I need a little more now than you're giving me, baby. Try."

She circles her hips into my next thrust with a wail. I feel her tightening. She's getting close. It's dirty pool to press her for more when most of her thoughts are wrapped up in pleasure, but I need her raw. I need her to admit this is more than just fucking.

"Stop pushing me." She shoves at my chest and catches me off guard.

I grab her wrists and hold them to the mattress, opening her to me. "Don't panic... I'm not pushing, baby. I won't ever hurt you. I just want more of you. I'll go slow. I'll be easy. Relax."

Even as I say the words, I know I've pushed my luck as far as I dare tonight. Disappointment is bitter, but I need to back down before she shoves me away altogether. Retreat feels like defeat, but I can't force her to share more than her body with me. It burns, but I'm going to have to be patient.

I reinforce my words with a glide down her body and a thumb across her swollen clit. She jolts and keens out, back arching. Her gaze bounces up to mine again, fusing us together as I pound my way inside her body—deeper, harder, faster.

"Noah!"

The sensual distress in her voice lights a new fire inside me. We have all summer. I'll reach her. I'm stubborn like that. Once she drops her defenses, she'll prove to me that she's feeling more than pleasure, too. But for now, I'll give her what she wants and needs and hope it's enough to bring her back for more.

"I'm here," I assure her. "Come for me."

Under me, she writhes and clamps down, her breathing choppy and interrupted. Then she lets out a scream that rings in my ears and squeezes all control from my cock. I can't help it; I follow her into a rocket-launchers-and-fireworks sort of bliss.

When it's over and she's panting beside me, I risk a glance her way. She's staring at the ceiling, face flushed. "For the record, I don't belong to anyone."

Before I can think of something to ease her fears, she disappears into the bathroom, shutting the door between us.

"Fuck," I mutter.

What is it with this woman? I have guesses, but I don't know for sure. She has deep scars on her heart, not from Simon Butler, but from something I don't understand. I'm almost looking forward to dinner with her brothers tomorrow night. Almost. If I can keep all my dubious conversational abilities from floundering, I might just get some answers.

When Harlow emerges from the bathroom a moment later, I'm waiting at the door. "I didn't mean to upset you."

"I know." She sighs. "I panic and… I'm just not ready for more."

She's too afraid to even consider it. "Maybe I'm not ready for less."

A frown furrows her brow. "I need to think."

With that, Harlow slips out of my grip and out of my bedroom. Reluctantly, I let her go. If I keep pushing, I'm only going to shove her out the door. Maybe I should stop trying to invest in a woman with more defenses than a military base.

Maybe…but I think it's too late.

With a curse, I hop in the shower to rinse off. I've never had a problem getting a woman. I've never wanted to keep one, so this problem is totally new. I have to figure out what it's going to take to persuade her I'm on her side. A tough gig if she won't open up enough to tell me why she's hurting.

After I towel off and head into the bedroom, I'm hoping I'll find her in my room, curled up in my bed. Every night, she pretends to fall asleep next to me. But she never does. Intimacy avoidance? Probably.

Tonight she's nowhere to be found.

I toss on a pair of shorts and head down the hall. Her bedroom door is cracked, and the lamp on her nightstand puts off a small circle of golden light. It's enough to illuminate the buds stuck in her ears and tears falling down her cheeks. She clutches a CD case to her chest, eyes closed. A pang racks my chest. The sadness on her face is killing me.

I stare as she finally makes her way under the covers and turns out the light. I can barely make out her shape as she sets the CD case down, rolls to her side, and drifts off a few minutes later.

I wait, watching Harlow until I'm sure she's crashed before I creep into her room and gently extract the buds from her ears. She doesn't protest. She doesn't stir at all.

The buds are attached to her phone. I take them both and slip them in my ears to give whatever she's hearing a listen. I hear a few notes fading away, then dead air. With a frown, I try to open the playlist and start from the beginning, but it automatically repeats and I hear a woman's voice. She prefaces whatever music is to follow.

"Hi, Harlow. It's Keeley. I know you don't want to talk. You're like your big brother." She gives a little laugh. "But sometimes we need help sorting out what's in our heads, and you know music is my language. I made this CD of songs I picked for you. If you don't need or want it, that's fine. But if something I've found helps you to recover after what happened or makes you want to talk, I'm here for you, sweetie. Maxon and I send our love. You deserve the best, and Simon Butler wasn't it. Anyway, I hope you enjoy."

Her sister-in-law's gentle if chipper voice trails off and the first song begins to play. It's old. Retro. Beats sliding down a scale, then tambourines and drums. I've heard it. I just can't place it right away. A woman starts singing about her lying, cheating boyfriend. It doesn't click until she sings that her boots are made for walking.

I have to smile. I don't know Keeley, but she's definitely got this tune right. Harlow had every right to let her dainty boots trample her ex on her way out the door.

That song ends, then another begins, this one more upbeat. It's definitely from a different era than the first. It's not familiar, either, and when another woman starts singing, I'm thinking I need to catch up on my chick rock. As I listen to the lyrics, the song is all about telling a deadbeat lover to kiss off in a tone that says she's not at all broken up about the split.

"'Goodbye to You,' huh?" I murmur. If Harlow had been singing this song, she would have called it "Eat Shit and Die."

I listen as the end trails off. Both songs have been appropriate to her situation…but neither should have made her cry.

The next song is also unfamiliar. The intro sounds like a guitar of some sort in an uneven beat, almost a Caribbean-style rhythm. I hear another female vocalist, her voice one I've heard before. Rihanna, I think. She sings that she can pretend she's not lonely but she'll be lying to herself and she'd give every dime she possesses to have what she's only been dreaming about. Is it possible Harlow feels that way secretly, deep down? Is there any chance she wants to be someone's one and only but is too afraid to admit it?

The next track on the playlist is a bouncy Michael Bublé tune I've heard on the radio about not having met the right one yet. Keeley seems really determined that Harlow needs and wants love. Does Maxon's wife know something about the woman in my house, who visits my bed, that I don't? I'm struck by one line, where Bublé says he knows that someday someone will make him work so they can work to work it out.

Is that what I need to do with Harlow? She keeps objecting, but is that because she doesn't really want me…or because she's trying to gauge my staying power in a relationship?

Interesting questions. I need to talk to Keeley. And her brothers. Hell, maybe Britta has insight, too. I'm not even sure why Harlow has become my mission in life suddenly. Maybe I'm avoiding the speech issue, which I can't fix, and focusing on the woman who I hope I can.

And maybe for the first time in my life I'm falling in love.

The catchy pop tune ends and another familiar song seeps into my ears. A Foreigner classic, a melody I've heard a thousand times. This is the one that made her cry. I recognize the notes now. Yes, in her life, there has been heartache and pain. Of course she has trouble knowing if she can face it again. I listen as the rest of the bridge slides into the chorus, Lou

Gramm's soulful voice rasping that he wants to know what love is, backed up by a large, harmonious choir. He also croons that he wants someone to show him.

The questions start rolling through my head once more, but I think I know what to do. I have to try with Harlow. Not just for her, not because I want to be the knight in shining armor who repairs the heart that someone—not her ex—broke. I feel good when I'm with her. Like I can be myself. Like she might always make me laugh. Like she's always going to turn me on. Like I could be happy for the rest of my days with her by my side.

Am I crazy? Am I distracting myself from my own problems? Maybe…but I don't think so.

When the song finally ends, I set her earbuds and phone on her nightstand. Her phone looks half-dead, so I plug it in with the cord dangling from the power strip on the floor. Then I stand in the dark and stare at her. I either need to be in or out. I either need to let her lick her wounds and work out her problems in her time and in her way or I need to be a force in her life that helps heal her. I can't keep pushing her if I'm going to leave in the end. I have to make a decision here and now whether I'm just the guy she's boffing for a few months until the real world comes calling again or if I'm going to find a way to make this woman trust me with her heart forever.

I know what my gut is telling me. Screaming at me. So instead of padding back into my room for a solid night of sleep, I take off every stitch I'm wearing and slide into bed beside Harlow. I curl my arm around her, doing my best not to jostle her. Then I plant my face in her neck so I can breathe in her scent and hope this is the first night of many I'll spend beside her.

I APPROACH TUESDAY night with both anticipation and dread. Harlow's family may have information I need but I'm sure they also have an agenda in mind. This dinner won't be purely social. They're going to examine and grill me, which would be fine if I knew for certain I'd be able to keep up my end of the conversation.

We park at her older brother's place, and a quaint sign hangs in the front yard, proclaiming it the Sunshine Coast Bed and Breakfast. A redhead in a golden sundress waits for us on the lanai, drink in hand. As we emerge from the car, a petite blonde sidles up beside her in a killer black dress. Harlow's brothers shuffle out after them, deep in conversation. Maxon parks himself behind the redhead and drops a kiss on the top of her head. She must be Keeley, which means the blonde is Britta. Sure enough, Griff cups the dainty woman's shoulders and whispers something in her ear that makes her smile secretively.

After I shut the car door behind me, I'm keenly aware of her brothers staring at me. I grab Harlow's hand.

"Advertising that we're having a fling? After last Friday morning, I think they know."

"No, I'm borrowing courage. Your brothers don't like me much."

"They just don't know you."

True. "But when I talk to them, I tend to lose my verbal ability. So this could be a really long evening."

Harlow turns to me, a little frown working between her brows. "I wasn't even thinking about you being anxious. I'm sorry." She squeezes my hand tighter. "I'm here for you. And look, no matter what they threaten, they can't kill and eat you."

I know she's right; they can't *do* anything to me. But if I want Harlow in my life for more than a few weeks, I'll have to deal with Maxon and Griff. Hell, I admit it; I want them to like me. I'd even settle for them tolerating me. If they hate me outright, their opinion might rub off on Harlow and make our already unsteady relationship even more rocky.

"I wouldn't be surprised if they want to," I grouse.

"They also want to rule the world, ambitious bastards."

"Stay with me tonight, will you? Just in case I…"

I grimace. She knows what I'm implying. It hurts to ask her for help. I used to give press conferences, do TV interviews regularly. Hell, I've even emceed galas for thousands. Now I can't trust myself to finish a sentence when it counts. I can only hope that with Harlow by my side, I'll feel less wound up and more able to carry on a conversation.

"Of course. I'm not throwing you to the wolves," she assures me so sincerely in a low voice for my ears alone before she raises her voice to something designed to carry. "I'm simply getting the family who cares about me off my back while assuring them that I'm not fucking my way out of a broken heart. Hi, guys. Keeley, Britta."

Maxon rolls his eyes. "Delicate as always, I see, little sister."

Griff groans. "Did you have to put that mental image in my head before dinner?"

"Hey, I've been in the same house with you and Britta when you've been busy, so I don't want to hear your complaining."

"We weren't loud," he objects.

Harlow snorts. "And the sky isn't blue, either."

"Ignore my husband," Britta insists as she comes forward to hug Harlow. "I promise I'll kick him under the table if he doesn't behave."

Keeley is right beside her, giving Harlow a quick squeeze. "And Maxon simply doesn't want to remember that you're a grown woman."

"Don't I know it," Harlow says. "In between nailing all the women in sight, he and Griff chased off every date I could have possibly taken to my senior prom. I'm still a little bitter." She levels a stare at her brothers. "You owe me, guys. Lighten up. Be nice to Noah. No biting. No baring of teeth. He came here voluntarily. Don't make him regret it."

Neither of her brothers says anything for a long moment; they both just eye me as if they're wondering how much they can trust me with their sister. Finally Maxon sighs and extends a hand.

Exhaling in relief, I shake it. "Good to see you."

"You're wearing more clothes this time, so that's a bonus."

Ah, the subtle dig. "Thanks. Now I know where your sister gets some of her charm."

He laughs out loud. Keeley and Griff join in.

"I like you already," Maxon's wife drawls. "Why don't you follow me into the kitchen and I'll pour you a drink."

"I'll go with you two," Britta says. "I'm not sure how much more knuckle-dragging I can take from our husbands."

They seem like potential allies, and I'm relieved someone from Harlow's clan doesn't hate me, but I'm not down with the idea of leaving her to deal with her none-too-happy siblings. "Will she be all right with them? They won't grill her too hard, will they?"

"Harlow?" Keeley laughs. "You should be worried about whether she'll skewer her brothers for acting like asses and whether they'll still have both their pride and their man parts intact after she's done."

Britta nods in confirmation. "Harlow is no fainting flower. Trust me. She can handle herself with them."

I cast her a glance over my shoulder as the women lead me to the kitchen. The trio of siblings is already deep in conversation, and my girl looks as if she's getting in most of the words. I relax and follow her sisters-in-law into the white, bright kitchen.

This may be my best opportunity, and I need to take advantage of it.

"What are you drinking?" Keeley asks.

"I don't care as long as you two can shed some light on what's going on with Harlow. Why is she so against...attachments?"

Britta slants a glance Keeley's way. I see on their faces they both know exactly what I'm talking about.

"How serious are you about her?" the blonde asks, her voice soft.

"I don't know yet. I like her, and I suspect that what I feel may be even deeper than that. I definitely want more than she's giving me now. She masks everything with sarcasm or sex. No offense, but I feel like the female in this relationship. She never wants to talk about feelings or anything beyond the moment. I know what happened with Simon must have been rough, but—"

"Simon is a symptom, not the problem," Keeley cuts in.

"Exactly," Britta agrees. "All the Reed siblings seem to have hearts shuttered extraordinarily tight until you pry them open. Has Harlow told you much about their parents?"

"Almost nothing. Her dad is a distant asshole and her mom was a stage-parent type, living vicariously through her daughter."

The women exchange another glance, this one full of secrets.

"There's probably more. Keep digging," Britta suggests. "Harlow hasn't opened up to either of us, so I can't say exactly what's going on with her. It may be simply a case of growing up in a house without much emotion. At least I hope that's all it is."

"Or it may be far worse," Keeley suggests. "For us, understanding the family dynamic was critical to understanding our husbands. But let me give you a suggestion: don't go there unless you're really, truly serious. Opening Harlow up won't be easy, not if she's anything like Maxon and Griff."

Britta nods emphatically. "You have to be invested before she'll even consider letting you behind her barriers, so if you're just going to leave, have mercy on her and simply enjoy what she can give you for the time you two have together. Don't push for more."

They're serious. This issue with Harlow—whatever it is—extends to the whole family. I already knew it wasn't simply Simon breaking her heart, but thought maybe it was her pride. Or maybe that she hadn't met anyone she could fall for yet. But to hear that her avoidance of feeling has possibly been going on for decades, that she's never learned to bare herself to anyone except sexually...

I blow out a breath. "I understand. Thanks. One more question, if you don't mind. How did you finally reach Maxon and Griff?"

"I walked away," Keeley said softly. "I couldn't live with someone who couldn't share his whole self with me. He still doesn't like yoga and he's been very slow to warm to the whole vegan thing, but I can handle that. I couldn't handle being in the same bedroom with him when he wasn't willing to touch me with his heart, too."

"Griff and I were separated for three years," Britta put in softly. "He left me abruptly one day after hearing some news and assuming the worst.

It took him finding out that we had a son together before he finally started asking himself some hard questions. The Reeds are stubborn and suspicious. They have a million ways to make you feel special one minute and like a stranger the next. If you decide you want to proceed, Harlow won't make anything easy on you. If she's been through half of what Maxon and Griff have, she won't open up and let you in without a fight."

When Keeley hands me a drink, I gulp half of it down. Holy shit, I have a lot of thinking to do. "Thanks for the insight."

"Our husbands could tell you more," she suggests.

But will they? "We're not exactly pals so far."

"Just like Harlow, you have to give them time. If you treat their sister right, they'll come around."

"Eventually," Britta adds. "We'll rope Harlow in for some girl time after dinner. Why don't you talk to Maxon and Griff then?"

A firing squad sounds almost as fun. But the ladies have shared with me all they can...or will. Now it will be up to me to persuade Harlow's brothers that I'm not a creeper or a douche simply out to bag their sister. At the thought of two-on-one time with them, my stomach starts seizing up. I begin to sweat.

This could be a long fucking night.

CHAPTER NINE

DINNER WAS EXCELLENT, dessert even better. I'm mentally counting the hours I'll need to pound in the gym to work off this much rich food when Keeley and Britta both leave the dinner table and start collecting plates. Harlow rises to help.

Then the predators pounce.

"Get your ass up and come with us," Griff growls in my ear as he leaves his chair and passes mine.

I glance over at Maxon. He's wearing an impatient scowl that says he's just been waiting for the opportunity to sink his teeth into me. Griff's expression is equally fierce.

So the smiles and jokes over dinner were all a show for the women. Now it's time for the lightning questions and the ass kicking I've been dreading.

With a sigh, I rise and debate what the hell I'm going to say. I won't win any brownie points with the dour brothers by spewing shiny bullshit.

As I follow them to the lanai, they drop into a pair of chairs facing the wicker sofa. There's a table dividing the room, and the situation feels totally like a them-versus-me thing. Like I'm on trial, and they're the judges, jury, and executioners.

I sink to the spongy couch cushions. "Before you say anything, I'll tell you why I hired Harlow if you can keep a secret."

That seems to catch them off guard.

"We can. Shoot," Maxon demands.

I take a deep breath, swallow, try to keep my head from getting fucked up. "I hired your sister to help me with some speech issues."

"Bullshit." Griff nearly lunges out of his chair. "I've seen your press conferences for years. You've never had any problem. Besides, you're not going to convince me that you haven't fucked my sister seven ways from Sunday. I saw you two that morning. I saw her big sex hair. I saw the whisker burns on her neck. I saw the way you touched her. So don't give me a story about some platonic crap that—"

"I'm not. I'm telling you that since my last major concussion I've had speech issues. Right now it's hard to talk to you, and I'm doing everything I can to hold my shit together. I can't function like this long-term, and I think Harlow can help. The fact that I'm trusting you with this information when it could ruin me should tell you that I'm serious about understanding her. I need your help. So far, I'm lost."

"If she's merely helping you, why do you need to decipher our sister?" Maxon snaps.

"Like Griff pointed out, we have more than a professional relationship. I really like your sister. I'm wondering if there's something more between us than a therapeutical rapport and a hot summer. She won't talk about that possibility, and Butler isn't the problem."

"I don't know if that's compelling enough for me to want to help you."

Leaning in, I stare down Harlow's older brother. "Were you in death-do-us-part love with Keeley after knowing her for five days?"

Beside him, Griff snickers. "No, he was still in the phase where he wasn't sure whether he wanted to strangle Keeley or just fuck her to death."

Maxon whirls on him with a scowl. "You're full of shit. Of course I wanted to fuck her way more. Most of the time."

Griff gestures to his brother. "See what I mean?"

"And what about you?" I ask to keep them on track. "Five days after knowing Britta?"

"I hadn't even touched her yet."

Somehow, I manage to hold in my sigh of exasperation. "Five days after you had?"

He bobs his head. "Yeah, I was still in the phase where I thought it was all about sex."

Maxon scowls. "You thought that for the better part of a year."

"That's my point." I lean in. "I'm not sure yet that I'm spending the rest of my life with Harlow, but what I *do* know? I'm intrigued and I'm not ready to give up on her. But she's frustrating the shit out of me. She barely admits she has feelings, much less discusses them with me. Can you either shed some light or give us a little space so I can figure her out and decide where we're going from here?"

The men exchange a long, silent glance full of bro-speak.

Finally, Maxon turns to me with a sigh. "We don't know what's up with Harlow. We've been wondering ourselves."

"And worrying," Griff adds. "Since my brother and I both got married, I thought we'd gotten closer to her."

"What he means is that since we both pulled our heads out of our asses and figured out this love thing is actually real, we've grown closer to Harlow. So when she burned Butler at their wedding so epically, it was great…but it was a total shock."

"The fact that she didn't tell us in advance and hasn't spoken to us about it since except to say that she's fine troubles us a lot," Griff puts in. "Sorry if we came off hostile. When you were just a guy who wanted to use her while she was hurting, I was ready to be a major pain in your ass. But if you're all about finding out where Harlow's head is and trying to help her work through it, count me in."

Maxon is already nodding before his brother even finishes speaking. "That's where I'm coming from, too."

I breathe out a sigh of relief. I managed an important conversation with Harlow's brothers without going mute. I'm calling that a huge win. The question is, how do I morph this into a meaningful victory that will help me unravel the mystery of Harlow?

"How do you think that went?" Harlow asks as she eases into the passenger seat beside me and I put the SUV in reverse.

"Good." I back out of the driveway, feeling exhilarated. It was actually far better than I expected. No, I don't have all the answers, but I have less pressure and more information than I had before. "What about you?"

"It was nice to see everyone. They seemed like they were in a good mood. And my brothers didn't murder you when you three disappeared for some bro-time."

"Nope. I was surprised too, especially when they mentioned that they used to be complete assholes."

"Oh, my god. Everyone hated them. You would have, too. They even stopped speaking to each other for three years over a stupid misunderstanding because they're both so stubborn and competitive."

"Seriously?" I would never have guessed that. They seem really tight. "What changed?"

"Keeley." At my confused glance, Harlow laughs. "Long story. But if not for her, I suspect my brothers would still be rivals."

I'm going to have to hear this whole story sometime. I also want to know how Griff didn't know he had a son for years. That sounds as if it involved a whole lot of hurt. And mule-headedness.

I'll bet it runs in the family, and I'm up against even thicker barriers than I imagined.

"Your sisters-in-law must have shitloads of patience and spines of steel."

"Yeah, they're badass. They've learned not to flinch, thank god. I can't imagine living with either of my brothers. They can be single-minded and unbending as hell."

Yep, definitely runs in the family.

"They said putting up with your parents was no picnic, either," I say experimentally.

Harlow fidgets in her seat. "No one ever accused Barclay and Linda of being a barrel of fun."

"So your mom was too involved and self-absorbed?"

"Pretty much. She wasn't *all* terrible, but as I got older I became aware that a lot of the nice things she did with and for me were for show."

I nod slowly and study Harlow to gauge her reaction to my next words. "What about your dad? You barely mention him."

Her entire body tightens for a moment. It's subtle but unmistakable. "There was a time I wanted to be a daddy's girl, like some of my friends. Then I realized that he was only interested in cultivating the Reed offspring with dangling penises. Apparently, brains reside there, not the skull—silly me—so my dad didn't think a little girl served much purpose in his life."

And his dismissive indifference had hurt. Harlow doesn't admit that, of course, but I see it in the press of her lips and the way she avoids my gaze. Has her father's attitude colored her relationships with all men?

"But he wanted you to marry Simon to help him?"

"Yeah."

No expounding on the topic. No saucy comeback. Just a flat statement of fact.

That isn't like Harlow. I'm rapidly learning with this woman that I should listen to what she says, but pay even more attention to what she doesn't—and won't. This conversation tells me I need to dig deeper into her relationship with her father.

"He sounds like a real bastard," I remark.

"Pretty much. My brothers were shaping up just like him. I'm really happy they're settled and seem so ecstatic with their lives now." She smiles sincerely. "And I'm thrilled that you didn't have a verbal issue all night. You felt relaxed and in control?"

More like really determined.

I can't miss her subtle shift in subject. I have to give Harlow credit; she's good.

"Enough to keep the conversation flowing," I remark. "It helped that your brothers weren't terrible to me."

"Since we're talking about Maxon and Griff, you should take that as a gift."

I am. But something else they said stuck out, something that's been playing over and over in my head. *Once we figured out this love thing is real*... Why would they think it wasn't? Okay, so their parents have a shitty, dysfunctional relationship that's ending but that can't be the whole story.

"How do you feel about your parents divorcing?"

"It's about time. They've separated a few times over the years, and I hoped they'd put everyone out of their misery, but then my mom would always run out of money and come crawling home."

"And your dad took her back in?"

"Totally. He relished those days. He rubbed her nose in the fact that he had the power. He enjoyed using it against her for weeks, sometimes months." She clasps her hands in her lap, fidgeting.

I'm poking at the edges of her comfort zone again. "Do you think they ever loved each other?"

She scoffs cynically. "I don't think they believe in love."

That would explain a lot. "Do you?"

Instead of a flippant reply, Harlow takes her time answering. "I think it exists. I mean, I look at my brothers. I would never have thought they'd meet women who could make them better men and completely change their hearts. It wasn't easy, that's for sure. But they made it work, and the only reason I can imagine either of them conquered their fears and got over their shit was because they fell in love. The kind that doesn't end. The kind worth fighting for. I'm really happy for them."

"What about you?"

"Me?" She laughs. "I'm not wired for love, Weston. My heart doesn't work that way."

But she wants a baby because she wants someone to love? I'm guessing she doesn't see the fallacy of her argument, and I'm not going to tango with her stubborn will now to point it out. My guess is she's never experienced romantic love and after watching her parents tear each other up, she's afraid of it. Simon Butler did zero to help the cause.

I do a gut check, ask myself if I should tackle Harlow, the emotional Mt. Everest. But I'm already sure that walking away isn't an option. This woman is under my skin. If we're skirting the issue of love after less than a week together, I doubt we can spend the whole summer wrapped around each other without the subject coming up again. Already, I want more from her than just a good time.

Yeah, that's a new one for me, too. But my instinct tells me I'm in the right place with the right person. Even Trace and Makuahine like Harlow. Maybe Fate dropped her in my lap. I don't know, but I've made a lot of decisions in life by listening to my gut. It's always served me well, and I see no reason to change now.

"Hmm," I answer noncommittally.

"What does that mean? Are you saying your heart does?" Her tone is skeptical. "If it did, you'd already be madly in love and married to your soul mate."

She sounds vindicated, as if her argument proves something to me about myself.

"I was married to my career for a dozen years. A pro athlete's life isn't an easy one. We're more than compensated for that, but I didn't want to drag a wife and kids through my absence half the year, the press and the injuries, the uprooting every time I might have been traded to another team. Now?" I shrug. "I want a personal life. I want something meaningful."

"Well, good luck with that." Harlow's cynical tone tells me she doesn't like the idea of me in love with another woman.

It's not much but she has *some* feelings for me. But I'm greedy; I want more.

When we make it home, she dumps her purse on the bar in the kitchen, then takes her phone and heads upstairs without a word. She's perturbed and preoccupied. Yeah, I'm getting better at reading her moods. The fact she hasn't mentioned sex tells me I'm making her think, maybe even making her feel. She doesn't want me close while she's feeling vulnerable.

Too bad.

After climbing the stairs to my bedroom, I strip out of every stitch I'm wearing, then stroll down the hall just in time to see her come out of the bathroom with a fresh face and an oversized T-shirt that says GIRLS DO SHIT BETTER.

When she sees me, her eyes go wide. "What are you doing?"

"Coming to see you."

"You've seen me." She gestures to her messy bun and her makeshift nightgown. "Nothing you haven't seen before."

"Take your shirt off."

Harlow sighs. "I'm tired. We'll fuck tomorrow."

I don't want her against her will, but I think she's hungry for me. She's eyeing me like I'm a piece of chocolate cake and she's been on a long, strict diet.

"All right. I'll just be in the shower masturbating to thoughts of you. If you change your mind…"

She gapes at me with wide eyes.

It's a mic drop moment, so I turn and pad down the hall—bare ass and all—to my bathroom and turn on the shower. I can't guarantee that my taunt will bring her running, but I have high hopes.

I've barely stepped in the shower, soaped up my hands, and started stroking myself with a long groan when she appears in the doorway, looking breathless. She stares at me through the floor-to-ceiling glass. It's fogged up but not so much that she can't see my hand working and my dick responding.

For a long, silent moment she says nothing, does nothing. Just stares.

I can't let that stand. Time to put on a show.

With my other hand, I soap up my chest and trail my fingertips down my ridged abs, then lower. Finally I cup my heavy testicles and throw my head back with a growl of need. Then I start chanting her name.

"Harlow, baby. Ah…yeah. That's it. Fucking stroke me. I'm so hard for you."

When I risk a glance at her, I see she's stepped closer. She's flushing. Her chest works up and down with choppy breaths.

I smile and I look right into her eyes. "When I get inside you, I'm going to fuck you so slow and hard, baby. Your toes are going to curl and you're going to scream your throat raw as we come together. Then I'll do it all over again."

At her sides, her fists clench. She presses her lips together and grinds her jaw as if she's trying beyond hard to resist.

"This doesn't mean anything," she vows as she yanks the shirt over her head and stomps to the shower door.

She enters the stall as a cloud of steam exits. I take her by the shoulders and drag her under the spray, fist in her hair, and bring her lips to mine. It's all I can do not to inhale her with my kiss.

When I push my tongue deep into her mouth, she stiffens, her palms flattening on my shoulders as if she can't decide whether to push me away or drag me closer. She can't control me—or the passion burning between us. It scares her. I feel it. But I'm not letting her go.

I change tactics, soften my grip on her tresses, lean back against the glass, and ease my lips away from hers until they meet hers with the merest brush.

Suddenly, she curls her fingers around my biceps and presses her curves against me like she can't resist.

Score.

Without warning, I turn her in my arms, plastering her back to my front. My aching cock settles in the valley of her ass, driving me absolutely insane. But I fight to keep my head in the game, cradling her breasts with both hands, dragging my lips over her shoulder, up her neck, settling against the delicate shell of her ear.

"Harlow, baby." I toy with her nipples, pinch them gently, flick them with my thumbs, gratified when her breath catches and she rests her head on my shoulder, arching her backside against my cock.

"Yes, Noah…"

It's a breathless plea that fires my blood. I slide one hand from her luscious breast to her flat belly, then down to her feminine heat. She's hot. She's wet—and not just from the shower spray. In fact, she's soaked and slick and ready.

I rub her clit slowly in dragging circles that I already know send her into a mindless frenzy and get her there fast. I press the other palm to the small of her back and urge her forward. Harlow doesn't resist. Obediently, she bends at the waist and braces her hands on the glass in front of us. Then I spread her feet apart, nudging them wide with my own. She rushes to cooperate.

Seconds later, I'm spreading her folds open with my fingers and tunneling inside her with a long curse of pleasure ripping from my chest. "Fuck."

Harlow arches and looks back at me, her eyes dilated, her cheeks beyond rosy. "More…"

I get a grip on my self-control, then twine my fist in her long, wet tresses, keeping her face twisted so she can watch me as I fuck her. "I'm going to give it to you, baby. Because no matter what you think, this does mean something."

"It doesn't have to."

"But it does. I know it. And you know it." I withdraw, then plunge in again, gripping the tile with my toes so I don't keel over in bliss. "Who are you lying to?"

Harlow starts to buck like a horse that hasn't been broken to a saddle. "You said it was sex. You said one day at a time."

"I did. But it's days later, and now this is more than just sex. I'm going to stay right here, so hard inside you, until you admit it."

She starts writhing, but I can't quite tell whether she's fighting me…or moving with me. "Fuck you."

"No, baby. That's my point. I'm going to do more than fuck you. Way more. I'm going to make love to you. I'm going to get down to your soul and fill you up."

Before she has a chance to object in earnest—and she will—I withdraw so slowly she can't help but whimper. Then I slide back in as if I have all damn day to fill her up—all while leaning over her back and circling her clit with my fingers.

"Feel me?"

Her breath is a harsh din above the pounding spray of the shower, but she doesn't reply. Instead, she merely sways with me, trying to speed up my thrusts.

"Do you feel me?" I repeat, my voice low and harsh. I don't know where this is coming from except a need to make her acknowledge that we're doing more together than scratching a mutual itch.

Harlow tenses, her fingers clawing at the glass as she tries to breathe past the pleasure. I know that's what she's doing. She's trying to hang on to her control. Trying not to admit that the love we're making is getting to her, too.

I stop everything—the slow grind of my deep plunge into her, the rhythmic torture of my fingers where she needs it most. I clench my jaw and grip her hips to absorb the punch of need that threatens to steal my breath. Denying her is killing me, but if I give her what she's aching for, Harlow will assume she has me where she wants me and won't think about this or us beyond the moment.

Her high whimper becomes a sharp cry of need as the lack of sensation hits her. "Noah...don't."

I'm not negotiating. "Do. You. Feel. Me?"

Breaths saw from her chest one after the other as she scratches at the shower glass again. "Yes. Damn you!"

It's a very reluctant admission, but I'll take it. "Good, this is me deep inside you, joining more than our bodies. Sharing more than fucking pleasure. I won't make you acknowledge that today, but I want you to hear it. I want that floating through your head as I send you crashing into orgasm. Afterward, I'm going to climb in bed beside you again. I'm going to sleep next to you. And I want to wake up beside you. No more crawling away in the middle of the night to sleep on the sofa down the hall."

"You snore."

"You hog the covers, and I don't care. I still enjoy curling up next to you."

"I don't sleep with anyone."

"Now you do."

"You're going to force me?"

I ease almost completely out of her body, making sure she feels every scrape of my shaft across her nerve endings, then give her nearly bursting clit a long swipe. "Persuade. You're always welcome to say no. Doesn't mean I won't try to use every way I know how to make you change your mind."

"What the fuck do you want from me?" Her angry words come out like a cry.

"I don't want anything from you. I simply want *all* of you."

Then I've got nothing left to say. I cut off whatever argument Harlow might have by plunging deep inside her again, strokes insistent, heavy, and in no particular hurry. Her breathless wails vibrate under my skin, grip my balls. Her body writhes, her hips working with my rhythm, trying to suck me deeper. She's sensual, responsive—like no woman I've ever touched. Holding out on her is so fucking tough, but if I can make her realize that we might be way more than a summer fling, it will be worth it.

"Noah…" She reaches down with one of her hands to pinch her nipples, one after the other. "I need more."

"I know. You going to let me give it to you?"

She catches her breath on a hard pant. A sob follows. But even with my fist in her hair, she manages a nod. "I can't take it. Please…"

Thank god, because I'm nearly at the end of my fucking rope.

"You're staying the whole night with me?"

"I'm dying here," she pleads with me for mercy.

When it comes to finding out why I can't get enough of this woman, I have none.

"All you have to do is say yes, baby. I'll let you fly. I'll make you come so hard. One little word… Give it to me."

Harlow clenches her fists, her body heaving as she tries to breathe and process my demand and drink in the growing ecstasy. I don't let up, I keep tunneling my way into her in long, strong strokes, igniting every pleasure point I can reach. I kiss my way up her back, then bite down on the sensitive spot between her shoulder and neck.

"Yes!" she finally capitulates with a cry. "Please, god, yes!"

That's all I need to hear. I have a whole night with Harlow and I'm going to make the most of it.

Finally, I unleash the pent-up passion I've been holding back. I sink in farther, harder, manipulating her nearly bursting clit, breathing against her skin as I exhale in long, harsh breaths. "Take me, goddamn it."

My own growl rings in my ears. I can't remember ever needing a climax more. I'm dizzy. Harlow turns me inside out. But I can't fall into the bliss alone.

The water at my back is turning lukewarm, and I don't give a shit. The only thing that matters is making this woman feel as if I'm going to be inside her forever. The way I feel right now, I would be so fucking happy to spend the rest of my days and nights right here, drowning in Harlow.

Oh, god. Am I in love?

Suddenly, she tightens, then grinds out a long, throaty cry as she clamps and bucks and gyrates her hips with me. She milks me. She takes my breath away. She robs my fucking soul.

I'm almost sure I'll never be complete without her.

That's my last thought as I spill inside her with a growling wail, gushing into her with all my might and losing myself in the process.

As I finally catch my breath, I slide my hands down her curves, worshipping her with soft, reverent strokes. "You okay, baby?"

No answer, just her back rising and falling with deep, heaving breaths.

"Harlow?" I ease from her body gently and cup her shoulders, turning her to face me.

Unmistakable tears run down her cheeks. She looks so fucking angry I almost step back. Almost... But if she's mad that I've made her feel something, I'm the only one who can soothe her.

"Don't do this to me!" She jerks out of my grip and steps back, reaching for the handle to the shower door.

If I let her get away now, she's going to toss up more walls between us. She won't allow herself to be vulnerable with me again soon—if ever.

"I'm not doing anything to you except showing you that you matter to me, damn it." I shut off the water that's gone cold, then take her arms in my grip. "You want to cry? I've got two shoulders and a chest to lean on. I've got two arms to hold you. I've got two ears to listen. And a heart that's open to you. All I'm asking is for you to open yours in return. Just a little, baby… Just try."

Before me, her face crumbles as if she's fought the good fight and just can't do it anymore. She dips her head to hide her face. Her shoulders fall in massive sobs. "No."

"Yes," I insist in soft tones and bring her against my body again.

"If I rip off all the Band-Aids just to make you happy, I'll fall apart."

"How do you know I won't put you back together, Harlow?"

She doesn't have an answer and when I step closer, slowly bringing her body against me and enfolding her in my arms, she crumples onto me, giving me her weakness. I give her back my strength. I don't know exactly what demons haunt her, but I'm beginning to suspect they're darker than anyone's imagined. I'm in too deep now to get out.

Not that it matters; I don't want out when everything in my soul tells me this woman belongs to me and I'll have to be the one to heal her and make her whole.

After long minutes, Harlow's tears taper off. She's limp and spent as I dry her body off, haphazardly put her wet hair into an elastic band, and tuck her into her bed beside me. She drops off in moments. Unlike the last time I crawled into bed beside her, she clings to me, wraps herself around me, and falls into sleep peacefully.

CHAPTER TEN

TWO DAYS LATER, Friday afternoon rolls around. I hate to leave Harlow when she's vulnerable. Since our lovemaking in the shower, she's been quiet, almost thoughtful. I slept beside her that night. I woke her up twice so I could be inside her again. She allowed me deep, clinging to me almost gratefully. I thought we'd turned a corner.

But when I woke at six the next morning, she was already in the gym, climbing the Stairmaster like it could take her far from me. All day—and all night—she gave me a wide berth. I let her…maybe more than I should have. I can't pressure her more or upset her too much. She has to decide on her own. And it seems as if she is. But boarding a flight to Honolulu this morning was damn hard. Will she be waiting for me when I get back? Or will she have disregarded our summer-long contract, cleaned out her stuff, and left?

I have no assurances and no way of knowing. But I can't force her to fall in love with me, simple as that.

Since I had a previous engagement, I flew to Oahu. Weeks ago, the high school I'd once attended and where I still hold most of the quarterback records asked me if I'd come lay some motivation on the kids just before finals and graduation. I owe that school for teaching me, for feeding me when my parents didn't always have the money, and for helping to shape me into the man I am today. Despite my worries, I said yes and hope I can keep myself together.

The visit is a surprise. No one knows I'm coming, and when I jog out to the middle of the gym floor, the kids all scream and shout. I say a few words I've rehearsed about determination, being true to yourself, and always doing your best, then we sing the school song together. I still remember it. Finally, I sign a few footballs for kids who play on the current squad and let girls half my age practice their flirting as I answer their pretend questions about pro sports and life's tough decisions. Then with a smile and a wave, I head back to the airport in Honolulu. I've got a plane to catch back to Maui. Back to Harlow.

I hope.

It's been a great afternoon, and I love being near my roots again so I can give back to my community. In fact, I left the school's athletic fund a nice donation before I departed. It feels good to be able to give back.

A couple of hours later, I'm savoring the high as I'm strolling through the airport, ball cap pulled low. Most people don't notice me. Tourists are heading back to the mainland. Businessmen are dashing to flights bound for Tokyo or San Francisco. No one is paying me much mind as I loiter in a seat in the corner at the gate.

Until a guy in his mid-twenties sits in the uncomfortable vinyl chair beside me. "Mr. Weston?"

I really don't want to draw attention to myself, much less a crowd. It's happened before. I was hoping that part of my life was over, damn it. "Yeah. Hey, I'm just catching a flight home and—"

"I'm not approaching you as a fan."

Despite being tall and broad, he's dressed in an impeccable suit, so I wonder if he's got some business opportunity in mind, maybe sports-related. "Whatever you're selling, I'm not interested."

"I don't want anything from you except information about Harlow Reed."

That snaps me to attention and whips up my protective instincts. "She's not up for discussion. Are you a reporter?"

"No. But according to the press, you're...together. I just want to meet her. Talk to her. Please."

This guy thinks I'm going to introduce him to my girl? No fucking way.

I hop to my feet. "This conversation is over."

"Wait. I don't think you understand."

Oh, I get it, all right. Waving a dismissive hand, I keep walking.

He follows. "I think she's my sister."

That stops me dead in my tracks. I snap my stare in his direction, scowling. "What?"

"My name is Evan Cook. My mother was Barclay Reed's secretary for three years. She died when I was five, but from everything I've gathered, they had an affair and that man is my biological father. Harlow and I were born three days apart." He clenches his jaw, looking as if he's trying to keep himself together. "I have no other family and…I just want the chance to know her."

I'd call bullshit…except he seems utterly serious. And when I look for some family resemblance to validate his claim, I can't deny that his eyes are the same green as Harlow's.

Oh, shit.

"Have you tried to contact her in the past?" I don't want to talk to this guy anymore if she's already slammed the door in his face.

"No. I only decided to get in touch with her about two weeks ago. But she's been impossible to find. Reclusive. Then I saw the news about the two of you. Social media said you'd had an appearance in Honolulu today, so I thought I'd try to talk to you first. I even bought a ticket to Maui in the hopes that she would see me…and you would help me break the news to her. I couldn't get a seat on this flight, but I'll be on the one after, that arrives late tonight."

Oh, fuck. How will Harlow feel about potentially meeting the product of her father's infidelity? Does she even know she may have another brother in the world?

As I sit again and he sinks down beside me, I'm torn.

"What about Maxon and Griff?"

"Who?" He looks confused. "I don't know them. My mom's journal mentioned my half sister. She wrote that Barclay's wife, Linda, was expecting a girl at the same time and that they'd eventually named her Harlow. If he had other family, I'm not aware."

"Have you tried to talk to your biological father?"

"Does he sound like anything other than an asshat to you? He knew my mother was pregnant. She said he was there the night I was born. But where was he after my mother was shot in a store robbery and I became a ward of the state of California? Child Protective Services contacted him and asked if he wanted to exercise his parental rights. He declined. If he didn't care then, I don't care now."

From the little bit I know about Harlow's father, I'm not surprised. I don't mention her older brothers again in case this guy is a crackpot. But if he's legit...will Evan come as a surprise to Maxon and Griff?

"All I'm asking is if you'll talk to her, find out if she would be willing to see me. I'll arrive about three hours after you. Here's my number." He hands me a business card. "I'm thinking of moving my home and the base operations of my firm to Hawaii, so I'll be here for at least a few weeks. I'd really like the chance to meet her. I won't take up more of your time."

With that, he stands and walks away, leaving me to wonder what I'll tell Harlow when she's already raw and shell-shocked...and how she'll react.

NIGHT HAS FALLEN by the time I pull up to my driveway. I peer at the huge house, trying to see whether Harlow is still here. From this angle, the place is dark. My heart pounds furiously. What will I do if she's gone? Call Maxon and Griff and insist they let me see her? Maybe. Probably. I can't let her give in to her fear and lick her wounds in private.

I can't give up on her. I've never had quit in me and I'm not about to start now.

Instead of hitting up the front door, I walk around to the patio and see Harlow perched on the sofa, playing her video game. My relief at locking eyes on her petite form still under my roof is palpable. I let out a pent-up breath.

Doing my best to seem casual, I stroll in through the open accordion doors and drop a kiss on her head. "Hi, baby."

She pauses her game and stands to face me. But she makes no move to touch me. "Hi. How was everything?"

"The high school visit was good. The 'after' part, we'll talk about in a bit. Did you eat dinner?"

"Yeah. I grilled some chicken and tossed together a fruit salad. I put leftovers in the fridge."

"Thanks."

I'll get to it eventually. Right now, I have no idea how I'm going to break this news to Harlow. I've wrestled with the decision to tell her and realized that Evan may want my help in breaking this to her, but he's not going to let me stop him. If I say no, he'll simply go around me—and maybe give her an unexpected shock she's not ready to handle.

She nods my way. "It's...um, been quiet all day. I just had a few phone calls with some colleagues about your next assessment. Tomorrow good? I want to nail down as much as possible before I decide on a course of therapy."

"Sure." I let out a breath. "Can I have a hug?"

Harlow fidgets, then nods. We meet halfway, and I wrap her in my arms. She's a little stiff but not resistant. I can't help myself from brushing a kiss across her lips, settling against her mouth for a heartbeat to feel her, before pulling back just enough to study her face.

"What's up?" She frowns.

I should realize she's getting good at reading me, too. "I need to talk to you. Why don't we sit?"

"If it's about the other night, I don't have anything to say. I'm still...processing."

I didn't expect her to profess her undying love. But at least she's not telling me to fuck off. I'm nervous that once I spring Evan on her she'll forget that she shouldn't shoot the messenger. But I can't control that. I have to do what's best for her.

I get dizzy and start to sweat. I recognize the symptoms. *Oh, shit. Oh, shit.* I can't freeze up now.

I rush to get the words out. "I met a guy in the airport says he's your father's son by one of his secretaries. The name Evan ring a bell?"

Harlow steps back and blinks in shock. Yeah, that did not come out smoothly. So much for breaking it to her gently. *Damn it.*

"What?"

Words start racing through my brain again, but it's as if someone stuck a cog in the spokes of the wheel that churn my thoughts from my brain to my mouth. I press my lips together mutely. Goddamn it. Of all the times to lose my ability to speak...

Harlow seems to understand and takes my hands. "It's all right. Breathe in and out. I'm not mad. I'm not even all that surprised. One of the reasons my parents are divorcing has to do with my dad's wandering penis. Obviously, my mom has no trouble with him sleeping around, since she told me to get over myself when I split with Simon. But during one of their fights a couple of months ago, all the ugly crap about my dad knocking up his current secretary came out. Mom is pissed about that. My dad seems proud and thrilled. My mother called it repugnant and unseemly. She asked what their country club friends would think if they knew. He said that if Amanda, his twenty-five-year-old assistant, had his son, everyone would think he's still the man."

He sounds like an absolutely assholic son of a bitch. My dad would never have dishonored my mother that way, especially with someone young enough to be his daughter. And if he had fathered children on other women, Trace and I would have been shocked and angered. Harlow merely shrugs cynically. My heart breaks for her.

"So...what does Evan want?" she asks. "Money?"

I shake my head and try to make my jaw work. I feel my thoughts steady. The dizzy, hot-clammy feeling recedes. When I squeeze her hand, it's better. "To meet you."

"Seriously?" She frowns skeptically. "To quote *Wayne's World*—a really underrated movie, in my opinion—'Yeah, and monkeys will fly out of my butt.'"

There's no way not to laugh at that.

"Hey, that's enough of that." Harlow wags her finger at me. "No making fun of my cinematic choices."

"I don't think *Wayne's World* is underrated," I manage to say and the words sound almost right. "I prefer a more highbrow comedy, like *Dodgeball.*"

Harlow laughs at me. "Oh, that's a socially important film, for sure."

"Um, hello. ESPN Eight, 'the Ocho.'" I wink her way, then turn serious. "The truth is, I think Evan really wants to meet you. He says he has no other family. I wonder if he wants you to be part of his." I hand the man's card to her. "He'll be in Maui in a couple of hours. This is up to you, of course. But he said he'd love it if you'd call."

She glances at the card before setting it on the coffee table. "I guess I shouldn't be surprised that my dad has another illegitimate child besides the one on its way. If you have a lot of sex with women who aren't your wife, it's bound to happen. I wonder if my mother knows. Or cares." She sighs. "I wonder how Maxon and Griff will take the news."

"Evan didn't know anything about them, only you. So if you decide to meet with him, your brothers will be a surprise to him as well."

She nods and pulls her phone from her pocket. "I need to call them. Will you give me a minute?"

I'd rather hold her hand and give her the support she needs, but Harlow isn't ready. As bitter as that is, I can't barge my way into her family business. "Sure. I'll head upstairs to change and be back in a bit. Let me know if you need anything."

I take a long minute picking out a comfortable pair of shorts and a loose tank. I rinse off with a quick shower, trying not to focus on the last time I wasn't in here alone. It's been three days since I made love to her—and I made her acknowledge me. She said she's still processing, and I don't know what that means. But letting frustration get the best of me isn't going to help.

I glance at the clock. About fifteen minutes have passed since I headed upstairs, so I risk creeping down. Harlow sits on the sofa, still staring at her paused game, unmoving.

She's in shock.

"Baby?" I rush to her side.

"Apparently Evan is for real, and I also have a sister I've never met. Her name is Bethany, and she's close to Griff's age. Maxon knew everything. He's known for months."

And his secrecy hurt. She doesn't say it, but I know. The grit in her voice tells me she chewed him a new asshole, too.

"Did he say why he didn't tell you?"

She lets out a heavy breath. "He didn't want to disillusion me. He knew I'd wanted to be a daddy's girl as a kid. He was trying not to color my opinion with the sordid details. Griff knows, too, of course."

Harlow doesn't have to tell me how alone she feels. I see it all over her face. She adores her brothers, and she feels betrayed that they've kept secrets from her, even if they meant to protect her.

"I'm sorry, baby." I take her hand in mine and kiss it, wishing I could take away her pain.

She shakes her head. "In his shoes, I probably would have done the same thing, especially since Maxon and my dad have had a strained relationship for as long as I can remember. He seemed to prefer Griff, even though they both worked for Dad as interns while in high school. He constantly belittled Maxon for not being macho and manly enough."

"What an awful thing to say to your own son, especially when he's still just a kid. Any reason he showed favoritism to Griff?"

"I don't know, and Maxon won't spill. But I'm sure it sucked. Just like I'm sure whatever Griff had to do to curry favor with the old man must have been dirty and underhanded since that's all Barclay understands. So my brothers learned to be unscrupulous, ambitious assholes from the best—at least until Keeley and Britta."

And until Harlow accepts that I'm here for her, she's handling all this alone.

"I'm sorry, baby." That her father is an asshole. That her brothers aren't forthcoming. That she's having to deal with an illegitimate brother when she's already in turmoil. "I wish I could say something to make it all better."

She shakes her head slowly. "You can't. I've known for a long while that Dad is a total bastard. With the age gap between us siblings, I didn't realize how much our father picked on my brothers. I thought I was the one who got the brunt of his displeasure."

My heart stops. Is Harlow going to tell me something? Is she finally willing to open up? "What displeasure? Baby, what did he do to you?"

Harlow jerks, seemingly startled by my question. "If you're thinking he touched me inappropriately or something awful like that, no. The truth is, he saw a girl child as useless in business, so when I wanted to intern, he laughed at me, patted me on the head, and told me my best bet was to marry well."

I gape at her. "Does this man know how smart you are?"

"I don't think he paid much attention to me once he saw that I lacked the requisite penis to house one's brains." She rolls her eyes. "Once I got older, he dolled me up and took me to functions, introduced me around…" She shakes her head. "You know what? He's just an asshole, and I don't want to give him more energy. I'd rather focus on now. I don't know whether to pity Evan growing up as the wrong-side-of-the-blanket kid or congratulate him for skipping a childhood with Barclay Reed."

There's more to this story. I can feel it. But like everything else between us, I can't force her. It's starting to frustrate the hell out of me. What will it take to make her trust me?

"Does Maxon want to meet him?"

"Yeah. I gave him Evan's contact information. We'll see. Maxon is all about family now. Well, not the parents, but he's ready to surround himself with people who matter. He also seems interested in finding out whether assholery is a genetic trait or a learned behavior, and I guess Evan will answer some of those questions for him. I'm sure Griff will go along, too. You know, scope out the long-lost brother together."

"What about you?"

She shrugs, then shakes her head and picks up her game controller. "I don't need anyone in my life, Noah. I'm better off alone."

I WAKE UP early the next morning. Harlow isn't beside me.

I don't need anyone in my life, Noah. I'm better off alone. Harlow's words resonate in my head. After the two brothers she trusted more than anyone shut her out, even to well-meaningly shelter her, I fear she really means them.

This damn woman is tying me in knots. How the hell am I supposed to reach her if she won't talk to me? If she refuses to even sleep in the same bed with me?

Creeping down the hall, I find her in her own room, curled up under the covers as if blankets can somehow ward off the hurtful people in her life. Or does she only mean to keep me out?

The frustration is bugging the shit out of me. Being under the same roof with a woman who only wants laughs and sex when I know we could have so much more isn't easy.

After tossing on running shorts and a pair of sneakers, I run out of the house and past the guard gate. The sun is just beginning to lighten the sky with vivid oranges and golds. I'm thanking every higher power imaginable that there are no reporters or paparazzi hanging out now. The new guard at the gate waves me out and I head down the deserted road, pounding one foot in front of the other on the pavement.

My thoughts circle and chase one another. Am I spinning my wheels with Harlow? Will she ever come around? Giving up seems logical. Why beat my head against that towering brick wall she has up around her heart? On the other hand, who in Harlow's life has ever truly invested in and cared about her? Not her father or mother. Definitely not her ex-fiancé. Not even her brothers until recently, if everything she's said is true. It begs one question: Who's been on her side? Who's been that someone she can count on, no matter what?

I don't think anyone. And keeping everyone out is her way of stopping potential hurt before it even starts. I don't blame her. But I also don't like it. Do I really want to be like everyone else who's let her down? Can I really imagine my life without her?

No.

Jesus, I think I *am* in love.

Well, hell…

After a three-mile loop around the estate, I walk back the last quarter of a mile, sweaty and exhausted and no closer to talking myself out of it. The sun is a blazing orange ball rising in the blue sky. It's going to be a scorcher, and I have a feeling summer will be no joke. But after a dozen seasons in Dallas, I'm used to heat and humidity. What I'm struggling with is the fact that days are sliding by, and while I've learned more about Harlow, I'm no closer to convincing her to trust me.

Something's gotta give.

The phone in my pocket buzzes, and I pull it free in case she's calling and wondering where I've disappeared. When I see Cliff's number pop up, I groan. Unless we're negotiating a new deal of some sort, he's never calling with good news.

"What's up?"

"Who the fuck is Mercedes Fleet? Where did you meet her?"

"Who?" I press the phone to my ear and struggle to catch my breath.

"Mercedes Fleet."

"I don't know her."

"Apparently you know her well enough to have knocked her up, at least according to her. TMZ broke the story an hour ago. They just called me for comment."

The bottom drops out of my stomach. This is one more problem I don't need. I search through my memory bank, trying to remember the last woman I had sex with before Harlow. I have to go back about three months. The party after my final Super Bowl win. I don't remember her name. Shit. I gloved up, but…nothing is foolproof.

Is it possible? What do I do now? And given what's up with her father right now, what will Harlow think?

"What does this woman look like?" I've been accused more than once of sleeping with some chick I've never touched. Some women like to brag about bagging someone famous, and I have to set the record straight. Or try. The truth is, too many people don't believe the denial. It sounds like weaseling, reeks of not manning up.

"There's a nice picture of her on TMZ, front and center."

"Hang on." I launch my browser and surf to the tabloid site.

WESTON'S LOVE CHILD ON THE WAY! screams the headline.

The picture below shows a woman standing behind a podium, microphones reaching to her lips and reporters leaning close as if no one wants to miss a word of her story. She's a beautiful woman with long, light brown hair, a slender frame, and stoic blue eyes. I scan the article. She claims we met at a Super Bowl after party at the St. Regis in Houston. I can't deny I was there. I was also stone-cold sober, so I know damn well she is not the anonymous brown-eyed blonde I fucked that night.

But several bystanders and even a former teammate place me at the scene and say they remember us talking before disappearing into one of the suite's bedrooms together. I'm baffled.

I lift the phone to my ear again. "I swear I don't know her. I certainly didn't get her pregnant."

"It doesn't look good, buddy. The network isn't happy. First that Harlow chick and now Mercedes. They're all for you being the man in the broadcasting booth, but women are a growing segment of NFL viewers, and they don't want to hear a guy led around by his dick, even if he is a football legend."

"Listen!" I growl. "I swear to god that I don't know her and I didn't fuck her. Why don't you try being on my side, goddamn it. I pay you enough." I huff in frustration. "Handle the PR on this. I've got to go."

Without waiting for a reply, I hang up on Cliff. If it's all over TMZ, then it's hitting other news outlets, too. It will be the talk of ESPN and other sports-dominated channels. It may even make mainstream news. Which means Harlow will hear about it soon…if she hasn't already. I can just imagine how she's going to take this. She'll lump me in with her sleazebag father and Simon. She'll assume I'm a man whore and an asshole. My denials will fall on deaf ears. She'll turn her back on me because she'll be too afraid to trust people, much less the guy she's known for barely a week.

I hold in a roar of frustration. What the fuck? I've got to get to her now, before the news reaches her. I need to explain. If I tell her I need her help… Yeah, inciting her sweet, natural empathy by asking for her assistance might keep her close. Maybe.

Shit.

I full-out sprint back to the house. There's a growing gaggle of reporters waiting for some scoop at the gate. They shout questions about this woman supposedly carrying my baby. The new guard, who understands his role, opens the gate. The tabloid press is still haranguing me as I dash through with a "no comment." The guy in uniform shuts the barricade behind me quickly.

The sun beats down on me as I run the last quarter-mile up to the house and crash through the front door. As soon as I step inside the entryway, I nearly trip over Harlow's suitcases. I hear her cursing from across the room and look up to see her dragging another piece of luggage down the stairs, her motions jerky and flustered. I step over the heap of her things and approach her. She almost collides with me, then shoots me a glare that's grim and red-eyed and resolute.

"Where are you going?" I demand.

"Anywhere that's not here. I'll stay with Griff and Britta until I can get back to California."

Like hell. "So you've heard the rumors? And you're believing this woman who says I met her at a party and knocked her up without first talking to me?"

"I'm not leaving because of you, Weston. Look, you've got your hands full, and frankly I don't need more drama. I'm not mad. You met her long before me, so what you did with her in February is none of my business. I don't think your mom is going to be thrilled that you've indiscriminately spread your DNA around, but..." She shrugs and reaches for her purse. "You'll figure that out, I guess."

I wrap my fingers around her arm. "I am not your father. Or your ex. I didn't do this."

She seems to lose some of her composure as she jerks from my grip. "Did you hear me? It doesn't matter. I didn't know you then. The truth is, I woke up this morning and realized I was done processing what happened a few days ago in the shower. I think this...fling means more to you than it does to me, and I'd rather not hurt you. So I'm going to do you a favor and leave. You're going to be great. I left the names of some fantastic therapists on the island—both speech and psychological. You may need both since anxiety seems to be a real trigger for you. Any of these people would be really qualified to help you." She gives me an entirely false smile as she gathers her luggage. "I wish you the best."

"This is bullshit." I jerk the bags out of her hands as fast as she can pick them up. "You're absolutely running away from me because you think I got that woman pregnant. You're scared to trust that I'm not Barclay or Simon."

"No."

"Hell yes. Look at me, Harlow. When have I ever hurt you?" She presses her lips together mulishly and picks up her big suitcase again. I yank it from her grip. "When have I ever done anything except try to help you?"

She doesn't answer, just grabs her computer bag and hoists it onto her shoulder. I grab the strap in my fist and jerk it behind me.

"Stop it!" she insists.

"You stop," I growl. "You're not leaving, goddamn it."

"Oh, I'm not? So you're going to keep me here against my will?"

"I'm not letting you run out over nothing." I lock the door behind me and lean against it, arms crossed.

Harlow is determined, but compared to me? She can't beat my size, strength, or persistence.

"I'm not running out. I'm getting out of your way and getting on with my life. That's it. So give me my bags and move so I can leave."

"Nope." I shake my head resolutely. "You don't get to do that. Did you forget? We have a contract. You've signed it. I've paid you. You're obligated to stay here with me until Labor Day."

She's a tiny thing, but her giant temper makes an appearance. "That's how you want to play this? So you are my father, after all? Besides the illegitimate kid on the way, you fucking think you know how I should run my life better than I do and you don't give two shits how I feel? Nice. Next you'll be telling me that I'd be better off marrying well, too. Never mind my aspirations or ambitions... So who, in your estimation, should I whore myself to for a ring on my finger?"

I won't let her manipulate the situation or my composure when she's only trying to push my buttons. "You want to marry well, baby? Marry me."

She scoffs and frantically grabs her luggage again, this time trying to scoop multiple pieces in her grip at once. "Yeah, right. That's not going to happen."

I divest her of her bags again, earning a screech of frustration from her.

"Give me one good reason why not," I challenge. "Just one."

"Hand that over." She reaches for her makeup case, but I set it behind me, too. "You want one good reason, Weston? Okay, you piss me off. We barely know each other and somehow you get under my skin and manage to scratch around and give me hives and—"

I laugh. That's not a reason to let her leave me. If I'm crawling under her surface and getting to her, that's a reason to make her stay.

"You think that's funny?" she challenges.

"No. But I think that makes us even. You get under my skin, too. You make me want you, make me need to understand you, hold you, heal you—"

"I'm not broken!"

She is, but not irreparably. "All right. But how many men have you dated you didn't care about at all? Who let you walk all over them? Who couldn't handle your backbone?" Her pause tells me the number is high, and she's aware of it. "I can handle you."

"I don't want a man who thinks he needs to try. When I agreed to marry Simon, I just wanted a decent guy to spend my years with, one who'd be there for me when it mattered. One who'd give me the children I want. I didn't care about adoration or devotion, just kindness and the appearance of happiness. I still want those things. I don't think you can give them to me."

"Try me."

She studies my face and frowns. "You're serious?"

"Completely."

"You're crazy."

"You didn't say you were looking for sane, baby. Marry me. You want a decent guy? I'm here. You want someone who will spend their years with you? I will. I'll always be here for you. You want kids? I will happily get you pregnant. I'll relish it. You might not care about adoration or devotion, but I'll give you those, too. I'll endeavor to be kind and do whatever it takes to make you genuinely happy, not just help you look as if you are. All you have to do is say yes."

"I've known you for nine days."

I shrug. "So? You listed off your wants, and I'm telling you I'll fulfill them. Who cares about the details?"

"I did the bride thing recently. Not looking to do it again. Now move so I can go."

"If you leave, tell me one person you know who's capable of giving you everything you want."

Her silence is telling.

"No one, right? You want to call Simon again? Or wait a few years and hope you meet someone better?"

She presses her lips together, and I can tell that she's thinking. One part of her would love to tell me to pound sand, but I'm dangling the life she wants most in front of her face. If I can't appeal to her heart, I can tug at her deep-seated desire.

Suddenly, she says, "You're already having a baby. You don't need me to have one, too. Move."

I stand my ground and grab her shoulders. "I have never met what's-her-name in my life. I did not have sex with her. I did not get her pregnant. We were at the same party at the same time, following the Super Bowl. I admit that. Maybe she decided to use that happenstance to see if she could extort money from me. I wouldn't be the first chump a gold digger tried to con. But I hope like hell you'd believe the word of the guy who's been your lover over the woman you've never met."

She falls quiet for a long moment. "What do you want?"

"Marry me."

"I'm not marrying anyone right now."

I try not to take it as a rejection. She's endured a big shock today, and I'm probably leaning on her too hard. Yeah, she's pushing back, but I expected that. I am talking to Harlow, after all. And after everything she's been through lately, she's entitled to lash out in pain. I'm hearty; I can take it. But the more I talk about tying the knot, the more convinced I am that we could be good together. I could make her happy. I could make her fall in love with me in return. In fact, I want that more than anything.

But I need more time. A summer may not be enough.

Trying to talk her into it for her benefit isn't working, so I change tactics. "Look, I could really use a wife. The network is getting itchy, and if I 'settle down,' it's more likely they won't rescind their offer. It seems like a shame to work on my speech only to find out that I might not have a position with the network after all."

"Marry the woman who's having your baby. That would solve your image problem."

God, this woman is stubborn as the day is long, and yet I still find her so damn fascinating. "She's. Not. Having. My. Baby. Get that through your thick skull. Marry me."

"The press would almost certainly think that I left Simon for you because I was cheating on him."

"Do you care? He was cheating on you in a big way and everyone knows it."

She lets out a long sigh. "No. I don't care about appearances. But you should."

"Why don't we make a deal? You marry me for a year. I'll give you a baby. On our first anniversary, we can reevaluate. If you want to stay, we'll continue on as we were. If you want out then, I'll give you five million dollars and custody, as long as I get visitation."

It's a huge gamble, and I could end up the worst loser. But this buys me at least twelve months with Harlow, maybe even a lifetime. A child would guarantee that we'll end up parenting together, so even if we divorce—over my cold, dead body—we'll always have our son or daughter in common.

Yeah, it sucks. I'm out of choices in my "better options" bucket.

"I don't want your money."

Another thing I like about her. She can be blunt and stubborn, sure. But she isn't greedy. She's so confident in her ability to make her own money that she doesn't want mine. "It's on the table if you change your mind."

She cocks a hand on her hip. "You could marry just about any woman you want. I have no illusions that I'm easy to deal with. Why me?"

If I tell her that I'm pretty sure I'm in love with her, she'll run screaming in the opposite direction. I have to play this cool. "We make sense. We get along. We have great sex. We share common values. I want to get on with the next stage of my life. You can help me with my speech, and the press already thinks we're an item. Introducing another woman now might send the network into a tizzy, not to mention my fans. Telling everyone that we're getting married suddenly turns you from the sordid, under-the-blankets fling to a legitimate staple in my life."

"What's in it for me, besides awesome sex? You can't guarantee me a baby. Neither of us knows for certain I will—or can—get pregnant."

"Any reason to think you can't?"

She shakes her head. "No. I have this friend who's been married for two years, and they're trying so hard...to no avail. Just saying it's not something we can predict."

"Fair enough. We'll try the fertility bit. If it doesn't work, I can still offer you some consolation: I know people in high places. I can open doors for you. Hell, I can introduce you to dozens of other players who probably need your help, too. If you want to jumpstart your career, I could do that for you in a major way."

She's silent for a long moment, like she's actually considering my impulsive proposal. But this is right. I'm sure. I know it in my bones. "Any catch?"

I pause, consider. "Two conditions: First, you have to put your all into making us work while we're together. No checking out because you think we're temporary."

"I wouldn't be a bitch for the sake of being a bitch. We'd both have to live with that, and it's too much effort."

"Glad to hear it. Second, you have to sleep next to me every night. If I'm in this house, you're in our bed."

She blinks, lips pressed into a firm line. I can tell she doesn't like it. "Why?"

"If you want to get pregnant, I have to touch you."

"So if I say yes to this ridiculous idea, I should be able to sleep in my own room once we get a plus sign on the pee stick."

I'm dying to know why she's so insistent about sleeping alone. "Nope. We'll have your health and the baby's to think about. I'll want to keep an eye on you both."

Harlow says nothing for interminable moments. Finally, she sighs and reaches for her makeup case just behind my feet. "I need to think."

When she turns with the case in her hand, I grip her arm to stay her. "For how long?"

"Give me...a week. I'll have an answer then."

CHAPTER ELEVEN

A FEW DAYS later, I'm pretty sure I'm going to lose my mind before Saturday rolls around. Harlow has been quiet. Preoccupied. She won't sleep next to or with me. I'm frustrated and jacked up as hell. It's been a long week without her—without touching her, without drowning inside her. I'm losing my mind.

Yesterday, we started another speech assessment—the most conversation we've had since I blurted that I want to marry her. This test is more physical and nonverbal than the previous ones. She stopped midway through to ask me questions about my proposal. Sharp, direct queries. I knew instantly she meant to ramp up my anxiousness to see how I'd perform. But when she hinted that she was leaning toward a no, I froze up and lost my shit. With a growl of frustration at this fucking unpredictable deficiency and her aloofness, I stomped out of the room.

Harlow tracked me down an hour later pumping iron in the home gym with an apology and a confession that she hadn't meant any of those less-than-subtle suggestions. The honest truth was, she's still thinking and she feels terrible for using our relationship to try to put me on edge. When she kissed my cheek, I knew she meant it. I also know she understands how much I want her in my life.

That woman having such a hold on my heart is unsettling, but I can't change it.

"Hey, Noah." She strolls into my office the next evening all dolled up in a sundress, wedge sandals, lip gloss, and curls. She's slung her purse over one shoulder.

I remove my earbuds and pause the game commentary I've been studying. "What's going on? Going somewhere?"

She nods. "Keeley is picking me up for happy hour and a little karaoke. She's convinced I need to get out. I think they just want to grill me about why I've been quiet lately."

I'd like to do the same, but I have to respect her space for another four days. Marriage—even for a year—is a big decision.

"Be home for dinner?"

"I don't know. Depends on how crazy my sisters-in-law get. I'll call you once I know."

I'd rather not eat alone and I don't love the fact that she's going to a bar while she looks so beautiful, but she's an adult. And I just want to marry her, not control her. "I'd appreciate that. Thanks."

With a nod and an awkward pause, she's gone. I miss the easy conversation we used to share. I wonder if proposing was a colossal error on my part. I don't regret it, exactly. But I wonder if, instead of moving us forward, she sees marriage as a threat to her independence or heart that is only setting us back.

Sighing, I stand. I hate the not knowing, and I swear I'll lose my mind before she puts me out of my misery—one way or the other.

Once she's gone, I prowl around the house. It feels huge and empty without her. It's still too big for two people, but when Harlow is here, she's humming as she cooks, shouting at the enemies on her video game as she's playing, or blasting music as she lies by the pool. This place is full of life when she's under my roof.

If she goes, it will be empty as hell. I have no idea what I'll do with this huge house. We haven't been together even two weeks, but it feels as if she belongs here and I'll be the interloper if I have to be here alone.

I pace, trying to imagine another scenario. What will our house feel like if Harlow lives here as my wife, round with our baby? Instantly, I'm hard and aching and wishing she'd decided to stay in so I could remind her of some of the ways we're best together. The last week without making love to her feels more like a year.

I need to stop this train of thought or I'll spend the entire evening in misery.

Flipping on the game console, I launch myself into the Middle English-style adventure and am just completing a side quest when I hear the slam of a car door. Who got onto the estate and how? The only people who are approved are family—hers and mine. Trace is working today. My mother doesn't like to drive the windy roads out to here. Harlow is with her sisters-in-law. By process of elimination, I'm not surprised when Maxon and Griff stroll into the family room through the open patio door.

"Knock, knock." Maxon raps his knuckles on the doorframe, then lounges against it negligently.

"Hey. Come in." I suck in a deep breath and try to calm my nerves. They know I've had issues, so it wouldn't be a shock if I stopped talking, but without Harlow here to interpret and referee, this might get ugly.

"Sorry to drop in unannounced," Griff says. "But when our wives said they were going to take Harlow out and shamelessly grill her for information about you two, we thought we'd chat with you about a few things."

Meaning they want to shamelessly grill me for information, as well.

"Sure." This sounds like an opportunity for me to sputter and choke, but I plaster a smile on my face and pretend that it's going to be great. "Beer?"

"I'll take one," Griff calls as he sits on the sofa.

"I guess I'll take water. My brother manipulated me into being the DD." When Griff flashes Maxon a grin, the older Reed grumbles. "Bastard."

After I get everyone situated, I turn the game and the TV off and sit in the chair opposite. "What's up?"

"We talked to Evan yesterday," Maxon informs me. "Over the phone. His story checks out. I even got brave and called my mother to ask her for information. She confirmed some of the story, so I think he's legit. We all agree to submit DNA swabs to be sure. The results should come back by the end of the week. But if he's really our brother…I guess the family just got bigger."

"Great." Why tell me?

"Did Evan say anything else to you at the airport?" Maxon quizzes.

"Just that his mom had been your dad's assistant and that she died when he was five. Your dad wanted nothing to do with him, so he became a ward of the state. I'm guessing he grew up in the foster system." I shrug. "That's it."

"Google confirmed all that, too. But there's more."

"Apparently, he's the founder and CEO of one of the fastest-growing tech infrastructure businesses in the U.S. He's worth billions."

"At twenty-five? Impressive."

"I don't know a Reed who isn't ambitious. It's been bred into us all. We come out wanting to conquer the world," Maxon says, and he's only half joking.

"Evan did say something about wanting to move himself and his operations to Hawaii. I'm surprised. This isn't a high-tech Mecca. Then again, he mentioned wanting family."

"That he doesn't know? It seems sudden," Maxon mused. "But maybe it's an orphan thing."

I frown. "When he approached me in the airport, he didn't explain why."

"Until we figure it out, we're approaching him cautiously. Clearly, he doesn't want money from us, but he wants something. If he's looking for close-knit camaraderie from the Reed clan, he's going to be shit out of luck."

It's probably none of my business, but if Harlow says yes to my proposal, I'll be the man who stands up with and for her. I just hope by opening my mouth, I'm not sticking my foot in it. "Your sister certainly thinks so, guys. The fact that you knew about Evan and Bethany but didn't tell her really upset her."

Maxon sits up straighter. "We just wanted to protect—"

"I know. She even admitted that in your shoes, she might have done the same." I feel my brain slowing. My jaw freezing. It's suddenly fucking hot in here, and I feel sweat breaking out across my neck and chest. But I manage to get a few more words out. "She was pissed."

Griff sighs, then looks at his brother. "I told you…"

"Fuck. Harlow is so independent. She used to be easygoing and rolled with the punches like a pro," Maxon insists. "Something changed after she went to college."

"Yeah, she grew up and realized she had an identity of her own." Griff shakes his head as if Maxon is an idiot.

"Maybe." The elder Reed doesn't sound convinced. "So is that why she's dodging my calls right now? She's annoyed that we didn't loop her in about Evan?"

"Probably." I refuse to candy-coat the truth. But I have to go for broke here. If I can bring Harlow back together with her brothers and enlist their help at once, I'd score big. Besides, they're going to find out sooner or later. But to have this conversation I have to talk.

I drag in a steadying breath, wait a few moments, hoping my state will improve.

The brothers exchange a glance.

"It's cool, man. We're not mad," Maxon assures. "You're just being honest. Relax."

Griff nods. "Exactly. We did this to ourselves. I can't blame you at all. Just say what's on your mind when you're ready."

Eyes closed, I nod and feel myself slowly let go of the stress. Finally, I feel everything that tensed up release.

"I asked your sister to marry me."

The silence that follows is deafening. Neither Reed brother moves or blinks, just stares at me. Do they want to beat the shit out of me or just think I'm certifiably insane?

Finally, Maxon rakes a hand over the top of his short, spiked hair. "I'd say you're fucking kidding us…but I can see you're not."

I shake my head.

"She said no." Griff sounds as if he's sure of that.

With a jerk of my head, I refute him. "She's said she'll give me an answer this weekend."

Another exchanged glance. Now they look impressed.

I don't mention how badly she wants a baby. If I do, one—or both—of them may plant their fist in my face.

"I'm shocked she didn't give you a full-out fuck no," Maxon admits. "Especially after Mercedes Fleet cropped up."

"I don't know that woman," I insist. "I didn't fuck her. I've never even met her."

Neither brother says a word. No idea if they're convinced. I don't have proof, just the truth.

"So why do you want to marry Harlow? As a shield from the press?"

"Hell no." Don't they get it?

"Well, it's not for the speech therapy. You can get more experienced help with that anywhere." Griff sips his beer. "So why?"

"Keeping it real? I've never been in love, but I'm pretty sure I am now. That notion scares the shit out of your sister. Why? And why doesn't she believe in love? Your wives both suggested I look at her relationship with your parents."

Neither brother seems to want to look at me for a long moment, then Griff sighs. "Probably a good place to start."

Maxon turns a shade of dull red. "Yeah."

Like talking to their sister, there's a wealth of information in what Maxon and Griff aren't saying. I wonder what they've endured with their parents.

"Maybe I should meet them."

Both brothers look at me in horror. "No!"

"Why would you want to do that?" Maxon spits.

"It's insane," Griff confirms. "And they'll just spend time figuring out how they can use you to their advantage. Trust me, if they did something to Harlow, they'll never own up to it, much less apologize."

There's a family history here I don't understand. Maybe I never will. But they're the experts.

I shrug. "I have to try something. Talking to Harlow can be like talking to a wall."

"Another Reed family trait," Griff quips.

Maxon nods. "I keep coming back to that first year of college. I noticed it that Christmas when I flew home for the holidays. Have you asked her about that time of her life?"

"No. I can try." But she's not speaking to me a lot right now, and if I interrogate her too much before she answers my proposal, I'm pretty certain her maybe will become a quick no.

"Don't. Let me get the girls to see what they can pry out of her. More soon." Maxon claps me on the back, then texts Keeley.

Griff sends off a quick message to Britta and quickly gets a reply. "They're on it."

It strikes me then that her brothers are actually on my side. "Thanks. You want Harlow to marry me?"

Neither says anything for a long moment. Finally Griff breaks the silence. "We want Harlow happy. As soon as I met Simon Butler, I knew he wasn't going to do the job."

Maxon nods. "He's too much like Dad in all the worst ways."

"But I think maybe you can make her happy," Griff says. "I've seen Harlow with boyfriends and lovers over the years. I've never seen her quite as in tune with one as she seems to be with you. There's something between you two. And frankly, if she didn't feel something for you, she would have given zero fucks about Mercedes Fleet and told you to shove your marriage proposal on the spot."

He's right. That whole paying attention to what Harlow doesn't say works for *everything* she's hiding, not just her secrets.

"Exactly," Maxon seconds. "And if sex brought you together, keep giving it to her, man. Don't give Harlow too much time to catch her breath. Or think."

I choke on my sip of beer.

"Never give her space," Griff agrees with a nod. "With a woman like her, you have to stay one step ahead."

Finally I manage to swallow. "She won't like me in her face all the time."

"You're right. That's not what I mean." Maxon shakes his head and scoffs. "Just focus on keeping her sated and smiling. Because as much as the Reeds are allergic to emotion, they're addicted to sex."

I'm totally happy with that approach. I have the upper hand in bed. So if I can make that advantage work in my favor, then hell yeah. It's on. And I'll do my best to pleasure her into saying yes.

ON FRIDAY AFTERNOON, I'm having trouble sitting across from Harlow in the home office. She's scanning her notes, absently piling her dark hair in a loose topknot and securing it with a pencil. The red bikini top she wore when we first met cradles her lush breasts. A moment later, she stands, and the flowing floral sarong around her hips emphasizes everything about her that's both delicate and curvy. I barely notice when she opens a thick tome, flips through, her brows knitting in a frown of concentration.

Even after getting out with the girls on Tuesday, she's distant. Maxon and Griff said their wives got zero information out of Harlow except a polite clap after Keeley finished singing. Harlow successfully dodged me most of Wednesday for meetings with some local therapists. On Thursday, we completed the assessment we hadn't earlier in the week. This morning, I had a TV interview with a local station on behalf of a nearby food bank. If it hadn't been for the generosity of others after my dad died, I might not have had three meals a day. I give faithfully and encourage others to do the same. After that, I had to run an important errand that required me to make a few phone calls so I could have a little privacy.

Finally home, I sit across from Harlow and watch her, wondering what the devil that woman is thinking under her studious facade.

"Baby?"

Head stuck in a book, she holds up a finger. "Almost done. I want to get this right since I know we're working against the clock."

She's not wrong about that. Cliff called me again yesterday to update me on the Mercedes Fleet situation. The woman wants me to acknowledge her baby and pay child support. I've refused. The news is still making waves on social media and in the sports world. My agent wants me to accept the deal before the network retracts it. I can't until I know whether I'll actually be able to fulfill the role. But I want the job so bad. I love football. I want to stay in the game however I can. Not to relive my glory days. I was never into that. This sport is in my blood. I know these players. I understand how the game is played better than most. I think NFL fans are the best, most loyal people. I'm not ready to walk away from any of it.

A few minutes later, Harlow sets the book aside. She sits across from me, clasps her hands, and levels a serious look my way. "Here's what I've come up with. You ready?"

"As I'll ever be." But am I? My stomach knots. Sure, her diagnosis could fill in the gaps, help me understand so I can move forward. This information might also terrify me with how hopeless my situation is.

"You might have some residual lapses in speech following your last concussion. I'm not discounting that possibility," she says. "I think it's more likely, however, that because you lost your ability to speak for a short time after your injury, you associate it with being unable to play the game any longer. That's a source of anxiety for you. And because of that, you found it hard to announce your retirement at your post-Super Bowl interview. The fact that you were unable to filled you with more anxiety, and something in your head clicked. The association was set. So when you get into tense situations, you have the disconnect between your brain and your mouth. It works the same with being really tired because I'm guessing that after the Super Bowl you were exhausted."

"You think I'm crazy?" That's what she's come up with?

She finally cracks a smile and looks at me with soft understanding. "No. And you're not defective, either. Nearly forty million Americans suffer with some form of anxiety, so you're hardly alone. I suspect your anxiety is a post-traumatic thing. It wasn't so much the concussion that disturbed you as it was your inability to speak afterward. Am I right?"

"Yeah."

"So that's it. When you start to experience anxiety, you associate the loss of speech with that, so the symptom kicks in. When you're calm and rested, it doesn't happen."

I get what she's saying but… "So you do think I'm crazy?"

"No," she assures, taking my hand.

It's the most contact we've had in days. I clutch her fingers in mine.

"What I think is that the loss of your career was something you weren't prepared for. Coupled with your injuries, which caused the problem, your anxiousness about the changes in your life are manifesting in this way. I've suspected this for a while, but I wanted to validate my thoughts, so my professors helped me to reach out to some people, a few even local, so I could get different perspectives. This is pretty much the consensus." Harlow rises and comes around the desk, never releasing my hand, before she sidles up to me and curls herself in my lap. "What this means is, we should experiment with ways to keep your anxiety and stress levels down—exercise, diet, meditation—that sort of thing. If we can't control it with those methods, we look at psychotherapy or medication. We search for what works."

I pull her into my arms and hold her close, closing my eyes to let her words sink in. I'm overwhelmed. It sounds as if this process won't be overnight. What if it takes months—or years—to work? I don't have that long. I need results now. "I'm not ready to turn down the job."

I'm barely able to get the words out. I feel both hot and frozen. The world is quaking beneath me, but I'm utterly unable to move.

"It's way too early for you to do that. And if the network job won't work for you, maybe you continue to cover football in writing. You'll find a way. But you're going to be fine. We'll work to keep improving your response, see if we can disassociate the stress with your loss of speech. I don't know how. This isn't my exact area of expertise, but I'm here." She meets my gaze. "And I'm sorry I tried to run out on you last week. We have an agreement, and I'm committed to helping you however I can."

Harlow doesn't say anything about my proposal. She still has until tomorrow to answer me, so I don't push. I can't help but think about how much easier it would be to handle my condition if I knew she was going to be around for at least a year—and maybe for a lifetime.

"So…what do we do now?"

"I'm making arrangements to tweak the groceries coming in. You should eat a lean diet of turkey and other tryptophan-rich foods, beef and anything else rich in B vitamins, salmon, whole grains, blueberries and bananas, all kinds of green and leafy veggies. You need to avoid processed sugar…" She winces. "And caffeine."

"No coffee?" The rest of the diet sounds fairly normal, but lack of java is a major issue.

"We'll wean you off, but it would be best if you started your day with a chamomile or green tea." She looks apologetic, and I have to remember that she's trying to help, not kill me. "We'll make sure you get sunlight every day. I want to try starting and ending your day with meditation. You already get exercise. How's your sleep?"

Without her beside me? "Surprisingly shitty lately."

"We'll try some valerian drops or capsules. If you've had adequate sleep, then—"

"I'll sleep better if I have you beside me."

I don't mean it to sound like emotional blackmail. She might take my words that way, but I'm simply giving her the truth.

Harlow pauses. Her arms tighten around my neck, and I feel her stiffen. "All right. If that's what you need, I'll be there."

I hold her tighter and bury my face in her neck. No, she can't help me, but somehow when I'm with her I feel so much more calm and whole.

Guess it's that love thing.

"Thank you. When do we get started?"

She pulls back and gives me a tremulous smile. But I feel her shaking and I don't understand.

Her voice is almost too chipper. "No time like the present. Let's do it."

CHAPTER TWELVE

AFTER AN AFTERNOON of cardio, healthy cooking, and some laughable attempts at guided meditation with a recording of a douchey British guy in my ear, Harlow tosses together a salad while I'm grilling some salmon. It's quiet. I wish I felt Zen, but neither of us have talked about what happens tonight. She'll sleep next to me because she agreed to, but it will cost her emotional grit. I don't understand why. I can practically see her bracing for it. The nice guy in me wants to let her off the hook. The ruthless bastard in me craves her beside me where I can give her so much pleasure she'll never refuse my proposal.

That probably sounds fucked up. She needs to make her own decision. But I'm getting desperate. I can't let this woman slip through my fingers.

We're eating at the bar in the kitchen when Harlow's phone lights up between us with a text from Maxon. Busy tonight?

I look at her. She shrugs at me. I'd rather spend the evening alone with her, but her older brother sends another message before we can talk.

We've got news.

Harlow doesn't hesitate. Should we meet you somewhere?

We'll come there. K?

After giving him a quick thumbs-up, she sets her phone aside. She barely nibbles on her dinner.

I lay my hand over hers. "You look worried. He didn't say anything is wrong."

"It's not like Maxon to be spontaneous. This must be big." She chews her lip. "I'm wondering if it's Mom and her boyfriend, Marco. Or Dad and his pregnant assistant. Or Evan, the long-lost illegitimate brother. Shouldn't those test results be back now? This shit is like bad tabloid TV, but it's my life." With a frown knitting her brow, she slants a cynical glance my way. "I feel like I was dropped in the middle of Crazy Town. Are you sure you want to marry into this family? Think hard."

I don't have to think at all. "Yes."

She sets her fork down and sends me a serious stare. "Why? Noah, I'm not the sort of girl to fall in love. Not with anyone."

I know Harlow thinks that, but her heart is too big to be closed off forever. "I heard you."

"But are you listening? I don't want to hurt you. I just—"

"Don't worry about me." If I have a year, I should be able to coax her into dropping her guard and falling in love.

Right?

Harlow gives me a nod she means to look assured, but I see the worry on her face. "I know, you're a big boy. If we get married, I at least want the honesty my parents never had. I don't want secrets or animosity or regret between us."

"Of course." Other players have fallen for a pretty face and a nice rack and ended up in hell because their bride was a heartless bitch looking out for her bottom line, but that's not Harlow.

"I mean, when you find a new lover, I'd rather you tell me than be blindsided."

When, not if. After her father and Simon, I can see why she'd think that her husband finding a mistress would be inevitable. "If we get married, Harlow, there won't be anyone else for me."

"Okay. Sure." She gives me a negligent shrug. Clearly, she doesn't believe me.

I take her hand. "I'm serious. To me, a marriage is between two people, not us and whoever flips my switch at the moment."

Harlow simply stares, looking as if she's trying to decide whether I'm a really good liar.

"I promise. We can make this work."

"Maybe we can since it's only for a year."

A year won't be long enough. I'm going to make sure it's not enough for her, either. "Just say yes. You'll see."

She doesn't answer, and silence falls between us. I'm looking for a way to fill it when the doorbell rings.

"That was fast," I remark as we both stand.

"Finish eating, "she says. "I'll get it."

When she opens the door, it's not Maxon and Keeley standing in the threshold, but Britta and Griff, hand in hand.

"Hey. What's going on? I didn't know you were coming over."

"Maxon texted and told us to meet him here. He said something was up," Griff said grimly. "We were only a few minutes away."

"If it's about Evan, Maxon hasn't updated me. Then again, I didn't know anything in the first place." Harlow turns away to shut the door.

"We didn't mean to leave you out," Griff assures her. "I'm sorry."

Harlow whirls on him. "Then don't do it again, okay?"

"Absolutely."

"If I had known you had no idea, I would have honored the girl code and told you," Britta promises.

That makes Harlow crack a smile, then hug her sister-in-law. "Thanks. Good to know I have *someone* on my side."

When Griff grimaces, I step into the awkward silence. "Hey, you guys. Come in. Can I get you anything?"

"We just came from a big dinner," Griff says. "Britta's mom is spending some grandma time with Jamie so we could have a date. Did Maxon say how long he'd be?"

"No." Harlow leads everyone to the family room adjacent to the kitchen.

"Eat the rest of your food," I murmur in her ear.

She shakes her head and picks up her plate. "I'm good."

"We didn't mean to disturb your dinner," Britta says apologetically.

"It's fine. Sit. Please." Her smile tells me having family around will soothe her, so as much as I'd rather be alone with Harlow, she needs this.

We're all settled with a drink and some small talk when a knock on the door has me hopping to my feet. I open it to admit Maxon and Keeley. The man's face is unreadable. He would have made a hell of a poker player.

"Hey, everyone." He shuffles into the room, Keeley's hand tucked in his as they settle on the sofa. "We've got some news and I thought we should all be together."

"Did the DNA test results come in?" Griff asks.

Maxon pulls a small FedEx envelope from his suit pocket. "Yeah."

That one word has gravity. They all understand if Evan is truly their brother, this will shake up their small, dysfunctional family.

"Open it," Harlow prompts. "We should know the truth."

"Yeah." Still, Maxon hesitates.

"Sweetheart?" Keeley murmurs.

"Don't worry," he says. "I just...don't know what to think. It's not Evan's fault that Dad is a dishonest, wandering-dick asshole. We can't blame the kid for his father's sins. Otherwise, Griff and I would be labeled grade-A assholes, too."

"But you're mad, anyway," Harlow supplies. "I get that."

"We have to be the bigger people here," Griff says. "If we cut him off because Dad was a son of a bitch, are we any better?"

Britta beams at him. "Thank you for listening to me."

He kisses her on the nose. "I do every once in a while, you know."

Maxon sighs. "Maybe Evan is a good guy. He seemed okay on the phone."

"But it's weird to wake up one day and suddenly be, like, I have another brother," Harlow points out.

"Exactly." Maxon points at her. "But this isn't about me—or any one of us. We have each other. He has no one, and we should give him the benefit of the doubt." He turns to his wife. "See, I'm listening to you, too."

Keeley bestows a smile his way and a kiss on his cheek.

I hang back, glad to see that the older Reeds—the happily married ones—are coming to the right conclusion. It doesn't escape me that Harlow is still unsure.

"Open the envelope." Griff nods at the mail his older brother holds. "Let's find out once and for all."

Even I'm holding my breath as Maxon rips it open and extracts the letter, his eyes scanning the page. He swallows, folds it up, then looks at his siblings. "He's one of us, no question."

The words reverberate around the room. The silence that follows is a bomb, and we all recoil, absorbing the news. Not that any of the Reed siblings seem surprised, but the news makes everything more real.

"Do you need to let Evan know?" I ask finally.

Maxon nods. "I guess we do, though he was already convinced. What's the etiquette for feeling out the brother you've never met to see if he wants to join the family? I never read Emily Post's advice on this kind of mess."

"Is there a right or wrong way for something this fucked up? I guess we just call," Griff suggests.

"If you'd rather deliver the news in person, you're welcome to invite him here, give him the news on neutral ground without any gawking onlookers," I suggest. "It'll be quiet. You guys can just…talk."

Maxon whips out his phone. "Griff?"

"It's a good plan." The younger Reed brother turns to Harlow. "But I don't want to bring him here if you're not comfortable."

She lets out a big breath, then nods. "If he's one of us, then…call and invite him."

With a curt nod, Maxon excuses himself to the patio, fingers tapping the screen of his phone. The silence in his wake is long and heavy.

"Does anyone want coffee? Tea? A big ol' bottle of booze to wash down this revelation?" Harlow offers with a wry tilt of her mouth.

Griff laughs as he follows her to the kitchen. "I'll take the booze."

Britta and Keeley both laugh. After I pour Griff a stiff Scotch and the ladies opt for iced tea, Maxon strolls back in with a sigh. "Evan had to go back to Honolulu. He'll be returning tomorrow afternoon. Who's free then? I know Griff and I should be working…but this is more important."

Keeley clings to her husband's arm. "I'm proud of you, putting family before ambition."

"It wasn't easy." He's only half joking.

She smiles his way, and I see the love between them bright and glowing and like it's been a bond between them forever. I envy them. I admit it. I want what they have and I want it with Harlow.

"I'm with Maxon," Griff says. "We make the time. Family isn't the shit show we grew up with. This is."

Harlow looks pensive but nods. "You're right. We'll be here."

I notice her pronoun—*we*, not *I*. It's a small but important detail. It gives me some hope.

We all gather around in the family room again, Maxon with a Scotch of his own now. Silence falls, and I search for a way to bring the room back up, but I doubt anyone feels like a rousing game of Cards Against Humanity.

Finally, Keeley claps her hands. "How about a little karaoke? Griff, you're exempt from singing."

He takes the good-natured jibe with humor. "Thank you. Everyone else's ears thank you, too."

Maxon grimaces. "Even if Griff doesn't sing, I'm not sure we're in the mood."

"Just one song," she pleads.

He smiles like a guy who can't say no to his wife. "What do you want to sing, sunshine?"

"Actually, I have the greatest song for *you* to sing."

Maxon shakes his head, his face full of *hell no*. "Like Griff, I shouldn't sing. But I love listening to you. Go ahead."

"Pleeeeasse. Do it for me. This once."

He gives her a long-suffering sigh as he gets to his feet. "I must really love you. How am I supposed to do this? We don't have a karaoke setup here."

"I have that Bluetooth mic in the car that will connect to my phone. Give me a minute." She dashes out the door.

We all watch her head for the car. I can't help but think she's a little zany.

"I'm going to apologize in advance, everyone. I'll sound terrible and probably break your eardrums," Maxon says with a shake of his head. "Fair warning."

No one assures him it can't be that bad, which tells me that the people who know him already know they're not in for a treat.

Keeley runs back in like she's got the wind at her back, carrying a white-and-gold-plated microphone with a box of dials and buttons wrapped around the handle, just under the head. She flips it on and connects it to her phone. Instant static fills the air.

After winces all around, she adjusts the settings and hands it to her husband with a huge smile. "Thanks, sweetheart."

"What have I gotten myself into?" He shakes his head good-naturedly.

"You'll see." Keeley's voice is full of excitement.

After a few pokes and swipes at her phone with surprisingly shaking fingers, she hands him the device. A cheesy electronic melody starts to play from the little speaker. It sounds a little like a sappy but unfamiliar ballad.

"What song is this?" Maxon looks confused. "There's just a yellow screen. No title. How will I do this?"

I peer over his shoulder, as does Griff. The men in the room all think they're going to solve the technical problem. Before we can, the screen flips to a bright blue and the first words that pop up make my heart stop.

"You're having my..." Maxon stops trying to butcher the melody as soon as he realizes what he's singing. "Baby? You're pregnant, sunshine?"

She tears up and nods frantically. "When I went to the doctor this morning for my 'flu,' he gave me the news. I wanted to surprise you after work, but when you got the letter about Evan in the mail, you seemed so tense and then... Well, we came here and started talking about family.

And I couldn't think of a better way to tell you that you're going to be a father and we're widening our circle than to share the excitement with everyone we love."

Maxon still looks stunned when Griff pats him on the back with a grin. Britta kills the music, then hugs Keeley with a little squeal. I look at Harlow and my gut twists. She's pasted on a smile for her brother. She's happy for him and his wife. But I know she's screaming inside.

"Well, since good news is going all around," Griff begins with a conspiratorial glance at his bride, "we'll add ours. Britta took a home test this morning. Looks like Jamie will be getting a brother or sister early next year."

Keeley gives a *squee* of excitement. "Did you get pregnant on your honeymoon?"

"I think so. I didn't want any more of a gap between Jamie and the baby, so I'm super-happy." Britta beams.

"Keeley and I have been trying since we got married. We didn't want to be too far behind you," Maxon quips.

"Congratulations." I hold out my hand to both brothers. After hearty shakes, I hug their wives and give them a congratulatory kiss on the cheek. The fact that they've included me in their family circle tonight makes me hopeful that Harlow's brothers no longer see me as the guy banging their sister, but instead as the man who hopes to marry her.

I turn to Harlow. Even as she's flashing a smile to Britta, she looks as if she's holding herself together by a thread.

The merriment lasts another agonizing hour. After a few toasts, the other couples leave for private celebrations of their own. As soon as I shut the door behind everyone, I turn to seek out Harlow. She's gone, racing up the stairs as if she can't get alone fast enough. I run after her.

WHEN I REACH Harlow's portal, I shove my foot in the doorway of her

188

bedroom before she can slam it in my face. "Baby…"

"Go, Noah."

"I'm sleeping beside you tonight. We made a deal." And if I'm right next to her, maybe she'll feel close and open up to me.

"Trust me, you don't want to be with me tonight."

I hear the tears in her voice and I'm more determined than ever. "Let me in, Harlow."

She jerks the door open with a frustrated sigh. Tears streak silvery paths down her face. "So you can tell me I'm a horrible human being? I don't know why I'm so happy for my brothers and their wives while I'm so miserably fucking sad for myself. I don't do pity parties, and I can't even understand why I'm blubbering like an idiot."

"You want a baby." In truth, she craves love and acceptance and an adoring family, but she's not ready to admit that.

"And it's not like I'm approaching menopause. It will happen when the time is right. I really am happy for them. Thrilled. My brothers deserve every bit of happiness they've got. I'll get over my shit. Just give me tonight alone."

Being alone is the last thing she needs.

"Why don't you come here, let me hold you?" I try to pull her in my embrace.

She twists away and wraps her arms around herself. "I don't want you feeling sorry for me."

I don't pity her because she's not pregnant. But this woman cries out for love and connection, even as she closes herself off. That hurts like hell. She's convinced herself a baby would fill her heart and satisfy her needs. Now that I've come to know Harlow better, I'm convinced she needs the picket fence, a passel of kids, *and* a smitten husband.

But I'll play it low-key for now. "I don't. How about a movie or a swim?"

"What's that going to solve?" Harlow scoffs.

Then she begins to eye me up and down. There's something going on in her head.

Suddenly, she whirls around and marches into her bathroom. She emerges seconds later, wiping away her tears with one hand and clutching a flat, rectangular container of plastic in a white-knuckled grip with the other. "Yes."

I'm confused, but the resolution blazing from her eyes tells me she's not agreeing to a flick on the 4K TV or a dip in the pool.

My heart pounds. "You'll marry me?"

"Yep. Let's do it. The sooner, the better. And these?" She opens the lid on the peach-colored container to reveal neat rows of tiny pills. "They're going in the trash. Last chance to back out."

Excitement grips my belly. This is fucked up; I know. Harlow becoming my wife for reasons that have more to do with my sperm than my heart isn't optimal, but I proposed to buy myself time. She's giving it to me, and I'm running with it. I'll figure out how to make this marriage about us and not just a baby after the vows are spoken.

"Never. Toss the pills."

Without a moment's hesitation, she opens her fist and the little container plops into the metal bin below with a ping. "Take off your clothes. I want you inside me now."

Her words light me on fire, and I have to clench my fists to keep from pouncing on Harlow here and now. "Two things first."

She's already sliding out of her clothes as if whatever I have to say isn't going to stop her. "I'm listening. Talk fast."

No way in hell. I'm going to make love to Harlow and remind her exactly who I am and how deep our connection is, regardless of how much she denies it.

As a wife, Harlow will totally be a handful.

Dashing out of the room, I sprint down the hall to my bedroom and yank out the box I stashed after my private errand yesterday. By the time I hit the threshold of my room, she's lingering just outside, not wearing a stitch.

I almost swallow my tongue. All that fair skin… Her rosy-tipped breasts hang natural and heavy above her slender waist, which flares out to a cocked hip, supple thighs, and an unobstructed view of the naked pussy I haven't been able to stop thinking about since the night we met. Harlow does something to me I can't even explain. Her attitude might be saucy and snarky, but she's one hell of a smart woman with a ginormous heart. I just need to get under the scar tissue surrounding it and show her how good our life can be.

I must be reaching her on some level if she wants me to get her pregnant. She must trust me more than she's willing to admit.

Knowing she wants me to start right here, right now shreds my self-control. I'm beyond eager, so I take her by the hand, jerk her against my body, then lift her onto the bed. She hasn't even finished bouncing on the mattress before I'm on top of her, shimmying out of my shirt.

"I planned ahead. This is yours." I pull the box from the pocket of my shorts. "If you're going to be my wife, I want you to wear this every day."

Harlow opens it and gasps at the ring I picked out for her. "It's…"

She doesn't finish the sentence, and I freeze. Too much? Not what she wanted? Ugly? "What?"

"The most beautiful ring I've ever seen." Harlow blinks, and I swear I see a sheen of tears in her eyes as she slides the band from the box.

It's a round center stone, about three carats, surrounded by a crown of smaller diamonds that add up to another carat combined. The band is thick, encrusted with three rows of diamonds, the two on either side small and flanking the stones in the middle that start at half a carat and incrementally graduate down to a quarter toward the bottom.

As I slide it on her finger, it fits perfectly.

"Oh, my god," she breathes.

Yes. It's that kind of moment. Chills roll across my skin. Now is important. This has gravity. I love seeing the mark of my possession on her hand. The view makes me harder than ever because now she's mine. "You like it?"

"It's extravagant." Harlow studies the ring, then peers at me, falling into my gaze. "I didn't need something this huge, but I love it." Her face clouds over. "I'll give it back when we divorce."

Like hell. "We're not even married yet. We can worry about those details later. Let's concentrate on setting a date. The sooner the better."

She barely misses a beat. "June tenth. That's in two weeks. We'll keep it simple."

Perfect. "I don't need anything more than for you to say 'I do,' baby."

"Huh. You need to do some doing, too, big boy." Her gaze wanders down my body, and she licks her lips. "Lose the shorts."

Harlow with determination and a plan is sexier—and scarier—than teary Harlow. I love both, but I'd always rather see her wearing that mischievous smile.

"Yes, ma'am." I scramble to my feet and doff everything I'm wearing, drinking in the sight of her tossed across my bed, naked and open, dark hair spilling, my ring glinting on her finger. "With pleasure."

She sighs as I lower myself on top of her again. My skin sizzles as our naked bodies meet. It feels as if it's been forever since I've really kissed or touched her. I'm dying to feel her all around me...but I don't want to rush. If I play this right, I've got the rest of my life to savor Harlow.

I twine my fingers with hers, locking them together. I want her so badly that I'm dizzy and sweating and about to climb out of my skin. But there's not a hint of anxiety now. I've got this part right. Now I just have to let nature take its course and hope that I can prove to her how happy we can be together so she'll never want to leave.

Pressing my lips against hers, I sink into everything Harlow—her scent, her flavor, her giving touch as she opens her mouth to me and welcomes me deep. Her taste bowls me over. I will never get tired of this, of her. In fact, I have a feeling I'm going to spend the rest of my life trying to catalog all the things about Harlow soon-to-be Weston that fascinate me.

Beneath me, she doesn't kiss like a woman who only wants sex and sperm. She makes love to my mouth with a moan, as if she's missed me fiercely, too. Clutching my hands tightly and curling her legs around mine, she seems to hug me with her whole body. I pour myself into her, with her for every peck, buss, and pucker, each slide of her tongue and catch of her breath.

I prolong the kiss, never wanting to let her go. She doesn't object or protest or try to hurry me along. I brush her hair from her face and press my lips to her cheeks, her chin, her nose, and her forehead. I hope she feels how much I adore her. I could tell her that I'm going to put her and our children—because there will be more than one—first. But she has no way of understanding a husband and father who both lives up to his responsibilities and keeps his vows. But I'll show her.

Soon, the lure of her scent draws me lower. There's a delicious pooling of that slightly floral vanilla smell between her breasts. Once I bury my face there and draw in a deep breath, my head whirls. Her breasts surround my head, and how do I not lave them with attention? I can't ignore those tempting, rosy tips. No way, no how.

When I slip one in my mouth, she rises up to me, all shallow breaths and exposed neck. She cups my head in her hands to hold me closer. My heart races. I don't even know how many women I've slept with in the past, but this grips me by the throat, by the balls...by the heart. She's a challenge. As my mother said, she's my equal.

My gut tells me she's my heart.

I switch my attention to the other nipple and give it a thorough working, gratified to feel it hardening even more against my tongue. Her breathing turns audible. Her body writhes as if she's desperate for more.

"Noah..."

"Yeah, baby?" I ask absently as I kiss my way down. At the flat of her belly, I linger and think about planting our child in her and watching him or her grow. I want that. I want to hold my son or daughter with Harlow by my side. I want forever.

But first I have to put my mouth on her pussy because her rich scent is filling my nose and flooding my bloodstream with raging need.

"Oh..." She pants. "God!"

As if she reads my mind, she spreads her legs under me, giving me complete access to the slick folds and feminine secrets in between. My oral fixation kicks me in the teeth, and I can't go slow. I shove her legs wide, sucking her clit into my mouth to tongue it while plunging my fingers inside her sweltering heat. She's like heaven, and I'd die from the pleasure of tasting her again if I knew I wouldn't be missing out on so much more of her.

Harlow is already close to the edge, hot and swelling, her flavor tangy and thick. I can't stop eating at her, taking her all in. I drag my hands down her body, gripping her hips and lifting her to my mouth, partaking as if I've never tasted anything sweeter. In my grasp, she arches and cries out. Her clit hardens. Her hands tighten around my head, plunge into my hair, and jerk, as if she can bring me deeper.

"Noah. Noah…" Her voice is a rising plea. She's right there, balanced on the edge, her body suspended under my hands and my mouth, ripe and ready and uninhibited. Then she bucks and screams my name. "Noah!"

Oh, fuck me. Harlow flows so sweetly, and I lap faster, deeper, dipping my tongue inside her as I work her stiff, screaming bud with my unrelenting fingers, wringing every last bit of pulsing ecstasy out of this orgasm.

When the tension in her body finally gives and she melts into the mattress with a sigh, I kiss my way up her body, dragging my lips up her abdomen, over one nipple before I lick my way across her jaw, then settle my lips over hers. In the same moment, I align the head of my cock and surge into her engorged opening with a groan of pleasure that tears from my soul.

God, I belong here. This is right. No, I probably won't get her pregnant tonight—what are the odds?—but I'm going to give it a hell of a try.

"Harlow, baby… I've missed you. You feel so good. Ohhh…" I grunt as I slide out and ease back in so slowly my back hunches and my toes curl.

She's not having any of my slow strokes. Under me, she lifts and swivels, encouraging me deeper, faster, harder. There's no way I can deny her. I have her beside me all night. I'll get hard again. I'll stay hard. I'll spend as much time filling her up as I can, tonight and every night she's mine.

Together, we set a savage pace, deep and fevered. I curl my fingers under her, grabbing her ass in my hands and bringing her to my hungry cock as I take her, teeth bared, with one hard thrust after another.

I'm not going to last. Jesus, it's been too long and she feels too good. When her nails dig into my back and her channel clamps down on me, I know she won't last, either. I'm praising any higher power listening as I plow into her, hips shaking, bed rocking, sweat pouring, swift and single-minded.

Under me, she breaks suddenly, jerking and howling out in a feminine growl of pleasure. I follow her seconds later, emptying every bit of my energy, soul, and semen inside her with a shout that makes my throat raw and my heart stutter.

After the sweltering bliss of release, I fall on top of Harlow with a sigh. She lifts limp arms around my neck. God, she's everything I didn't know I was looking for—sweet yet sarcastic, selfless yet standoffish. She will both keep me on my toes and make my life interesting. The last few years had seemed gray, shallow, lacking. I assumed it was the grind of football or knowing that retirement was on the horizon. But nothing changed inside me until I met Harlow. She's the sassy ray of sunshine I've needed.

Her lashes flutter open and she gives me a glittering green stare. "I think we should do this every night before the wedding and even more often afterward."

Yeah, maybe it's just about getting pregnant…but that's not what her eyes tell me. Something soft shines from her face. It's more than adoring. I'm thinking—hoping—maybe she's well on her way to being in love with me, too.

"You got it," I promise, hoping she doesn't change her mind.

CHAPTER THIRTEEN

A FTER A DAMN busy day, I'm feeling worn out but surprisingly accomplished. This morning, we stopped by my mother's place to tell her we're getting married. She beamed and hugged us both, oohing and aahing over the engagement ring. Then she nearly choked when we told her we plan to tie the knot in two weeks. Thankfully, she recently helped my sister organize her wedding and volunteered to do the same with Harlow. They're planning to get together tomorrow to launch into the details.

Both my mom and my fiancée—it's oddly thrilling to call her that— were ear-to-ear smiles. It did my heart good to see them together, looking excited as they discussed the ceremony that will begin the rest of my life with Harlow.

Then I called Trace and left a message for him. He's been scuba diving for the last six days with his buddies in some far-flung place in the South Pacific and probably won't have cell service until Wednesday, when he gets home. But he knows to call me once he reaches civilization again.

Then I dropped Harlow off at a bridal shop so she could scout out the wedding dresses. She refuses to wear the monstrosity her mother picked for her wedding to Simon, which is fine by me. While I waited, I walked the beach, cap pulled low. An hour later, she left the store grumbling that she didn't have six months to order a dress and nothing off the rack works for a short girl. She wants everything to be perfect on her wedding day. I'm taking that as a good sign. She didn't plan much of the aborted ceremony, but she wants to be in charge of this one. If our marriage was merely an exchange of a temporary wife for a baby, she wouldn't care half so much. I promise her my mom will have some ideas about the dress situation, and if worse comes to worst, my Aunt Lahela is one hell of a seamstress.

Once we arrived home, we intended to hit the gym downstairs and work out, but as soon as she appears in a small pair of black spandex shorts and some bra thing that's stretchy and tight across her breasts while leaving her midriff bare...iron isn't what I want to pump. We end up naked, entwined, shouting out our pleasure on the rubber floor.

Will today be the day Harlow conceives? That possibility excites the hell out of me.

"We should do that again. I want you to be convinced I'm giving you my full"—I slide out and thrust back in—"effort."

She pants out something between a moan and a laugh at my teasing. "I almost believe you. But maybe we should do it one more time so you can *really* persuade me...oh. Yeah. Just like that."

I thrust deep once more and Harlow's sentence melts into a moan. As we rock and grind, she clings to me, yet it feels as if she has fewer walls between us. Sex is one place we've always been in sync, and today we're even more together than yesterday.

Afterward, we realize we're running way behind if we're going to host her family for dessert at eight. But a quick shower becomes a quickie in the shower instead. I'm dressed and hauling ass downstairs as Harlow fiddles with a round brush and a blow dryer. The doorbell rings.

I open it to find Maxon and Keeley wearing big smiles and carrying a bottle of sparkling white grape juice and a carrot-pineapple bread with icing. Britta and Griff are right behind them with a passionfruit tea she recently discovered and chocolate Chantilly cake. After hugs all around, we set up in the family room. With everything they brought and the banana bread pudding Harlow made early this morning, I'm likely to end the evening in a sugar coma. I'm okay with that.

Before we cut into anything, Harlow runs back upstairs and returns clutching two large bags, then hands one to each of her sisters-in-law.

"What's this?" Keeley asks with delight.

"Just a little something to say congratulations." Harlow smiles.

She's fond of her sisters-in-law, and I see the gracious woman I've come to know, not the sad one who's envious and torn and defeated. Harlow is kind and thinks of others. Sure, she's human. I understood her hurt last night. I'm glad to see her on an even keel today. I'm even more relieved she hasn't changed her mind about the wedding or the baby. I hope some of that—whether that's her resolution or just me—is making her happy.

"You didn't have to get us—" Britta gasps. "Wait! Are you... Are you wearing an engagement ring on your finger?"

Harlow glances my way, and I grin at the crowd. "As a matter of fact, she is. I asked and she said yes."

Both Keeley and Britta jump to their feet, gifts forgotten as they share the joy of Harlow's good news with hugs. Maxon and Griff both shake my hand.

"You sure you want to do this?" Maxon teases. "My sister isn't easy to handle."

"She's not. But she keeps life interesting."

Griff shakes his head. "Said no man who wanted to stay sane ever."

I laugh and they welcome me into the family with a hearty backslap before turning to embrace Harlow.

"Congrats, little sister," Griff says with all sincerity.

"Thanks. I'll consider myself smarter than you since it didn't take me years to figure out that I should marry him."

"Yes, but I didn't almost walk down the aisle with the wrong person, sister dear. That was one hell of a wedding..."

"Yeah," Maxon agrees. "I love YouTube. I can see Simon's *oh-shit* face over and over. The moment he realizes he's completely screwed and publicly humiliated is particularly sweet."

"You never liked him." Harlow rolls her eyes.

"Nope," her older brother confirms. "Wanted to punch his boring, average face when we met because he wasn't there for you."

Griff nods in agreement. "Douche extraordinaire."

"Not to mention Dad's lap dog." Maxon grimaces. "You didn't need that."

I'm guessing they don't feel that way about me or they would be sporting more scowls than smiles.

"I'll do my best to make your sister happy," I promise as I slide my arm around her and pull her close.

"But you could help," Harlow insists, then slants a glance at me. "Noah and I haven't had time to talk about anything except a wedding date but...Maxon, I hope you and Keeley would let us have the ceremony at your place, on the beach where you and Griff both tied the knot. Is that okay?"

She seems to be asking me as much as she's asking her brother and his wife. They're enthusiastic, and I'm good with whatever she wants and whatever makes her happy.

"Absolutely," Keeley answers for them. "We'd love to host your wedding there. Maybe we'll make getting married on our lawn a new Reed family tradition."

Harlow laughs, then turns to me. "What do you say?"

"Sure, baby. I don't care so much where we get married as long as we do."

"Then it's settled. Thanks." She curls up against my side, flings her arms around me, and turns her face up for a kiss.

I can't remember another time she's invited my affection. She's never shy about initiating sex, and I'm down with that. But I'm always the one to give her a hug or a kiss that has nothing to do with getting busy. Sure, this might be for show, but her expression glows sincere.

I kiss her with a lingering brush. "You're welcome."

Before I can kiss her again, the other women hustle her to one side of the room and launch into wedding plans. Keeley and Britta both volunteer to help. Her brothers suggest the officiant they used. Texts start flying. Next thing I know, we have a florist to meet on Tuesday afternoon and a photographer who does stunning work booked. Thankfully, he had a cancellation and could slot us in. As we're discussing Britta's mother doing the catering with the help of a rented staff she's used for other events at Maxon and Keeley's resort, the doorbell rings.

Evan.

Celebrations have been dominating the conversation, but the sudden silence reminds us all why we're gathered.

Harlow stands and lets out a nervous breath. "I'll answer the door."

"I'll get it," I insist. "My face is the only one familiar to him."

Everyone nods collectively, acknowledging my point, so I head to the entryway and yank open the door to find Evan standing at the threshold. "Hey. Come in."

He gives me a curt nod, looking nervous, dressed in a sharp gray suit and perfectly polished wingtips. "Thank you for inviting me. Quite a place you have here."

I shrug. "Pro football paid well."

He doesn't say anything more, so I pull the door open wider. He turns and his stare falls on the gathering. Everyone is standing. Maxon and Griff come forward, hands outstretched, and introduce themselves.

"Happy to meet you in person," Evan murmurs.

Harlow hovers nervously behind them. "Hi. I guess…I'm your sister."

"It's nice to meet you, Harlow. I wish it was under less awkward circumstances."

She nods. "It's pretty weird to wake up one day and find out I have an adult sibling I never knew about."

He sends her a faintly apologetic smile. "I grew up knowing about you, but my mother's journals never mentioned Maxon or Griff. I don't know if she was in the dark or simply didn't have anything to say about them…"

"Well, we all have some catching up to do," Harlow says. "Come in. Sit. Do you want coffee, tea, or sparkling juice? How about dessert?"

"Coffee, please. Black. Nothing sweet, thank you." He takes in the gift bags and the cake. "Are you celebrating an occasion?"

Maxon and Griff exchange a glance before the younger brother nods proudly. "Our wives both recently learned they're expecting. This is Britta." After they shake hands, he turns to bring the redhead closer. "And this is Maxon's wife, Keeley."

"She's our resident songbird," Harlow puts in.

"Or karaoke addict. I'll own up to either one," she says with a self-deprecating grin.

Evan gives the ladies a stiff nod. "Congratulations."

"We're also celebrating the fact that Harlow and I got engaged last night."

"That's good news, Mr. Weston, Harlow."

"Noah," I correct. "No formality here."

"Noah, then. I can see why you're celebrating," he intones. "I hope you'll be happy together."

The words come out, but he looks bleak as hell.

"We'd love to have you come to our wedding," Harlow ventures. "If you're free."

I'm proud of her for opening up and including Evan, giving the brother she doesn't know a chance.

"Absolutely," I second and take her hand in mine. "We'd love to have you. We're doing this quickly, on June tenth."

"I'm available. I'll be there. Thank you." He relaxes in his seat, looking pleasantly surprised.

"And feel free to bring a date," Harlow adds. "If there's someone special, we'd love to meet her."

He sits up straight, his spine becoming a steel rod as his face closes up. "My wife and our unborn child died a month ago in a car accident."

The air leaves my lungs the same way it leaves the entire room. No one says a word, and I'm sure they're all as speechless as I am.

"Oh, god. I'm so sorry." Harlow finally breaks the silence as she races to Evan's side and enfolds him in a hug.

Her compassion warms me almost as much as her kind heart.

Evan's arms circle around her stiffly, as if he isn't used to comfort. As if he's allowing her embrace not because he wants it but because he doesn't want to risk hurting her feelings. He looks at me as if to ask if the hug meets with my approval. I nod, and something about the entire exchange pangs me in the chest. Jesus, what has this man been through? His dead eyes say that, in the blink of an eyes, his life has become pure hell.

Keeley and Britta are right behind Harlow, sighing and offering their condolences.

Maxon frowns. "I'm so sorry."

"We had no idea." I see the sheen of tears in Keeley's eyes. "I can't imagine—"

"You don't want to," Evan cuts in. "I'm sure you're all wondering why I've left Seattle suddenly and decided to put down roots in Hawaii. The truth is, my late wife encouraged me to meet you, Harlow, since we started dating at fifteen. I put it off. I didn't want to be the illegitimate kid who destroyed your fairy-tale family."

Maxon and Griff both scoff.

Harlow shakes her head. "Oh, no issue with that. Barclay Reed is a terrible human being and a worse father. You were better off, trust me."

He pauses, considering. "And I didn't want you to pity me for being the poor, orphaned bastard."

This man doesn't want anyone to feel sorry for him, ever—even in loss. He still seems uncomfortable with the ladies hovering near his personal space and offering their sympathy. I wonder how he's been coping with his grief over the last month. Does he have an outlet?

"We feel sorry for what you've gone through, but pity is in short supply in this family," Harlow says matter-of-factly. "We've all been through shit."

"Some that would make your blood curdle," Griff cut in.

Evan nods in acknowledgement. "I saw the YouTube video of your wedding, Harlow. I'm sorry your former fiancé lacked morals and integrity. You seem too nice for him."

"She is," Keeley assures.

"I'm better off without the ex," Harlow assures with a toss of her hand. "And much happier with the new model. My—our—father chose the last one, but I picked Noah."

Her possessive words warm me, and I press a kiss to her temple.

Britta lays a hand on Evan's arm. He freezes up, then visibly forces himself to relax.

"How can we help you?" Griff's soft-spoken wife asks. "Is there anything we can do to make your move or your first days on the island better?"

"Do you have a place to stay?" I ask.

"Thank you. I'm fine," he tells us. "My assistant, Nia, is coordinating the details of having my things shipped over. For now, I'm in a hotel. I'll find a place eventually."

"What are you looking for?" Maxon asks. "Griff and I are Realtors, so if you want to buy, we're happy to help."

The other guys fall into a conversation about areas around the island and debate the pros and cons of condo versus house, while the women start their own conversation about weddings and babies, punctuated by Keeley and Britta opening their gifts from Harlow—pretty pink boxes with a decorative water bottle, an anti-nausea wristband, energizing bath bombs, and a journal to capture the journey of their pregnancy.

After hugs among the ladies and some very practical talk about island housing, Evan stands. "Thank you for including me in the evening…and making me feel welcome."

The Reed siblings all get to their feet. Maxon sticks out his hand. "You're not alone. Come visit any of us at any time."

Keeley nods and gives him a business card with the details about their bed-and-breakfast. "If you need an ear or a song or a homemade cookie, stop by. There's always someone there."

"Britta and I would love to have you for dinner some night so you can meet your nephew. Jamie is nearly three."

"And he's all boy!" Britta teases. "Really, please come over."

"We're also looking forward to having you at our wedding," Harlow adds. "I'll text you the details. We're getting married too quickly for invitations, so that will be the 'formal' invite."

Evan takes a deep breath, looking overwhelmed but more at peace. "Thank you. Becca was right. I should have gone out of my way to meet you all sooner. I appreciate all your kindness and hospitality. I know it's odd to suddenly incorporate me into your family...but I'd like that very much."

With those words and a reserved nod, he departs, leaving us all in somber silence.

AFTER THE FAMILY heads home, Harlow is unusually quiet. She doesn't argue or twist away when I enfold her into my arms and pull her to bed with me. Though there's no one else in the house—or within a mile radius—she whispers to me. How sad she feels for Evan, how angry she is for thinking of herself while her brothers and their wives shared their baby news. Then she confesses how directionless she was feeling until she met me. From her, that's high praise, almost as if she's admitting that she needs me. I listen, murmuring my sympathy for all her half brother has lost and assuring her that she's being too hard on herself. Her feelings are real, and it's better to admit them and deal than to shove them down as if they never existed. Makuahine taught me that—or tried. The knowledge usually serves me well.

I fall asleep cocooned in deep contentment. I'm getting through the concrete around Harlow's heart...I think.

Either sleep did her a world of good or she's putting on a hell of a front this morning, because she's so chipper it almost makes my teeth hurt.

"Here's your green tea, sleeping beauty." She sets a mug on my nightstand, looking too beautiful for a woman who's probably been awake less than fifteen minutes. Her inky hair tousles around her slender frame, wrapped in a silky pink robe that ends at mid-thigh and reminds me why I think she has some of the most gorgeous legs I've ever felt wrapped around me.

I grumble, glancing dubiously at the mug. "There's not enough caffeine in that to wake up a gnat."

"I expected you to be grouchy. The first few days will be rough. I have all kinds of ways to help you cope. I've been doing a lot of research and I've learned so many awesome tricks. We'll get through this. Up! Time to get started."

With a groan, I close my eyes. "Aren't you getting together with my mother to talk about your wedding dress?"

"Not until two this afternoon. It's only eight now. So we have hours to figure out what relaxes you."

Oh, goodie.

"Sex?" I suggest.

"We'll get there. But I'd like to give some of these other methods a spin, see what works for you when you're alone, because I won't be in the broadcasting booth with you. And if I was, the NFL would get NC-17 fast."

She has a point.

With a sigh, I stumble to my feet. "I'm not fond of you right now."

Harlow laughs. "I'm sure you'll get over it. And if not..." She shrugs. "Well, you won't be the first person to dislike me. Is this the first time you're realizing I'm a morning person?"

I knew, but this seems like cruel and unusual punishment when I can't have coffee. "Ugh. Can you tone your smile down just a bit? It's blinding me."

My teasing makes her smile brighter. "Nope. Sexy ass up! Let's go. Hey, at least I'm not talking about PT. Yet."

"I'd prefer that." Because with Harlow's unpredictability, I never know what she'll do next.

"Ha! I'll remind you of that later. Drink your tea, toss on some comfy clothes, and get moving."

Grumbling, I put on a pair of gym shorts and a wife-beater. She's already opened the doors in the bedroom to the Pacific. It's going to be another beautiful day in paradise.

"You know, I'd be more relaxed after another hour or two of sleep."

She shakes her head. "First, you don't have any time to waste. Doesn't the network want an answer?"

They do, and she knows it. "Secondly?"

"If we're going to have a baby, buster, he or she won't give a shit when you want some z's. If we get pregnant quickly enough, you'll be able to help me through the first few weeks at least. Two a.m. feedings, colic, days and nights reversed… All the fun stuff."

Harlow sounds as if she's really looking forward to motherhood, even the not-so-fun parts. In truth, I'm looking forward to our kid, too.

"All right." I reach for the steaming mug that looks like moldy water or strained vomit. Green liquid just isn't appealing and the smell isn't fantastic. "Why green tea? Isn't black stronger?"

"Because it contains L-Theanine, which helps soothe the rough edges of anger or anxiety. It has a little bit of caffeine, but not what you're accustomed to, so we'll be supplementing with extra water to flush your system out and get you over the caffeine withdrawal faster."

I'm not looking forward to the headaches. Despite feeling grouchy, I know Harlow is going to a lot of trouble to help me. "Okay, I'll choke it down. Then what?"

"Choke? I wouldn't make you do that. I poured in some local honey, as well. Helps with any allergies you might have. Plus, it contains a compound that helps reduce inflammation in the brain, which may reduce depression or anxiety. And if you're feeling like you want to up your glam factor, it's also a natural skin moisturizer when applied topically. We can do masks later," she says with a wink.

"Pass." I give her a hard shake of my head that makes her laugh as I start sipping the tea. Surprisingly, it isn't terrible. "So if we're not having sex—and I protest that, by the way—what's next?"

"A healthy breakfast, including fresh mangos. They contain linalool, which helps reduce stress levels."

I love mangos, so I'm digging that. "Sounds good."

"Then we're going to try a few new things. But you have to hurry. We have less than thirty minutes before the first therapist arrives."

"First therapist?" What the hell does she have planned?

"You'll see. Hustle!"

With that, she's gone, her light footsteps resounding down the stairs before I hear her rattling around the kitchen.

Quickly, I brush my teeth and splash some cold water on my face. While the tea doesn't taste terrible, it's not jolting me awake like a good cup of steaming java. It's going to be a long day.

With a sigh, I head downstairs to find Harlow setting down a plate of scrambled eggs and sprouted-bread toast, along with a bowl of fresh sliced mango. She makes one for herself and we dig in, discussing wedding details. If she can find a dress, then we've got the major bases covered. We'll text invitations to a select few. I really don't want this to turn into a media circus, so the fewer people we advise, the less likely our nuptials will be crashed by the press.

I have to ask the question that's been lingering in the back of my head since she agreed to marry me. "What about your parents? Are we inviting them? I know your relationship isn't close…"

"I can't think of a reason I should. I know that probably sounds terrible to you, but if you met them, you'd get it."

"Shouldn't I do that before we tie the knot?"

"I'd rather spare you."

There must be one hell of a story here. I'd think she was exaggerating except that Maxon and Griff sounded equally anti-parent.

"I appreciate that, but I didn't ask you to. I'd like to get to know them." And draw my own conclusions.

I may never understand this woman unless I meet them. Other than our wedding, I don't know if I'll have an opportunity. As far as I know, they haven't reached out to Harlow since I met her, so unless it's an "occasion," I doubt they'll bother. It completely boggles my mind. I can barely go a day without talking to my mother. Harlow has gone weeks.

She drags in a breath and picks at her eggs. "They'll both try to take advantage of your money and celebrity. They'll figure out in two-point-two seconds what's in it for them and work like hell to exploit you."

It's such a harsh charge to level against the people who raised her. Harlow turned out all right. So did Maxon and Griff. I'm confused.

I set down my fork and snag her stare. "What happened? What did they do to you?"

"Besides being utterly self-centered? The list is long and ridiculous." She tosses her hands in the air. "It's ancient history. It's just...I know who they are. I'd never want them to look at you and see the means to climb a social ladder or make more money. Don't give them the chance."

I sigh, both touched and pissed off. On the one hand, Harlow is protecting me from people she thinks would try to use or harm me. It's sweet but unnecessary. I learned how to shed sharks and hangers-on years ago. Instead of worrying about the boo-boos I'd never let those people inflict on me—or her, ever again—I wish she would open up. I'm more convinced than ever that something terrible, something that altered her life and her psyche, happened at the hands of these people. Same with her older brothers.

I need to know what.

"Thank you, but I'll be fine. I still think we should invite them. They are your parents."

"My mother will try to take over everything."

"We'll tell her it's already planned. Then there's nothing for her to get her fingers in."

Harlow hesitates. "Maxon and Griff don't want to see them any more than I do. And what about Evan? What an awkward way to meet the birth father who never wanted him. And his wife, who despises the guy for nothing more than being born."

"Maybe. Or maybe it's the sort of occasion that supports family unity and they'll come together when they meet."

She snorts, then covers her mouth apologetically. "Sorry. It's just...

Really, you don't know them."

"I want to."

Her face closes up. "Why? If we're only going to get divorced—"

"What if we don't? What if we stay married, have children, and live happily ever after?"

She backs away from me. "I'm not the girl for that shtick. If you're peddling fairy tales, you should find Cinderella."

But I want Harlow.

I also want to understand what the hell made her need to protect herself. I'm more convinced than ever that her parents are the answer, and her brothers may be right when they say something happened during her first year in college. I'm going to dig until I get information, because her spirit is too bright and her heart too big to live behind barricades for the rest of her life. Unfortunately, I have to do it slowly, subtly, or she'll force more distance between us.

Why couldn't I have fallen for a simple girl?

Because a woman like that doesn't do it for me. Maybe that makes me an idiot or a glutton for punishment, but I love Harlow as she is— complexities and all.

"We'll talk about this later. Where are we taking this therapy next?" I slant my gaze out the window, pretty sure she'll pounce on the subject change. "The great outdoors look pretty gorgeous today."

"Maybe later. Finish up. Emil will be here soon."

"Who?"

"Your yoga instructor. Keeley swears by him, says she's taken a few of his classes. He doesn't usually work on a Sunday, but I told him that you required privacy and would pay well." She smiles. "Just an FYI, he's gay."

I shrug. "I don't care."

"Keeley seems to think you'll be his type."

"I'm taken," I point out.

Harlow breaks into a laugh as there's a knock on the door. "That must be him."

I wolf down the rest of my breakfast and turn to find a man in gauzy white capri pants, a black tank that shows off his ripped arms and shoulders, and a flashy smile. "Well, hello there…"

It's a long freaking hour after that. We clear off some space on the shady back patio and get down to posing. The only thing yoga reminds me is that I'm not a human pretzel. Holding my body in unnatural positions while trying to breathe isn't calming. Half the time, I'm not sure whether I should fend off Emil's flirting or beg him for mercy.

To his credit, I'm sweating at the end of the hour. He leaves me a paper with some stretches he wants me to work on until he sees me again on Tuesday—oh, joy—then with a wink and a flirtatious grin, he's gone.

"I don't like yoga," I say as soon as the door shuts behind him.

Harlow, who was way better at imitating Gumby than me, tsks. "You have to give it a try."

"I did."

"A real try. A couple of weeks at least."

She's attempting to help me. I keep that in mind. "Fine."

"Good. Now let's try some other hacks for relaxation I found. I was looking for strategies you can employ when you're in the booth and feel yourself getting wound up." She dashes across the room and opens the drawer, yanking out a box. "These are yours."

After a little wrestling, I open the package with a frown. "Squeeze balls."

"With helpful sayings." She pulls them from their slats, where they were nestled in cardboard. "See?"

The blue one says YES! I CAN DO THIS. BE QUIET. BE CALM. BE KIND is painted across the green one. The yellow one reads FOCUS. LISTEN. BREATHE.

"They'll fit in your suitcase when you travel. You should be able to slip one in a suit pocket without it being too conspicuous. It's perfect."

I'm not sure how much good squeezing a round bit of foam will actually do me, but she's doing her best. For her sake, I owe her the same.

I palm the blue one, giving it a firm mashing with my fingers. Actually…it's kind of tactilely interesting. "Sure."

"Oh, I forgot something else." Harlow dashes upstairs and returns moments later with a shallow rectangular box. "You should use this every day."

When I open the lid, I see a brown leather journal. It's well made and masculine but... "You want me to write down my thoughts and feelings?"

She nods. "I know what you're going to say: Why am I doing this? My brothers would laugh and complain this much reflection isn't alpha male enough for them, too. But hear me out. Since this is a new phenomenon for you, I think it behooves us to keep track of your mood, surroundings, and conditions when you start to have a situation that makes you feel panicked and start to shut down. If we're keeping track of everything, it's possible we'll find patterns and can help you avoid places or people that trigger you."

It sounds kind of horrible to spend time every day in self-reflection, but I guess not doing it is how I managed to waste months vacillating between denial and relative agony before I finally decided to do something. And it's taken extra time to pin down what bothers me and when it bothers me...and maybe she has a good point about being precise and helping myself avoid shitty situations.

"All right. I will see if I can find my deep-seated emotions or whatever will help me and put them down on paper."

"Thanks. If you try writing every morning, even just for five minutes, you'll feel better that you've purged anything that may be bothering you. If you still have residual tension after that and yoga, then you can squeeze your balls." She winks. "The foam ones. But hey, if you'd rather squeeze the ones between your legs..."

"Nope, I'm good."

She laughs. "I also have some aromatherapy candles on their way. Citrus scents should help calm you by increasing the amount of norepinephrine in your system. They're small, so you'll be able to take them with you to games if you need one. And if your peer in the broadcasting booth doesn't mind."

I can only imagine how many sportscasters and play-by-play guys will flat out laugh at my fruity candles. But you know… Fuck them if they would rather give me crap than help me succeed.

"Thanks, Harlow. Really. I'm not sure how much of this I'll like or will stick, but you're making me step outside my comfort zone to see what might make my life more livable. I appreciate that."

Her smile is slow and looks relieved. "You're welcome. I really do want to help."

"I know. I appreciate your effort." I take her hand. "I wish you'd let me help you, too."

Her mouth twists. "What do you mean?"

"Get you through whatever has convinced you that love isn't possible for you. That there's nothing more than sex and common goals between us."

She looks away. "We have other things to do today. I have this crossword app you can download, which should help divert your thoughts when you feel them seizing up. I also hear that getting a pet—"

"Harlow, listen." I take her shoulders in hand. "Nothing is more important to me than helping you."

"I'm fine. Besides, you don't owe me anything else. You're already paying me."

"I'm not trying to exchange favors here. I'm trying to open up your world so you can see what you and I have together is special."

Her eyes slide shut. "Don't go falling for me, Noah."

"It's too late." I swallow and go for broke. "I love you."

CHAPTER FOURTEEN

THE FOLLOWING MORNING dawns. I roll over, not surprised to find Harlow gone. I remember her beside me for at least a few hours. After the abrupt end of our conversation, she retreated outside with music and her earbuds. I didn't expect her to sleep beside me, but she did. And she woke me wanting to make love—fevered, clinging, silent. Emotion pinged off of her, vibrated in every touch. I wanted so badly for her to talk to me, for the intimacy to be a prelude to her admitting that she has feelings for me. Instead, she wordlessly shouted at me with her body. All I could do was hold her, tell her mutely that I'm here for her and hope she'd understand. Hope that she'd open up to me.

After the sex, I conked out, so I don't know if she slept the rest of the night beside me. I certainly don't know where she is right now.

I drag my ass out of bed and realize it's after nine. After a quick brush of teeth and groping around for some clothes, I jog downstairs. I don't hear anything—no music from the kitchen, no rattling around of pots and pans, no ethereal video game music. Hell, I don't even hear the ocean, which means she hasn't yet opened the patio doors. That's not like her. Downstairs, the lights are off, the blinds closed.

Harlow is nowhere.

Heart thudding, dread gripping me, I dash up the stairs, charging to the bedroom she used to occupy alone. Has she packed up and slipped out? Was I getting too close? Was it too much, and she decided to flee?

At the top of the landing, I thrust open the door to find her belongings exactly where she left them. The woman herself is sitting on a chair in the corner of the balcony, looking out over the mountains that rise up in the center of the island. With one hand, she's gripping the arm of the chair so tightly I wonder if she's using it to keep herself upright. I can't see what she's doing with the other.

"Harlow?" I ask cautiously.

Because something is wrong. Definitely, utterly wrong.

She jerks in acknowledgement but takes a long time coming to her feet and facing me. When she does, she's clutching something in her hand, pressing it against her chest.

"Baby?" I creep closer. I don't want to scare her, but something tells me not to leave her alone, either.

"Noah." She looks paler than normal. She looks stunned.

"I'm here," I assure her. "What's going on? Tell me and I'll—"

"I'm pregnant." Slowly, she uncurls her fist and shows me the home pregnancy test folded inside. A pink plus sits in the middle of the little window. "It's the third one I've taken."

When she glances over at her nightstand, I see two others sitting there. I rush over and grab them. One says the word PREGNANT in the middle of the stick. The other shows two thin lines in the viewing field.

Shock freezes me. If she said she was actually Minnie Mouse, I would have been less bowled over. How? When?

Carefully, I set the tests down. "We only started trying three days ago. Is there any chance Simon—"

"No. None." She licks her lips. "I'm guessing this happened weeks ago, after we ditched the condoms. I'd been taking the pill less than a week, but I was so early in my cycle that I never thought this could happen."

I blink, my thoughts racing. I wouldn't have guessed that was more than marginally possible, either. Clearly, we were wrong. And I'm totally fine with that. Inside, I want to do a crazy-happy man dance. We'll definitely still be together when this baby is born. I'll have at least a few months with my son or daughter. We'll bond as a family, and Harlow will see that I'll be here as a husband and a father.

Everything would be fantastic—hell, perfect—if she looked remotely happy.

"Baby, isn't this what you wanted?"

Slowly, she nods. "I just didn't expect... I realized on Saturday that my period was late by a couple of days. I didn't think much of it. The stress of everything that happened with Simon, all the stuff happening between us"—she shakes her head—"meeting Evan, focusing on your anxiety issues... There's a lot going on. Plus, introducing and stopping the pill in the same month was probably messing up my system, right? So this morning, I borrowed your rental and grabbed a test at the drugstore, just in case. When it came out positive, I wondered if it was wrong. It had to be. I hear they can be unreliable. So I ran out and grabbed two more— different brands—thinking that surely they would come out negative."

But they hadn't. She's in shock. Since we wanted to conceive, I don't know why she seems as if she's not processing this development with a huge smile and a celebratory whoop.

"I'm happy as hell they didn't." I risk reaching out to her and gripping her shoulders because she doesn't look as if she should be alone right now. "Harlow, we're going to have a baby. Our baby."

Finally, she meets my gaze. Tears well, and her eyes are green pools of worry. "I'm scared."

"Of what? I'm here. We're getting married in eleven days. Everything is perfect."

She swallows and nods slowly, but I can tell her brain is racing ninety to nothing.

"There's nothing else to worry about," I assure her, stroking her arms up and down.

She eases away from me and wraps her arms around herself, looking down and away. Looking anywhere but at me. "I didn't think I'd feel this way. I thought I was over...what happened. That I'd pushed all the bad memories aside. But...what if I lose the baby?"

I frown. I don't want to discount her fears, but I don't want her fretting over a mere possibility. Other things about her response disturb me, but I have to break this down one worry at a time. "You're healthy. We can start doing all the right things to ensure you keep this baby. We'll see a doctor ASAP and follow his advice to the last letter. There's no reason to think you'll miscarry. Is there?"

When Harlow blinks, tears roll down her cheeks unheeded. "It wouldn't be the first time."

With a sob, she falls to her knees.

Shock rolls over me as I kneel next to her and take her in my arms. "You had a miscarriage?"

For long moments, she can't answer me. Every soft cry and ragged pant that comes from her mouth and steals her breath stabs me in the heart. A thousand questions roll through my mind. I want to know. I *need* to know. But I wait until Harlow is ready to speak. She's fragile, and instinct tells me she'd ten times rather run away than divulge something this painful. The fact that she's reaching out for me, burying her face in my neck and holding me while she sobs, tells me she's trying. It tells me that, at least on some level, she trusts me.

"Yes," she finally manages to squeak out.

Dear god.

"How long ago?" Was it Simon's baby? Or someone else's?

"I had just turned nineteen when I found out. I didn't mean to get pregnant…"

Her first year of college. Maxon pegged the time frame right. I hope like fuck some frat boy didn't play games with her or seduce her and not give two shits when she had to deal with the consequences. "Oh, baby. I'm so sorry to hear that."

"It hurt."

Physically? Emotionally? "I know."

"You don't know. You can't! I wasn't even sure how I felt about the baby and before I could make up my mind…"

Her pregnancy ended. Her someone to love unconditionally was gone.

"I'm sorry. So, so sorry." It's not much but I don't know what else to give her now beyond my deepest apology and sincerity.

She dissolves into racking sobs. "I haven't spoken a word of it since the day I lost the baby."

Not once? She's bottled it up all these years? Yes, that's like Harlow. She shoved her pain down, which is why she still has unresolved feelings years later.

And she chose to tell *me*. That speaks volumes. So does the fact she's already worrying about this baby. Harlow is older now, her situation more stable. We're going to be fine. Great, even. She'll be a fantastic mother. I'll be the kind of father my dad was before he passed away. We'll have a happy, wonderful life. If I can help her heal.

First, I have to calm her down. "Harlow, deep breath. This isn't good for you or the baby. You have to relax for me."

She nods...but the agony of her sadness lingers thick between us, echoing in every one of her cries. I try to soothe her, rub her, whisper to her and reassure her. Nothing.

Finally, I take the pregnancy test from her hand and kiss the top of her head. "I'll be right back."

Rushing around the house, I gather everything I think might help her. Within minutes, I dump an armful of stuff in my bedroom, then head back to hers, scoop her up, then lay her in the middle of the bed.

When I ease back, she grabs me tighter. "Don't go."

My heart stops. She never wants me to see her vulnerability, but now she's not only allowing me to stay while she's falling apart, she's begging me to. "Oh, baby, I'm not leaving you, just setting up a few things to make you more comfortable."

With a nod, she releases me and sniffles, trying to stop her tears.

Dashing around the room, I light the citrus candles she found to help me. I downloaded an album of all the soothing atmospheric music from the video game she's been playing and I meant to surprise her when the time was right. As much as I'd love her delight, I'd far rather see her calm now.

As the strains of the wind instruments fill the room, I put the happy yellow squeeze ball in her hand and read it. "Focus. Listen. Breathe."

"What if I lose this baby, too?" she asks, eyes so full of worry and misery that my heart breaks.

I caress the hair from her face. I still have so many questions about her previous miscarriage. Now isn't the time. "We'll try again. We'll see the doctor, find out if there's anything else we should be doing. I'll take care of you. I'll stay here and hold your hand and tell you every single day how happy I am that you came into my life because I always knew I had the capacity to love...but I never knew I would fall for someone as perfect for me as you."

A fresh wave of tears racks Harlow. "You're ruining me."

The words sound like an accusation, but I hear surrender in them. I feel it when she flings herself against me. With those words, she's admitting something. She's opening doors between us.

"You ruined me the night we met," I admit softly.

Harlow jerks back. "I'm not that girl. I won't make an idiot of myself over a guy. I don't cling."

She's so adamant, I immediately back down. "You're never an idiot and you don't cling. But if you lean on me for support when you need it every now and then, there's nothing wrong with that, baby."

Somehow my soothing tone seems to have the opposite effect. "I don't commit, damn it."

Because she's afraid to.

I take her by the arms and pull her against me. "You didn't in the past. I don't know what happened with the guy who got you pregnant so young, and you don't have to tell me until you're ready. Maybe he left you when he found out. I don't care about him. But I love you. You're having *my* baby now. And I'm staying. Get it through your head that I'm not the guy from six years ago. I'm a man who understands responsibility and knows what he wants. I want you and our family, Harlow." I slide one hand down to her still-flat belly. "Try to believe in me. In us."

"I don't know how," she admits with a whimper, crying against my chest.

Her admission breaks my heart. She doesn't trust much of anything or anyone—not her parents, not the institution of marriage, definitely not the father of her unborn baby because that ended badly once before. But she wants to trust me. She hasn't run away. She's beginning to tell me her truth and give me her pain. It's more of her heart than I had yesterday.

"I'm patient. I'll help you figure it out. I'll show you that I'm not like your father. I'm not like the guy who knocked you up and ran out. We're getting married, and I'm here."

"For a year," she mumbles, sounding as if that fact makes her miserable.

Telling her again that I love her or want to be with her forever won't work. They're words. For all I know, someone else told her those same things before he turned out to be an asshole of the highest order. Actions speak louder, and I'm going to have to find a silent way to shout my love.

"For at least a year. If I have my way, it will be forever." When she opens her mouth to speak, I lay a finger over her lips. "Don't say anything. Don't argue. And don't tell me I don't know what I feel. Just let the words sink in. Repeat them to yourself a few times. Remind yourself what I said when you feel worried or alone. If you do it enough, maybe you'll start believing that I mean what I say. If not, I'll show you every day that I do. But one way or another, I'm going to convince you that we're meant to be together."

THE FOLLOWING DAY, Cliff begins buzzing my phone at six a.m. I really have to introduce him to the concept of time zones and that mine is six hours behind his.

Groping around on my nightstand, I reach for my cell, gratified to see Harlow still slumbering beside me. After hoisting myself up and snagging my shorts from the ground, I exit the room and press the device to my ear.

"Hi, Cliff. Why the fuck are you calling so early?"

"I know it's morning."

"The sun isn't even up yet. I shouldn't be, either." I sigh. Cliff wouldn't call without a reason, and I should get down to it instead of bitching at him. "What's going on?"

"It's the network. Mercedes Fleet keeps giving interviews…and she gave one that ran this morning with the 'intimate' details of your hookup."

"The one that never happened? She's making this shit up out of her head."

"There are witnesses who said they saw you go into a bedroom with her…"

"I didn't," I swear. "I've never met her. I would remember doing her if I had, so those people have faulty memories or are being paid to remember incorrectly."

"It's your word against hers, man. And I have to tell you, right now it doesn't look good."

"I want a DNA test. That will prove I'm telling the truth."

"That was going to be my next suggestion…if you're really sure you never—"

"Ever. I did not touch her. I want this test ASAP so I can prove to the world that I'm being straight-up honest."

"I understand. We'll have our legal team reach out to her and start the negotiations to have a NIPP test conducted. She's more than eight weeks pregnant if she conceived when she says she did. But it will still take a week to get the results once her blood is drawn. In the meantime, the network is nervous. Mr. Chickman—remember him, the president, COO, and executive producer—is seriously considering retracting the offer. I've spent all morning talking him out of it. You need to accept now."

I can't. Sure, Harlow and I have a plan in place to keep my anxiety in check and we'll be following up with a doctor later this week, but I'm not ready to commit to the job. I'm still not certain I can even do it. Nothing like failing miserably on a really public stage… There's no coming back from that.

"When I'm ready, Cliff. Not before."

"Goddamn it, Noah. I worked for months to broker this deal and it's about to dissolve under your feet like quicksand."

"Then maybe it wasn't meant to be." Saying the words is like stabbing myself in the chest. I love football. I miss football. I'll be gutted when July rolls around and training camps start in earnest without me. I fucking want this job. If it weren't for my unpredictable loss of speech, I would have agreed to the deal weeks ago. It's sweet and right up my alley. "I have a lot of things going on here."

"Like what? What's more important than this gig you practically begged me to secure for you?"

I feel like a shit to keep secrets, but I skip telling Cliff about my issues. He's professional and really good at his job, but I don't want a word of this breathed to the network, even inadvertently. They will worry. And there will be leaks. No thanks. I just want my problem solved so I can accept their offer and move on.

"Why are they in such a hurry to get this done? I don't need to be in a booth for months."

"That's what I've been telling you. This shit with the pregnant hookup has them worried about your image. The NFL has had its share of…let's say less-than-sparkling domestic relationships in the press."

I know that. It's been a black eye on the league for a while. "Look, the thing that's more important right now than saying yes to this job is the very thing that should make them feel better. I'm getting married." I don't mention the baby just now. It will make his head spin.

"What? That brunette you've been seen with on the island?"

"Harlow. Yes. We haven't made any announcements because we don't need the press crashing our wedding. It's going to be small and quiet. We'll send out a press release after the ceremony. I'll text you details if you want to come to Maui for the event."

"You're important to me, Noah. I'll be there. You know, I think this is a great strategy. She's educated and beautiful and you look good together. She'll be an asset and she should make the network feel better about your hound-dog ways. Smart move, buddy. Glad you thought of it."

Cliff seems happier, so I don't bother arguing with him about my reasons for marrying Harlow. He's not a hearts-and-flowers sort of guy, so if I tell him I'm deeply, truly, madly in love, he'll simply snort and tell me that it's a great shtick.

"I try. Let the network know that we've spoken that and you're satisfied I'm not going to be an image problem for them."

"Will do. It would help if you reacted publicly to Ms. Fleet. She keeps running off her mouth to anyone who will give her press and you haven't said anything beyond the brief statement you let me issue denying her claim."

"I don't think we should say anything more until the results of the DNA test come back. Why give her the attention she's seeking with this stunt and encourage her to double down? After the prenatal paternity test results, I'll have plenty to say."

"All right." Cliff sighs. "I hope like hell that woman's blood proves you right. I'll see about asking Mr. Chickman to be patient. Can I tell him you're getting married?"

I grit my teeth. "If you have to. If nothing else will save this deal. But I'd rather keep Harlow's name out of the press for as long as possible, and I fear that if we give the head of a sports news organization exclusive information about my upcoming wedding, it will become a circus."

"True. I'll do what I can. Don't forget to send me the details about your ceremony."

"You got it. Hold Chickman off a little longer, and this will work out. I believe that."

CHAPTER FIFTEEN

D AYS RUSH BY, and I'm finally able to wake up with one thought resounding through my head: It's my wedding day.

The last week and a half has been a whirlwind of activity. My mother and Harlow's sisters-in-law got together to design a wedding dress for my bride that I'm assured fits her style perfectly. My aunt dropped her life to make it in record time. I own a tux, but asked Trace and Harlow's brothers to stand up with me, so they've rented theirs to match. She asked one of her sorority sisters, as well as Keeley and Britta to be her brides-maids. It's a sunny, breezy day. Not a cloud in the sky.

I wish I could say everything was perfect, but I've got some worries. Since discovering that she's pregnant, Harlow's mood has been day to day. She's happy at times, and our visit to the doctor was full of smiles. She seems a little anxious about losing the baby still, especially late at night when she's tired and asks herself if she should be slowing down. She can be moody first thing in the morning, which evens out as soon as we start journaling, doing yoga, and engaging in other visualization or breathing exercises. The best thing? She wants sex. All. The. Time. It's so awesome that I'm more than happy to deal with whatever mood Harlow is in because she's always putting a smile on my face.

But other issues in life still hang over my head. Mercedes Fleet came forward with a list of demands mere days after Harlow discovered she was pregnant. Through lawyers, I saw her ridiculous list of "must-haves." I placated her until she finally agreed to that damn DNA test. Interesting that she dragged her feet… But yesterday, she finally gave a blood sample. Within a week, I'll be off the hook. Harlow and I haven't talked about the whole mess any more. I don't know whether she believes I didn't get that woman pregnant. The worry niggles at the back of my head.

The last complication is her parents. Harlow finally agreed to let them attend the ceremony. Maxon texted their mother with the details last night. Griff contacted their father. I'm curious about why they each chose a parent to interact with, but they must have their reasons. In both cases, her parents said they would be there but they didn't appreciate the short notice or being unable to bring their current significant others. That was another one of Harlow's demands. They also won't be participating in the ceremony.

"You ready, man?" Trace barges into the bedroom at Maxon and Keeley's utterly charming bed-and-breakfast. We have a gag order on all guests and staff for the big event, but we'll release pictures and information afterward.

I wonder if my soon-to-be brother-in-law and his lovely wife have any idea that this will thrust their sleepy, burgeoning little business into the spotlight and that they'll soon be busier than they imagined. Smiling to myself, I turn to my brother as I zip my fly. "Just have to put on my shoes. Hey, could you give this to Britta to give to Harlow before the ceremony?" I found a beautiful necklace with three diamonds—one for me, one for her, one for the family we're creating. "Tell her it's my wedding gift and I'd love for her to wear it during the ceremony."

"Sure." Trace takes the box from me, then reaches into his tuxedo jacket to pull out a flat rectangular package wrapped in tissue paper with a colorful red and silver bow. "This is from Harlow, for you."

I tear into the delicate wrapping and find a picture of the two of us taken last week when we barbecued with her family at my place. The sun slants over Harlow, lighting her up as she tosses her arms around me and kisses my cheek. I'm smiling from ear to ear. Her engagement ring glints in the golden shimmer of light. We look damn happy. Even better, the frame around this image is made of gorgeous sun-bleached wood and engraved with the words TOGETHER IS A WONDERFUL PLACE TO BE.

I hold the gift tight in my fist and choke up, hoping like hell this is her way of saying she loves me. Because she hasn't said that out loud. "Tell her I said thank you."

Trace claps me on the shoulder. "You picked a good woman. I wish I could meet a woman half as awesome as Harlow."

"You will," I assure my brother. He's a good guy, after all. "How are things looking out there?"

"Gorgeous. Keeley and Britta have this wedding shit down. And the officiant is a dead ringer for Uncle Ano, right down to the big belly and straggly beard." Trace laughs. "Both men had a chuckle about that. The flowers are beautiful. The photographer is ready. The cake looks scrumptious. And your bride seems nervous but...man. Your jaw is gonna drop. She's gorgeous."

I wish like hell I could talk to Harlow and reassure her, but Keeley and Britta have been uber-protective and determined to maintain that damn tradition of the groom not seeing the bride before the wedding.

"I can't wait. Let's do this."

"Cool your jets, brother. You've got ten minutes. But it's just adorable to see you so eager," he pokes fun at me, then claps me on the shoulder. "Congratulations. I know your life with Harlow will be happy."

I try not to remember that she's still talking divorce in twelve months. I'm going to move heaven and earth to keep her beside me and so ecstatic she'll never want to leave.

"Thanks, man."

As I pack the picture and frame she gave me in my duffel, Trace leaves to deliver my gift. Time is tick-tocking with the speed of frozen molasses. I double-check my pockets to ensure that I have everything I need for my plans at the reception. I don't know her parents or what exactly they've done to her, but the necklace I gave her was a simple token. The real wedding gift I'm hoping to arrange is one intended to give her long-term peace of mind.

When I speak my vows, I'll be promising to love, honor, cherish, and protect Harlow. I take that seriously.

Finally, Maxon and Griff wander into the room.

"You ready?" Griff asks. "Palms sweating?"

I'm cool and ready to bounce. "Nope. Just impatient."

Since I've got a few minutes before the ceremony, I decide to share my plan. I want their approval, especially since I realize this will affect them, too.

"So…I want to give Harlow peace. She's been through a rough couple of months."

"What do you have in mind? Extended honeymoon?" Griff winces as if the thought of what we might do on said newlywed getaway is painful to consider.

"Not exactly, no." I blow out a nervous breath. "I don't know all the details, but I think you were right. Your parents might be part of her problem."

"Told you," Maxon returns.

"I had no doubt." Griff shakes his head, his face tight with loathing.

Relief that they're listening winds through me, and I warm to my subject. "Since I don't know if she'll truly be able to feel peace until they're gone from her life, my plan is to make them go away."

Maxon grins. "If Harlow doesn't already love you madly, she will after this, I suspect. My mother will jump if you offer her money. My dad is playing a shell game with the bulk of their wealth, and I think she's panicking that she will wind up virtually penniless when the ink dries on their decree."

"And aww…her boy toy will go away and use his penis to bilk some other woman old enough to be his mother out of her divorce settlement." Griff rolls his eyes. "What a shame."

The younger Reed brother really doesn't like his mother. No doubt, there's one hell of a story there.

"Dad is less motivated by money," Maxon spits. "He loves it, but he's far more interested in pussy. And avoiding public humiliation. Hey!" His eyes light up. "I could tell you a few stories you could threaten to spill to the press. Anonymously, of course, so it doesn't come back to you. It's verifiable information. Throw in a hooker or two, and he'll probably go quietly. Most of Harlow's life he said he didn't have use for a 'splittail.'"

I haven't even met this man and I seriously want to punch his face. I want to make him feel the pain Harlow has felt, which he clearly never bothered to care about.

"Lay it on me. I'm happy to use whatever you can tell me."

Maxon's grin is full of glee as he fills me in on Barclay's sexual exploits with secretaries, employees…and the daughters of some of his best friends. He has to talk fast because it's a lot, but by the time Trace sticks his head in the door with a thumbs-up, I've heard enough to nail this bastard to the wall. And I can't wait.

I head out to the makeshift altar—a huge arch wreathed in a burst of colorful tropical flowers. The ocean roars at my back, and there's a simple white runner between two rows of chairs on the front lawn, overlooking the beach. About twenty people are gathered to witness the ceremony to be presided over by a guy who really does look like my uncle Ano. My family fills one side of the seating. Harlow's side is virtually empty, so I don't have to guess who her parents are. They're sitting in the front row three chairs apart, looking somewhere between uncomfortable and disdainful. Assholes. Everyone else—even my agent, Cliff, who never celebrates anything—looks excited to be witnessing our happiness unfold.

I feel at peace. I know the next year won't be easy but I'm all about seizing opportunities. Harlow *will* be mine for the rest of our lives.

As soon as I'm in place with Trace at my side, the piped-in music stops and Keeley walks up the aisle, bouquet in hand, beaming. She sets her flowers aside and grabs the mic that's been arranged up front. Her beautiful, almost haunting voice fills the air around me with a vaguely familiar tune. I know I've heard it on the radio, but I can't place it. I wish like hell I could when Keeley sings of today being the first words of a lifelong love letter. When she belts out the lyrics "I choose you…" I start humming along with the Sara Bareilles tune.

Harlow's friend Kiaria strolls up the aisle in an azure dress that clings to her arms just off the shoulder and molds to her delicate curves. Britta proceeds down the aisle next in a similar dress in a complementing shade of blue.

Keeley finishes the song, then falls into place near the rest of the bridal party, mic still in hand. We left Maxon's bride in charge of the music and so far she's chosen fantastically well.

When the next song starts, I know right away it's "I Will Follow You Into the Dark" by Death Cab for Cutie. It's an unusual choice, but Keeley's delivery of the lyrics is emotional, her voice caressing every note and wrapping it in something special before she moves on to the next. I look across the lawn, back toward the house, breath held as I wait for Harlow.

It seems to take an eternity, but I finally see her come toward me in a flowing white dress that hugs her slender waist and ruffles at the shoulders before crossing in a gentle *V* above her cleavage. A flower at her hip where the fabric gathers gives way to waves of white chiffon waterfalling down to pool around her feet. The diamonds I gave her glitter and sparkle at her neck, making her look every bit as feminine as the white lily tucked behind her ear, bright against her raven hair. I nearly choke at how beautiful she looks. How radiant. I've cried very few times in my life—my father's funeral, my first Super Bowl win...and today. Seeing Harlow come toward me, willing to give me potentially the rest of her life, hits me square in the chest.

"You should see your face," Trace leans in and whispers. "You love that woman."

I don't answer, just smile. Yeah, I do and I don't care who knows it. And as Harlow comes closer, I see her glowing, her gaze fixed on mine. The windows to her soul look wide open. Tears perch on her lash line, threatening to spill, but the happy curl of her lips makes her expression infinitely sweet. I'd love to freeze this moment in time, so ripe with hope, and stay forever.

The song ends after the first verse when Maxon and Griff deliver their sister into my hands and I curl my fingers around hers. The men join

Trace, and the officiant in the vest with the loud Hawaiian shirt underneath welcomes everyone to the beginning of our lifelong union of happiness.

Harlow glances my way again, and our gazes connect. The ground staggers beneath my feet, and I turn dizzy, a little sweaty. She can read me, so she squeezes my hands and raises her shoulders as she inhales before slowly letting the air leave her, encouraging me to follow along. After a few breaths, it helps and I feel calm flow over me again. I'm going to speak my damn vows today. Nothing will stop me.

The ceremony is everything I imagined, and it seems as if I've barely had time to blink before we're sliding rings on each other's fingers and being pronounced man and wife. Harlow smiles up at me before she leans closer and her eyes slide shut. I wrap my arms around my wife—it feels awesome to call her that—and kiss her with all my heart, silently telling her that it's the first day of the rest of our lives together.

When we break apart, I raise our clasped hands above our heads with a whoop. Our guests cheer—except for her parents. I ignore them as we race back down the aisle and head toward the massive tent set up on the other side of the wide yard.

Inside the reception site, a champagne waterfall flows, the cake is ready to cut, the deejay is already grinding out celebratory tunes. I hold my wife close before the rest of the wedding party arrives. "Hello, Mrs. Weston."

She raises a brow at me. "How do you know I haven't changed my mind? Maybe I want to go by Reed."

I know she's teasing me since we discussed this. Well, I insisted she change her name. It's the only thing I asked for. If she feels as if she's belonged to me from the beginning of our union, I'm hoping she'll find it easier to stay for the rest of our lives.

When I growl at her, she laughs. "Gotcha, Mr. Weston."

"That's husband to you."

With a nod, she moves in for a kiss that's sweet and slow and full of promise. "So…husband, how long do we have to stay here and make nice before we can get out of these clothes so we can get sweaty together?"

"Still can't get enough of me after this morning? And last night?"

"Never," she says softly.

God, I must be smitten because all I can do is hold this woman close and kiss her breathless.

"Hey, get a room," Maxon shouts as he, Trace, and Griff enter the tent, Keeley and Britta beside them.

I give him a good-natured laugh. "So the day you got married, you wanted to shake hands and dance and mingle without any thought of being alone with your bride whatsoever?"

He scowls. "Shut up."

With a rosy blush, Keeley laughs. "He's often surly, but that day… I swear he was barely civil to guests about two hours into the reception. I had to coax him into cutting the cake before he grabbed me by the hand and led me off to the bedroom."

Everyone laughs as more guests fill in. I introduce Harlow's siblings and their wives to my family, and they all start chatting immediately. Everyone seems to get along, find something in common, despite coming from really different places and backgrounds. I couldn't ask for more.

Then Barclay and Linda Reed creep into the tent, glancing around, looking extremely out of place. As soon as Harlow spots them, she tenses.

"Relax. It will be all right," I assure her.

"They're going to make a scene. Because we planned everything without my mother, she will criticize every bit of this ceremony. She expresses her hurt by hurting others. My dad… I have no idea how he'll retaliate, but it won't be pretty."

I lead her to a quiet corner and take both her hands in mine. "I want to give you another wedding gift."

Harlow immediately touches the necklace at her throat. "You don't have to get me anything. This is already more than I need. It's so beautiful, by the way. Thank you."

"You're welcome. But I want to give you something you *really* want. The thing is, you have to tell me if you can live with it. Because once it's done, it will be damn hard to undo."

She frowns. "What do you mean?"

"I can make your parents leave you alone for the rest of your life, probably your brothers, too. They're okay with my idea. If you don't want them in your life ever again, all you have to do is say the word."

Surprise transforms her face. "Really? It's so...sudden."

"I know. So if it's not something you want, I won't do it. If it is, then I'll make it happen."

"That's going to cost you a fortune, I already know. I can't let you—"

"Money isn't the issue. I don't care how much I have to drop if having them out of your life will give you peace of mind."

Harlow's face fills with emotion, with gratitude. Lips trembling, brows knitting, cheeks turning red, she looks seconds away from crying. "You don't even know what happened with them. Why would you do this for me?"

"Because they're the kind of parents who weren't there for a nineteen-year-old girl who needed their help. And because I love you. My job now is to make you happy, and I intend to do it so well you'll never want to leave."

Tears roll from her eyes and down her cheeks. "It probably sounds terrible because they're family and we're supposed to stick together. But that's not the sort of parents they've ever been. I don't want them anywhere near our son or daughter, and I'd be forever grateful not to have to see them again."

I'm relieved that I read her right and she's not offended by my offer. "I have paperwork and a checkbook. I'll take care of it."

The tent fills up quickly after that. We eat dinner, toast our union, cut the cake, have our first dance. Every time I see one of Harlow's parents trying to approach her, I whisk my wife into another conversation or activity. It doesn't escape my notice that Linda Reed has spoken to no one, as if she finds all these people beneath her, even her own daughters-in-law. Barclay has ignored everyone at the reception except my agent, Cliff. Clearly, Harlow's father has figured out that my professional right hand can open doors and he's determined to fast-talk and suck up until Cliff gives him the time of day.

Hours have passed, and it looks as if Harlow's parents are getting seriously annoyed that they have had no part of the ceremony and have not been given a moment of the bride's time. Other guests have finally found their own fun on the dance floor and have stopped making friendly overtures toward the standoffish couple.

That's when I approach them alone at their table. "Mr. and Mrs. Reed, I'm Noah Weston."

Barclay stands, all charm and smiles. "Our new son-in-law. Welcome to the family. We're glad to have you and if you're making our little girl happy—"

"I plan to. Let's take a walk. It's loud in here, and I'd like to talk to you."

"Sure. Anything. And if you're ever looking for business opportunities, I know some amazing venture capitalists—"

"I'll take that under advisement." As I step to the opening of the tent, Barclay and Linda follow me. I gesture them out to the breezy Hawaiian evening, glancing back at Harlow nestled between her two brothers, looking at me with her heart in her eyes.

With a nod, I exit out the flap and lead her parents toward the parking lot. They're going to leave as soon as we're done talking. I'll insist on it.

"What can we do for you, son?" Barclay asks.

That's something I *never* want him to call me again. My dad was the most selfless, loving man I've ever known and I can't imagine how Maxon and Griff have learned to become good men with this self-serving shitbag as a father. "I'd like to make you an offer."

Barclay is all smiles. "Love to hear it."

When I glance Linda's way, she curls her artificially enhanced lips up as much as the Botox allows and wraps her bony fingers around my arm, eyes widening as if she's an ingénue, not a cougar. "We're definitely all ears."

"Excellent." I work myself loose from Linda's grip. In no way, shape, or form do I want to give that woman any idea that I'm interested in her overtures. "Harlow would like peace and happiness in her life. It's come to my attention these are two things you've never cared whether she's had in the past. That changes now. Mr. Reed—"

"Barclay, please. Harlow has misrepresented her childhood, I'm sure. She had the best of everything—schools, clothes, cars. The truth is, she suffers from a bit of leftover teen angst."

It's all I can do not to call bullshit as I throttle the asshole. "I tend to believe my wife. She desires your absence from her life. In exchange—"

"That's absurd," her father insists. "We had no intention of barging in on her honeymoon. Of course we'll give her a few weeks of privacy while she settles into married life."

"Exactly." Linda sends her soon-to-be ex-husband a sidelong glance as if she's reading him so they can plot, then sidles closer to me again. "We were thinking that we should have a lovely cookout for Fourth of July. Or perhaps later that month we can celebrate my birthday together as a family."

"No. She desires both of you absent for the rest of her life."

"What?" Linda looks shocked and perplexed. "What stories has that silly girl been telling you?"

I know of few women who are less "silly" than Harlow, and her mother's question only pisses me off more.

"Details are unpleasant and unnecessary. Let's get down to business. Mrs. Reed, if you'll sign an agreement to walk away from Harlow and abide by it, I'll give you five million dollars—evenly divided over the next ten years."

The woman's blue eyes widen with a gasp. She licks her lips, looking nervous.

"Linda…" Barclay growls in warning as if he knows she'll be tempted.

She ignores him. "You'll put that in writing?"

"I've already got it right here." I extract the agreements I had drafted, which are sealed in envelopes. "If you sign tonight, I'll give you a twenty-five-thousand-dollar bonus."

"No," Harlow's father answers for his estranged wife.

"Yes," she snaps defiantly, then whirls on him.

"We value family too much."

She scoffs at his clenched-teeth assertion. "When have you ever given two shits about your children unless they could somehow help you? Never." The woman turns to me. "I'll take it."

"I forbid it," Barclay insists, fists clenched.

That makes Linda laugh. "You don't have that power anymore. If I want to escape you, I need money, you tight-fisted bastard. Our new son-in-law has just given me the means to say sayonara to you forever. I'll see you in court, of course. After all, I helped you make most of that money and spent more than one evening on my back with your sweaty colleagues to make deals happen, so I'm entitled to half."

Holy shit. Linda isn't exaggerating, either. Not if Barclay's face is any indication. That's how much this man wanted money and power, enough to whore out his own wife?

"Prenuptial agreement, remember?" The man smiles acidly.

"It's ancient," she insists with a stomp of her foot.

"But binding."

"We'll see. In the meantime, I'm taking Weston's money and spending my life with Marco, a *real* man who gives a damn about someone besides himself."

"He'll give a damn about you as long as you have cash, Linda. As soon as it's dried up, so will his affection."

"You don't know anything about us." She turns back to me. "Where do I sign?"

"It's not quite that simple," I say, glad the bickering twosome finally gave me an opening. "Mr. Reed—"

"I don't need your money."

"You don't." I nod. I've had this guy investigated over the past couple of days. He's got a healthy bank balance to go with his rotting heart. "But as I understand it, you're about to close on big deal with some slightly reluctant owners of a lucrative family-owned business. Great product, by the way. With the right exposure, it will take off and make everyone millions. You have an obviously good nose for business."

"I do, which is why if you stop listening to whatever nonsense Harlow is spouting, you'll see that you and I can make serious bank together and—"

"How would an openly religious family feel about knowing that you have a nasty predilection for seducing your very young secretaries and getting them pregnant? How would they feel about knowing you have two illegitimate children and another on the way?"

"You have no proof!"

"I do. Evan Cook bumped his DNA against Maxon's. We have the test results. I'm also in the process of tracking down your other daughter, Bethany, right now."

"That was decades ago. I'll tell them I'm a born-again man."

"Well, I also have a sworn statement from one of your more recent assistants, Liselle. She signed an affidavit that you hired her at twenty and had her pregnant a few months later. You fired her when she had an abortion and refused to warm your bed again. You're on the verge of settling her lawsuit, aren't you?"

"You bastard! What do you want?" He flushes red, green eyes flaring as if he'd like to get violent.

But Barclay is too smart for that. As much as it clearly chaps him raw, he knows I'll annihilate him if he throws down.

"I want you to sign an agreement that, in exchange for my silence on this matter, you'll never speak to Harlow again unless she makes a written overture to you first, which I will have to approve and have my lawyers vet. This offer is only good tonight. If you leave the reception before agreeing, I'll be leaking the information of your indiscretions the second you drive away." I turn back to Harlow's mother. "And you won't get a dime unless your husband falls in line—and stays there. So I suggest you start talking him into it now. I'll give you two minutes to discuss."

It doesn't even take them that long to come to a consensus. They start whispering furiously before I've even walked away. Thirty seconds later, Barclay clears his throat. "Fine. We'll sign. That whore of a daughter never lived up to her full potential. I'm happy to dump her worthless ass in your lap. You can take care of her now. But you mark my words…" He points a finger in my face, and it takes every ounce of my self-control not to punch the smarmy sneer off his lips. "She will be nothing but a disappointing albatross who drags you down. Enjoy that."

IT'S LATE WHEN we leave the merriment. Harlow and I finally retire to the suite Maxon and Keeley reserved for us. A big tester bed draped in pure fluffy white, almost like a cloud, beckons. As we reach the threshold of the room, I hear the revelers fading in the background. Harlow fidgets by my side.

When I lift her into my arms, she clasps her hands around my neck and relaxes into my hold. "I can't believe we're married."

"We are. And now I'm going to make sure you don't forget it."

Even in the low, flickering light of a dozen candles scattered around the room, I see her flush as I kick the door shut and carry her across the room while her shoes drop to the bamboo floor in a tumble.

"What does *male ána* mean?" she asks about the decorative sign on the door.

"Wedding." I set her on her feet at the side of the bed and draw the gauzy white drapes shut.

"That's fitting, then." Her voice shakes. "You know, Maxon and Keeley have done a lot to spruce up this place in a short time and I think they—"

"Do you really want to discuss their decor right now?"

Harlow presses her lips together. "No. I'm just…nervous."

"You're not alone," I assure Harlow as I bring her close again and whisper in her ear, "*Aloha au ia 'oe.*" When she searches my face for the meaning, I tell her in low tones, "I love you."

"Noah…"

She's afraid to admit she loves me, too. I'm almost convinced she does. A hundred times in a hundred ways every day, she says or does something to prove it. For whatever reason, the words are trapped in her heart. But I have a year with her now. I'll coax them out.

"Shh. *Nou No Ka 'I'ini.*" I untie the delicate white sash around her dress and let it flutter to the floor. "I desire you."

Before she can answer, I place my fingertip at the hollow of her neck and trace my way down to the hint of cleavage visible above her dress. Her eyes drift shut with a sigh.

"Touch me," she murmurs. "I want you so much…"

I lower the zipper down her back. "In good time, *wahine.*"

"Wife?" she asks breathlessly as the dress clings only to her shoulders.

"Exactly."

Seconds later, I push the fabric down one arm, then the other. The gown slithers to her feet, revealing a gift that leaves me hard and aching and amazed that this woman is *mine.*

"You looked beautiful in your wedding dress, but this…" I blow out a harsh breath. "Whoa."

I have no words to describe Harlow standing before me in a creamy-white baby doll made entirely of transparent lace—except the silk covering her nipples and the underwires supporting her plump breasts. A big bow at the bottom of the silk shows off her tiny waist and the long line of her flat abdomen before tapering down to the flare of her hips and the shadow between her thighs, barely covered by a gossamer strip of peekaboo silk.

I'm going to lose my mind before I get my hands—and my mouth—on all of her.

"You're beyond gorgeous," I finally finish. "But what you're wearing is dangerous."

She raises a brow at me. "Dangerous? It's not the kind of outfit I'd wear if I wanted to Krav Maga your ass."

"It's the kind of outfit you wear to seduce a man." My fingers skim down, knuckles brushing the swells of her breasts. "And trust me, you're going to get fucked."

"Oh? I thought you'd make me feel tender and adored, like a delicate flower, on our wedding night," she baits me with a flutter of her lashes.

"I will," I assure her, caressing her hair back from her face before cupping her nape. "When we leave here in the morning, you'll have no doubt I value you above everything else. But you'll also be wrung out, deliciously sore, and smiling."

"You say the sweetest things, you big hunk of romance." She winks.

I chuckle as I undo the bow of her nightie and watch it loosen around her body. "I'm the most romantic bastard you'll ever be married to."

As the garment falls into my palms, I lean in to kiss my bride again, the way I've wanted to since the officiant said I could earlier this afternoon. As before, our lips meet, slow and sweet, clinging and brushing. A spark. A tingle. A thrill racing through my body as I peel away the rest of her clothing and leave her in nothing except the diamonds I bought to fasten around her neck and the ring I put on her finger.

"That may be, but…aren't you overdressed?"

I send her a lazy grin as I shrug out of my suit coat, bow tie, and shirt. Harlow's breath catches as she caresses her way up my bare chest as if she can't stop herself from touching me. I let her palm my shoulders and my pectorals as I unhook the fastening at my fly and yank down my zipper. I toss everything onto a nearby chair and face her, wearing absolutely nothing.

"This what you had in mind?"

She eyes my cock, saluting her at full staff. I had her last night…and this morning—hard. It doesn't matter, though. I'm beyond eager to sink inside Harlow again, to make our union official in every way.

"I think you'll have to come a bit closer," she coaxes.

"Why don't you get on the bed, lie on your back, and spread your legs for me?"

She blinks…but I don't change course.

I haven't forgotten her reaction to my subtle hint of dominance our first night together. I've waited, bided my time until I thought she trusted me enough to give me not only her body but her free will for a night. I'm not sure how she'll react, if I'm asking for too much, too soon. But some part of her wants a man she can trust, who will take care of her in every way. I'm hoping she'll let me start here and now.

"What?" She sounds somewhere between shocked and breathlessly aroused.

"You heard me."

A hint of thrill dawns on her face as she shuffles toward the mattress and tumbles back, eyes wide and on me. She parts her thighs shyly. I can see a mere hint of the pink slickness between. "Like this?"

Her question has my stare jerking back to her face. She's biting her lip, and that rosy pout is making me think all kinds of sinful thoughts about how to put her lips to good use.

Jesus, I've barely touched her and my chest is heaving. Even the suggestion that I could command a woman as independent as Harlow floods my system with desire. It runs thick and hot through my veins.

"Wider. Show me your pussy. Show me what's mine."

Bracing her feet on the edge of the bed, she flares her legs farther apart, giving me a glimpse of everything wet and feminine and rosy in between. She's aroused, too. I know her body well now. I know when she's swollen and pouty. Already her clit looks hard. Harlow is ready. Hell, she's eager.

A thousand urges pelt me at once, but one towers over the others. I need this—need her—now. Face to face. Heart to heart. Lips connected. Bodies joined.

I caress my way down her thigh and drag my fingers through her glossy folds, gratified by the catch of her breath. After leaning in for a kiss, I sit beside her and grab her wrist, giving her a gentle tug. "Straddle me."

Without hesitation, she tosses one thigh over my hips and rises onto her knees, positioning herself above my cock. I hold myself in place, nestling my head at her opening and aligning us. When she tries to slide down my length, I hold her hips, make her wait.

Harlow loves every position. She's enjoyed sex against a wall. She shivers when I take her from behind. She loves the way I kiss her when I'm on top. But after hundreds of hours making love to this woman, I know that nothing sets my wife on fire more than her impaling herself on my shaft as I guide her hips while she rides me.

When I drag my lips up her jaw and skirt the edge of her lips, the seconds tick by. I dive into her mouth. Our tongues tango as I cup one breast, teasing her hard nipple with my thumb. I taste her growing need. She starts to whimper, shifts restlessly, and tries to sink onto my cock. I tighten my hand on her hip to stay her.

"Not until I say so, *wahine*."

"But Noah…"

"Not until you admit you want me."

"I want you. So much. So bad." She shakes her head at me. "All the time. You know that."

I do. She's never shy sexually, always willing to reach out day or night to tell me that she desires my touch and aches for the satisfaction I give her. It's one of the reasons I feel so connected to Harlow. Not a day goes by that we don't get lost in one another.

"Not until you admit that you're mine."

She peers into my eyes, as if understanding that I'm finally asking for more than her body. "I'm your lover and your wife." Her exhalation rattles as if my demand has stirred her nerves again. "And I'm yours, Noah Weston. Only yours."

Primal satisfaction roars through my body. I desire this woman with every cell in my body, every beat of my heart. And right now, I need to know that she belongs to me.

The next demand comes harder. "Not until you tell me how you feel about me."

I'd give almost anything to hear that she loves me, but I can't insist that she say it if she's not ready. I want her words—whatever they are—to come from her heart.

Harlow opens her mouth, closes it, swallows. In my grip, she trembles. The movement is almost imperceptible…but I feel her.

"It's okay, baby. Whatever you're going to say, it's fine. Just talk to me."

For a moment, she closes her eyes, almost like she's afraid to admit defeat. Then she sucks in a rough breath and nods. "*Kāne*… Did I say that right?"

"Husband?" I give her the translation of her Hawaiian word in English. "You said it perfectly."

"I love you."

Joy buoys me. She said the words freely, every syllable soft but heartfelt.

I let out a whoop. "That's what I've waited to hear—for so long."

"I know. I tried not to," she says solemnly. "Fall in love, that is."

"Oh, I'm aware." I cup her cheek. "But I'm so glad you lost the battle with yourself. I'll never make you regret it."

"Tonight, when I saw my parents, when I realized what you were willing to do for me simply so I'd have peace…it all clicked. I couldn't keep you at arm's length because of anything they had done to me in the past. I couldn't compare you to Simon, either. And I couldn't punish you when you've done nothing but try to make my life better every day, in every way. You've tried to heal me and understand me and… It hit me when I saw you strolling back to the reception tonight after talking to them, whistling and looking so self-assured. You're not the kind of man to make yourself bigger on the back of someone else's degradation. You're fair when treated fairly. You're kind and funny and…everything I dreamed for as a little girl and didn't think existed in this world."

Hearing the cynicism in her voice give way to hope—and knowing I had something to do with that—makes me feel a hundred feet tall.

"Thank you for being so honest. I wanted to make you happy."

"You have. More than I ever dared to wish for."

She's looking at me so solemnly, so sweetly. I can't not touch her.

"Oh, baby…" I move in to kiss her.

She braces her hands on my chest. "Wait. Let me finish. I want to tell you everything I haven't yet, everything that's been holding me back. My…past. But not now. This is our wedding night. This is our night to celebrate us. I don't want to take that away."

Her words wrap around my throat and nearly choke me. I can't swallow. I can't speak. Harlow is willing to give me all the secrets she's been protecting so fiercely? She's well and truly mine now. That makes me want her even more.

"All right. You're right, tonight should be about us. But I want to hear everything you have to say soon. If it upset or affected you, I want to know about it."

She smiles softly. "And that's why I couldn't stop myself from falling in love with you. You're here not for just whatever you can manipulate out of the situation but simply for us."

"Always." I cup her face in my hands. "Now can I kiss you?"

Tears sheen in her eyes. The sob she's holding in becomes a laugh. "The sooner the better."

I can't stand being even a breath apart from this woman for another moment. I seize her mouth with my own and nudge her body down onto me, letting her impale herself at whatever pace pleases her. When every inch of me is enveloped inside her, the connection is more than physical.

My tongue fills her as my cock does, and she shudders. I feel her heart beating furiously against mine. Harlow clings to me—fingers, thighs, lips. Eternity whispers through my head; she's mine now and this is right. It's the sweetest music ever. My wife challenges me. She selflessly helps me cope and recover every day. She makes me laugh and moves me in ways I never expected a woman to. And now she's finally given me her heart.

I manage to tear my mouth from hers, band my arms around her, and rock with her. Lust scorches my blood as my heart threatens to explode. "Hearing your feelings was the sweetest wedding gift you could have given me. Say it again."

"I love you."

The words are something just above a whisper as if they still scare her on some level. But she's braving her fears, opening up, and trusting me.

She's becoming one with me in every way. I feel like a king.

"I love you, baby. Dear god, you have no idea…" I rock inside her and groan, working to get deeper and fill my wife full of every bit of me that I can—cock, heart, love.

Harlow moves in earnest above me now, sliding up, then working the sensation down my length until I'm shuddering to hold back. As much as each sway and gyration of her hips undoes me, I can't climax before Harlow. I won't.

Lying back, I grab hold of her hips to pull her onto me completely and hold her still. "Don't move unless I tell you."

She keens in protest. "But I'm close."

"I know." I feel her tightening around me, clenching, clamping in desperate need.

Holy shit, she's going to undo me if I don't keep ruthless control over her every move.

"Noah…" She thrashes around to steal more sensation.

With one hand, I dig deeper into her flesh in warning. With the other, I tangle my fingers into her hair and force her to look at me. "Stop. Tonight, you'll come when I want you to come. You'll come because neither one of us can hold back for another second. And when that happens, you're going to tell me you love me again. I'll shout it back to you. Then you'll collapse against me, panting and sated and sleepy. But I'll just grab you again and start all over…" I press up beneath her, inching deeper inside her, gratified when she gasps because I know exactly where her sweet spot is and precisely how to stroke it repeatedly so she falls apart in my arms. "Do you understand me?"

"Yes. Please. Yes…"

"Please what?" I look into her eyes, telegraphing how much I need to hear her say who I am to her.

She meets my stare. Our gazes fuse.

"Please…husband."

God, she's perfect. She knows me, reads me, understands me. Harlow Weston utterly completes me.

That's my last thought before I drive up inside her again with a roar, pistoning again and again against her most sensitive spot until she cries out. "Come now!"

Harlow does without hesitation, shattering above me with a face full of desperate passion. She's holding nothing back now. She's giving me everything—and I suddenly feel the difference between every other time we've had sex and tonight, when we're making love not only without physical barriers but without mental ones, too.

"I love you..." she cries out as her body shudders with completion.

"I love you, too!" I release and empty every bit of myself inside her, then bring her close to hear our heartbeats slow together with a sigh of satisfaction.

Tonight is the first night of the rest of our lives together. I have to believe that nothing can tear us apart now.

CHAPTER SIXTEEN

A S HEAVENLY AS our wedding night was, the follow morning turned to hell. News of my marriage to Harlow spread like all gossip does— quickly and with bite. By the time we had breakfast with Maxon, Griff, their wives, and little Jamie, the press was already surrounding the parking lot. Getting to the car proved difficult. Sliding inside and driving away turned out to be nearly impossible. Their shouted questions were somewhere between salacious and insulting, about everything from my "busy" sex life apart from my wife to barely veiled sneers about our relationship while she was engaged to Simon.

As much as I'd love to go off on them, they're doing their jobs and losing my shit does no good, so I stick to my canned response. "Harlow and I are newlyweds and we would appreciate some privacy so we can enjoy this time in our married lives."

I hoped more than believed that would be the end of the incident.

"Mercedes Fleet says your wedding is a publicity stunt and a way to avoid your responsibility to her baby."

Of course she said that. I would, too, if I was trying to exploit someone else for my own gain. I wish this woman would just stop. I'm guessing she got unexpectedly pregnant. Maybe she can't afford this baby. Or maybe she got pregnant by a hookup who won't acknowledge her. It's possible she simply wants to put a famous man's name on her child's birth certificate. I don't know. But she needs to be honest with the press—and herself.

"I've never met, much less been intimate with, Mercedes Fleet. That's all."

And that's the last time I'm repeating myself, damn it.

As I'm finally able to duck in the car and slam the door, I glance at Harlow. She looks a little rattled.

"You okay?"

She gives me a nod that looks more confident than I think she feels. "Let's get out of here."

That's going to be a feat since a handful of reporters seem intent on blocking the road so they can continue to shout questions at us. But after I start the engine and rev it a few times, they get the message and back away.

Finally, we're making our way down the road. I know the press will be waiting for us at the security gate when we get home, but at least we'll have privacy once we make it inside.

"This will die down," I assure Harlow. "After the test results come back negative, Ms. Fleet will be exposed as a fraud. The press rarely apologizes or admits it was wrong to run with a story when they had no facts to support it. But they will go away and chase the next juicy tidbit as soon as they find it."

"Have you lived with this since you went pro?"

"No. Usually, I get a few cameras in my face after a game or before a big event. But it's never been this intense. That's why I know all the attention will disappear as soon as there's no more steak to feed these hounds."

"But it's your word against hers. I don't know why they don't wait until the facts are in."

"Because that doesn't sell papers or generate clicks."

She sighs in frustration. "That sucks."

It does. And it suddenly occurs to me that we've only talked about the paternity suit in practical terms since the day the accusation came to light. "Do you believe me, Harlow? Do you think I got her pregnant?"

"I thought you had when it first happened and that you simply didn't want to tell me."

"Like Simon. I get it."

She nods. "Even my dad has that nasty habit. It's like he gets off on knocking up girls half his age and…"

She's revolted and angry. I met the man, so I at least have a glimmer of understanding. When her experience with men has been so negative, trust is thin and believing my claims of innocence can't be easy. I'm trying to see this situation from her perspective. But she has to see it from mine, too. If she loves me, I need to know she trusts me, as well. No, she wouldn't blame me for something that happened before we met. But she would blame me for lying to her about it now. If I wasn't telling the truth and Harlow found out, everything I've spent weeks building with her would crumble in so many pieces I wonder if I could ever put it back together.

"I don't understand the man." I grimace. "But I completely get why you might have had difficulty believing I didn't get that woman pregnant at first."

"I was sure you had that day it came to light. And I was angry when I had no right to be. I'm sorry about that."

I take a left onto a wider street and head west, sending her another glance. "But you believe me now?"

"Of course. I mean, unless you were super-drunk that night—"

"No. I had a beer or two, but I wasn't wasted. After my concussion, the doctors told me to drink only in moderation and I've followed their direction. And I've *never* been so drunk that I didn't remember taking a woman to bed, much less doing all the stuff she claims."

"Then I see no reason you'd lie. And why would you demand a paternity test if you were? Logically, it doesn't make sense. Even without all that, I'd believe you." She reaches for my hand. "We hadn't known each other long the day her claims went public. I overreacted because…you were getting to me and that scared me to death. I was so afraid I was falling for someone who was like my dad or my ex. I wasn't really mad at you. I was furious with myself."

I give her hand a squeeze. "I understand. It just means a lot that you believe me now. Proof that I've been nothing but honest is coming, baby."

She smiles my way. "Thanks, but I already know."

Just like that, my Sunday starts looking up. Once we get home, my family comes over for an early dinner before Trace boards a plane the next morning for a few days of meetings in San Francisco.

The shit hits the fan and splatters everywhere on Monday morning when Mercedes Fleet gives her most salacious interview yet, revealing details of the things I supposedly can't resist in bed and the ink I've never showed in public. The first claim…she's guessing. She has to be. Besides, what guy doesn't like a blow job, followed by some down-and-dirty penetration? But the description of the tattoo on my hip is something else entirely. It's an elaborate compass, a tat I got after a few years in the league to remind myself which direction was home so that I'd never lose my way. The ink on my shoulders, arms, and ribs are all well photographed. But the compass was just for me.

How the hell does this woman know about it?

I try to block the worry out, work on reducing my anxiety and upping my mental calm. Harlow stays beside me, helping in every way she can. I need it now more than ever. I'm starting to worry that if this liar gives more interviews like the last and I don't accept the network's offer before I'm ready, I'll never have a chance at a career in the broadcasting booth and I'll have to leave football way before I'm ready.

The call I've been fearing comes on Monday night. Cliff didn't board his plane back to New York because Gus Chickman, who runs the network, wants to see me. In person. As soon as he can get to Maui.

Cue the interrogation.

Shit.

I'm pretty sure this chat is make-or-break.

"You're going to be fine," Harlow assures me in a soothing voice as we finish dressing for a dinner meeting on Wednesday night at one of the steakhouses on the island. "I'll be right beside you. We'll tell them you've been busy wooing me, then planning a secret wedding. After our honeymoon, you'll definitely give their offer the serious consideration it deserves and you'll have an answer to them in less than a month. We've rehearsed this, so it will be as smooth as butter."

"Yeah." I try to sound sure of myself, but I'm nervous as hell. What if I freeze up when I need to defend myself most? I know Harlow will step in and smooth things out…but how will that look to Chickman?

On the way to the restaurant, I don't complain when she puts on soothing instrumental music I swear only gets played in elevators and funeral homes. To my wife's credit, the relaxed tempo of the flute-heavy tunes helps me focus on my thoughts and talk myself away from the proverbial ledge. I also practice my breathing on the drive and take a lot of moments to touch Harlow—a squeeze of her hand, a caress of her knee. Just having contact with her calms me.

When we arrive, the valet takes my keys and manages not to gape at us for too long, which is a blessing. But he can't keep his eyes off of Harlow, and it annoys the hell out of me.

I step into the punk's line of sight and force him to stop ogling my wife. "We good here?"

He blinks, seeming to realize that he's staring at Harlow in her strappy blood-red dress. "Um, yes, Mr. Weston. Sir. There's no problem."

"Glad to hear it."

I don't mean to be hard on the kid. He's maybe all of twenty-two, and my wife is a vibrant beauty. But not every man who comes to this place with a gorgeous woman on his arm will be so understanding. Hell, I'm not sure how much I can be. This is the first time I've discovered how much I don't like random men gawking at Harlow.

She approaches with a smile for the kid and wraps her fingers around my arm, flashing her wedding ring. "Thank you."

Her soft voice rings in my ears as we head to the door.

"Was I an asshole?" I whisper.

Harlow holds up her thumb and forefinger a fraction of an inch apart. "A little bit. Wound up or jealous?"

"Both," I grumble, knowing I need to get my shit together. "Sorry."

"The good news is, I'm not leaving you for a kid I met in a parking lot two minutes ago and Mr. Chickman is here because he *wants* to talk to you, because he *wants* to have you on board. If he didn't, he would have given Cliff the kiss-off speech already and asked your agent to pass it on to you."

She makes valid points. I'm so lucky to have her in my life. "Damn, I married a smart woman."

"Don't you forget it."

With a laugh, we enter the restaurant to find Cliff and Chickman already sitting at a table in the corner, exchanging words over a glass of Scotch. Their conversation looks too heated to be casual. As we approach, they stop arguing abruptly. My agent pastes on a wide smile that reeks of bullshit.

My nerves torque up. Sweat breaks out between my shoulder blades. This could go sour really fast.

"Hi, Noah." Cliff and I shake hands before he nods in my wife's direction. "Harlow. Good to see you again."

"Likewise." She gives him a gracious smile.

Then Cliff makes the introductions.

I've met Gus Chickman once or twice in passing over the years. He's a football fan himself and he's cheered me through a couple of Super Bowls, I'm told. I've got that working in my favor. Instead of focusing on everything that's gone wrong with the Mercedes Fleet situation, I have to remember that the man who wants to hire me actually likes me.

Or he once did.

The network executive and I exchange a few pleasantries before I help Harlow into her chair. Chickman isn't smiling, but he isn't glowering either. Maybe the situation is still salvageable...if I can keep my shit together.

After the waiter comes to take our drink orders, the television bigwig leans across the table and stares at me. "I asked for this meeting because as charming as your agent is, I need to hear from you, Weston. Do you want this job or not?"

Cliff pats him on the back. "Gus… Gus, we've talked about this. Of course Noah does. Most likely, he'll say yes. He's just been—"

"I want to hear from Weston."

When the older man drills me with his blue eyes, I nod. "I'm very seriously considering your offer. I hope you'll appreciate that the last few months for me have been hectic. Getting married isn't something that happens without a lot of consideration and planning, so—"

"Agreed, but we don't make this sort of substantial offer to everyone before we've actually heard them perform in a booth. Your last couple of press conferences weren't your best, but I've listened to you speak many times over the last dozen years. With your knowledge of the game and your insight, I think you can do this job better than anyone."

"Thank you. I understand I've kept you waiting longer than you anticipated. You've made me a lucrative offer, and I grasp the gravity of that. Because I've had big things going on in my personal life, I wanted to be one hundred percent sure I could deliver on everything you expect before I agreed to anything."

"What does that mean? I just expect you to talk." The old man glares, his forehead gleaming with a thin sheen of perspiration. "Are you really considering walking away from football altogether? Or is there some other reason to think you can't do the job?" He leans in with narrowed eyes. "Did that last concussion mess you up more than you're letting on?"

"Um…" I start sweating, too. Profusely. The need to swallow makes me shut my mouth. My stomach feels as if I took it apart with a chainsaw and tried to hold it together with a rubber band. A million words zoom through my head, but I can't seem to speak a single one. So I shake my head and hope he believes me.

But really, if I can't muster an eloquent defense, why would he?

Harlow understands my predicament and reaches under the crisp white tablecloth to wrap her fingers around my knee and give me a comforting squeeze.

"Then what's the damn problem?"

I still can't answer. I try to pass off an expression that says I'm attempting to put my thoughts into words, but I'm sure he can see a drop of sweat rolling from my temple.

"Out with it, Weston," he insists. "Is your personal life too much to keep up with your job responsibilities? Because we should talk about that. The executives in my sports division aren't happy with all your splashy news lately. You had a reputation as a man whore early in your career. I decided to offer you this job at this pay because you'd seemed to clean your act up in recent seasons. But since your antics with Mercedes Fleet came to light, I've had a very nervous board of directors. Say something that will help me put them at ease."

I could. Normally, I'd love to. Right now, I can't say anything at all.

Clenching my fists, it's all I can do not to pound them on the table in frustration. Since I have to keep my shit together, I turn to look at Harlow. She's been holding back, letting me run things unless I needed her.

Now, more than ever, I do.

She squeezes my knee again, then turns her most charming smile on Chickman. "Other than being worn out after an eventful weekend, Noah is fine. We'd planned to take at least this week for a honeymoon, so the fact that he's having dinner with you tonight instead of keeping his promise to his new wife ought to tell you he's very serious about your offer. But he wants to give it its due consideration. It's a long-term commitment. The fact that he wants a few weeks without a media spectacle distracting him so that he can be entirely sure is not something that should make anyone nervous. Your board of directors should be relieved he's being so serious and cautious. If he says yes, they can be completely certain he means it."

God, she's wonderful. Perfect. She both scolded and reassured Chickman in the same speech. No wonder I love her so much.

"Furthermore, if I thought for one moment that Ms. Fleet's claims were true, I would not have married Noah. Maybe you saw the YouTube video of my last attempt at marriage? If you did, you know I won't accept my fiancé knocking up some other woman. Ms. Fleet is an attention seeker, and you're giving her far too much validity by even listening to her claims. You're a smart man. Haven't you ever dealt with someone trying to get their fifteen minutes of fame by climbing on your back and riding your coattails for all they're worth?"

When he flushes a guilty red, I drag in a deep breath. *Score, Harlow!* The woman should have been a trial attorney. This performance tells me that if we ever get into a gnarly fight, I'm likely to lose.

"Thank you, Mrs. Weston," Cliff cuts in, jaw clenched. He's annoyed that Harlow is doing his job for him right now—and doing it better. "But I've got it from here."

I glare at my longtime agent. Where the fuck does he get the idea that Harlow doesn't have a voice at this table? That she can't speak for me if I want her to, if I can't do it myself?

Harlow shrugs. "I just thought it was important to share what Noah and I have discussed and—"

"Sure," he says dismissively, then turns to Chickman. "Like Noah explained to me, the wife is a great asset and a perfect front. Smart, lovely, educated. This marriage will keep the Mercedes Fleets of the world from being taken too seriously in the future, and Noah will use his utmost discretion with other women. Right, buddy?" He claps me on the shoulder. "She was a smart business move. Good choice."

I drag in growling breaths of fury. Cliff is way out of line, making Harlow sound like a prop instead of the woman I'm going to love madly for the rest of my life. I've known Cliff for a decade. He doesn't love anything except a smoking deal and he'd say anything to get one done. I can't point that out now, but Harlow is smart. She'll get it.

Still, I feel compelled to stop his shitty behavior.

"What the hell?" I manage to blurt out. More words are behind those, piling up in my throat, dammed by anxiety and anger.

"I'm just relaying what we discussed, Noah," Cliff assures. "You promised me she'd be good for your image, and now I'm in total agreement. I'm sure Mr. Chickman is as well."

"Absolutely." The network executive winks my way.

"Well, since my work here is done and you boys don't need me to conduct business, I'll leave you to it." Harlow smiles graciously and rises to her feet.

I grab her by the hand, swallow, force out one syllable. "Sit."

"Don't be silly. You get business done. Mr. Chickman has flown all the way to Maui from New York to talk to you. I'm sure he has a network to run and can't be gone any longer than usual. I'll take a taxi back to the house."

"Harlow…"

"I'm fine."

She's not fine. Not remotely. I see it on her face. She handled Cliff's snub and insult with grace, but her smile is as artificial as Chickman's toupee. My agent is a hustler. She couldn't possibly take his BS about her being an asset to cover up my affairs seriously.

"I'll go with you." I stand.

"Don't be silly." She shakes her head.

"My red-eye leaves in three hours," the network executive states baldly. "We discuss this now or I'll have to rescind the offer."

"See?" Harlow says with a sparkling smile as she grabs her purse. "Lovely to see you, gentlemen. Good evening."

I stand and take hold of her arm. Nothing on her face conveys that she's upset or pissed off, but I sense something deeply wrong. "Baby?"

"Do what you need to. You've got this. I understand. Don't worry." A brittle wave later, she slips out of my grasp and exits.

I'm left staring after her, dread rolling through my gut. What, exactly, does she understand?

I'm not sure. In fact, I'm worried as hell. That woman wouldn't have left my side when she knows I'm having verbal trouble unless something had gone horribly, terribly wrong.

"Noah, buddy…" Cliff stands and urges me back to my chair. "Mr. Chickman's time is limited, and the little woman will be waiting for you back home. Why don't you sit down so we can get everything ironed out?"

With a frown, I do. I don't have a choice if I want to cover the sport I love come this fall. But as soon as I get home, I'll talk everything out with Harlow. That will be enough. Right?

SIXTY-FIVE MINUTES LATER, I dash inside the front door, glad business is done for the night. I rushed dinner along and managed to give Chickman a promise that I'd make a splashy announcement in a few days with my exciting news. Let him interpret that however he wants.

"Harlow?" I shout from the entryway.

No answer.

Foreboding rolls through me as I glance around the dimly lit house. The pictures of little Jamie she stuck to the refrigerator the other day are gone. So are the random hair ties she usually leaves lying on the coffee table so she can get her hair out of her eyes for serious gaming.

Shit.

I try not to panic. She's often tidy. She sometimes declutters random-ly. Maybe she came home from the restaurant and decided to pick up a little.

"Harlow?"

Still nothing.

Dread knotting my gut, I run upstairs and barge into the bedroom she used to sleep in alone. When I fling open the closet door, it's completely empty. No sexy red dress. No hanging row of short-shorts and sexy tanks. No pile of shoes at the bottom screaming in loud colors and gleaming with bling.

Oh, fuck me.

When I dash to my room, the few garments she'd moved into my personal space are all gone, too. Her toiletries are missing from the bathroom. Her scent still lingers…but the woman herself is utterly gone.

This cannot be the end of us.

With shaking hands, I pluck my phone from my pocket and call her. Her voice mail greeting plays right away, telling me to leave a message. I squeeze the device as shock rolls over me. She won't even talk to me, hear my side of…whatever's gone wrong? No, she's simply picked up and left. I'm still not sure why. Yes, Cliff was a prick and painted our marriage as a business transaction, but doesn't she see that he just wanted to get the deal done and was willing to say pretty much anything to both make it happen and be the bigwig?

Maybe not.

"Baby, where are you? What's going on? You're upset and I want to talk this out. I want to fix it. I want—"

"You can't," Harlow says suddenly, stepping from the shadows to lean against the doorframe.

She's changed out of her killer red dress and now wears a T-shirt that says BE BRAVE. BE BOLD. BE YOU. A Harlow with a message on her chest is a Harlow with something on her mind.

I pocket my phone and approach her. "What do you mean, I can't? Are you saying I can't fix it? Baby, Cliff is an asshole and—"

"I know. But I understand everything now." She sighs and sways into the room.

"What does that mean? You don't understand anything if you think I used you to make this deal happen. Newsflash: it was already on the table before you walked into my life.

"But you needed me to improve your image after Mercedes Fleet started alleging you're the hottest lay outside of porn and that you two are having a love child."

That might be true but… "I didn't use you."

"Maybe not. Probably not." She presses her lips together in regret. "But the whole drive here and the time I spent packing up, I couldn't stop wondering if I was just a smokescreen to you. A way to get ahead in business. I tried to talk myself out of it. You're not my father and all that. But what I ultimately realized is that I'm not ready to trust anyone that completely, least of all myself. So…Maxon came by and took all my things. Griff is on his way to pick me up. I'll return the money you paid me for speech services, and you don't owe me anything more when we divorce. Don't worry. I won't rock your boat and start proceedings until our anniversary. You'll be great in the broadcasting booth, I'm sure. I believe in you."

I'm crushed and so fucking confused. "No. No, baby... I believe in *you*." I grab her shoulders. "Don't leave. I love you. I—"

"And I can't guarantee I'll ever be whole for you, so it's better if I let you go now. Before I hurt you any more."

"What does that mean? You are whole. You're everything I need. We've been doing great until tonight and I don't understand."

Harlow sits on the side of the bed and closes her eyes. "I owe you an explanation. I didn't tell you everything about my miscarriage." She lets out a rough breath. "When I went away to college, my dad got me a part-time job with a man named Jeremy Ronald. He had a small company with a unique computer technology my father wanted to launch big and exploit. I didn't know when I walked in the door that talks had been stalled for months. Or that I was butter meant to grease the wheels so they'd start to turn again. My father just told me to work for the man and 'be nice.'"

"He pimped you out?" I know that's what she means and I'm instantly horrified. She was barely more than a child.

"See, you understood that much quicker than I did. I started that job with all intentions of being the best assistant he could imagine and giving him my all. I just didn't know he didn't mean behind a computer, but on my back." She frowns, not quite looking at me. "I was young, and he was handsome, charismatic. When he made a pass at me, I was dumb enough to be flattered. He wasn't married, and so what if he was older than me?"

"How old?" I snap. It's all I can do to hold on to my temper. Because I know where this story is going and I want to kill this man I've never met.

"Thirty. I was eighteen. He seemed so worldly and funny..." An acidic, self-deprecating twist of her lips wrings out my heart. "And I couldn't believe that a man like that thought I was beautiful and interesting. The love of his life, he said. Yeah, I was that stupid."

"Never stupid. You were naive, baby. Trusting."

She finally looks at me, and I see something so vulnerable on her face it hurts me. For the first time, I see the most fragile parts of Harlow. And I see how close she is to breaking apart.

"I was a virgin," she whispers.

Oh, fuck. "Baby, I'm so sorry. You deserved better than to have your father sell out your innocence for a business deal."

"It's actually worse than that. Before I left for college, he insisted I go on the pill." She swallows. "I took them faithfully and I was so shocked when, a few months into my affair with Jeremy, I realized I was pregnant. I told my mother first. She didn't say a word, just handed the phone to my father, who congratulated me. I still didn't get it, even then. Not for years, in fact. But I'll get back to that.

"After we hung up, my father called Jeremy, full of plastic outrage and demanding to know if my boss intended to 'do the right thing.' Jeremy was furious. The second I arrived at work, he ordered me into his office, called me a manipulative whore for trying to trap him, and fired me. I left in tears. And I never saw him again." She drags in a breath as if she needs the courage to continue. "I quit school and transferred to a campus closer to home. I'd barely walked in the door when my father started in on me. Apparently, I was a stupid bitch because I couldn't even manage to make Jeremy fall in lust with my pussy long enough to get the deal done. Two days later, I miscarried."

Fury roils and bubbles inside me. I should never have let that bastard leave our wedding reception alive.

But right now, Harlow needs me more than I need to right her wrongs.

"Listen to me. Your father took advantage of you. He's a sociopathic bastard who doesn't deserve a daughter as wonderful as you. You're funny and beautiful and so smart."

"Not smart enough. I let him manipulate me twice. Simon was his idea. I'd already decided not to go through with the wedding. I was only staying around long enough to let the video play so all of our guests would know exactly why I was running back down the aisle. As my father and I lined up at the back of the ballroom, he said he'd talked to Simon about my desire for a baby and that I should ignore my fiancé and stay off the pill. After all, the placebos he'd gotten me in college had very nearly done the trick. They would have if I'd just been a little better in the sack."

Shock pings through me. Who does that to their own daughter? The kind of man who sees her as nothing more than a bargaining chip in a quest to pad his bank account. Rage grips my throat, squeezes my chest. Death is too good for that man.

Then I realize what she's saying to me. "You were never a business deal to me. Ever."

She shrugs. "You're probably telling me the truth, and I may very well wake up one day and regret this. But I'm not ready for unconditional trust. I don't know when I will be. At least I leave understanding so much more about what love really means and with a baby finally on the way. I'm so much better for having known you. You'll have moved on before I'm whole enough to think about love again. I hope you find the woman who's worthy of you, Noah Weston. You deserve the best."

With an apology on her face, Harlow turns to go. My heart crashes against my ribs as I grab her wrists and tug her against me. "I have the best, damn it. I have the most amazing wife in the world. Don't.go. Please."

As I seize her mouth in a crushing kiss, I feel the wetness on her cheeks. Harlow is breaking both our hearts because she's so afraid to believe in love, so afraid she'll wind up used and alone.

I clutch her, push my way into her mouth, and kiss her like I'm never letting go. She's everything to touch, to taste. When I dig my fingers into her hair, I do it with a silent plea to stay and believe in herself. To believe in our love.

Her body shudders as she kisses me in return and clings to me for a terrible, wonderful second. Then she steps back with a shake of her head and teary eyes that confess leaving me is destroying her.

"I'm sorry," she whispers. "I love you."

She tears the ring off her finger and lays it on my nightstand before whirling around to disappear, feet thudding as she runs down the stairs.

I chase after her. "Harlow!"

The front door slams. By the time I yank it open again and follow her into the dark night, I'm too late. Griff is driving her away with a grimace and a wave of apology.

I'm left in the driveway as I watch the taillights disappear, worrying I made the biggest mistake of my life by staying at that dinner tonight and wondering if I'll ever hold my wife again.

CHAPTER SEVENTEEN

T HE LAST FORTY-EIGHT hours have been an absolute daze. Harlow is gone. I keep turning around and expecting to see her glued to her video game or dancing as she preps a meal in the kitchen or scanning some textbook for clues about how to help my speech-anxiety screw-ups. But I find her gone every time, and the realization that she left flattens me all over again. The bed feels fucking empty. I've taken to sleeping on one of the sofas downstairs because I can't be in the space where I once made love to Harlow without needing her again.

I've called. I've apologized. I've explained. But my wife isn't blaming me. She's blaming herself. How do I fix that?

Maxon came by my place yesterday to have a drink and a chat. He doesn't know what happened or where Harlow's head is, but he knows she's torn up. Griff called this morning to gently troll for information. I didn't tell either of them much. This is something my wife and I have to work out together.

With every hour that drags by, I wonder if that's possible.

"I don't want to pry," Griff said in all sincerity when he rang. "But I've never heard my sister cry herself to sleep. She won't say what happened, just that you two didn't fight and it's not your fault."

My options to help Harlow process are limited. I refuse to do something lame, like send her flowers. She might appreciate them for two seconds, but they won't heal what hurts her. I'm not entirely sure what will, except maybe time, but that's unacceptable. I don't want to spend another moment without her. Maxon and Griff both seem to have overcome somewhat rocky upbringings with those selfish pieces of shit who raised them. Maybe…Harlow needs to talk to people who share her common experience, who have walked through the fire and come out whole in spite of it.

"Can I ask you a personal question?" I finally said to him.

"Shoot."

"Did your parents do something terrible to you growing up?"

The silence on the other end of the line speaks far louder than if Griff had shouted. I hear him swallow, struggle to answer. "Harlow has things to work past, too?"

Boy, does she ever. "Yeah. What about Maxon?"

"He hasn't said a lot, but based on what I know and what I've observed, it's a fair guess."

But as close as the brothers were, neither knew the trials the other had endured? Maxon and Griff are in a better place now, sure. They've embraced love and moved on with their lives. I think Harlow could tip either way…but she'll err on the side of caution—and loneliness—unless someone gives her a shove in the other direction.

"I'm going to ask you for something I have no right to, but if I don't, I doubt I'll ever get my wife back."

Griff lets out a rough sigh over the line. "You want us to tell her our stories and persuade her to tell us what she endured in the hopes that it will help her."

I can't call Harlow's brother slow. "If she can see that you two have been able to move past whatever happened and that you aren't letting that stand in the way of your happiness, maybe she could heal. She doesn't feel whole or ready or sure of herself."

"Maxon has been saying for a while that he's sure something happened her first year of college."

"He's right." I can't say more than that without betraying her confidence. Harlow needs to tell her story herself. But will she?

"Fuck." I hear a loud crash that sounds very much like Griff slammed a door or punched a wall. "I should never have left her with those two vipers. I should never have believed that they saw her as the pretty princess of the family whom they'd never sully or touch. Maxon will blame himself, too."

"There was probably nothing you could have done then. But you can absolutely help her now. Please... This is really my last hope. If Harlow won't forgive herself and let this go, I'm going to wind up divorced at the end of a year and spend the rest of my life fucking miserable and alone. I know none of that is your problem—"

"It's Harlow's. She *needs* you." Griff pauses. "I've always wondered why Harlow wasn't the 'love' type. As a kid, she was into princesses and weddings and all that fairy-tale stuff. And always babies. I thought she'd marry young and happily, have a huge family and... Goddamn it. After high school, she seemed to stop dating. Simon was a surprise. I couldn't imagine why she was eager to marry someone she didn't love." He sighs. "Her running out on the wedding was epic. I wish you could have seen it."

Me, too.

"But?"

"I've never seen her as happy as when I've seen her with you, and the woman staying in my guest bedroom right now is so fragile I barely recognize her."

That hits me like a blow to the gut, so hard I can't breathe. "You gotta help me, man."

"I'll do what I can. She's planning to fly back to San Diego on Sunday. She was offered a job before she came here. She's talked about taking it."

Oh, god. If she leaves for California, getting her to come back to Maui—to me—will be between difficult and impossible.

"Anything. Please."

"I'll call Maxon now. We'll have a heart-to-heart intervention and see if we can't help you both. I spent three long, miserable years without Britta because I couldn't get over my shit. I want more than that for my sister. If two people ever belonged together, it's you."

We rang off after Griff promised to call me tomorrow. The next twenty-four hours are going to be torture. I haven't shaved in two days. I can't even remember the last time I ate. I've done nothing except for lift weights until exhaustion set in, catnap, and think of ways to win my wife back.

The sun has come and gone by the time I look up again. Hours have passed, and I don't even know what I've done with them except for think of Harlow and wish again that anxiety hadn't seized me at the worst possible time. Calling Cliff to curse him out should have made me feel better. Or at least like I had accomplished something. The only satisfaction I got was in knowing I did the right thing in telling my agent that if he can't respect my wife and treat her with the deference he's shown me, then he needs to get the hell out of my life and career. He called me later to tell me that he'd left Harlow a voice mail explaining and apologizing. Not that it made a difference. Why would it when she's not upset with me, merely convinced that believing the worst for even a moment means she's not ready to love me. I'm not expecting a perfect wife, just Harlow.

God, I could think in circles for hours.

A knock at my front door pulls me out of my reverie. I glance at my phone. Who the hell could be stopping by at nine o'clock at night? Since the list of approved visitors is small, it's one of a handful of people. I'd love to see my wife…but I'm not holding my breath.

With a groan, I lurch off the sofa and tug open the door. Trace fills the doorway with a stack of mail in hand and a solemn expression full of sympathy. "Hey, bro. I came to cheer you up. I got off the plane about two hours ago. Makuahine told me that you and Harlow have…separated. I can't even imagine why. You love her and she loves you."

"It's complicated."

He strolls in and sets the mail down, shaking his head. "If it's this Mercedes Fleet situation, couldn't Harlow have waited until the test results came back?"

Test results. It's Friday. I should have them already.

"It's not that simple," I answer as I grab my phone and open my email. The paternity problem isn't the reason my wife left me...but it didn't help. "In fact, it's a huge complication because Harlow is pregnant. We'd planned to wait a few weeks before we told the family. The wedding was enough, but now...I guess I might as well let the cat out of the bag. So not only have I lost my wife but I'm losing my son or daughter. I didn't think that would hit me so hard but it's got my fucking chest in a grinder."

"You're not giving up, right? Fight for her, man."

How do I get her to fight herself on my behalf?

A glance at my screen reveals an email from the independent lab we hired to process the blood results. With a shaky breath, I open and scan the response. Then I frown. None of what they're saying makes sense.

"What's wrong?" my brother asks, easing me into a chair. "You turned a shade of pale I've never seen on you."

"The test results are *inconclusive*? What the hell? I never touched that woman. I never even met her. The test results should be fucking zero and I don't understand why they're not."

"Yeah. Didn't the lab tell you it would either be ninety-nine-point-nine percent yes or zero percent no, nothing in between?"

I nod. "Wait. The lab technician wrote a note at the bottom. Maybe this will explain." But it doesn't. "Okay, they're saying the DNA structure rules me out as the father. Oh, thank god." I breathe a huge sigh of relief. I can't wait to shout these results to the world. And to my wife. No, they might not change her mind, but at least they'll prove I'm no liar. They'll prove that I'm not like her father or Simon. "But the results are inconclusive because there are some striking DNA similarities."

As soon as the words come out, something clicks in my head. I stare at my brother. We look a lot alike, enough that Trace is often mistaken for me. Is it possible that Mercedes Fleet believes Trace was me that night? The reason that others at the party thought they saw the two of us hit the bedroom together? And the explanation for the lab finding DNA similarities?

"Fuck, did you sleep with this woman at the Super Bowl after party?"

Trace frowns as he staggers back to the sofa, suddenly turning his own shade of pale. "I-I don't…know. I remember this one blonde. As soon as I walked in with you, she was all over me. Who was I to say no? But after we hooked up, we drank. A lot. Then one of her friends dragged her out. And that's really the last lucid thing I remember. There's this fuzzy picture of a brunette all flushed and panting in my head. I don't even have a face. I thought it was a snippet of a dream after I passed out, but… Holy shit."

"Do you have a tattoo of a compass on your hip?"

Suddenly, he grimaces. "Yeah. I saw your ink during that shoulder surgery you had a few years back. You don't remember telling me that you'd had it done to remind you of the way home?" When I shake my head, he goes on. "You were just coming out of anesthesia. I liked the look and the idea of it, so you let me snap a pic and I got the same ink a couple of weeks later. After that, you were busy rehabbing and living in Texas. I guess I just didn't remember to tell you or…" He rakes a hand through his dark hair. "Was that sex dream real? Oh, my god. Did I get that woman pregnant?"

I'm thinking it's a distinct possibility. "I suggest you contact her and the lab and find out for sure. I'll be reaching out through lawyers to indicate that since the child isn't mine, I expect her and her demands to disappear. What you do from there is up to you."

"But if that's my child…" He swallows. "He or she is family. And my responsibility."

"Yep." Not much more I can say, and I'm happy my younger brother came to the right conclusion.

"Holy shit."

"You already said that," I point out.

"It bears repeating."

I can't argue with that. "Want a beer?"

He might need one after realizing he probably fathered a child on a woman he can't even recall.

"No. The last thing I need is *not* to have my wits about me. That may have already gotten me in trouble. I need to figure out exactly what I'm going to say, what I'm going to do if the test turns out positive. And I need a stone-cold sober head to do it."

Another good call. "I'll help you however I can."

He turns to me, looking anxious but resigned. "Thanks. I'm only sorry I didn't put everything together sooner and save you any headache with Harlow."

"It's cool." I clap him on the shoulder. "And I'm not giving up on Harlow."

I'll make these results public so the scandal will die down and Mr. Chickman's board of directors will climb off his back. But mentally, I've already moved on. I'm thinking of ways to help Harlow see that I'll love her even if she's imperfect. That I'll always value her above all else.

CHAPTER EIGHTEEN

Harlow

"**H**I, BABY. IT'S Noah, leaving you a message. Again."

His rough, sleep-deprived voice guts me. Why hasn't he given up on me? I'm defective when it comes to love. Sure, I can care. I can totally help when someone else needs me. But when the time comes to lower the walls and give my heart, I freeze. I *feel* love. I want to open myself up. But like Noah's issues between his brain and his mouth, there's this block between my heart and my ability to trust. I don't know how to conquer it. Some days I feel strong. But when all it takes to shatter my fairy-tale castle is a few sentences from a total asshole doing his best to make money, my strength is obviously an illusion.

I'm not ready to love.

Still, I can't bring myself to stop listening to Noah's voice mails. I grip the phone tighter and close my eyes, pretending he's beside me and I still have the right to throw my arms around him, bask in his warmth, and kiss him with all my might.

"Listen… In spite of what Cliff said to Mr. Chickman, I married you for one reason only: I love you. I would never put a negotiation or a paycheck above you. But those are just words to you, I know. I'm sure your father and Simon have given you plenty of platitudes and empty promises in the past. So tomorrow before you fly back to San Diego, I plan to hold a press conference and announce that I'll be turning down the network's offer."

"What? No!" I shout at the recording as if he can hear me. "You can do the job."

But he can't hear me. I left him.

Because I didn't live up to my end of the contract we signed. Because I didn't honor my vows. Because I couldn't trust in love when things got tough.

"I'm doing it to prove that you're more important to me than anything," he says in my ear.

I close my eyes in shame. Nothing makes me feel more terrible than Noah giving up the future he wants because he thinks he needs to prove something so I'll love him the way I should. He doesn't have to prove anything, damn it. I know Cliff is a hustling asshole saying whatever he thought would get the deal done most expediently. Even when I left the restaurant, I was half convinced of that. By the time I'd packed my bags and left Noah's estate, I was eighty percent certain the man I'd married had never once said he'd tied the knot with me to land a multimillion-dollar job. The following morning, I was even less convinced that Noah was that sort of shitbag. Now that the weekend has rolled around, I'm almost completely sure he had nothing to do with Cliff's BS at all.

But it's that sliver of doubt that worries me. Given all that, can I ever be the wife and partner Noah needs?

"I know you're probably thinking that I've progressed enough to function as a color commentator. Maybe you're right. Still, I have this...difficulty to overcome. It won't be an overnight process. I could probably do it now that you've taught me so much about how to cope. The thing is, I don't have anything left to prove to the NFL, football fans, or the public. Just you. I wanted you to know that before you leave Hawaii—and me. I also need to make one thing clear: If you ever miss me, want me, decide you love me, I'm here. I'm waiting. I've never loved anyone the way I love you and I never will. And if you'll give me the chance, I'll help heal your bruised heart. Like my speech problems, it won't be a quick, easy fix. That's okay. You accepted me—faults, speech glitch, and all—knowing I'd make progress but never achieve perfection.

That's true of you, too, and I'd happily accept your fears and flaws if you ever want to come back. If not, then…good-bye, *wahine*."

The subtle click in my ear when he hangs up has so much finality my chest implodes. I did the right thing for him, to save him more of this wretched pain later. But right now, I'm feeling so weak. All I want to do is pick up the phone, apologize, hear him say that he loves me again. Tell him how much I love him in return…

A soft knock on the guest bedroom door at Griff and Britta's new place breaks my reverie. "Come in."

Britta sticks her head inside, soft platinum hair a beacon of light in the near darkness. After a heart-to-heart with Maxon and Griff this afternoon, I came in here to shut the door, shove in my earbuds, and process. Since then, night has fallen. So has my mood. It's been a heavy day.

"I thought I'd check on you. I kept your dinner in the oven when you didn't answer earlier."

"That's sweet. Thank you, but I'm not hungry." Way too much on my mind.

"How are you handling everything you and your brothers talked about earlier?"

"I'm still in shock," I admit.

But I also feel closer to them.

After lunch, they pulled me into Griff's study and sat me down. They both confessed everything Mom and Dad had inflicted on them growing up. I'm still reeling.

Our twisted father insisted on making his sons "men," so he offered to get them laid at sixteen by whatever secretary he was boffing himself at the moment. He's belittled Maxon since my oldest brother turned him down, then treated Griff like the favorite son because he'd repeatedly partaken. Why had Dad done it? Because the old man wanted his boys to share in his depravity? Because Barclay thought that somehow made it all right? Because he wanted carbon copies of himself? I'll never know or understand.

Griff didn't get off easy, either. Our self-centered mother used his desire to be loved to manipulate him so she could whore him out in order to climb a stupid social ladder.

My brothers' admissions floored me. Didn't our parents care at all?

No. They're self-absorbed monsters. Sociopaths. I can't think of another reason people would care so little about their own kids' psyches. They feel superior, and all the "little people" below them are irrelevant, even their own children. I don't comprehend at all. The baby growing inside me is tiny, the size of a grain of sand, but my number one instinct is to protect him or her. I'd lay down my life to shield this kid's innocence. My parents couldn't wait to exploit ours.

After hearing my story, however, my brothers are nothing but supportive and protective. After we all purged, we shared tears, followed by laughter at all the stupid ways we've tried to cope over the years. But Maxon and Griff have turned into great men and even better husbands. I left that study reeling and confused…but certain there's hope for me yet.

"Can we come in?" Britta opens the door a bit wider, and I see Keeley standing there, face looking unusually solemn.

They mean well and they want to comfort me. I can't say no. They're awesome women and some of my best friends. "Please."

They shuffle in. Britta sits on the bed next to me, Keeley in the fluffy chair in the corner. Both stare as if they have more to say. But something has been tugging at me, and I have to know…

"Did you two already know everything my brothers told me today?"

They glance at one another as if confirming their own suspicions.

"I've known what had happened to Maxon or a while. But even though I was Griff's confidante for years and I knew he'd been through a lot, he never told me about the summer that almost destroyed him," Keeley murmurs. "I still don't know all the details."

Britta shakes her head. "Griff finally told me what he'd been through the day we got married. But despite working for Maxon for years, he's never confided in me. He's always been a respectable boss mixed with a dash of protective older brother."

He would have never sullied Britta with his sordid past. Same of Griff with Keeley. It's exactly why they never told me, either. Well, that and their own respective shame. Neither wanted me to look at them with horror, disillusionment, or pity. And I can only imagine that's why they never told one another.

But now everything is out in the open, and the truth has brought us even closer as siblings. I understand my brothers so much more now. I also understand the fortitude it took them to overcome the past my parents heaped on them and embrace the love of their spouses.

Can I do that with Noah?

I want to. God knows I close my eyes at night and imagine I'm beside my husband. That he's just a reach of my arm away. That he loves me and our baby and…

Then I open my eyes to the dark and realize I'm alone. Because I'm afraid. And I'm crushed.

With my sisters-in-law staring at me, the truth hits me. I have two choices. I can either keep bowing to the fear that I can't love Noah the right way or, like he said, I can accept that I'm not perfect and simply do my best.

Would it work? We did pretty good for a few weeks. I'd been there with and for him until things got heavy. Until Noah unwittingly hit my vulnerable spot. Maybe I could do it again in a bigger, better way.

But what if I can't? What if it's not enough? What if I hurt him irreversibly in the end?

"Thanks for everything, you two," I tell my brothers' wives. "Your support has meant a lot to me these last few days."

"Anytime. But Noah loves you," Britta says.

"I know."

He's never given me a real reason to question that. And when I consider that fact, I wonder again if I'm crazy to throw away the kind of adoration and devotion most people spend their whole lives wishing for.

"I'll say what Britta is too polite to tell you," Keeley cuts in. "You're being a moron."

Despite the pain tearing through my chest, I have to laugh. "I deeply suspect that."

That doesn't mean I know how to just get over myself. Does anyone? I've met people who were their own worst enemy and wondered why they couldn't find their fucking gumption and just fix it. But I get now that life isn't always simple. Fear isn't rational. Getting over your internal scars enough to carry on again is a bit like committing to a lifestyle change. And like a diet, it doesn't work instantly. It's a concerted effort, a commitment—an adjustment of mindset.

I don't lack grit. I could definitely live with Noah again. I'd love to…at least for a while. But what happens if I fall off the wagon? How badly will he be hurt? And what if I drag our baby through our breakup? This isn't just about him and me anymore.

Is the joy worth the possible price later, especially since I fear Noah will pay so heavily?

"I know you're probably tired of me dishing out songs for every occasion but music really helps me think." Keeley shrugs. She is who she is. "If you'll open your phone for me, I'll download you some music I picked that might help you."

She means well, and it can't hurt. Why the hell not?

As I hand her the device, I look Britta's way. "I think…I'd like to talk to my brothers again. Are they still here?"

The sisters-in-law glance at one another again, this time as if they're trying to decide who's going to be the one to impart bad news. Finally, Britta sighs. "Maxon and Griff both received calls from the FBI about an hour ago. I knocked but… Your dad has been accused of embezzling from clients for the last twenty years. They're alleging that your mom aided and abetted him. They've both been arrested. Your brothers were asked to come in and give statements as family members and former employees."

As if the day wasn't already full of revelations… This one steals my breath and grips my chest. But should I actually be surprised? If Barclay and Linda Reed weren't above using their own children for their gain, why would they hesitate to abuse clients?

273

"Oh, my… Wow. I should have seen that coming."

Keeley gives me an apologetic grin. "That's pretty much what your brothers said. The FBI indicated they might need to talk to you at some point, but maybe not since you never worked for your father."

I don't have anything to add to a possible embezzlement indictment, but if they want witnesses about my parents' character, I have plenty to say. I'm not vindictive…but they have a lot to answer for as parents and human beings. Maybe this is Karma's way of getting things done.

"Whatever they need, sure."

Keeley nods and hands my phone back. "The playlist is downloaded. I bookended you with the Beatles. I hope these songs help you."

I'm about ready to launch it and start the packing I've been avoiding before tomorrow's flight when the doorbell suddenly rings.

"And that will be Evan," Britta says, rising to her feet.

"You invited him over?"

She turns back in the doorway. "No. He called and asked if he could see you."

I can't imagine why, but before I have a chance to ask, she's out the door.

Keeley stands and gives me a hug. "We'll set him up in the study. Head in there when you're ready."

"Now's as good a time as any." I shrug.

"You might want to fix yesterday's smudged mascara. And put on a bra."

I have to laugh at myself. I've been so up in my head that I totally didn't think about taking off my old makeup or the fact that I didn't have the mental energy to get fully dressed today.

"I'll do that." I give her a self-deprecating roll of my eyes. "Tell him I need to clean up, then I'll be in."

"Sure thing." She's back to her bubbly self, which I appreciate because the mausoleum mode dragging down the whole house has got to go.

"And thanks for everything," I say. "I don't know how my brothers lucked into you two ladies, but they should be damn thankful."

Keeley winks my way. "Britta and I never let them forget it. We'll occupy Evan with embarrassing stories about Maxon and Griff until you're ready."

I laugh as she slips out of the bedroom, then head to the adjoining bathroom and stare in the mirror. And stare some more. Oh, hell. I *am* a mess. I'm so grateful Keeley said something. I don't even look presentable enough to socialize with anyone's pet.

Dialing up the music she downloaded for me just now, I turn up the volume and cut on the shower. I'll be quick, but it's going to take some repair.

The first song to blare through my phone speakers is "The Long and Winding Road." Paul McCartney's iconic voice, complete with that little break in the first line, is unmistakable. By the time I'm soaping up, my tears are falling down. I should feel noble about my decision to separate from Noah now and save him the pain later, but I don't. I'd love to change my mind but...all the fears that made me leave in the first place are still there. Sure, progress not perfection, and all that. But what if it's not enough?

As I'm rinsing my hair, a song I don't recognize begins to play. It's kick-ass, beginning with a serious guitar riff. Then a woman with a high-pitched, almost fragile voice belts out that she wants to dream again and this time she's not scared because she's unbreakable. The lyrics resonate, pinging and bouncing inside me, connecting deep. She sings a quick bridge about fear being the crutch that holds you back and turns your dreams to dust.

Oh, hell. She's right.

Noah won't use me. I know that now. He's also willing to take me back. What's keeping me from running back to him right now is nothing more than my own anxiousness and worry.

As my thoughts roll on, so does the song, shouting that all I need to do is trust.

So simple. But so damn hard.

Shoving aside the shower curtain, I wipe the water from my hand enough to tap the screen of my phone. The tune is "Unbreakable" by Fireflight. I'm definitely listening to that again. After hearing the vocalist's resolve, I know I need more of my own.

And I have to remember to thank Keeley later for telling me so in her way.

The next song up begins with a totally different guitar sound than the last, this one a gentle sway like a breeze-tossed palm. It's unmistakably Elvis saying that he can't help falling in love. Yeah, I couldn't help it, either. When he sings the eloquent plea to his love that she should take his hand and his whole life, too… That's another sob I can't stop. Everything Noah said to me boiled down to that message.

And I still walked away.

I have this terrible feeling I've made the biggest mistake of my life.

I have to get out of the shower and not keep Evan waiting anymore. Maybe…I need to call Noah to talk, too.

As classic Elvis drifts off, I cut the faucet and hop out of the shower. I refuse to cry over this mess I've made anymore. I'm going to figure out how to be happy and start doing it.

The King fades, leading into John Legend. "All of Me" is a beautiful song with a beautiful message. That man loves his woman, the same way my husband said he loves me—with all my curves and edges and my perfect imperfections.

Damn it, that starts the waterworks again.

Grabbing a pile of comfy clothes from my suitcase, I scramble into something I hope is presentable—along with a bra—as the ballad mellows into another fitting choice on Keeley's part. Katy Perry's "Unconditionally" captures the essence of the way I'm supposed to love my husband in return. When she croons about letting go of the fear and just being free, I laugh through the fresh sting of tears. Keeley isn't subtle in delivering her message, but she's effective.

As I wrestle a comb through my wet hair and wrangle it into a bun, George Harrison sings me out with "Here Comes the Sun." It's the vocal equivalent of light peeking through the darkness. Upbeat. Happy.

Hopeful. Keeley—and the Fab Four—are telling me that everything will be all right.

The collective message of this playlist isn't lost on me. I've put Noah and myself on this long, winding path to misery, which will only get longer unless I decide that fear will no longer break me. If I'll embrace the fact that we both fell in love and believe that he loves all of me uncondi-tionally, my long, cold, lonely winter will be over.

I sigh as I stroke some lip balm across my mouth. Keeley is probably right. And now I'm feeling like a total coward. What if Maxon hadn't gotten over himself enough to admit he loved Keeley? What if Griff hadn't worked past his anger enough to marry Britta? What kind of loser does it make me if I don't even try to make my relationship with Noah last?

Yeah… I have to talk to him.

After rushing out the bedroom door, I race down the tiled hallway and approach the study to ask if I can borrow someone's car because I've got to go. Instead, I hear Evan talking—and his words stop me short.

"So I don't see any other choice. I've given this a lot of thought. I'm going to have to buy a wife."

Is he kidding?

One of my sisters-in-law chokes. Britta, I think, since Keeley has no trouble finding her voice.

"That's not really legal. You know that, right?" Maxon's wife points out.

"It's merely a business transaction."

Okay, he's not kidding.

"So is prostitution."

"Keeley makes a good point," Britta says softly. "I'm sure you'll find someone special again someday. No one will replace Becca. She was your only girlfriend and your first love. It will take you time to recover and you'll have to work through your grief before you can fall in love—"

"No. I don't want love. I will simply offer someone young, socially adept, and mildly attractive the position as my wife in exchange for stability, fidelity, and financial security. A housekeeper and a cook can't meet all my needs."

"Can't you hire a hooker for sex?" I stroll into the room with a frown, unable to stay out of this conversation.

He frowns my way. "I want children someday. For obvious reasons, a prostitute won't serve my purposes. A surrogate won't work, either, because I want my son or daughter to live with both a mother and a father. Rather than hire someone to help me navigate corporate galas and fundraisers that exhaust the introvert in me, as well as a cook, a housekeeper, a Girl Friday, and a hooker, I can simply buy a wife. It's far more logical and cost effective." Evan rises to his feet. "Hello, Harlow."

I swallow as Keeley and Britta both stand and head for the study door, shaking their heads.

"Well, good luck with that plan," Maxon's redhead says in a tone that more than conveys she thinks he's being a dumb ass.

"The right candidate is out there," he assures me. "Not every woman marries for romantic reasons."

Britta gives him a tightly polite smile. "Let us know if you need anything else."

Griff's wife doesn't know what to say, and I don't blame her. I'm kind of at a loss for words, too.

"Thank you for your hospitality." My half brother nods.

"And before I forget, thank you for the music, Keeley," I say softly.

Her face brightens. "Did it help?"

"Actually…yeah." I smile, and she claps her hands with a little squeal of delight.

After the women back out of the room, I hug Evan awkwardly before we both take our seats.

"How would your late wife feel about you hiring someone to take her place?" I challenge.

"Becca understood me as no one else ever has or ever will. I loved her with my entire heart, and I buried my soul with her and our unborn child. But Fate or God or whatever you believe in has decreed that I should keep living. I'm having trouble doing that," he admits.

"It may take more than a month to adjust. It must be a terrible shock and—"

"Unimaginable. Becca was my rock, my crutch…my sun. But I have to be practical. I work fifteen hours a day, often seven days a week. I don't have time to grocery shop or cook or pay my bills. I can't run errands, drop off dry cleaning, deal with the tax assessor. I don't function well at parties where I need to be charming. And while I don't have the time or inclination for romance, that fact has done nothing to mitigate my sex drive. After dissecting the problem, I came to the logical conclusion that I need a wife who understands what our relationship is…and isn't."

Before Noah, I would have completely understood his point of view. If his prospective bride came into the marriage with all the facts and her eyes wide open, the arrangement would have made total sense to me. In fact, I probably would have applauded Evan for his out-of-the-box thinking.

But not anymore. Now, I'm horrified.

And that should tell me something about how connected I am to my heart.

"You don't ever want love again?"

He drags in a deep breath. "Would I like it? Very much. But I've loved deeply and totally. I believe it's something we're only entitled to once in our lives and only if we're very lucky. Though Becca was taken from me too soon, I had my chance. I won't have another, so my heart is now closed. Would it be better to marry someone on a pretense?"

"No, but I don't think you should shut yourself off to the possibility that—"

"It's not possible." He raises a dark brow, and I'm struck by how much he looks like a Reed, like a younger blend of Maxon and Griff. He acts like one, too. His bravado hides a pain he doesn't want to show and I can't really fathom. "I could ask you the same question. In fact, that's why I came here tonight. I heard you left Noah and your sisters-in-law told me a bit about why. I have to say, I'm shocked."

"Well, join the club. Griff said roughly the same thing. Maxon just asked me if I'd lost my damn mind."

"Smart men. I would do or give *anything* to have Becca back for even a day. I won't waste your time asking if you love Noah because I know you do. And I won't let you insult my intelligence by hearing you insist otherwise. You're throwing your chance away." He grabs my hands. "Stop before it's too late. I'll never love another day in my life, and I fucking regret that I let my wife drive to her appointment in that rainstorm because I was too busy to tell the windbag on my phone to shove his sales pitch up his ass and take her myself. I certainly treasure the time I had with her, but what's worse is regretting every moment we'll never share—the children we'll never have, the adventures we might have taken, the gray hairs we'll never fret about together... Don't throw away what might be a lifetime of love together." He stands suddenly. "I've overstepped my boundaries, haven't I? Did I mention that I'm not good socially?"

His words—and the emotion he's forcing himself to bury—bring me to tears, and it's all I can do to hold myself together. I can't imagine how much admitting that cost him emotionally. But he's right.

And I've been a terrible idiot.

"You did mention it, but you didn't overstep. Thank you for looking out for me and for being so honest."

"Of course. You and your brothers, along with your spouses, have been more family than I've ever had. If Rebecca could see me now, she'd be smiling." We hug again, this time much less awkwardly than our greeting. He tugs at my ear fondly. "Go get your husband. I can't be happy for myself anymore, so you be happy for both of us."

THE FOUR SEASONS in Wailea is a gorgeous paradise and someday I'll stop to appreciate it. But today I only care about my husband. His press conference starts in three minutes and I have to get there before everything goes horribly wrong.

I ached to see him last night, but after Evan's departure, Britta and Keeley were rattling around the house, worried about my brothers' return from wherever the FBI had taken them. Besides, I wanted to take time to be one hundred percent sure of my decision.

So we watched a funny chick flick, baked brownies, and stayed up until the guys came in after one a.m., utterly exhausted. But they were smiling. They'd been able to add surprisingly helpful information for the FBI, and the case against our parents is now looking tight, according to the special agent who interrogated them. All it took was for one whistle-blower—one of my father's former assistants/mistresses—and their entire scheme began to crumble. They're both in custody and it doesn't look as if they'll be getting out anytime soon.

Maybe I should pity them or feel sadness that my parents are probably going away for a long time. But no. They're getting what they deserve. They won't be able to hurt anyone again. My brothers and I, along with our spouses and future kids, can finally be a family without their dark presence in our lives. We can finally look to the future.

And after sleeping on it and listening to Keeley's playlist again, I'm more sure of the future I want than ever.

I scramble down a series of hallways and wonder why these places are always like a maze. It's frustrating. Parking was a bitch, and I just want to reach Noah, say my piece...and let the chips fall.

When I approach the meeting room, reporters are already jammed into the space, double-checking equipment and jockeying for the best angle. No one notices me as I slip in the back, hair pulled into a braid, borrowed ball cap low over my face.

My heart is pounding and my palms are sweating. This could end fairy-tale happy...or Greek-tragedy sad. The fear I haven't learned to tame yet still nips at my heels with a hundred what-if questions and the accompanying doomsday scenarios. I shove them all down.

I'm choosing to embrace love.

Right on schedule, Cliff files into the front of the room, to a bank of mics set up at a podium behind a long banquet table. Noah is right behind him.

My heart stutters. If that sounds trite, I don't know how else to describe my chest seizing up in joy at the sight of him, then pounding again simply because we're in the same room together.

When he steps out of the shadow, he looks as big and Alpha and sexy as hell as usual. But he also looks exhausted, resigned. Grim.

I did that to him. Never mind if I might hurt him in the future. I've brought him pain now. And that's something Noah Weston, football great and amazing husband, should never feel because of me. All season, he should be in the booth, providing the best color commentary for the sport that's made him the man he is. The rest of the year, he should be letting me give him all my love and devotion.

He'll give everything up if I don't stop him. And he's willing to do that. For me. To prove something I don't need him to.

That realization tears at my heart.

Cliff steps behind the podium and taps the mic in the middle with his finger. It's definitely hot, and the screeching feedback has reporters covering their ears. Then he clears his throat. "Ladies and gentlemen, Noah Weston has a major announcement about his professional future. The message is prerecorded. He will only take questions afterward about the video."

A tech dressed in a collared shirt with the hotel's logo springs into action and taps a few keys to launch whatever they recorded onto the screen behind us as the lights dim.

I know what Noah's announcement is, and I'm not having it. This is my moment. It's now or never.

With my insides churning and chugging, I push away from the wall, tear off my ball cap, and stride down the middle aisle like a badass bitch with a point to make. "I know you said Noah would take questions after the announcement, but how about a comment beforehand?"

My husband's head jerks up. He sees me. Our gazes meet, and a zip rolls down my spine. Brutal relief rips across his face as he stands. His eyes pierce me with hope and something that's unmistakably lust. "You have something to say?"

Every camera suddenly swerves and points in my direction as I smile out my love to Noah. "Yeah. Wanna hear it?"

Noah doesn't bother walking around the table. He leaps over and meets me halfway across the room. I hold out my arms to him and he takes me into his own. Our bodies meet. His heat seeps into me. His musky scent is arousing, but it's also as familiar as coming home. He clasps me so tight I can barely breathe, but I don't need to. I have the man I've realized I can't breathe without.

"Why are you here, baby?" he whispers in my ear.

"Because I can't let you give up this opportunity."

He pulls back enough to scan my face. "Is that the only reason?"

I shake my head solemnly. "Because I can't live another minute without you. Forgive me?"

"Already done." Apparently he doesn't care any more than I do who sees how elated we are to be together again. Euphoria slams me as his mouth crashes down on mine and he reminds me that I belong to him.

I'm going to kiss this man every day for the rest of my life. I'm going to tell him that I love him. And when I feel uncertain or scared, he's going to tell me everything that's in his heart. But I'll never let him go again.

"I love you," he murmurs against my lips.

"I love you, too," I assure him as I sniff back tears, then whisper for his ears only. "You'll never have to wonder again if it's true or if I'm ready to be with you. I do and I am. I called the firm that offered me the job in San Diego and turned them down. If you'll have me, I'm staying in Hawaii. With you."

He looks as if he's struggling to keep the press conference macho enough for the sports crowd, but he'd rather be alone with me, telling me exactly how he feels with his words—and his body. "Thank god. Oh, baby... Yes."

Noah's face clouds over with that mixture of love and need that tells me if I don't wrangle control of this situation, I might find my clothes flying off because he's too eager to touch me to wait. In truth, I'm eager, too. But I don't want an audience. I very much want to be alone with my husband so I can atone and worship him in every way he deserves.

"Hold that thought, big guy. Let's make an announcement."

"What do you think I should be saying to these eager reporters?"

I brush a kiss across his mouth again. "Why don't you let me get you started? Take over when you're ready."

I don't say *if*. I know Noah will be able to speak and get his message across just fine.

He cocks his head, clearly intrigued as we stroll, hand in hand, to the front of the room, behind the podium. "You do that."

Cliff shoots me a wary stare that says he's waiting for me to tear his balls off. He should be. But I won't...at least not today. No promises about tomorrow.

I give Noah's hand one last squeeze, then step up to the mic. "Good afternoon, everyone. As some of you know, I'm Harlow Weston, Noah's wife. He's gathered you here this afternoon to let you know that he'll be accepting a job to provide color commentary he was offered earlier this spring by Mr. Gus Chickman and his esteemed network. Noah will do a fantastic job, and he's thrilled to be continuing to serve the sport he's loved his whole life." I send him another glance, and he beams back at me with pride, so I forge ahead. "I'm making the announcement for Noah to bring attention to an issue that doesn't get the airtime it deserves. Too many players in this great game suffer concussive injuries and head trauma that can lead to lasting damage. I'm proud to tell you that my husband and I met because he hired me professionally as a speech therapist so he could accept Mr. Chickman's offer with an open heart and an open conscience. He may occasionally struggle, and I ask that you be patient and remember that, unless you've had more than a handful of concussions, you can't understand what he's enduring. We're hoping to use our platform to not only elevate the sport, but the wounded warriors who have played it bravely and paid a price they never anticipated. Noah and I are also thrilled to announce that we're expecting our first child and now that the situation with Mercedes Fleet has been resolved, we'll be taking an extended honeymoon before his exciting new job starts." I turn to the man I love with all my heart. "Ready to take questions?"

The smile he turns my way is one I'll never forget. He's relieved to have his secret out. He's grateful I did the heavy lifting, just in case anxiety tied his tongue in knots. Most of all, he feels blessed that we're going to live the life we promised one another on our wedding day.

"Thank you, Harlow. I'd love to." He squeezes my hand, takes a couple of calming breaths, and palms a foam ball he extracted from the back of the podium. "But first I have to thank my wife for her wisdom and all she's done to support me, for the joy she's given me, and for reminding me today of all the reasons I fell for her. Progress, not perfection."

"Progress, not perfection," I chime back, wanting to kiss this man more than I can ever remember. But he needs his moment in the spotlight, and I'm so happy he's taking it.

The next forty minutes are a whirlwind of questions, and Noah answers them both perfectly and patiently. He sounds smooth and relaxed, joking with reporters—looking nothing like the fatigued, washed-up athlete he did before the press conference began. He oozes confidence and charm as he provides enough details about the role he'll be playing with the network, the nature of his speech issues, some of the therapy we've been employing, as well as announcing that we'll be starting a players' assistance organization to give advice and direction in the event a player, current or former, needs help, direction, or an ear.

I've never been prouder of him.

The inevitable question about my parents' arrests arises. He lets me field that with a vague answer that the investigation has just begun, no criminal charges have been filed yet, and that I know very little about the allegations because I haven't been involved with my parents in quite some time and never with their business.

Finally, the rapid-fire queries slow, and Cliff steps in to end the press conference. With a wave, we clasp hands again and file into the back room, away from reporters' prying eyes and his watchful agent.

"You came back to me. I'm so relieved." He cups my face in his hands and searches my face for answers. "What changed your mind?"

"I realized I was an idiot."

"You were afraid."

I nod. "Of getting hurt. Of hurting you. Of how much I love you. So many things… Then I realized that I was hurting you anyway. All of my brothers talked to me, even Evan. Keeley came to my rescue with songs, and Britta gave me space when I needed it. These last two days, my family has been there. But something still felt missing, and that was you. I'm not whole without you. It's hard for me to admit that."

"I know. But your trust means so much to me."

"You've done nothing to make me doubt you. It was all in my head. And I had to decide whether to make us both miserable or fulfilled for the rest of our lives." I cock my head with a little grin. "I think I chose well."

"I know you did. What shall we do now, Mrs. Weston? Go home and celebrate naked?"

"We're awfully far from home. Isn't this a hotel? Can't we just get a room?"

"We could, but I want you in our pool, on our dining room table, and wrapped around me in our bed."

"That sounds"—I sigh, contentment brimming inside me that's so bright and sharp I'm almost painfully happy—"perfect. I want you inside me, next to me, a part of me forever."

"You've got it, baby. You can have me however you want me. Once we're both sated, which may be a few decades from now, can you show me how to kill that damn Draugr Deathlord who keeps whipping my ass on that fucking video game?"

I toss back my head and laugh. I might not be good at love with the usual guy in the usual way. But I think I'm going to be damn good at loving this one for the rest of my life. "You're on."

Noah brushes a kiss over my lips. "You know what I thought the first time I saw you?"

"Tell me," I whisper.

"That I had no idea when I purchased my dream home that it would come with the woman straight out of my fantasies."

His words make me smile. He makes me glow. With Noah, I'm sublimely happy. "Well, now I'm your reality, big guy."

"And I'm so blessed."

I join our hands, thumbing his wedding ring, gratified that he's still wearing it. He thrusts his hand into the pocket of his pants, pulls out my wedding ring, and begins fitting it on my finger again. "I've been carrying this around because I can't stop thinking of you. Do you, forever this time?"

"I do. Forever and always. I promise."

"I'm going to hold you to that."

"You can hold me to that, hold me down, or just hold me tight. I'll always be yours."

The End

Read on for excerpts from Shayla Black!

MORE THAN WANT YOU

More Than Words, Book 1
By Shayla Black
NOW AVAILABLE!

A fresh, sexy, and emotional contemporary romance series by Shayla Black...

I'm Maxon Reed—real estate mogul, shark, asshole. If a deal isn't high profile and big money, I pass. Now that I've found the property of a lifetime, I'm jumping. But one tenacious bastard stands between me and success—my brother. I'll need one hell of a devious ploy to distract cynical Griff. Then fate drops a luscious redhead in my lap who's just his type.

Sassy college senior Keeley Kent accepts my challenge to learn how to become Griff's perfect girlfriend. But somewhere between the makeover and the witty conversation, I'm having trouble resisting her. The quirky dreamer is everything I usually don't tolerate. But she's beyond charming. I more than want her; I'm desperate to own her. I'm not even sure how drastic I'm willing to get to make her mine—but I'm about to find out.

This book is the first in the More Than Words series. The books are companions, not serials, meaning that backstory, secondary characters, and other elements will be easier to relate to if you read the installments in order, but the main romance of each book is a stand-alone.

This book contains lines that may make you laugh, events that may make you cry, and scenes that will probably have you squirming in your seat. Don't worry about cliffhangers or cheating. HEA guaranteed! (Does not contain elements of BDSM or romantic suspense.)

"THIS WILL BE our last song for the set. If you have requests, write them down and leave them in the jar." She points to the clear vessel at her feet. "We'll be back to play in thirty. If you have a dirty proposition, I'll entertain them at the bar in five." She says the words like she's kidding.

I, however, am totally serious.

Keeley starts her next song, a more recent pop tune, in a breathy, a capella murmur. "Can't keep my hands to myself."

She taps her thigh in a rhythm only she can hear until the band joins during the crescendo to the chorus. Keeley bounces her way through the lyrics with a flirty smile. It's both alluring and fun, a tease of a song.

Though I rarely smile, I find myself grinning along.

As she finishes, I glance around. There's more than one hungry dog with a bone in this damn bar.

I didn't get ahead in business or life by being polite or waiting my turn. She hasn't even wrapped her vocal cords around the last note but I'm on my feet and charging across the room.

I'm the first one to reach the corner of the bar closest to the stage. I prop my elbow on the slightly sticky wood to claim my territory, then glare back at the three other men who think they should end Keeley's supposed sex drought. They are not watering her garden, and my snarl makes that clear.

One sees my face, stops in his tracks, and immediately backs off. Smart man.

Number Two looks like a smarmy car salesman. He rakes Keeley up and down with his gaze like she's a slab of beef, but she's flirting my way as she tucks her mic on its stand. I smile back.

She's not really my type, but man, I'd love to hit that.

Out of the corner of my eye, I watch the approaching dirtbag finger his porn 'stouche. To stake my claim, I reach out to help Keeley off the stage. She looks pleasantly surprised by my gesture as she wraps her fingers around mine.

I can be a gentleman…when it suits me.

Fuck, she's warm and velvety, and her touch makes my cock jolt. Her second would-be one-night stand curses then slinks back to his seat.

That leaves me to fend off Number Three. He looks like a WWE reject—hulking and hit in the face too many times. If she prefers brawn over brains, I'll have to find another D-cup distraction for Griff.

That would truly suck. My gut tells me Keeley is perfect for the job.

Would it be really awful if I slept with her before I introduced her to my brother?

MORE THAN NEED YOU

More Than Words, Book 2
By Shayla Black
NOW AVAILABLE!

I'm Griffin Reed—cutthroat entrepreneur and competitive bastard. Trust is a four-letter word and everyone is disposable…except Britta Stone. Three years ago, she was my everything before I stupidly threw her away. I thought I'd paid for my sin in misery—until I learned we have a son. Finding out she's engaged to a bore who's rushing her to the altar pisses me off even more. I intend to win her back so we can raise our boy together. I'll have to get ruthless, of course. Luckily, that's one of my more singular talents.

Sixty days. That's what I'm asking the gritty, independent single mother to give me—twenty-four/seven. Under my roof. And if I have my way, in my bed. Britta says she wants nothing to do with me. But her body language and passionate kisses make her a liar. Now all I have to do is coax her into surrendering to the old magic between us. Once I have her right where I want her, I'll do whatever it takes to prove I more than need her.

WORKING TO TAKE my fury down ten notches, I try to stay practical, scan the yard. I don't see any children. Is Jamie already asleep? Maybe so. It's ten thirty. Do little kids go to bed early? I don't know. I didn't consider that sooner. Damn it.

Now what do I do? I'm hardly in the mood to stand here and toast the bride.

Britta isn't hard to find since she's the only blonde among a sea of native Hawaiians in bright, tropical prints and sandals, clinking glasses and smiling.

From a distance, she's wearing a pencil skirt in a sedate gray that clings to a curve in her hips she didn't used to have. Her ass looks lusher, rounder. Her hair, though wrapped up in some classic twist, looks longer or thicker—something.

The lust that hits me is stronger.

She's talking to a pretty brunette who's about her age. The striking woman hugs her, joy evident in her huge smile. Britta replies. I can tell because she still talks with her hands. She's graceful, as always. Not surprising. She entered college on a dance scholarship.

I remember watching her move on stage for the first time. The beauty of her dance stunned me, the way she was aware of her every muscle, the complete control she had over even her smallest movement. Pale tights and a flowing scrap of chiffon flirting with her thighs gave me a hard-on from hell. I was her boss at the time. She'd just begun to work for Maxon and me. I appreciated her smarts in the office and her talent on stage, sure. But more than anything, I wanted those slender thighs wrapped around me while I fucked her. I told myself to back down. She was so young. Everything about her screamed hands off. I didn't listen. I corrupted every bit of her purity. Then I walked away, leaving her with a pregnancy she hadn't planned for, and myself with a mountain of furious regret.

I wonder how much she's changed. Is she bitter now? Withdrawn? Maxon told me that I broke something in her. Fuck. Is she angry? Does she hate me?

How many beds has she slept in since mine?

I swallow the question down. I have no right to ask.

Besides, do I really want to know?

I keep staring at her, watching her slender shoulders as she laughs gently. I hear the sound rising above the din of conversation. It's good to hear her happy even though I'm so fucking sad.

No one else has noticed me. I need to approach her, think of something rational and non-confrontational to say. Or turn around and come back tomorrow, when she doesn't have a whole bunch of company who will gawk at me the minute I demand to see my son. When she isn't celebrating her pending union to another man.

But I can't make myself leave. I just stare, willing her to look at me.

Suddenly, she stiffens. I see the moment she becomes aware of my presence. She tilts her head toward her right shoulder. I see the jut of her chin. She pauses for a sliver of a second, as if she's not sure she truly wants to know if I'm just beyond her line of sight, making her senses flare.

"Britta," I call out to her.

At the sound of my voice, she whips her head around, as if she's heard a ghost and is eager to dispel the notion I could be standing ten feet behind her.

Our eyes meet. My breath stops. God, she's still so fucking beautiful to me.

In that moment I know one thing: no matter what's happened, how long it's been, whatever Britta thinks—she's still mine.

A gasp falls from her lips. She drops her drink, her face going pale in an instant.

The woman she was speaking to frowns in concern and grabs Britta's shoulders, shooting me the evil eye.

Yeah, I'm the bad guy here. Everyone knows it, even me.

I take a step toward her, and that seems to pull her from her daze. She waves off her concerned friend and darts in my direction, bearing down on me with something between shock and fury.

Her eyes are still such a stunning shade of blue, almost turquoise, like the warmest ocean waters near the shore. They're the first thing I noticed about her. Blue-eyed blondes aren't terribly unusual, especially in Los Angeles, where I spent my childhood. But everything about Britta is different. Her eyes are slanted and slightly far apart, framed by heavy lashes. The effect is exotic, sexual. Her pillowy mouth sucks me in next, bent with an exaggerated bow on top and a puffy curve on the bottom. I still dream of that mouth. I remember every time I kissed it, every pleasure it ever made me feel. Tonight, she's exaggerated her pouty lips with a soft

293

gloss that makes me want to tell everyone else at this gathering to fuck off so I can eat it from her now.

No one else has lips as enticing or soft as Britta Stone. Believe me, I've looked. A lot. But when I really want to torture myself, I close my eyes and stroke my cock to a memory of her eyes flaring wide for me while her mouth opens to let loose the gasp of orgasm she can't keep in anymore.

Any wonder I'm harder than hell?

Any wonder I want her back?

"What are you doing here?" she hisses in demand.

How did I find her house or why did I choose this moment to invade her life again? I'll spare her the boring details of both. "Somewhere in the back of your head, you must have known this day would come. I want to see my son. Where's Jamie?"

Her eyes flare wide with shock. Her chest caves in, as if my words are more of a battering ram than a question. She braces her left hand over her heart. She's wearing a round diamond solitaire on a simple gold band. The sight of another man's ring on her finger makes me homicidal. Someday, somehow, some way, I'm going to remove it and replace it with my own.

"Griff…"

When her face goes taut, I see she's fighting worry and tears. I want to do something—hold her, reassure her I don't mean to take Jamie away, wrap her in my arms and kiss her until she forgets about the world.

But when I reach for her, she jerks away. "Don't. Why would I know this day would come? He's two and a half, and before tonight you never showed any interest—"

"I found out he exists an hour ago. It took me three minutes to coax your address out of my brother and fifty-two minutes to drive here."

She stares at me in blinking shock.

DEVOTED TO PLEASURE

Devoted Lovers, Book 1
By Shayla Black
Coming July 3, 2018!

The first in an all-new sexy contemporary romance series from *New York Times* and *USA Today* bestselling author Shayla Black.

Bodyguard and former military man Cutter Bryant has always done his duty—no matter what the personal cost. Now he's taking one last high-octane, high-dollar assignment before settling down in a new role that means sacrificing his chance at love. But he never expects to share an irresistible chemistry with his beautiful new client.

Fame claimed Shealyn West suddenly and with a vengeance after starring in a steamy television drama, but it has come at the expense of her heart. Though she's pretending to date a co-star for her image, a past mistake has come back to haunt her. With a blackmailer watching her every move and the threat of career-ending exposure looming, Shealyn hires Cutter to shore up her security, never imagining their attraction will be too powerful to contain.

As Shealyn and Cutter navigate the scintillating line between business and pleasure, they unravel a web of secrets that threaten their relationship and their lives. When danger strikes, Cutter must decide whether to follow his heart for the first time, or risk losing Shealyn forever.

ABOUT SHAYLA BLACK

Shayla Black is the *New York Times* and *USA Today* bestselling author of more than sixty novels. For nearly twenty years, she's written contemporary, erotic, paranormal, and historical romances via traditional, independent, foreign, and audio publishers. Her books have sold millions of copies and been published in a dozen languages.

Raised an only child, Shayla occupied herself with lots of daydreaming, much to the chagrin of her teachers. In college, she found her love for reading and realized that she could have a career publishing the stories spinning in her imagination. Though she graduated with a degree in Marketing/Advertising and embarked on a stint in corporate America to pay the bills, her heart has always been with her characters. She's thrilled that she's been living her dream as a full-time author for the past eight years.

Shayla currently lives in North Texas with her wonderfully supportive husband, her daughter, and two spoiled tabbies. In her "free" time, she enjoys reality TV, reading, and listening to an eclectic blend of music.

Connect with me online:
Website: shaylablack.com
VIP Reader Newsletter: shayla.link/nwsltr
Facebook Author Page: facebook.com/ShaylaBlackAuthor
Facebook Book Beauties Chat Group: shayla.link/FBChat
Instagram: instagram.com/ShaylaBlack
Twitter: twitter.com/Shayla_Black
Google +: shayla.link/googleplus
Amazon Author: shayla.link/AmazonFollow
BookBub: shayla.link/BookBub
Goodreads: shayla.link/goodreads
YouTube: shayla.link/youtube

If you enjoyed this book, please review it or recommend it to others so they can find it, too.

Keep in touch by engaging with me through one of the links above. Subscribe to my VIP Readers newsletter for exclusive excerpts and hang out in my Facebook Book Beauties group for live weekly video chats. I love talking to readers!

OTHER BOOKS BY SHAYLA BLACK

CONTEMPORARY ROMANCE

MORE THAN WORDS

More Than Want You

More Than Need You

More Than Love You

Coming Soon:
More Than Crave You (Fall 2018)

CONTEMPORARY EROTIC ROMANCE

THE WICKED LOVERS (COMPLETE SERIES)

Wicked Ties

Decadent

Delicious

Surrender to Me

Belong to Me

"Wicked to Love" (novella)

Mine to Hold

"Wicked All the Way" (novella)

Ours to Love

"Wicked All Night" (novella)

"Forever Wicked" (novella)

Theirs to Cherish

His to Take

Pure Wicked (novella)

Wicked for You

Falling in Deeper

Dirty Wicked (novella)

"A Very Wicked Christmas" (short)

Holding on Tighter

THE DEVOTED LOVERS

"Devoted to Wicked" (novella)

Coming Soon:
Devoted to Pleasure (July 3, 2018)

SEXY CAPERS

Bound And Determined

Strip Search

"Arresting Desire" (Hot In Handcuffs Anthology)

THE PERFECT GENTLEMEN (by Shayla Black and Lexi Blake)

Scandal Never Sleeps

Seduction in Session

Big Easy Temptation

Smoke and Sin

Coming Soon:
At the Pleasure of the President (Fall 2018)

MASTERS OF MÉNAGE (by Shayla Black and Lexi Blake)

Their Virgin Captive

Their Virgin's Secret

Their Virgin Concubine

Their Virgin Princess

Their Virgin Hostage

Their Virgin Secretary

Their Virgin Mistress

Coming Soon:
Their Virgin Bride (TBD)

DOMS OF HER LIFE (by Shayla Black, Jenna Jacob, and Isabella LaPearl)
Raine Falling Collection (Complete)

One Dom To Love
The Young And The Submissive
The Bold and The Dominant
The Edge of Dominance

Coming Soon:
Heavenly Rising Collection
The Choice (March 27, 2018)

THE MISADVENTURES SERIES

Misadventures of a Backup Bride

STANDALONE TITLES

Naughty Little Secret
Watch Me
Dangerous Boys And Their Toy
"Her Fantasy Men" (Four Play Anthology)
A Perfect Match
His Undeniable Secret (Sexy Short)

HISTORICAL ROMANCE

The Lady And The Dragon
One Wicked Night
Strictly Seduction
Strictly Forbidden

BROTHERS IN ARMS MEDIEVAL TRILOGY

His Lady Bride (Book 1)
His Stolen Bride (Book 2)
His Rebel Bride (Book 3)

PARANORMAL ROMANCE

THE DOOMSDAY BRETHREN
Tempt Me With Darkness
"Fated" (e-novella)
Seduce Me In Shadow
Possess Me At Midnight
"Mated" – Haunted By Your Touch Anthology
Entice Me At Twilight
Embrace Me At Dawn

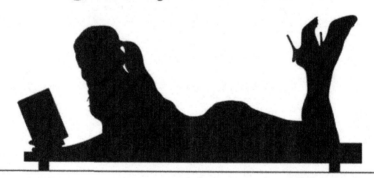

CPSIA information can be obtained
at www.ICGtesting.com
Printed in the USA
LVOW13s0758140718
583547LV00023BA/527/P